QUEEN OF THE TEES

QUEEN OF THE TEES

JOHN NICHOLSON

Nick Guymer Series

No.2

2nd Edition
Published by Head Publishing
Copyright © John Nicholson 2014

Edited by Sarah Winterburn
2nd Edition edit by Robert Marcum

Printed by Berforts Information Press Ltd

ISBN 978-0-9926640-1-5

http://www.johnnicholsonwriter.com

For Dawn
For Mam
For Teesside

"The rivers of our lives,
flow into the waters of time.
But who are we?
Where we are?
Are there any signs?"

CHAPTER 1

'Hey! Hey you! What the hell do you think you're doing?!'

Nick Guymer jumped out of his car and ran towards 33AndAThird, his friend Jeff Evans's second-hand record store.

A girl, maybe 18 or 19 years old, was emerging from the door holding a Tesco carrier bag. Ordinarily, this wouldn't have been suspicious, but it was 7am on a Sunday morning, the new light of the day only just breaking across the inky blue-grey Harrogate sky.

As he shouted, the girl, with little more than a glance at him, began to run. Nick slammed the car door and instinctively took off in pursuit. She had a 15-yard start, was a fast runner and sped away from the shop at the bottom of Commercial Street, crossed the road and headed off down Franklin Road, a typically grand, leafy stretch of Victorian houses with big sash bay windows.

He was fit but this kid could really shift and was about 25 years younger. Catching her up seemed unlikely but he could keep pace enough to maintain sight of her. As he ran, he pulled out his phone and found Jeff's number on speed dial. He answered right away.

'Where have you got to? Have you slept in, you lazy get?' he said in a similar Teesside accent to Nick's own.

'I'm chasing a lass who was robbing your shop, as it happens,' Nick said in gasps, keeping his sights on her in the distance, dressed in black jeans and black puffa jacket.

Jeff laughed. 'Bollocks. It sounds more like you're humping some lass.'

'Jeff, I'm telling you...I'm fucking chasing this kid who was coming out of your shop as I arrived to pick up the boxes of albums.'

'Eh?! Have they taken any records?'

'No, she just had a carrier bag with her. Something was in it, though,' he panted.

As he talked, she turned right onto Grove Road and out of his sight. He managed a spurt of pace to make sure she wasn't out of sight long but 10 seconds had passed before he reached the turning and as he headed east, he couldn't see the thief. He kept going but knew it was pointless; she'd probably disappeared into the cemetery. He stopped and got his breath back.

'I've lost her. Fuck it. How much money did you have in the till? That must have been what she was going for.'

Jeff laughed. 'Nick, son, I run a shitty second-hand vinyl record shop so there's never any money in the till! Whatever she hoped to find, she'd have been sorely disappointed unless she's a big Procol Harum fan and wanted all their early singles on the Regal Zonophone label, 'cos some bloke brought them in yesterday afternoon.'

'Aye, that'll be it. The town is full of thieving Procol Harum fans...shit...I'm knackered.' He rested on a garden wall, rivulets of sweat running down his back.

'Well, when you've put your lungs back in, I need those boxes of records over here - the car boot has already started.'

Nick had been collecting a few boxes of records for his best mate to sell at a car boot sale at Harrogate Rugby Club on Claro Road. For some reason, car boots always began at an unholy early hour and ended just as sane people were having their Sunday breakfast.

'I'll be there as soon as I can,' said Nick, walking back.

Jeff did car boots every week as a way to shift commonplace, uncollected or knackered vinyl albums at a pound or less, records that would just clutter up the shop otherwise. Nick often helped him out - he was a major collector of vinyl records and car boots were good places to seek out bargains. It was also a good excuse to get out of the house and away from just sitting in front of a computer, which was pretty much all he did the rest of the time. Being a football writer had its advantages but getting regular exercise wasn't one of them.

Back at the store, he pushed at the still-open door, went in and flicked on the strip lights to look around. It was a small, square space filled with racks of records and cardboard boxes on the floor. The walls were covered in the rarest records, which had been slotted into transparent PVC covers. The till looked intact; it hadn't been opened or robbed. Nothing seemed to have been obviously disturbed or stolen. Maybe the kid was just trying her luck.

Jeff had sorted out the records for the car boot and put them in six boxes by the door. Nick put them into the back of his old BMW, wedged the door shut and drove the short distance to the rugby club.

'Aye, aye, here he is, the Sweeney!' said Jeff, opening up the boot of the BMW and carrying the boxes to the table. 'Would you recognise her if you saw her again?'

'Never saw her face for long, she was young-ish but yeah, she was tall and skinny, leggy sort of lass. Good runner, very fit, too fit for me.'

'It's weird, 'cos I've never had a break-in before. I always thought that was because Harrogate isn't especially full of toe-rags who want to steal old albums smelling of joss sticks.'

'Well, I don't think she took much. I couldn't see anything obviously missing. But she had a Tesco bag and there looked to be something in it.'

Jeff moved the boxes into alphabetical order and put up a cardboard sign advertising records for a pound. As soon as he'd put them out, a few middle-aged men moved in, flicking through the boxes with the experienced gimlet eye of the long-time record collector. Someone picked out a couple of Stevie Nicks solo records and some Fleetwood Mac and handed over a fiver. It was the sort of stuff that Jeff couldn't sell in the shop because it was too mainstream for his regular punters.

Nick had made a flask of green tea.

'Do you want a brew?' he said, pouring out a steaming cup.

'Is it proper tea?' asked Jeff, happily getting rid of a Meatloaf record for a proffered 50p.

'It's green tea, not Tetley's, if that's what you mean.'

'I can't be doing with that, man. I need tea so strong that you can stand a spoon up in it. That bloody hippy stuff is as weak as cat's piss...though how weak cat's piss is compared to any other animal's piss, I'm not sure. I bet dogs piss is stronger. Fox piss is probably even stronger than that. There should be commonly accepted scale of piss strength in order for us to make accurate analogies.'

'How is green tea hippy stuff? I'm drinking it, not smoking it,' said Nick.

'It just is. You're alright, I'll get something from the burger van in a bit; I'll just deal with the early rush first.'

Someone bought a copy of Linda Rondstadt: Greatest Hits for 50p. Nick rested against the boot of his car, stretched his legs and massaged his sore hamstrings. The playing fields were nearly full now with cars still arriving in a steady stream as people unpacked all manner of stuff from rolls of bubble wrap, 1950s repro furniture and children's clothes to Gordon Ramsay cookbooks, indefinable bits of metal, foot spas, old coins and catering-sized tins of peaches.

He really, really liked car boots and it was the only sort of shopping he enjoyed. Somehow, it seemed more real to buy things off a table in a field than from some expensive retail unit in a shopping centre - a return to the medieval origins of retail where you turned up in the marketplace and sold what you had. There was something pleasingly democratic about it as anyone who had a spare fiver could become a retailer for a few hours. No annual rent and rates to pay, no insurance or health and safety legislation, no staff wages to find, just you and your stuff in the open air.

There were a lot of regulars who did car boots as as a primary or secondary income. Others were in really desperate financial straits and had to try and sell a little slice of their life in order to get through another week of existence.

The field was a bit wet and muddy underfoot but it hadn't dissuaded a large crowd from turning up to peruse the heaps of clothing, electrical goods, gardening tools and all manner of other unwanted flotsam and jetsam disgorged from various houses. It was a tribute to society's eager overconsumption that there was a seemingly infinite amount of stuff to shift most days of most weeks, almost everywhere in the country.

On the far side was a familiar figure wrapped in a big wool coat and black wool scarf, laying out boxes of books.

'Hello, Nick, how are you this morning?' asked Susan Rutherford as she neatly placed books in rows on her stall.

'Good thanks, Susan, how are you? You must have to get up early to get here at seven all the way from Malton.',

She gave a weary shrug of her shoulders.

'Oh I don't sleep much after half-five these days. Anyway, it's usually worth it, I sell more books in Harrogate than anywhere else. How's Jeffrey this week? I hope he's not been out drinking heavily again. He had a terrible hangover last week. It's not good for him.'

Susan was Jeff's aunt, his mother's sister, and often fussed over his lifestyle choices.

'He's his usual hairy and slightly odd self but at least he's not actually drunk. Not yet anyway. He's selling records over there.'

'Ah of course,' she said. 'Will you remind him to come over and see me if he can get away? His mother wants him to pick some things up for her.'

'Yeah, of course.'

He looked through her stock - there was a lot of old novels in worn linen covers from the turn of the previous century and battered old paperbacks of classics, none of which looked like the usual car boot fare. She even had a small poetry section, which is a difficult sell in a good book shop, let alone on a bleak October morning on a field usually used for rugby.

'I put something aside for you,' she said, taking out a small yellow and black paperback book: Pictures of the Gone World, by Lawrence Ferlinghetti. She knew he collected volumes of beat poetry.

'That's really good of you, Susan. I love Ferlinghetti.' How lovely for someone to remember what you liked. He gave her a fiver.

She half-smiled and nodded, her long grey hair blowing messily in the stiff westerly.

'I thought you would. That's an early edition too, printed in San Francisco.'

'Fantastic - a real bit of history. Thanks again Susan, that's rather cheered me up.'

'Oh well, we all need cheering up sometimes,' she said with a smile.

'Yeah, my therapist would probably agree with that,' he said ruefully.

'Therapist?'

'Oh. Yeah. Don't tell Jeff...he doesn't know about it. I've been going for a while. I get these...err...depressions and stuff. I'm trying to work it all out.' He shrugged, wishing he'd not mentioned it. She looked at him with a world-weary expression and then unexpectedly reached out and put a cold hand to his face and nodded.

'I understand, Nick. Being happy isn't a common condition for some of us. But you're a good chap. I can tell. Everything will be fine.'

5

He felt a bit embarrassed as she just stood there, her hand on his face, looking at him with tired eyes. After a couple of seconds he put his own hand on top of hers and said, 'I'll be alright, I think. Thanks, Susan.'

'Try and keep love in your life,' she said, eventually withdrawing her hand. 'That's my tip for you.'

'That's a nice thought Susan, thanks. Speaking of that actually, my girlfriend has just started her MA in history at Durham. She's dead excited about it. She's a mature student, though she hates being called one. She says it makes her sounds like she's a pensioner...not that there's anything wrong with being a pensioner, like,' he said, shutting his mouth after extracting his foot.

Susan was a visiting lecturer in archaeology at Durham University. She'd been full-time head of department until recently but was now in her mid-60s and looking to retire.

'She made a good choice to go to Durham. You're never too old to learn something new. What is she doing her MA in?'

She thrust her hands in her pockets as the wind blew, but her long grey hair wrestled around her head in a knot. Some car boots were held despite awful weather and people would still turn out. She searched for a woolly hat while he talked.

'Well, that's why I mentioned it. She's doing Romano-British history. She majored in Roman for her first degree, so she's picking it up again. That was your period, wasn't it?'

Susan nodded and smiled a somewhat weary, watery smile as she kept putting out books.

'Well, I may see her then. What's her name?'

'Julie Wells.'

'Julie Wells, righto. There are often cross-overs between the history and archaeology departments and that's a very interesting period, a time of great change in Britain. I'm still occasionally involved in the Boudica Society and...'

'...yes, Julie's very interested in all that. Boudica and err...Cartimandua, is it...the err...what's it called now, Brig something...'

'The Brigantes tribe?'

'Aye, that's it. Apparently, women were allowed to inherit property and that, which was bloody unusual for the time. But then you'll probably know all that already.'

She gave a wry smile.

'Ah, I see. Is she coming at it from a feminist perspective?'

'Well, she's always been interested in women's lives and culture, so I guess she is. She's old school, y'know, when it comes to sexual politics, like...'

'What does "old school" mean?' asked Susan, her eyebrows knitted in a frown.

'Old school? Oh, I mean she's hardcore...err...by which I mean she's a believer in the 70s-style feminism y'know, very anti the patriarchy and gender stereotypes, girls in pink, boys in blue...all of that,' he said, worrying that he was saying the wrong thing. Was Susan a hard-line feminist? 'I mean, I agree with her because it just seems fair and she'd kick my backside if I didn't.' He grinned. Was that OK? He didn't really want to have a gender politics discussion in a muddy field before eight in the morning.

'Ah, I see,' she said, pulling on a cerise-coloured woollen hat. 'Well she should look in on me some time and introduce herself. I still have an office up there, she's welcome to drop in for a chat if I'm around; or if she joins the archaeological society, I'll meet her at some point, I'm sure. '

'Great, I'll let her know.'

'If she's interested in Boudica, the society meets soon for our monthly debate. Tell her to look out for it. There are notices in the department and on the website. It's often a lively affair. Our next one should be especially so...I'm not really looking forward to it to be honest, but I was asked and I said I'd do it, for the young students if nothing else.'

She was well-spoken with a crisp, clear voice without a hint of an accent to betray her upbringing on Teesside. Nick had first met her a couple of years ago when she'd started doing the car boots in Harrogate. She bought and sold books as a hobby, an outlet from the stiffness of academia, perhaps.

There was a high-brow air about her, the air of a woman who had spent her life in the halls of universities, but there was also a hint of the slightly mad cat woman, too. She wasn't the least bit snobbish or unapproachable though, and it was surely the privilege of specialist academics to have an unworldly quality. You couldn't spend your life in a muddy trench looking for history in the soil while being overly concerned with more modern, mundane matters. He would have liked her as a teacher or lecturer. Recently she had seemed more withdrawn. As he was currently in therapy to try and alleviate his own depressive moods, he had wondered if she was similarly afflicted, but it wasn't something you could really ask in a windy field with the smell of frying onions from the burger van in the air. Maybe one should, but he certainly couldn't.

'I'll tell her about the Boudica thing when I speak to her tonight. I'm sure she'll come along. In fact, if I'm up there visiting her, I'll come along too.'

She rubbed her hands together as a dry, chilly breeze blew.

'I've got some green tea in a flask if you want some to get warm,' said Nick, 'I always bring some with me, it's always cold on this field.'

'That's kind of you but no thanks; I don't really like green tea. It's supposed to be very good for you, isn't it? I find it too weak. I'm rather stuck in my ways, I'm afraid. It's not a good quality, I know.'

'Jeff finds it totally unacceptable, too. He calls it hippy tea. Only me and Julie seem to like it.'

That made her smile, and he was glad to see her smile as it made her look less washed-out and tired.

She took out a pair of red fingerless gloves from her parka coat pocket, put them on and began shuffling books around on the table. A few people looked at her bargain box of 50p books.

'Okay, well, it was nice to see you Susan. I'm sure Jeff will come over later. I'll see you soon. Take care.'

'You too, Nick. Be strong. Everything will be alright.'

He smiled and walked away. What an interesting lady she was. He wandered around the car boot. Most of the stalls were selling kid's toys and clothing, a few specialised in old tools and furniture. Someone had a box of vinyl records sitting on the ground which always made his heart leap. Records - you had to look through them, just in case, even though it was usually all Jim Reeves, Leo Sayer, Abba and battered copies of The Sound of Music. But if you didn't look, you missed the occasional gem.

Skimming through at speed he could see it was all 80s pop music, Culture Club and Simple Minds. Nothing for him there but sitting on the table was one seven-inch single. By instinct he picked it up. It was on the red Polydor label, 'Good Time Girl' by Stone the Crows, a rock band led by Maggie Bell in the 70s. Nick had their albums but not any singles. It always quickened his heart to see something he wanted.

'How much for this?' he asked.

'Ten pence, mate,' said a big old bloke. It wasn't valuable, but it was hard to find. Ten pence was a bargain. It was these small victories that gave him pleasure as a collector. He didn't go out of his way to buy rare stuff, though it was nice if it came along. He was more interested in amassing a huge library of music and now had over 10,000 vinyl albums, singles and CDs but it was nowhere near enough.

Jeff was now eating a burger and had a polystyrene cup of tea and a doughnut in reserve.

'Before you start, don't tell me I'm eating too many carbs,' said Jeff as he approached.

Nick ignored him; he didn't go on about being low-carb as often as others went on to him about it. It wasn't like it was a religion.

'Sold much?'

'Just offloaded six Carpenters albums for a whole two pounds and the second and third Chicago albums for a quid each. Big time, baby, big time! Thing is, they're all good albums - Tony Paluso's guitar on the Carpenters stuff is brill...Terry Kath on the Chicago albums...I mean, this is top-quality sounds I'm all but giving away here. I hope I'm appreciated.'

'Isn't it amazing that people pay 10 quid to download new albums when they can buy old ones on vinyl for a few pennies?'

'It makes no bloody sense at all. If no-one ever recorded any more new music there's still plenty of stuff to listen to. I've not even heard all the albums I want to hear that were recorded in 1966 yet, let alone any other year.'

Nick held up the single he'd bought.

'Ah, bit of 70s blues rock, nice. 50 pence, was it?' said Jeff.

'A bargain at 10 whole pennies.'

Jeff whistled. 'Sweet meat, baby.'

'I was talking to Susan,' he said as he held up the slim volume of poetry. 'She had this for me. Bloody great.'

Jeff squinted at it: 'You're the only man I know who didn't get fed up of poetry at school.'

'I love Ferlinghetti. Even the title of this, Pictures of the Gone World, just sounds brilliant.'

'Hmm. It sounds like a 25-minute track by the Grateful Dead to me.'

'Susan says you've got to go over and see her. Something about picking up stuff for your mam. She's a funny old bird isn't she? Susan, I mean. Sort of unworldly,' said Nick, resting on the boot of Jeff's car. 'I really like her. She said something really good to me.'

'Oh, aye, what?'

Nick waved his hand. 'Oh, it doesn't matter. Just a little bit of philosophy, maybe.'

'Ah, right, I'll go over when it's a bit quieter. Aye, well she spent years in trenches with a trowel, didn't she? She was always good to me when I was a little kid. Took me on days out away from the Teesside smog to Scarborough and Whitby and bought me fish and chips. A chap doesn't forget such things. Anyway, academics are always overfocused like that - unlike you and me, who are in no way overfocused on obscure rock bands of the 70s.'

He pulled a comedy face, eyes wide open and mouth agape, like he was a hypnotised dog. 'So what have you been up to?'

'Not much. Just the usual writing gigs,' said Nick.

'Uh huh. Have you actually been out and done anything?'

'Err...no. Not as such.'

'Typical of you, that is. I bet you've not even spoken to anyone for days, have you?'

'Err...no. No, I haven't. Not actual face-to-face talking. Not since I last saw you.'

'That was six days ago, man.' Jeff shook his head. 'You need a social life.'

'I know. I should make an effort, but I just get into my own head and the time passes. Days fly by. I dunno where they all go. Trouble is, I sort of like it.'

'You're a weirdo, you know that? I thought you were supposed to be getting out of your old habits?'

'I am. But I keep going back to my default mode.'

'Hey, did I tell you I'm shopping for a bike?'

'A push bike?' said Nick.

'No, 'course not. They don't make them in my size. I mean a big brrmm brrmm bike. I've always fancied one just for tooling around on locally. Just an old second-hand job, like.'

'Do you know anything about bikes?'

'Aye, they've got two wheels...'

'Very good, you can't go wrong then.'

'...one wheel at the front and one at the back.'

'And they run on bananas.'

'Aye, everyone knows that. It's why so many monkeys ride them. So if you want to have a look at some with me, I'm off up to that Suzuki place on the Ripon road later.'

'I can't, man, I've stuff to do. Anyway, I know even less than you about bikes. Two wheels, you reckon, eh?'

Things had gone quiet after the initial rush to pick over new arrivals' stock.

'Hey, thinking on, did you say that robber ran off with a Tesco bag?' said Jeff, from behind his doughnut. Nick nodded while looking at the sleeve of the Yes album, Going for the One.

'Yup, that's all she had with her when she legged it.'

Jeff nodded, sugar sticking to his beard, and then shook his head in amazement. 'You know what was in that bag?'

'No idea.'

'Potatoes! They've nicked my mam's spuds. I got them at the Starbeck car boot yesterday morning off that farm lad who often does the boots. You know which one, his family have a farm out by Wakefield and he turns up with a trailer piled high with potatoes. He actually looks like a potato, come to think of it. Maybe farmers turn into what they grow? Anyway, I got two bags of potatoes and some vegetables.'

'Vegetables? You don't eat vegetables, do you?' said Nick.

'Not unless it's in the course of sexually adventurous love-making, and even then I draw the line at aubergines...'

'...well, you've got to have moral standards.'

'Exactly. But who the fuck steals potatoes?'

'Juvenile delinquent chip-shop workers?'

'Ah. Whatever happened to juvenile delinquents? They were all the rage when we were growing up in the 70s. You never hear of them these days.'

'They've evolved into chavs, I think. But I just can't see anyone, no matter what you want to call them, thinking, ah look at that, Kerr's Pinks, I'll have them. It's carbohydrate crime. I mean, even in your shop there are things worth more than the price of potatoes.'

Jeff pulled his long hair back behind his head and fastened it with an elastic band to keep it from blowing in his face.

'It seems less likely than me selling, or even giving away, this copy of Boney M's Greatest Hits,' he said, holding up the record. 'They could have taken The Pretty Things' debut album I've got in there, that's worth a couple of hundred quid.'

'Hey look, who's that talking to Susan?' said Nick, pointing across the field.

Jeff squinted. 'I don't know. He looks familiar, though.'

'She doesn't look best pleased with him. Maybe it's a punter trying to get a cheap deal.'

The man was tanned and had closely cropped silver hair. He looked like he was in his late 50s or early 60s. Susan was waving a dismissive arm in his direction as though she was telling him to go away.

'Might just have a wander over there and make sure she's OK,' said Jeff, emerging from behind his tables.

'Good thinking. I'll fend off any vinyl-hungry punters for you,' said Nick.

He watched as Jeff strode across the field. The man turned as Jeff approached and held out his hand to shake. He looked too well dressed for a car boot. Car boots largely attracted the skint, the tight, the weird and the bereft. Nick was all of the above. As it was cold and very early on a Sunday morning, normal people with regular lives were unlikely to attend, so it was odd to see a regular, prosperous-looking member of society there. He really stood out in a Barbour coat and expensive tan leather boots. By the look of Jeff's body language, there wasn't going to be any trouble. He had his hands in his jeans pockets and was nodding. Meanwhile, Susan was busying herself with some books as though staying out of the way. After five minutes Jeff returned.

'Everything OK?' said Nick.

'Aye, I thought he looked familiar. That's Martin James, Susan's ex-husband.'

'Oh, right, it looked like they were arguing about something.'

'Yeah, he wants to collect some old papers from the house, up in the loft apparently. She wasn't happy with when he wanted to get them or something. Not convenient for her...no love lost there, like.'

He pulled out a hanky and blew his nose.

'How long have they been divorced?'

'Must be the best part of 20 years. I remember him being around when I used to stay with her in the summer holidays. They were married in the early to mid-70s - both worked at Durham Uni. He's actually still working full time, he was saying, up at Teesside University, he's a history prof, like.'

'You'd think he'd have got all his stuff out of the house in 20 years, wouldn't you?'

Jeff snorted and shook his head. 'Aye, you would, like. He's a nice-enough bloke. Bit smooth, but then everyone is smooth compared to me and you, aren't they?'

'True. We are definitely not smooth. We're the anti-smooth.'

They stayed at the car boot until 11am, when things began to thin out. Jeff counted the money he'd taken. It came to £65.50, but more importantly, he'd sold nearly 100 albums.

'I reckon I can get all of these in my car now,' said Jeff. 'Are you coming on to the late boot in Starbeck? Hopefully I can shift another 50-odd.'

'Much as I'd like to stand around in the cold for a few more hours in

Starbeck, I can't, I've got an appointment at 12.'

'I'm hoping that young Linda Blake is there. I usually get a place next to her,' said Jeff.

'Young Linda? She's probably the same age as us.'

'Nah, she's only about 38 or 39, that counts as young to me these days now that I'm in my mid 40s,' Jeff said, scratching and then smoothing down his bushy beard. 'I'd like some red-hot lovin' with her if at all possible, and what better place to woo a lady than at a car boot while standing next to someone who is selling animal protein in bags labelled "brown meat" and "white meat"?'

'An irresistibly romantic setting, for sure. Are you in with a chance, like?'

'I reckon so. She's always friendly and laughs at my jokes and no-one is ever friendly and laughs at my jokes except the mentally ill and you. They usually just think I'm a big hairy nutter.'

'Yeah, but you are a big hairy nutter.'

'...but in a nice way,' Jeff said, pulling another face and rolling his eyes up into his head so only the whites of his eyes showed.

'I'll see you tonight in Jack & Danny's if you're not ensconced in her love nest by then. Don't forget to go and see Susan before you split.'

'Aye, I'll go over there when I've packed up.'

Nick drove away from the rugby club and back to his apartment in the Dales Mansion on York Place, found a space in the car park and walked across The Stray, a large open expanse of parkland-style grass that runs through the centre of Harrogate. He took some deep breaths as he walked, inhaling in the cool October air, a stiff breeze blowing in off the Pennines.

He had been going to see his therapist, Marc Lewis, since the spring but he wasn't yet quite convinced that therapy wasn't just one big massive con designed to pick open your psyche and discover as many problems as possible in order to generate an awful lot of money but no solutions. But all the same, he did accept he needed some sort of help.

The problem was long standing. He suffered from depressive episodes, which in recent years had got much worse, and for most of his life he'd struggled to have emotional connection with people,

14

finding himself considering what to say and feel in social situations rather than having any natural empathy or engagement. Not with everyone and not all the time, but enough for it to be a problem. This had made it hard for him to share his life with his ex-partner Julie when she had moved into the Harrogate flat. A toxic mixture of his depressions and his cold, introverted moods had eventually forced her to move out and back to Teesside after 18 months. That was now over a year and a half ago. They had been together for three years prior to moving in together, so to see it fall apart after just 18 months under the same roof was totally crushing for both of them and he carried a lot of guilt. So much guilt that it had driven him to seek out professional help.

The previous spring, while sorting out his dad's estate after he had died, they had begun to rebuild things by sort of dating each other again, albeit at a distance, and he had started to confront his demons, but he still felt no more able to cope with having a normal husband-and-wife, live-under-the-same-roof arrangement, even though he wanted to. Changing who he was seemed impossible.

Marc Lewis had his offices in a large Victorian house on the opposite side of The Stray to Nick's apartment. Nick greeted the receptionist, a woman in her 20s with small features and thin lips. She recognised him and smiled.

'Hello, Mr Guymer,' she said in a lilting Yorkshire voice.

'Call me Nick. Only the police call me Mr Guymer.' It was a line he used all the time in place of proper interaction.

She laughed a little. 'Okay, Marc will see you now Mr Guy...err...Nick,' she said, nodding at him.

He licked his dry lips and walked into the large office feeling a little nervous; he usually did before these sessions. Talking about himself wasn't his idea of fun and it really hadn't got any easier yet.

Marc Lewis was in his late 20s or early 30s. Dressed casually in a white open-necked shirt and dark navy jeans, he had heavy beard stubble and very hairy arms but a quickly receding hair line. He was what Jeff would have called a 'hairy baldy' and put Nick in mind of a short-haired version of Metallica guitarist Kirk Hammett.

He smiled and held out his hand but his shake was weak and damp, which made him seem insubstantial. After some pleasantries, they sat opposite each other in leather-backed armchairs next to what had originally been a large open fireplace. Marc Lewis had poured them both a glass of water.

'I think we've made some interesting progress in recent weeks, Nick. So let's have a chat about your relationship with your mother.'

Nick exhaled deeply. 'Well, I got on better with her than with my dad. As I've talked about before, dad was just distant and seemed unconcerned about me for my whole life, but mam was nicer to me, especially when I was younger. She looked after me well when I was small, or that's what I feel, anyway. Then when I was 13 she started getting ill. They wouldn't tell me what it was really but I know it was something gynaecological. She had a hysterectomy and that meant she was in hospital a lot and because my dad ignored me most of the time, I was just in my room and on my own. I'd play records and read when I was wasn't doing school work.

'Did you miss your mother?'

He swallowed the water and nodded. 'Yeah. But only selfishly.'

'What do you mean?'

'I mean I missed her not being at home to cook me food and to hear me talk about what was happening at school.'

'Well, you were a young boy, that's natural.'

'When I was 14 or thereabouts I think her physical illness started to lead to psychological problems. She was upset a lot. I'd find her crying and I wouldn't know why. She'd disappear to bed and was really tired. I used to think she was putting it on or doing it for attention and for a while it rather annoyed me, which wasn't very nice.'

'Again, Nick, you were a boy. You couldn't be expected to know about mental health issues. Did anyone discuss her problems with you?'

'No, never. No-one did. Even when she went into hospital.' God, he hated having to revisit this stuff. He'd brushed it under his psychological carpet for a long, long time but knew he had to spill his guts to get to the heart of the matter. 'She never got well after that and was always in and out of hospital for one thing or another right until I left home. Dad used to pretend it was nothing, but it obviously wasn't nothing, All I could think to do was ignore it and carry on as if everything was fine. I just got my head down and got into my music and books and poetry. I hardly even went to hospital to visit her because I hated it, hated seeing her there and because it frightened me a bit. I just wanted everything to be normal so I pretended things were normal.'

Marc Lewis made notes as he talked. 'So really from the time you started to go through puberty, your mother wasn't in your life much?'

'On and off but no, not really. Even when she was there, she was sort of absent.'

'Would you say your parents helped make any big decisions for you? About going to college or anything like that?'

He laughed a little bitterly. 'I made all the decisions about...well, about everything. I decided to go to college, I decided where to go and what to study. They didn't really even know anything about it. I just announced stuff like that and they went along with it without questioning me. I actually thought I was quite lucky at the time. Other kids parents made interventions in their lives but mine never did, so I could do what I wanted. But obviously, now I'm older, I can see that was actually really irresponsible of them, especially when I decided going out drinking most nights was a good idea despite not even being 16.'

The therapist nodded. 'So from age 13 you've virtually raised yourself without any parental guidance. That's very hard on you. It's no surprise you developed coping mechanisms such as a tough emotional shell and an instinctive disconnect from things that might harm you. You had to be brave.'

'Brave? No, I wasn't brave. I just had no choice. I just had to get through. Some kids have it a lot worse than I did and that fact actually makes me feel like I'm sitting here and just moaning on.'

'Where it rates on some sort of notional scale of neglect isn't really relevant. It doesn't mean these were not important years in making you the adult you grew into being.' He added a couple of notes to his pad. 'It's my view that you haven't really left your emotional teenage self behind. You're stuck in that survivalist frame of mind; that emotional instinct to protect yourself has become a reflexive dogma, almost.'

That did make a lot of sense.

'Is your mum still alive?'

'Yes, she's in a psychiatric ward again at the moment. She's heavily medicated a lot of the time. I go to see her occasionally, but not that often. She's spaced out and her memory is threadbare. It's sad, really.'

'In a way, I think this is worse than if you lose a parent. She's there but she's not there, in many ways. I can see why it'd be upsetting and why you ended up with the issues you have. Tell me this, do you feel lonely?'

Nick sat back and looked up at the plaster rose on the ceiling of the old Victorian house. He thought he knew the answer.

'Not really. I can survive on my own easily. Before today I hadn't even talked to anyone for nearly six days.'

'Really? Interesting. That doesn't bother you?'

He shook his head.

'So you don't feel lonely, then?'

Nick moved awkwardly in his seat. 'Maybe I feel alone rather than lonely. Is that different?'

'You tell me.'

'When I was sorting out my dad's estate earlier this year, I realised I felt very angry and bitter towards him, and my mam, too, to a lesser extent.'

'Why?'

'I've talked about this before, Marc.' He felt uncomfortable.

'I know, but let it come out again.'

'I was bitter at them for abandoning me. I was a kid. I needed help to grow up but I didn't get any help from anyone. I was alone. Maybe I do still feel alone but then, we're all alone in our own heads, aren't we?' He could feel emotion rising in his throat as he talked and a veneer of water glazed his eyes.

Marc Lewis nodded, his fingers placed together under his chin. 'This is what I was getting at. Those of us with good parental relationships can count on their support all through our lives. They're on our side and will support us and help us, not just in childhood. You don't have that. You sought that kind of reassurance and comfort in drinking and in your music and books.'

Nick closed his eyes. 'They are what raised me. Rock music is my family. I really mean that. Sometimes, I feel that music is my only constant, true friend in life. It's always there for me and never lets me down and doesn't judge me. The spirit of it, the...the...fucking guts of rock n roll, that is my religion, it's my spiritual being y'know...I worship it - I know that sounds mad to anyone who doesn't feel like that about music - I know some people just like a tune to hum or whatever, but to me, it's at the root of everything. I know this will sound mad but it's really what I understand as God. The Holy Rock 'n' Roll. It's the most profound thing and I draw strength from it almost every day. It fills up a massive hole in me and has done since I was a kid.'

Marc Lewis nodded. 'Do you think we might call that hole loneliness?'

Nick shrugged but said nothing, his emotions welling up inside him again.

'OK, let's move on a little. Tell me about your relationship with Julie and how you'd like that to progress in the future,' he said, looking at his notes from previous meetings.

Nick blew out air, desperately fighting his reflex not to say anything much.

'We're dating, really, almost like it's a new relationship. We agreed we couldn't think about living together until I was in a better place mentally.'

'But a few hours together now and again is not enough for you or her?'

He looked away and tried to unravel his feelings.

'We usually get on great and I'd love it to be like that all the time. But you can't have a relationship with someone if you keep just shutting down emotionally and that's what I do. And then there's my depressions. I'm not sure they're anything to do with my childhood, though, Marc. I think they're something chemical or hormonal.'

'Indeed, but such things can be brought on my distress or trauma in childhood or at any time, really. Healing one can help heal the other.'

'I can usually feel it coming on. It's like a black shadow moving over me, an impenetrable cloud. I can be fine one minute and then I go down into this mental hole, sometimes for an hour or two, sometimes for a day or two, during which I'm just...well...it's not good. I can't talk. Everything annoys and stresses me out. It's not fair to anyone else to have to sit with this silent, brooding shell of a human. I often can't even speak and I won't answer the phone or the door. It all feels too intimidating. It's not just a mood, it's my entire existence.'

He sat back and glanced at a clock on the wall, hoping the hour was nearly up. His hands were sweating and he felt upset at having to rake over the breakdown of his relationship again. It felt like picking off an emotional scab that may have healed over for a very good reason.

'Do you feel alienated from people, from the world?'

Nick leaned forward, trying to be honest as possible.

'Look Marc, I just don't feel stuff like normal people. I have no emotional connection at times when, often only in hindsight, it seems that I should have had. It makes me seem crass and uncaring...no, it doesn't make me seem like that, I am like that. I know that. So much so that I try to pretend that I do connect, but I don't, really. It's an act. It's all intellectual and not emotional at all. I don't want to be like that. It's taken me years to even realise this, though.'

'I think you judge yourself too harshly. Julie obvious sees qualities in you that you don't see in yourself. She still wants to be with you, so you must offer her something. You obviously connect with her even if you think you don't. Tell me, were you ever violent towards her?'

'God no. Not once, not even close. The thought of it appalls me.'

'Are you violent to yourself?'

'Self-harming? Maybe. In a way. I nip the skin on my arm and I dig my nails into my hand to calm myself down sometimes. The pain is...it's sort of nice. I've only started to do that in the last year, though.'

He held out the palm of his right hand; it was covered with red marks made by his own nails.

'Does that draw blood?'

'A little, sometimes,' he mumbled, ashamed of himself and hating even having to tell him. 'Cutting myself with a blade does sometimes feel attractive when I'm really down, but I've never done it. Not yet, anyway. But I can see why people do it. I bet it releases the...the pressure, somehow, or the pain maybe.'

'Hmm, that concerns me greatly. You must call me if you ever get a strong urge to cut yourself. It may help you to remember that people are not always finding emotional connectivity with other people quite as easily as you imagine they are. They're just playing roles, too - saying the right thing, et cetera. Your idea of what is normal may in part be a cause of your stress. This is quite common, you become so sensitive to your own perceived failings that you imagine everyone else is getting on fine and you're the odd one out, when that's not really true and the normal human experience is much closer to your own without you actually realising it.'

'Nobody does this. Or only crazy fuckers,' he said, gesturing at him with the palm of his hand. He stared at the carpet, feeling upset.

'Okay. I do hear what you're saying. Tell me, what do you think are your best qualities?'

That caught him by surprise.

'I feel pressure to say something but I can't think of anything,' he said after some thought.

'Take your time.'

'I know a vast amount about rock music and football and I can write OK. That's all that comes to mind, but that's all just a symbol of my dysfunction. A good and giving, open person would be doing things for other people, being a useful member of society, and I'm not that.'

Marc Lewis interjected. 'Let me help you. I think you're a funny guy. You can make witty, quick, clever comments. It's a very attractive quality. I'm sure Julie thinks that. I bet she laughs at your jokes, doesn't she?'

'Yes, she does and only she ever says anything complimentary to me, so thanks for saying that, but really all of the joking is just a defence mechanism to keep the world at bay.'

'We all have to deal with the world, Nick. Your problem is that you're unhappy with the job you're doing of dealing with it.'

Well duh. How the hell was this of any use to him or to anyone else? The human psyche, by the time you're 46, is so twisted and dense that you surely can't unravel it. This was a waste of £85 an hour. He could buy a lot of records with £85 that would surely be better bloody therapy. But he kept quiet now and listened.

'One important thing therapy teaches us is that the more you try to self-consciously change, the more you will stay the same, and I think that's where you're at. You badly want to change and trying to change only sends you further into your usual behaviour spirals. To really change, you have to open up to different ways of being and let them change you in the long run, rather than just try to impose a new set of rules on your old self. You need some practical strategies to release the self you want to be.'

Those kinds of phrases were incredibly grating. They sounded glib and reeled off by rote. The jargon of therapy and psychoanalysis, like all jargon, seemed designed to keep the tourists and amateurs at bay.

They stood up.

'You're doing well, Nick. Don't be so hard on yourself,' he said, nodding earnestly. 'You can change and grow but don't force it. Just allow new influences to get a foothold and flourish. Think outward not inward, if you can.'

As Nick left the office, he realised he'd been sweating profusely. His armpits were sodden and now cold and clammy in the brisk breeze. He headed for home grinning and singing Pink Floyd's song, 'Brain Damage'. Surprisingly, he felt better just for talking about all the shit in his head. He'd never said it out loud to anyone quite like that, not even Julie.

He'd just got home, put on the kettle and made himself a ham and boiled-egg salad when his phone rang. It was Jeff.

'You'll never guess what's happened now,' he said, a hint of incredulity in his voice.

'You're not ringing from that lass's bed, are you?'

'I wish. No, I've just got in and I've been robbed, Nick! Fucking robbed!' Jeff had a small flat in the centre of town where he lived on his own.

'What? As well as the shop?!'

'Yeah.'

'But...but... that's surely not a bloody coincidence, is it?' said Nick.

'What's been taken?'

'That's just it, nothing. The lock had been popped but I can't find anything missing at all and anything valuable has been left...well, OK, I've not got anything valuable except for records, but there was a Visa card on my desk, and they left that.'

Nick could hear him walking around his flat.

'Hang on...' Nick could hear Jeff was rummaging in something, '...fuck me...ha ha...this is so weird. They've only taken a carrier bag of vegetables!' he guffawed incredulously.

'You're taking the piss,' said Nick, knowing Jeff liked a joke.

'Honestly, I'm not. I had a carrier bag of cabbage, carrots and onions in my cupboard and that's gone.'

'Did you get that from the car boot yesterday as well?'

'Yeah, I left the other one with spuds in in the shop because it was for my mam, she'll pick it up on Monday, or she would have done if chummy hadn't had it away on her toes with it. Then I brought two more home, one of potatoes which I emptied into the rack, and the veg which I left in the bag.'

Nick began scribbling notes. He wrote a lot of notes. It was a way to keep some sort of order in the chaos of life.

'See, that's not a coincidence either, is it? They took a carrier bag of spuds from your shop. Now they've taken a second bag. Someone wants those bags for some reason.'

'What silly fucker wants my veg and why?'

'I'm pretty sure they don't want your veg, Jeff. They want something that they think is in those bags. Like you say, no-one steals root crops.'

'But there was nothing else in there.'

'Not as far as you know. But that can't be the whole story, can it? I'll see you in the bar later. We'll try and work this out.'

He stared out across The Stray through a large picture window. Something weird was happening to Jeff. This clearly wasn't any ordinary robbery.

CHAPTER 2

Nick pushed open the door to Jack & Danny's, his regular watering hole in town. It was dark inside and a nice place to retreat from a busy Sunday afternoon. They had a good classic rock jukebox and attracted an older clientèle who were not likely to get drunk on brightly coloured pop, cause trouble or, worse still, demand to hear pop music. This was a very good thing. He got himself a sparkling mineral water and double tequila, poured one into the other and took a seat by the window.

Jeff soon arrived, bustling along in his usual maelstrom of long, greying straight hair, beard and loose-fitting clothing. At 20 stone and being six foot three, he was a big presence in all but the largest rooms.

'Now then, Mr Guymer, still committing that heinous act of tequila abuse, I see. If you keep drinking that I'm going to ring up Cuervo Gold, tell them what you're doing and get them to send the tequila police down here to arrest you.' He jabbed a fat index finger at him.

'You're always going on about my tipple of choice. I think you're in love with it really. You're just in denial,' responded Nick.

'Aye, maybe you're right, maybe it's my inner Mexican lady boy.'

He sat down opposite him with a pint of lager.

'So did you call the police about the break-in?' asked Nick.

Jeff shook his head and flicked his hair behind his ears. 'Nah. No point. I'm not going to make an insurance claim, largely because I don't have any insurance, and I can't see Plod being bothered about a bag of spuds, can you?'

'I've been thinking about that,' said Nick, turning a beer mat around in his hands. 'Like I said on the phone, no-one steals bags of potatoes and vegetables, so they must have been looking for something else.'

Jeff nodded while taking a drink. 'Aye, go on...'

'When you got those bags at the car boot, what did you do with them?'

Jeff stared off into the middle distance to think.

'Nowt. I just bought them from the lad, took them back to my pitch, put them on the ground next to the car while I was selling, then packed them up and went home. I left mam's bags with the records in the shop and took the others home, tipped the potatoes onto that vegetable rack thing in my kitchen cupboard and left the other bag on top of them. That's the one they stole. '

'Who was the pitch next to?'

'I was in the corner as usual, so Linda Blake was on my left and there wasn't anyone on the other side, but across the way were the usual couples selling kids' clothes and stuff.'

'Could anything valuable have fallen in the bags from another stall?'

He shrugged. 'There's nowt of value at a car boot, is there? Mostly it's people selling crud for pennies. There's a bloke who sometimes buys and sells gold and silver stuff, but that's about it.'

'Well, someone thinks you've got something worth stealing. There's no other explanation, there's no way that both your places being broken into on the same day and the only thing taken is some potatoes and vegetables is a coincidence. It's not some sort of vegetable addict looking to get their kicks...something's not right, I just can't work out what it is,' said Nick, arms folded, his face set in a frown.

'Ah well, bollocks to it. I don't see what else we can do. There was no damage done really, it's not like they shit on my bed or something,' he said, taking a big drink of lager. 'So what else did you get up to today? You said you had an appointment. What was it? Pox doctor?'

'Obviously, yeah, I do usually go to a pox doctor on a Sunday but today I was actually at a bloke called Marc Lewis's place.'

'Who's he, like?'

Nick inwardly winced. He'd hidden it from his best friend for long enough. It was time to be more open, to stop hiding. 'He's my...oh fuck it, he's my therapist, Jeff. And don't fucking laugh!'

'Therapist? Who are you now? Woody Allen?' asked Jeff, grinning.

'I didn't tell you about it because I knew you'd take the piss. I've been going for a while now.'

Jeff bellowed a laugh.

'Of course I'd take the piss but that doesn't mean I don't love you, darling,' he said. 'So what prompted this? You're not going to get the old cock lopped off and become a woman, are you? If so, can I have the first dance?'

'Yes, I'm really a woman called Cindy from Bridlington and no you can't, I know you, you'll be feeling me up within seconds.'

'Well hello baby! No, come on...seriously man, what's it all about?' He tugged at a silver earring he wore through his right lobe.

Nick had kept it to himself because he'd wanted to see how it all worked out, but also because he felt awkward and embarrassed.

'I'm just trying to work a few things out, that's all,' he said, trying to be nonchalant, hoping to brush over it quickly.

'Things like what?'

Nick sighed. 'Just...just...relationship stuff, y'know.'

Jeff raised a fat forefinger into the air, which was his way of saying a light bulb had gone on in his brain.

'Ah ha...I wondered if this was to do with the fragrant Julie. Has she sent you to a shrink?'

'No, she bloody hasn't. It's my idea,' said Nick, feeling indignant. He knew Jeff had never really warmed to Julie when she lived in his apartment, thinking she was a bit snobbish and sensible. Nick also suspected he was jealous of her because naturally he spent much more time with her than with him. Jeff and Julie occupied two different worlds in his life.

'Look Jeff, it's no big deal. I'm just trying to work out why my brain works the way it does. Why I'm a bit of a solitary...weirdo...why I can't really...I don't know...connect with people easily.'

Jeff shrugged. 'There's nowt wrong with you, son. Nowt that a skinful of drink won't fix, anyway. You've always been a bit quiet sometimes. You used to bring in bloody Leonard Cohen records to play at school dinner time. How the fuck was that going to help us get through a day?'

'I was an arty sod, wasn't I? I liked the words, and anyway, just because I've always been a moody sod, like, doesn't make it healthy and no, getting wasted on the drink won't help it, man. If anything that's making it worse. It's bigger than that. I've got to grow up and be...be a man about it, or be a grown up or whatever. I've been a kid for too long, running from my issues rather than confronting them.'

He sighed again, his skin crawling with awkwardness.

'Aye but, for good or bad, it's who you are. I mean, no offence son, but you, like me, are a nerd. We're overfocused on shit that other people have never heard of, mostly to do with obscure rock bands of the 60s and 70s. We're not built for chit-chat about soap operas or the price of cookers. Of course we seem weird to the Straights.'

Nick sighed. 'I know that, I'm not trying to be someone else, I'm just trying to be a better version of me... look man, I want to eventually give living with Julie another shot - if she'll let me, which is by no means a given - and I want to not fuck it up this time. You really don't understand how messed up I am, man, partly because you're also a loony. It was brutal what I did to Julie, mentally, I mean. You weren't there. I never hurt her physically but you know, mentally, shit, I tortured her. I reduced her to a scrunched-up ball of tears, weeping in the corner of the room, and the more upset she got, the worse I became. It wasn't just us falling out over her not liking Hawkwind or something. It was...it was profound, man. No-one should have to suffer that. So I've just got to be a better man for her and I'm bloody determined that I will be and if it takes talking to a shrink, then that's what I've got to do. I'll do whatever it takes.'

Jeff held his hands up in surrender. 'Hey, fair enough son, but that break-up wasn't all about you being a moody twat; she wasn't perfect either. She provoked you a lot of the time, she didn't understand you. I saw it with my own eyes. She was on your case all the time.'

Nick scowled and waved his comments away. 'Just shut up, man...you don't know the half of it. I know you're trying to be on my side but...this is grown-up shit, man...I've got to sort it out for myself...and I can't drink it off my mind like I'm 18. Look, let's just talk about something else. Therapy is probably all bullshit, anyway.'

'Well if you're going proper bonkers, I can probably get you a good-quality straitjacket at the car boot. There's nothing you can't buy at that one in Starbeck.'

'I'll keep that in mind. Now what about this Linda Blake? Are you any nearer to setting up your stall on her pitch, as it were?'

'Bloody hell, that's a tortuous metaphor, even for you. Here's something I bet you didn't know about her...'

'...I don't know anything about her so nothing would surprise me, not unless she's actually Johnny Giles in a blonde wig and dress. That would surprise me greatly but even then, I reckon I'd soon get over it.'

They both laughed.

'How can you say that? She doesn't even look like Johnny Giles! There's a hint of Rodney Marsh about her in his QPR pomp but that's all good. Turns out she's actually from Teesside. Not far from our old stomping grounds actually, Hartburn Village.'

'Bloody hell. It's a small world, eh. How long has she been down here?'

'Since she was 18 - she went to Leeds University but her folks and the rest of the family are all still up there.'

Jeff cracked his knuckles. 'Aye, I'll have her under my spell soon enough, I reckon.'

'Are you sure? She might not like talking about records that came out on the pink Island record label, Jeff. Some weirdoes don't.'

'Hey, give me credit, there's more to me than obscure records...not much more, that much I'll give you...but a bit.'

They laughed again. It felt better to laugh. They didn't do serious very well at all.

'Hey, I'll tell you what. Do you fancy a free dinner and piss-up?' asked Nick, reaching into his jacket pocket and pulling out a card.

'Whoa ho! Does the pope like a kiddie-fiddler?' said Jeff before frowning and repeating those words back to himself. 'Hang on, that wasn't right, probably blasphemous too, actually, still, hopefully god will forgive me. What I mean is, err...of course I bloody do. What's the gig?'

'You know the Northern Sport Writers Awards?'

'Not really, no.'

'No, well, why should you? It's an industry thing, really. I've been nominated for 'Northern Sports Writer of the Year' and 'Northern Football Writer of the Year' and there's a big dinner at the Teesside International Hotel where they announce the winners. I can bring two guests. Obviously I'm taking Julie, but you can come, too.'

'Get in. In my head, I'm already there. Well done Mr G. Anything that gets a chap a free feed is a small victory in life. It should be a good nosh-up. Wonder if there's a free bar...'

'They'd not be so stupid. It'd bankrupt them - a room full of northern journos and a free bar, it'd be a recipe for disaster. You'll get wine with the meal, though. It'll be cheap plonk, I should think.'

'Free plonk is the finest tasting wine to me, son. So what do you win, if you do win?'

'Some sort of cheaply engraved trophy, I imagine. Still, it's nice to be nominated. It's never happened to me before. So we'll go up together if you like. It's a week on Wednesday.'

'Cool. Thanks, man, is it a jacket and tie job?'

'Yeah, it's quite posh, so put your best bin bag on.'

Jeff saluted and nodded. 'Mind, Julie will bloody love all of that; an expensive hotel, bit of nosh, champers, getting those lovely breasts of hers all dressed up. That's all right up her strasse.'

Nick smiled. Jeff was right, she would love it. Having grown up on one of Stockton's roughest estates, she was still a sucker for a touch of upmarket living.

'By way of thanks I'll even buy you one of your Gay Mexican abominations,' said Jeff, getting up, '...and I won't even take the piss out you for drinking it.'

Monday was a big writing day for Nick. He had two columns to write about the weekend's games as well as opinion pieces for various websites. Early in the evening, he called Julie at her home number in Norton, one of the nicest areas of Stockton.

It rang twice and she picked up.

'I was just thinking about you while I was peeling a cucumber,' she said, a laugh already in her voice.

'I'm not sure whether I should be flattered or insulted.'

'Depends on what I do with the cucumber, doesn't it?'

'Ah yes, a simple life spent at home with only the love of a good cucumber for company, you can't beat it. Well, you can, but it just snaps in half.'

She gurgled a rude laugh. 'So what's going on in Harrogate?'

'Someone stole Jeff's potatoes,' he said flatly.

'They did what?'

'They broke into his shop and then into his flat and stole a bag of potatoes and some veg.'

She laughed out loud. 'Are you using potatoes as a metaphor for something?'

'Nope. They stole actual potatoes and veg. I don't know why. It's the oddest thing. But that wasn't why I was ringing. I've actually been nominated for a couple of Northern writer awards and they're holding...'

'...you've been what!?'

He repeated himself. She gave a small cheer and clapped. 'That's brilliant. Brilliant. Well done, you. It's no more than you deserve.' It made a tingle ripple from the back of his neck to the base of his spine.

'Well, it's hardly an Oscar but...yeah it's quite an honour really. The thing is there's a big do at the Teesside International a week on Wednesday when they hand out the awards and I wondered if you'd like to come with me. It's a big dinner.'

'Eeee god, yeah, I'd love that, it sounds class, like,' she said lapsing into the broad Teesside accent of her upbringing on the Hardwick estate.

'It's an evening gown type of thrash, so you'll need to dress up a bit and I'll have to dig out my best suit.'

'That won't fit you now. Not since you lost all the weight.'

Since she'd moved out he'd changed to a low-carb diet, dropped 50lbs and put on quite a lot of muscle. It seemed to have given him more energy and, though he thought it was probably a sort of mid-life crisis, it had made him feel a bit better about himself at a time when he was badly in need of feeling something positive.

'I know, I was thinking of getting it taken in.'

'Nah, that's no good, it's two sizes too big. Buy yourself a new one. Do you want me to help you pick one out?'

It was the sort of thing she liked to do but he really disliked, especially with someone else in tow. Shopping for clothes had caused a lot of arguments in the past. It was best avoided. These were the sort of lessons he was trying to teach himself.

'No it's OK, I might have a look in town this week, see what I can get.'

'I know what I'm going to wear already. I've just got this original 1920s dress, it's the sort of thing they wore for parties in big country houses.'

'A flapper's dress?'

'Yeah. I look like Lady Muck in it; black silk and chiffon with lace sheer sleeves. It's class, man.'

He was pleased that she was pleased. They didn't meet up every week, mostly just when Middlesbrough had a home game, though they talked on the phone regularly. Although they were both in their forties, in some ways it was like teenage dating again, which he rather liked. They'd agreed earlier in the year that they'd operate a no-sex policy, fearing it would change things and put pressure on them just as they were repairing their relationship and he was getting his head together. Nick now suspected this was more his issue than hers and that she was prepared to resume a much more physical relationship than the occasional kiss, cuddle and grope. She'd always had a more powerful sex drive but their almost platonic friendship was working well for now.

'Right, well I'll come up next Wednesday afternoon and we'll get a cab over there for a 7pm kick off.'

'Would you like to stay over?' she asked. He searched for information or implication in her tone but couldn't find any. Stop over-thinking it, just be natural.

'Well, I invited Jeff as well, so we can get a hotel room if you want,' he said, immediately pleased with himself for knocking the ball back into her court.

'Don't be daft, that's just a waste of money. You two can crash on the floor or sofa for one night.'

'Thanks, Jules. What about the Boro game this Saturday? We're playing Everton. Shall I get us tickets?'

'Yeah, great. Oooh, while I remember, I'm going to a meeting of that Boudica Society on Saturday night.'

Nick interrupted. '...Ah, I was talking to Susan Rutherford about that at the last car boot.'

'Who?'

'Jeff's Aunt Susan. I've mentioned her a couple of times. She sells books at the car boots.'

'Oh, yeah. I remember. It's a woman called Diane Edwards in

charge now and she runs this Boudica Society thing. A woman on my course said I should go along and take a look. She reckons they're all a bit crazy.'

'That's funny, Susan said you should check it out, too, when I told her you'd gone back to university.'

'Right, well, it starts at 7.30 so I'll have plenty of time to get down there after the football.'

'Can I come along?'

'Oh yeah, of course, that'd be good for us to do something that isn't football. I wasn't sure you'd be interested.'

'Yeah, it sounds intriguing. A room full of mad people is always my idea of a good night out. I'll drive us down there after the game.'

'Cracking. I'll see you on Saturday then.'

He was going to tell her about the session with Marc Lewis but then decided against it. The chat had gone well; better to end it while the going was good.

'Ta ra, lovely Mr Guymer,' she said, in a sing-song voice, obviously happy. When she was happy, Nick was happy, but happy meant being vulnerable. If they fell out it would throw him into a trough of misery that, in the dark of the night, feared he really could not survive. He'd spent the last year and a half getting his head together and becoming emotionally self-sufficient again. Being in love was a bloody complicated and difficult state of being. Did the pros outweigh the cons?

He was just filling a kettle and thinking about Julie when the phone rang again. Momentarily, he thought it was her calling back, but it was Jeff.

'I hope you're not ringing to have phone sex with me,' he said, picking up the phone, which was exactly what he would have said to Julie too.

'Some fucker has broken into my car!' said Jeff, breathlessly.

'No! Don't tell me you had a shopping bag in there?'

'Yes, Nick. Yes, I fucking did!' he yelled.

'Yer kiddin', aren't ya?' But it was obvious he wasn't joking.

'It was just some shopping in a Tesco bag and they've fucking knocked out the driver's side window and taken it! Tomatoes, bread,

Tabasco sauce and a packet of sausages. What. The. Fuck?! Someone is taking the piss.'

Nick didn't know what to say but scribbled down notes as Jeff ranted.

'The bags of potatoes and veg you bought from that car boot were Tesco bags, too, weren't they?' he asked

'Yeah, yeah, so what?'

'Did you have any other shopping bags in the car? Like from Sainsbury's or Waitrose?'

'Waitrose?! I'm not made of money, son. I don't eat organic chicken raised on crushed sapphires or whatever it is they do...but yes, I had a two Morrisons' bags on the back seat with 12 cans of Stella in each. They had a special discount on. They never took them.'

Nick bounced his Biro on its nib on his pad of paper. 'See, that proves it's the Tesco bags from the car boot that they want. They thought it was one of those.'

He drew a circle around and around on his pad.

'I just wish these stupid fuckers would leave me alone!'

On Saturday Nick drove into his old home town of Stockton and headed towards the suburb of Norton where Julie lived. Its origins as a village dated back nearly 2,000 years. She owned a flat in a large Victorian house which had been converted into six apartments in the 1930s. It looked out on Norton Green, an expanse of grass around which most of old Norton was arranged. He rang the bell and he heard her coming down the stairs. She pulled open the big wood and stained glass door.

'Hiya, mister,' she said, smiling and giving him a quick hug. She had on her Boro scarf, black leather bike jacket, close-fitting black jeans and black boots. With her fair blond hair spilling down over her shoulders, her turquoise blue eyes and full, smiling lips, he'd always known she was out of his league. She stood just an inch shorter than his 5'10" and had also lost weight since they had lived together. She always smelled of Calvin Klein's 'Escape for Women'. It was the smell of comfort, excitement and guilt.

'Hey, Jules! You're rockin' an old-school 80s heavy metal look. This is very good.'

'It's a bit of a throwback to my biker days. I've even got my old Guns N' Roses t-shirt on underneath the jacket, sweet child of mine. I think I'll start wearing more black, it hides my sagging arse. I fancy us today; I'm going for 2-1. Everton are rubbish away from home.'

'I like your optimism. I never expect us to win. It always seems so unlikely. If we're off form then I expect a big loss, if we're on form, I expect it to end at any moment.'

'Miserable sod. We have the powerful, firm, rippling buttocks of the Yak on our side, not to mention the giant mountain of flesh that is Mark Viduka.'

'That is true. The cost of feeding parmos to those two is probably single-handedly keeping the local economy afloat.'

It was a good game, with Boro taking a first-half lead through a Yakubu penalty before missing a second penalty, then going two goals up through Viduka. Nick, speaking out of long and bitter experience, said that this was too good to last and so it proved on 77 minutes when Tim Cahill pulled one back. Bloody hell. The last 10 minutes were tense enough but then the fourth official put up the board for injury time and it read eight. Eight! There'd been a stoppage when something had been thrown on the pitch but eight bloody minutes? Christ. There was no way Boro could hold out under the battering they were getting. But somehow they did and ran out 2-1 winners, only their second win of the season. They walked out of the ground and back to the car feeling emotionally drained.

'Why do we put ourselves through this, Jules?'

'It's character forming.'

'Aye, we've got so much bloody character after 35 years of watching the Boro that we don't know what to do with it.' They got back from the game in time to have some bacon and eggs and then took off again for Durham.

'It must be odd for you being a student again,' said Nick, as he drove through the dark and damp night.

'It is, like. You feel really old next to all the freshers, man, they seem so young.'

'But acting like they're all grown up.'

'Of course. Bless them. Away from home for the first time, having sex and being drunk a lot, usually at the same time, just like we both did; it's a great tradition. For me like, just spending time in lectures learning stuff feels like a real luxury. Not like work at all. It's so brilliant not to have to go to work in a sodding office in a suit. Mind, this Boudica Society thing should be interesting. Apparently they've got a bit of a reputation. Someone was telling me yesterday that it's full of a mixture of hard-line feminists, crusties and the sort of people who do historical re-enactments.'

He laughed. 'That's a potentially interesting combo. They could re-enact great feminist battles from history - throw themselves under the king's horse and all that.'

'I think that's what they do - I heard something about how they'd done the ransacking of Colchester by Boudica's army. I don't know how, like, as there's not much detailed historical record, and how do you re-create ransacking without actually doing a lot of ransacking?'

'Ransacking is a good word, isn't it? So much nicer than slaughter or mass killing.'

'Ah, well, I can tell you, me being a top history wonk and that, technically, the word ransacking doesn't mean killing.'

'Ah, right, I stand corrected, Professor...so they're all firebrand radicals...how radical can you be in archaeology or history, though?'

'Maybe we'll find out tonight.'

'Actually, Susan Rutherford asked if you were coming at your studies from a feminist perspective. Maybe she's part of a Durham feminist cabal.'

'Ooh, I hope so. I like a feminist cabal, sounds very early 80s. And what did you say to that?'

'I said I didn't know if that was part of the research but that you'd always been interested in the history of   women's culture and politics.'

She nodded. He felt relieved he'd got it right.

'Although I've only been there a couple of weeks, I get the impression that most young female students would hate to be called a feminist these days. They think that means you have to hate men and have hairy armpits and wear ugly non-sexist trousers. Quite frustrating to someone as old school as me. It's a shame. I think they're confused about it, really. Being a feminist is a bloody good thing to be. We need more feminists and less buying into the usual patriarchy bollocks.'

'I once saw some graffiti on a wall at Newcastle Poly that said, and I quote, "The patriarchy is a cunt".'

She burst out laughing. 'That's very clever. Or very something. What was it Paul Simon said about the prophets writing on subway walls?'

'Newcastle was good for graffiti in the late 70s. Someone had written "best friends really aren't, they destroy things" on the side of the city hall. I always loved that.'

'That sounds born out of bitterness. I'll tell you what my favourite was - you'll remember it in Stockton.'

'It wasn't "Cyclops Arsepickers" was it?'

She howled in laughter and slapped her leg. 'Yes yes, that's it. On the bridge down from the Dovecot Arts Centre. I loved "Cylcops Arsepickers"!'

'I did, too. Surreal and yet very specific somehow. I always wondered who did it and why.'

'It was genius...anyway, so yeah, being an older feminist at University in this day and age doesn't feel very cool.'

'Here, you're a woman and one who has lovely tufty armpits, tell me, what is it with women's hairy armpits? Why are they such a problem for everyone? There's this huge industry dedicated to the removal of so-called unsightly hair. I've never understood the aversion. It's all natural, isn't? Same with pubic hair. All this waxing and shaving is a waste of time and money. Put me down as firmly in favour of armpit and pubic hair on women, Jules. Call me old fashioned but body hair is what separates adults from children and getting rid of it genuinely seems weird to me. When we were teenagers in the 70s, a glimpse of pubic hair was brilliant. Having a pube caught on your fingernail after a bit of a rummage in a lasses knickers was the most exciting thing ever. Never understood the obsession with wanting to getting rid of pubes.'

'Yeah, but you're quite unusual these days. You're right, no-one cared about it when we were kids, but some men are freaking weird about women's body hair now, like it's unclean or something and that's given women a complex about it. So now we feel we have to change ourselves from our natural state, not just for fashion but just to be socially acceptable. I really don't see why I should be judged harshly for having hair on my legs or anywhere else, I really don't. It still annoys the hell out of me. Women grow hair on their legs, under their arms and between their legs, end of story. Why can't we just be allowed to be what we are without someone thinking we're some sort of hirsute witch?'

'I totally agree. I hope you've never removed any of that hair for me.'

'I did when we first met because I assumed you'd think me weird otherwise and I didn't want to scare you off with my extravagantly thatched bush. Ha Ha. Once I knew you were cool about it, I've let it all grow unfettered!' She burst out laughing again. 'So don't go shaving your bollocks on my account either, lad. Get a shift on, we'll be late. We'll park by the cathedral and walk down to the Museum of Archaeology by the riverbank.'

It was a cold misty night as they hurried down a footpath to the bank of the river. The Old Fulling Mill was lit up. They were just in time.

Inside around 30 or 40 people were standing around drinking some sort of punch being ladled out of big glass bowls. It was quite a turn out. As Nick and Julie entered they all turned to look. They were a bit of an odd bunch; mostly it looked like a gathering of the female nerds. Some seemed to have dressed up for the occasion in an approximation of 2,000-year-old garb. One stood out especially. She had bright henna-red cropped and spiked hair, reminiscent of David Bowie on the Aladdin Sane cover and stood at least six foot tall with broad shoulders. She was an impressive figure and, judging by the coterie of women that stood around her, was some sort of leader of the society. She spoke quietly with a small blonde woman sitting in the front row, who she addressed as Sophie.

There were just three other men present, hippy-looking types who were probably just there because there were 30 or 40 women in the room. It was a strategy he'd deployed as student, having been the only lad in a poetry reading group.

Julie recognised an older woman from one of her classes and led him over.

'Hello, Georgina. This is Nick. How are you?'

She was about 50 and had short hair and wore a jumper decorated with Gothic patterns.

'Julie, hi. Hello, Nick. Welcome to our little get together. We're just waiting on Diane and Susan arriving. Have you got your briefing notes? No? Here have mine, I'll get another copy.'

She handed him an A4 sheet titled, 'Queen of the Tees?'. It was to be a debate between those who took the view that Boudica was born into the Iceni tribe in what is modern-day Norfolk and those who believe she is of the north, from what is now Teesside. Wow. That really appealed to his Teesside patriotism.

'This is really interesting stuff, Georgina. Is there much evidence for Boudica being from this region?'

She threw back her head and laughed. 'That is what we're here to debate and discuss, Nick. Yes indeed, yes indeed.' She rocked back and forth on her heels with more amusement than seemed strictly appropriate.

As she talked, a skinny, leggy girl with short hair entered the room and appeared to be looking for someone. She looked very familiar. Eventually, she pushed open a side door and left the room. A minute later the lock dropped in Nick's mind - she was the girl he had chased through the streets of Harrogate. She was the potato bag thief! What the hell was she doing here 70 miles away? He turned to tell Julie, who was in still in conversation with Georgina, but before he could say something, Susan Rutherford came in through the door alongside a taller, broader, slightly younger woman who must have been Diane Edwards. She walked with her shoulders back and led with her chin. She was dressed in a floor-length green velvet and gold brocade coat and wore an embroidered Edwardian smoking hat - the sort of hat middle-aged rock stars wear to hide the fact they're going bald. This curious ensemble made her look like a gothic, Merlinesque sort of figure.

By contrast, Susan was a smaller, academic-looking, mole-ish woman with small features, wearing a grey waterproof coat and carrying armfuls of papers.

As they arrived, the assembled people all applauded and some even cheered. Here were their heroes, the stars of the show.

'These people are all really wrapped up in this thing, aren't they?' said Nick into Julie's ear. 'Look at them, they're really excited. It's like a football crowd only with middle-class punch-drinking kids.'

She raised an eyebrow. 'I told you, a lot of people think they're crazy. Someone said it's more like a cult.'

'They were right, but y'know, it's good...bonkers people are fun...as long as they don't have knives.'

'I wouldn't be so sure with this lot,' she whispered back in his ear.

He turned to look for the leggy girl again but she'd gone. Maybe he'd just imagined she was the same kid that he'd chased. After all, how could it be the same person here? It made no sense. He must be imagining it. He waved at Susan across the room and she acknowledged him with a nod of her head but seemed preoccupied with her sheaf of notes. She looked very tired, with dark rings around her eyes. A pair of doors were opened into the debating room. Someone made a whooping noise like a fox's yelp in the night; it was immediately picked up by others and turned into a mass call-and-response session with the red-haired girl leading the way, holding a long, carved oak pole above her head. It was a piercing and somewhat eerie noise as they all started to move forward with Diane and Susan at the head of the pack as though being led into an arena for a fight.

'Let's sit at the back so we can see these people in action,' said Nick. 'Some of them seem very hyped up almost like they're ready for a fight, though I can't see this lot actually fighting, not until they take their glasses off anyway.'

'No, it's not exactly like coming out of the away end at Cold Blow Lane in 1984, is it?' said Julie with a laugh.

They sat on the back row of a block of portable seating raked on a low slope. Two lecterns stood at the front of the room. Diane took the left one, Susan the right. The yelping continued. Two women in ancient-style garb began beating out a rhythm on the wooden floor with long staff-like poles, which others picked up on, stamping their feet in time. Thump-thump-yelp, thump-thump-yelp. For a moment it sounded like they were going to break out into a chorus of Queen's 'We Will Rock You'.

The tall girl with Bowie-red hair stood front and centre and conducted the incantations for a minute or two, twirling her stick as she did so. After two or three minutes, she motioned with her hands to settle down the audience and the noise dropped away to silence immediately. She ruled the room.

'Hello tribes, and welcome. As many of you already know, I am Florence Farrell - a fiercely proud Brigante. Welcome to the monthly Boudica Society debate. We welcome members of all tribes both old and new. Tonight is the big one, the one I know many of us have been waiting for. We have with us the two biggest hitters in the world of Boudica research. Both proud members of the Brigante tribe, too. Diane Edwards, who many of you know is Head of Archaeology here at Durham University and a long-time advocate of our Boudica having northern roots. In her new book, The Queen of the Tees, she details her search for our queen and comes to a stunning conclusion with which I'm sure you're already familiar: that Boudica was born and raised as a royal Brigante here in the north of England!' She could barely contain her excitement.

This brought many of the assembled to their feet whooping, whistling and doing the fox yelp. Diane smiled and raised her hand in recognition of their support.

'Our other speaker today is Professor Susan Rutherford, who was Head of Archaeology here until 2005 and who wrote what some consider to be the definitive history of Boudica over 20 years ago. She has lectured all over the world on Boudica and she's now a visiting professor here at Durham. Without doubt she is one of the country's greatest Boudica experts. Susan held Diane's position here at Durham until last year. Born and raised in the heart of Brigante country near the Tees, she maintains the classical theory that Boudica was likely to have been an Iceni from Norfolk.'

Boos rang out at notion. Nick looked at Julie and made a face to say, 'What are these people like?'

Julie frowned and looked around her at the booing crowd. There was hostility and even anger on some faces.

Florence Farrell continued, a wide smile on her face, clearly enjoying the febrile atmosphere. 'Can I have some order amongst the tribes, please? Thank you.'

Nick mouthed the word 'tribes' at Julie. She shrugged.

'Diane will speak first and then Susan and then we'll take questions from the floor. So without further ado, Diane.'

There was more whooping and clapping. Nick looked at Susan, she had her head bowed, looking at her notes. For a moment he wondered if she'd dropped to sleep.

Diane Edwards stood up, still resplendent in the long velvet coat and smiled. 'Thank you, Flo. We've called tonight's debate "The Queen of the Tees?" with a question mark and that question mark is important because the truth is, at the moment, we have no categorical, evidential proof of where Boudica was born, where she died or where she is buried. Until the day we unearth her grave, we will never know for sure. However, as some of you know, it has been my ambition to find out more about the woman I call the People's Queen. It is my contention that Boudica was born into a noble family in this region and that she was, initially at the very least, close to the Brigante tribe, possibly even considered a royal member. She was also close to their leader, another powerful woman: Cartimandua. I also strongly believe that her body was taken back to her homelands in AD 61 and buried here. I will explain in detail why and where I think she may lie.'

More fox yelping. Two women stood up and clapped. One punched the air. A few others shouted at them to sit down. Susan looked up wearily. Presumably she had seen this sort of behaviour before. Why was she putting herself through this?

She continued. 'The Queen of the Tees will be published later this month. In many ways it's the culmination of my life's work on Boudica and I'd like to read a couple of extracts for you.'

As she was reading, everyone was held in rapt attention. Those who agreed with Diane were nodding in agreement with her words; some seemed every emotional, as though they had invested a lot of themselves in the Boudica story, as though she was a combination of cultural and historical hero - a woman inspired by injustice who led an army against a powerful overlord.

Diane Edwards presented a detailed case for Boudica's roots being in the north, with only her later years spent as part of the Iceni tribe in Norfolk. The Brigante tribe were spread all across the northeast and down into modern-day Yorkshire and they were renowned for their noblewomen being on an equal footing with men, able to inherit land and property. She made reference to texts by a Roman noblewoman accompanying her husband to York in the first century who wrote of a 'great tribal leader, a fierce flame-haired woman who makes even strong men cower' - a woman from the 'wild northern lands'. She went on to narrate a Roman historian's accounts of the local tribal leaders they had found when they first came to Britain, which she claimed contained a reference to Boudica's family as some kind of local royalty in the northeast. But it was when she moved on to discussing where her body was buried that matters got even more heated.

She suggested two potential places. One was an iron-age fort at Stanwick, now near Darlington, which had been created in AD 40 and had grown into one of the most important strongholds in the entire country, the tribal capital of the Brigantes.

'The other location I have in mind, and again this is laid out in more detail in the book, is a site just outside what we now know as Norton-on-Tees.'

Julie turned to Nick with her eyes wide. 'Maybe she's buried in my back garden?!' she whispered.

Diane then went into great detail about Anglo-Saxon burials founds near Mill Lane in Norton in the early 1980s, which she said dated from the AD 400-500 period but which were near to an older site held to be holy by the Brigantes. This she cross-referenced with a Roman historian called Burgundia, whose History of the North Lands in the East mentions the site as being a centre of 'worship and a burial place of great significance'.

She spent another 10 minutes on other post-Roman historians who made reference to the same place and even suggested it had been destroyed at a later date by an early Duke of Northumberland because it was still a focus of Pagan worship rather than the Christian church, leaving only a copse of old yew trees behind today as evidence.

Her case, though incredibly detailed and meticulously researched, was essentially some speculation and a lot of assumption. It was presented with a flourish but it was, at least potentially, a castle built on sand. It clearly needed some hard evidence but presumably she lacked the funds for a proper dig at the site.

She sat down to huge applause and stamping from most of the room. Clearly, Diane's view was the popular one, the fashionable one, perhaps understandably so.

'I feel sorry for Susan having to speak to this lot,' said Julie. 'I'm not sure they're in a mood to listen.'

Florence Farrell then introduced Susan to a few boos and general mumbling. She stood and put her papers on the lectern, peering over her glasses critically to survey the audience before speaking.

'I know many of you here believe in Diane's theories and I admit, she does set out an exhaustive case. She has done as much research as it is possible to do. However, as attractive as these ideas are, and as a Teessider myself I recognise they are very attractive, the fact remains that there is no hard evidence, as she herself acknowledges.'

Several people began booing and slow hand-clapping on hearing this. Susan raised her voice.

'I have spent the last 40 years researching Boudica, Cartimandua, the Brigantes and the Iceni as well as many other tribes and have found nothing to prove that Boudica is from this region nor brought here on her death. Some think she is buried in Wales, or London or the West Midlands. No-one really knows. We're entirely dependent on the Roman historians and they tell us absolutely nothing about her burial or her birth or even anything about her life up to the point of the rebellion she led. As regards to Stanwick Hill fort, that was almost certainly built by the Brigante Queen Cartimandua and she collaborated with the Romans; she was pro-Roman, whereas Boudica fought them - she was their sworn enemy. I don't think Boudica's people would want her to be laid to rest in the hill fort of a pro-Roman. The Norton theory is mere wishful thinking, I'm sorry to say. All sorts of places came and went as focal points for worship and burial in these times, some formal, some informal and we can't really know why, let alone assign any such place to Boudica or indeed to anyone else. The question I must keep asking is "where is the hard evidence?" A few references here and there to a powerful woman in the north lands is simply too vague. It maybe Boudica, yes, but it may well not be, too.'

There were a lot more boos now. Susan ploughed on regardless. Her voice was clear, well-spoken, without any trace of her Teesside roots and without the kind of rhetorical flourishes that Diane deployed. Her delivery was one of the measured academic.

'Boudica has always stirred up deep emotions. She is a hero to many of us. However, because there is a lack of detail about her and her life, it allows us to impose any theory we like upon her, to imagine she was something she was not: that she is almost a modern woman for modern times. But she was not. She was not of the people, in the common sense, rather she was royal born and very much of the elite and she led a rebellion of almost unparalleled brutality that we would find unacceptable today, even as acts of war. For example, it was on her order that when her armies ransacked London, the noblewomen were to have their breasts cut off. Imagine that splashed over your newspaper headlines today. I know many of you see her as a leader of what today we might call the sisterhood but no...no...she was not, or at least not in the sense we understand today. She was a wronged woman; her daughters were raped, yes, but she was a bloody and ruthless warrior.

'However, and we must always remember this, While there are many reasons to be excited by Boudica, she was not a skilled warrior queen. Her demise was caused as much by her lack of military nous as anything else, if we are to believe the Roman historian Tacitus. People today all too often want her to be something that she was not. She was a great figure, who fought against the odds, and we are right to draw inspiration from her, but we must do so from the basis of truth and not fantasy. I could talk longer but I fear you are not in the mood to hear what I am saying. I fear you look upon Boudica as though she is a football team and you are its fans. I see the attraction but it is blinding you to important truths.'

A woman next to Julie stood up and shouted 'traitor!' The booing grew louder.

Susan, now visibly upset, got to her feet again and began shouting, 'You are fantasists!'

'Oh my god, she's lost it,' said Nick, moved at seeing her so agitated.

Susan raged at the woman who had called her a traitor, shaking a small, tight fist at her, leaning forward and shouting with all the power her small body could muster.

'You are committing one of the worst crimes you can commit in historical and archaeological analysis and that is to bend the truth to fit your desires. It is...it is dishonest! My life has been dedicated to this work and with all due respect you are just...just a silly girl who thinks a historical figure is something to cheer and boo. It is intellectually demeaning to you and to me!'

She screamed the final sentence at a high pitch which settled the restless tribes down a little. The power of her emotion was striking. But just as the fervour had subsided a little, the woman who had shouted 'traitor' piped up again.

'Just fuck off!' she shouted contemptuously in a Geordie accent. Uproar again. Susan looked somewhere between furious and tearful.

Florence Farrell rapped on the floor with her stick to restore order.

'Please, please let us make our language appropriate.' Again they all went silent right away.

'It was appropriate!' shouted the Geordie again, to a ripple of laughter. Florence laughed heartily, too.

'I thought Susan was rather good,' said Nick, who had applauded her loudly.

'That certainly took some guts,' added Julie, 'but it's a bit like bear-baiting here...it's not nice. Susan's right, it's more like an Old Firm game.'

Florence continued. 'Okay, so we're going to take some questions from the tribes now. Hands up, please, and say your name and tribe so we know who you are and where you're from.' A woman next to Nick strained her arm up into the air as though she was 11 years old and wanted to desperately answer a question in class. Florence pointed at her with the carved oak pole, wielding it like a rapier with an extravagant flourish. It invested her with great authority as she walked up and down, patrolling the floor during answers like a 21st-century version of a warrior queen.

'Fran Carter - Coritani. What is Diane's theory on why there hasn't been a dig to look for Queen Boudica's burial? Is it a conspiracy by the Iceni followers?' She spoke with an East Midlands accent.

Nick looked at her. Was she crazy? She looked perfectly normal; a regular middle-class kid in her early 20s. This might be some sort of elaborate game of role play, but it was a game driven by some really powerful emotions.

Diane stood up.'Yes, there is a conspiracy to keep Boudica in Norfolk. Yes, I firmly believe that - '

This incensed Susan again; she got to her feet, raised both hands in the air in horror and then waved them dismissively at Diane.

'Oh Diane! How can you say that?! That's just absolute nonsense and you know it! I know what you're trying to do, you're just trying to excite these girls, trying to exploit their youthful energy and sense of romance. It's dishonest what you're doing here, and cruel, too; but worse, worse still, it is academically fraudulent!'

She turned to the person who posed the question and tried to speak calmly.

'There is no conspiracy, my dear, no. Why would anyone want that to happen? All historians and archaeologists are seekers of truth.'

This in turn clearly angered Diane and she flushed pink in the face.

'Really? I beg to differ, Susan. The establishment in our disciplines like the facts to remain unchanged. There is a well-established view of Boudica which you were largely responsible for creating and of which you are chief custodian and perpetrator...'

'...there is an established view based on the evidence! That's why it's the established view!' shouted Susan, now a shade of cerise that looked unhealthy, a small fleck of spit arcing into the air as she did so.

'No! No! No!' said Diane at the top of her voice to more howls of support, now wagging her finger at Susan. 'I won't be silenced on this. We have consistently failed to get funding for a dig at Norton, while other far less important projects have gone ahead!'

'Not true. Not true at all!' shouted Susan, shaking her head.

'It is true! It happens time and again! The county archaeologist is your personal friend. He won't sanction a dig due to your influence.'

She spat out the word personal with real bitterness.

'Fantasy!' dismissed Susan with a wide wave of her hand. 'He turned it down because there's nothing to suggest it will produce any results. My so-called influence is merely to properly represent the facts - if that is an influence, and it damn well should be, then I am guilty, but I have done nothing wrong in the slightest. '

Boos and stamping broke out again. Florence Farrell looked around the room, her green eyes wide, surveying the response of the crowd.

Diane turned to her audience. 'The answer is yes, there is a conspiracy. I am sure of it. And Susan is at the heart of it!'

Florence pointed her stick at another woman in the audience who stood up and above the noise shouted at Susan, 'I've heard rumours that you performed an unofficial dig in Norton years ago. Is that true?'

Susan shook her head vigorously, her beetroot-coloured face contrasting sharply against her silver hair.

'This is all more fantasy. I have heard that, too, but it is all rubbish. I have not performed an unofficial dig. I would never be so unprofessional. It is an accusation totally made up by my enemies to try and discredit me. I've always believed it was fabricated by those who seek to change the accepted wisdom on Boudica.'

Diane Edwards was now equally puce in the face with pent-up anger. The two of them stood 10 feet apart hurling accusations at each other, both of them seemingly uncorking a lot of bottled emotion, as though this was all being aired for the first time.

'Susan, you know as well as I do that these rumours exist because your ex-husband told me and told several other people that you had done precisely that in 1996. You know that! It is not me making up stories or anyone else. Don't be so paranoid!'

'Whatever he said to you or anyone else was not true. He's a bitter man who wanted to create trouble for me so he invented a silly story to get you all worked up, knowing fine well you would want to believe it was true, but it wasn't true then and it's still not true today.'

The fox yelping and stamping broke out again and the whole room was soon in uproar once again.

'Why do these kids care so much about this?' asked Julie, shaking her head.

'I think it's like Susan says, they're supporting a football team; it's irrational but you get a sense of belonging. It is exciting, I mean, it's mad but it stirs the blood.'

Susan sat back down and began to collect her notes. Diane Edwards was on her feet, patrolling the floor restlessly with Florence at her side waving her stick. There was another question, this time from an older woman who seemed less angry.

'What are the economic implications for relocating Boudica to Teesside? Has any work been done on that - tourism and so on?'

Diane nodded.

'Let's be clear about this - it would lead to the economic regeneration of Teesside. Millions would flow in from visitors every year if we could find the gravesite and thus relocate Boudica to Teesside once and for all. Millions! The whole region would benefit from the rebranding of the area. That's why I called my book The Queen of the Tees. She is our queen and on behalf of us all, I demand that we see her returned to us!' She reached a pitch that provoked a huge roar of approval. Susan looked on, her chin jutting out in defiance.

Julie stood up. 'That's all very well, Diane, but Teesside has a proud industrial past and needs an industrial future, too. How many people are going to be employed in the heritage industry? Not many, and they'll doubtless mainly be part-time jobs. Thinking a visitor centre and a museum will form the basis for an economic revival is naïve. It's all very romantic and I'd love it to be true as much as you, but you have to be realistic. There will be a lot of work for you and for other academics but it won't employ many ex-steel workers, will it?'

As this didn't obviously side with either Diane or Susan, it seemed to confuse the crowd a little and they didn't know whether to support or oppose.

Susan shouted 'Hear hear' and clapped.

Diane ignored Julie's comments and ploughed on with her conspiracy theme.

'This region has always been ignored by governments and by the London establishment. It's always been the case in the past and it is the case today. If there was evidence Boudica was buried in London, we'd have dug several sites by now, that I can assure you.'

'But there is no evidence!' shouted Susan getting to her feet, furiously yelling. 'We can't conduct expensive archaeological digs on nothing but your whims!' She was so vehement she did a little leap off the ground as if to volley her words home with greater intensity.

'Whims! Whims! I have conducted exhaustive research, I have uncovered references in texts and I have spent years doing it. These are not mere whims, this is proper historical research. You continue to be a major obstruction to progress, Susan, and I believe you like it that way. You do not want to cede your pre-eminent position to me or to anyone else. You are, at heart, being selfish and you know it.'

'Oh really? This is pathetic! It is beneath me to have to endure this childish nonsense. You've always been like this, and it's why you are not taken seriously. I have had enough of this, enough of all of you!' cried Susan desperately, gathering her papers and walking out to a chorus of booing and more cries of 'traitor!'. Then the thump-thump-yelp cry struck up again. As she departed, the whole place was in a ferment. Some women jeered at her aggressively as she walked out, others were laughing; no-one was indifferent. It was riotous.

'Come on, let's have a word with the poor old girl,' said Nick, getting up. Julie followed him down the steps and out of the room. Susan was hurrying out of the door. They ran after her and caught up on the riverside footpath.

'Hello, Nick, I did see you earlier. I'm sorry you had to see all that in there. It got rather out of hand as I feared it might do. I really shouldn't have indulged Diane's invitation, nor got so caught up in my emotions. I thought I could defend my corner but...well, you saw what happened.'

She cleared her throat, still looking very emotional and upset, nervously rubbing her temple with her finger tips. Nick put his hand on her shoulder and patted her to try and offer some comfort.

'I thought you were very brave,' said Julie as they walked.

'Brave? Stupid, more like. I knew it would end up being like that. I shouldn't have agreed to do it really. Vanity, I'm afraid. ' She let out a big sigh, her head bowed.

'They seem to see Diane as some sort of all-vanquishing hero...and what's all this tribes business?' said Nick.

'Oh, that! It's all absolute nonsense, an affectation. They are pretending they're still part of the ancient tribes of Britain. They do re-enactments, that sort of thing. The hard core of them are like a gang really. They're the ones who lead all the chanting and such. It's silliness. I mean, it's nice that the young are passionate and engaged about history and archaeology, but Diane is exploiting that and I fear she is warping their minds or at least playing to their basest instincts. Someone should teach them a lesson. Teach them some respect. Without respect we have nothing.'

'Indeed. They seemed a bit out of hand. Diane's view certainly seemed to be popular,' said Nick as they walked up to the cathedral. 'Nothing against what you said, though. I thought you made an awful lot of sense.'

'Of course she does, she's a world expert in Boudica,' said Julie.

'Diane's ideas are more glamorous and satisfy the modern lust for...for...a kind of historical soap opera. She is a good researcher and a fine archaeologist but she has a blind spot about Boudica.'

She took out a small white handkerchief and blew her nose, silently.

'I got the impression she was rather bitter and angry,' said Julie.

'Bitter? Hmm, yes, probably. We are all bitter. Life makes one bitter, does it not?'

'And that's why she clings to the story about the unauthorised dig?' said Nick.

'Hmm yes...well, you'd have to ask her about that, it suits her to believe what she wants to believe...' she stopped beside an old Mini and unlocked the door. 'Well, it was nice to see you both. I hope it didn't put you off, Julie. I thought you made a very good point in there, my dear, but I'm afraid this was not academia's finest hour.'

'Don't be silly. It was enlightening in its own way,' said Julie, touching her on her arm. 'Are you OK, Susan? Would you like to go for a cup of tea somewhere?'

She gave her a watery smile. 'Yes, I'm fine, Julie, and thank you for your kind concern. I'm just very tired. I really must go home and make some plans. Goodbye to you both.'

They stood and watched her drive off.

'Oh, bless her. I really like her,' said Julie. 'She's like someone from a different era. More 1906 than 2006. But she seems very sad and alone. Hasn't she got a husband or partner?'

'No. She's divorced, kids live abroad. All academics. There was some big rift or bust-up y'know...families et cetera.'

'Uh, god yeah, bloody families,' groaned Julie.

'Yeah, I like her too. She's got nice manners, even when she was getting mad and shouting, you couldn't imagine her telling them all to just fuck off. She is like something out of a 1950s film. But she looked totally exhausted by the end of it all,' said Nick, as Julie took his hand.

'Well, I suppose if you can't belong to a bonkers society at college, when can you?' said Julie.

'True, I joined something called the Anti-Music Society at college. It was run by a lunatic Scotsman and was just an excuse to make an atonal very loud racket on musical instruments in the name of art. Actually, I wouldn't mind a go at that again now.'

Nick drove them back to Julie's flat and went in for tea.

'The next home game is a week on Sunday - the Newcastle game,' he said, looking at the fixture list in the programme.

'Ah, the local derby.'

'Yeah, I've never felt it was a proper derby, though. We've tried to pretend it is but Newcastle is too far away for a derby. '

'When I was little, my dad always said Hartlepool and Darlington were our local derbies, not Newcastle or Sunderland.'

'He was right. I'll get us tickets for that. Right, I've got to be going, it's already after nine and I've got to be up early for this bloody car boot that Jeff's roped me in for. I'll see you on Wednesday for the awards do, Jules. Remember to put your drinking trousers on, or drinking dress as the case may be.'

'I'm already looking forward to seeing you win the big prize.'

He finished his tea and she gave him a big hug, nuzzling into his neck, her arms around his waist, kissing him on the lips, holding him against her hips for long enough for him to get aroused. She knew what she was doing and he could feel her breath quicken a little as they embraced. She gave him a final peck on the lips.

'Oooh, I wish you could stay.'

Stay meant sex.

'Well, I'll be back up on Wednesday. '

She nodded and smiled and took another kiss from him. He took one last deep breath of her and then drove off south in the dark. He'd thought he was a bit crazy until he'd seen some of the Boudica Society women. As he drove he thought again about the girl he'd seen coming out of Jeff's shop. It was her. It definitely was her. She had been at that meeting, in the darkness of a northern night on the A1 he was certain and he was certain that it was a very strange coincidence. Very strange, indeed.

CHAPTER 3

Nick woke up early for the car boot, walked into town, bought Jeff a posh coffee and a flap jack from Costa and went round to his flat. Jeff opened the door looking like he'd been dragged through a hedge by a tractor.

'Here you go, big man, I got you your favourite triple mocha beta blocker or whatever it's called and some unhealthy, sugary oat thing that is pretending not to be a biscuit; just to help you face a new day of tuber and veg theft.'

Jeff's scowl lifted and he took the coffee from him. 'Owee in...ah, overpriced, pretentiously titled brown liquid, the day is looking up already. Thanks old boy. Just what I need. And it's not long until the pubs open. I choose to stay alive for another day.'

His flat was small and, like his shop, full of vinyl records stacked in boxes against every wall. It smelled odd, like a wild animal was living there, which in a way was true.

They went into the kitchen, where Jeff poured the coffee into a big glass cup.

'See, I'm quite civilised, really,' he said, wiping some spillage from a small Formica kitchen table.

'Where's the cupboard that they took that bag from, then?' said Nick, looking around and sipping from his cup.

Jeff pointed to a pantry door behind him.

It was a shallow cupboard with three shelves playing host to one tin of processed peas, a plastic tub of salt and a tin of kippers. Underneath was a three-tiered plastic rack holding mostly potatoes and a couple of onions.

'So this is where you tipped the Tesco bag of potatoes from the car boot?' said Nick, getting onto his hands and knees.

'Yup. The bag they took was on the top, that was the veg I'd got, but I'd already tipped out the spuds onto the rack. They sweat if you leave them in a plastic bag too long, much like a chap's knackers in those nylon underpants we had in the 70s.'

'Speak for yourself; I had massive white cotton underpants. Mother thought man-made fibres were common. They were so big, if you got a decent erection you could have used them as a makeshift ridge tent,' said Nick, distracted by the dirt at the bottom of the cupboard.

He pulled the red plastic rack to one side. There were mouse droppings around the edge of the cupboard in amongst old bits of onion skin, dust and other detritus that had fallen from the rack over the months and years. Jeff wasn't one for cleaning out cupboards, or anything else for that matter.

'Have you got a torch? It's dark in here.'

Jeff disappeared and returned with a massive portable halogen light which bathed the whole room in pure white light.

'Fucking hell, I wanted a torch, not Pink Floyd's light show! You've not got an inflatable pig as well, have you?' said Nick. It illuminated the whole cupboard perfectly, so he pulled the plastic rack right out and looked at the floor.

In amongst the heaps of muddy grey dust was something more solid. He pushed the muck away and with his fingertips picked up what looked like a gold-coloured pin.

'Any idea what this is?'

Jeff took it from him and held it up between his thick forefinger and thumb.

'I know nothing about such things but this looks a bit like the pin off the back of a badge.'

Nick pushed more dirt aside and felt something hard. It was a three-inch, T-shaped piece of metal which looked very old and decayed, covered with blue-green oxidation. Alongside it was a more intricate piece of metal over three inches long and two inches wide. It was a lattice work shaped into some sort of symbol or insignia, also blue-green with oxidation.

He held the three items in his hand and showed them to Jeff.

'What do you reckon?' he said. 'They look like crusty old bits of metal to me. They can't be what the robbers were looking for. They're worthless, surely. They must think these are something else, something valuable, like. '

'Hmmm, I reckon they're old, though.'

'Yeah but that means nothing, does it? You see people on telly with bits of pottery that are 2,000 years old and it's worth less than some shitty 1950s pot.'

Nick flipped over the brooch and held the gold pin across the back. It fitted perfectly.

'See, this must have been attached,' he looked at it closely, 'and I think it's only just broken off recently. Look, you can see the gold underneath the green where it was attached. It probably got broken in the bag under the weight of the spuds. '

Jeff took it and squinted. 'You reckon it's gold? Could be brass, couldn't it?'

'Maybe, but it looks like gold to me. This other piece...I reckon that's part of some sort of fastener which you clipped the pin onto once you'd put it through your coat or whatever. '

'Aye, like the better-quality badges you used to buy at Newcastle City Hall when you saw a band. Cheap ones just had a little lip of metal to rest the pin under but the nicer ones had a little anchor mechanism. I had an enamel UFO badge like that. I lost it after passing out at a Wishbone Ash gig. Bloody Southern Comfort, it still makes me want to puke when I smell it.'

'I tell you what you should do, you should show this to your Aunt Susan. She must have unearthed all sorts over the years on archaeological digs. Seems likely she might have an idea what this is or at least how old it is. Or if not, she'll know someone who does,' said Nick, getting up on his feet.

Jeff scratched his beard. 'Yeah, good idea, but who the hell would want these and why? Even if they are gold, they don't weigh much and won't be worth more than a few quid. 'Tis weird shit, dude.'

'Life is full of weird though, isn't it? You should've been at the Boudica Society meeting me and Jules went to last night, it was fucking mental. Susan got really upset.' He recounted the highlights of the evening. 'But the really weird thing was that I'm sure I saw the lass who broke into your shop there.'

'Gettaway with you, you didn't, did you?'

'I know it sounds weird and I only saw her briefly, but I'm sure it was her. She disappeared before it all kicked off, though. I thought, nah it can't be...but the more I think about it, the more I'm sure it was her.'

Jeff stood and stared at him, thinking. 'Even I can't come up with a mad theory about that.'

'Nope, me neither. Maybe she's a skint student from round here who fancied a bit of robbing. It doesn't seem likely, though.'

'No that doesn't seem likely. Still, poor old Susan, eh. You wouldn't think these learned folk would be as rabid as your typical football fan, would you?' said Jeff.

'These were. Why don't we go over to Malton tomorrow morning to see her? Then if she can tell us what these things are or if they're worth anything, you can give them to the police and get the potato thieves off your back.'

Jeff saluted him. 'That, captain, is a very good idea.'

Once the car boot was over and after he'd helped Jeff pack away records, Nick went home to do some work on his latest book, a history of football in the north-east of England, called Northern Lights. This was where being the kind of person who was happy to be quiet and alone for hours, days or weeks really came into its own. He worked until after midnight without interruption, lifted some weights for half an hour, took a shower and went to bed. He didn't wake until 8.30am and drank tea looking out at the rush-hour traffic that he was delighted never to be caught up in. Harrogate was a busy, well-to-do and vibrant town, full of money, history and pretension. It was often where rich people from Leeds moved. Some parts of the town were as expensive as Mayfair. It wasn't uncommon to see £100,000 cars sitting in the slow-moving morning traffic, which perfectly illustrated the impotence of owning a high-performance car in Britain.

His morning walk was another of his life's rituals. Existence was, at its core, chaotic. You had to give it some bones or it was just a loose and baggy monster and would get away from you. This is why he needed habits and routines. Most people had these imposed by work and family but in his case the former was fairly loose and the latter non-existent so he had to find his own structure.

He walked out of town on the Otley Road, took Harlow Moor Road north and then back into town past Valley Gardens. The wind was blowing in rain from the Pennines, pushing fragments of slate grey clouds across the sky. At 10am, Jeff called by in his old Ford van to take them to Malton.

They headed out of town on the A59 with some Todd Rundgren playing on the old cassette player. Flat farm lands gave way to the more rolling fringes of the Yorkshire Wolds the further east they travelled. Malton lay just off the A64 between York and Scarborough.

'Hey, I'm going to buy a suit tomorrow for the awards do,' said Nick.

'You in a suit?!' Jeff exclaimed.

'I know. It's not my natural habitat, but I can't turn up in jeans and a Flying Burrito Brothers t-shirt, now can I?'

'You bloody should.'

'Why?' asked Nick.

'You should be true to yourself and you sir, you are a scruffy git. Mind, you'd have to suffer Julie's wrath. She'd not be seen dead with you at a posh do like that if you turned up in a t-shirt, but you know that doesn't mean you shouldn't.'

That really annoyed Nick; he was tiring of Jeff's sniping at Julie.

'Look, don't be a cunt about her Jeff! Unlike us, she's got standards. That doesn't make her some sort of stuck-up harridan and she's not got a bad word to say about you and god knows you've given her enough reason to have over the years,' he said defensively. 'So have some bloody respect. You seem to forget that I'm in a relationship with her...some sort of relationship, anyway.'

'She's always wanted to change you, that's why you had all those problems,' said Jeff, shaking his head.

'According to you, yes, but that's bullshit. Shut up, I don't want to talk about it. You know fuck all,' he said, now annoyed. He wanted to change and changing wasn't a bad thing, was it? You could change for the better, or at least he hoped so. It wasn't a proper grown-up relationship with Julie yet but it felt like it was heading down that road and it was only happening because he was consciously trying not to make the same mistakes and because, to some degree, she was, too. He knew Jeff wouldn't understand that. He thought not changing was something to be proud of.

'Don't lose your shit, dude, I was just taking the piss,' said Jeff. 'I shall be wearing my dinner jacket. It cost £10 from Age Concern last year, lovely quality it is. If you want to wear a suit, you wear a suit.'

What he hadn't told Jeff was that he wasn't just going to buy any old suit, he was going to buy an expensive designer suit from David Watts, an upmarket menswear store in town, and that he was doing it because he knew it would both impress and please Julie.

It was exactly the sort of thing he would have refused to do on principle when they lived together. He had been wilfully protective of his studenty, scruffy appearance as though it was almost a moral issue. He'd dug his heels in over nothing, almost by reflex, always fighting against, against, well, against something. Buying a nice suit was, he hoped, a physical manifestation of the mental change he was trying to make. After all, she'd only been trying to help him.

Change the subject.

'Aye, so that Boudica Society thing me and Jules went to was mental. Susan could just about hold her own, though.'

'Yeah, you were saying that yesterday. Well she's old school, isn't she? You know, brought up to argue your corner, be polite but firm. Kids like her brought up in the 40s and 50s with rationing, they've got a good perspective on life, if you ask me. Even the middle class like her had it tough compared to today. She's always been very level headed y'know. Sensible, I suppose. It's underrated, is sensible.'

'Aye, it's the sensible people who get stuff done so that the fuck-wits like me and thee can go out to play. Does she get on with your mam?'

'They've always kept in touch but they're very different types of people. Mam is more outgoing and loud, as befits a woman who is a boozer. She's the anti-Susan, really.'

'And she lives alone?'

'Yeah, I don't think there's been anyone since she divorced Martin, though she never took his name. I always liked that.'

'Isn't that the point of getting married, though?' said Nick.

'What? Changing your name?'

'Yeah, that's the gig. That's the convention you're buying into, isn't it? I mean, I like that she didn't change her name as well but then I'm no fan of the institution of marriage...or at least, it's not for me and Jules.'

'I never really liked him even though I only met him a few times. He's OK but a bit up himself. I always thought he was a strange choice for her.'

'People marry inappropriately all the time, don't they?'

'Aye, well she's got a couple of kids but they're academics abroad. When my mam remarried after dad had snuffed it, I was about 16 and, if you remember, I was an absolute swine. I was boozing and generally deploying a scorched-earth policy. But she was really nice to me. She even let me stay over down here in Malton during the summer holidays. She treated me like a human and not some pubescent nightmare, so I never forgot that. She even used to sub me money at college even though I was usually only skint due to two things...'

'Lager and records?' said Nick. It was a fair guess.

'...there you go...lager and records, indeed. So I've always kept in touch with her over the years, though I never saw much of her until she started doing the car boots. She's super brainy. Massive IQ. Big giant brain. They reckoned she was the head honcho academic in her field, y'know...the Romans and all that what's-her-name business.'

'Boudica, you mean?'

'Aye. She was like a world expert on all of that. Do you say it Boo-Dicker our Bo-De-Cee-Ah?'

'The former, I think. Yeah, that came out at the meeting. I got the impression her successor, this Diane Edwards woman, has eyes on her crown. She's pushing this whole Teesside angle.'

Jeff started hitting the cassette player, which had jammed. 'Aye well, they all want their own gig, don't they? They want to put their stamp on the academic world. Remember that teacher we had in sixth form? Big Stan? He was an expert on that book Tristram Shandy.'

'Laurence Sterne's classic. Actually, I once talked to Susan about that book - she had an old copy. Oh yeah, I remember him, he was good. Bit of a freak. He had wild hair and a beard.'

'He was a freak alright, smoked grass, I reckon, he had that vibe. But I remember some kid going on about some rival theory about something in that book and Big Stan went mental because it was in opposition to some idea he'd had...it's all territory to them...they want to be the one whose theories are held to be the definitive ones and go down in all the text books as the Grand Fromage.'

By 10.30am it was a lovely bright and sunny morning as they drove into Malton, but with a stiff easterly wind making it feel cold, the sort of wind that the expression 'it'll blow the cobwebs away' was designed to describe.

Susan Rutherford lived on Middlecave Road, a leafy street to the west of the quiet market town, where years could pass without much happening at all.

'If you wanted a picture that perfectly illustrates the word respectable, it'd be of the houses on this sort of road,' said Nick as they drove towards Susan's house.

'Oh aye, this sort of place is about as rock 'n' roll as digestive biscuits. It oozes tartan slippers and sensible anoraks, doesn't it? Hey look...getting in that red sports car...talk of the devil, it's Martin James, Susan's ex,' said Jeff, pointing as they went past.

Nick looked out of the passenger window as they went past a man getting into a classic Porsche 911 and recognised the smart, tanned man.

'Oh, yeah. Nice car.'

'That's a mid-life crisis car if I ever saw one,' laughed Jeff. 'I'm only surprised he's not got a ponytail and an 18-year-old Russian girlfriend.'

'He's a bit, y'know, designer fashions if you ask me.'

'So am I, as long as I can buy designer fashions at a car boot...'

'...for under two quid.'

'...for under two quid yeah, obviously...and that's top whack, mind. You can't even get designer fashions in my size - not unless Armani have started a range of capacious tarpaulins.'

They parked outside Susan's large, detached Victorian villa. It was set back from the road by a gravel drive and large, tall privet hedges on all sides.

'Did you call to let her know we were coming?' asked Nick, getting out of the van.

'I sent her an e-mail last night. Tried calling this morning before I picked you up but there was no reply. I left a message saying we had something we wanted her to have a look at. Didn't bother going into any detail; I mean, it might be nothing, mightn't it?'

They crunched down the gravel driveway on foot.

As they approached the door, they could see it was off the latch and ajar.

Jeff knocked and called out. 'Susan! It's Jeff and Nick!'

He listened but there was no reply. He knocked again. 'Susan, it's Nick and Jeff!'

The draught from a breeze threatened to shut the door but Nick wedged his foot in the gap. 'Susan?!' He thought he heard a thud or some movement inside.

'She's probably out the back,' said Jeff. He peered in. 'Susan it's me!' he called out. But there was no reply. 'She must be in the garden, I'll go round and have a look,' he said. 'Just go on in, she won't mind.' He walked off around the side of the house.

Nick went into the house and called out Susan's name again but there was still no reply.

A parquet-floored hallway with a big blue-and-red patterned rug led down to the kitchen at the far end with rooms off each side. It was a big house. A career in archaeology must have paid well. He felt a bit uncomfortable walking into someone's house uninvited. The walls were covered in various framed photos of teams of academics on projects, mostly in trenches and fields. By the look of the haircuts and clothes, these dated back to the late 60s.

A front room led off to the left. He looked in, no-one was there. He walked further down. 'Susan, are you in?' he called and looked into the back room, beginning to feel quite spooked by the silence.

There she was.

For a long heartbeat he just stood and stared while his brain clicked into gear and allowed him to understand what was in front of him.

She was lying on the floor in an unnatural, crumpled position, her legs folded and twisted under her as though they were made of melted wax. Her head was lying on an ornamental fire surround and her long grey hair spilled out onto the hearth.

Nick ran to her, his heart racing now. What did you do to check if someone was alive? He touched her neck; it was still warm. Did that mean she was still alive or only just dead? Find a pulse. How did you bloody well do that? He fumbled with her wrist.

'Susan. Look at me...Susan,' he said, taking her hand. There was no response at all. He looked closely at her mouth and chest; she wasn't breathing.

Jeff walked in at that moment. 'She's not out the back...what the fuck is...Susan!' he stood, mouth agape. 'Is she ill? Has she passed out?'

Nick tried in vain to find a pulse again. She still wasn't breathing so being the wrong side of the mortal veil seemed the only likely option.

'Just call an ambulance, Jeff. Go on! Now!' he said, with urgency but not wanting to shout. It felt wrong to shout when you were next to a dead person, as though she could hear and be disturbed. Jeff was in shock, he looked dazed. 'Get your phone out and do it! 999!' Nick hissed at him as he eventually backed off into the hallway and began dialling.

His mind was whirring over at high speed as he looked at her lying with her head on the fire surround, her eyes closed. It was very odd having a dead body right there in front of you. Interesting really. The stillness and silence was remarkable. The ultimate stillness. Literally without movement. It was not the stillness of sleep or unconsciousness but the final stillness and more deeply still and silent because of that. Never had it been more obvious that the body was merely a vehicle for the person and Susan Rutherford had certainly vacated hers. Everything she had ever been, every thought, experience and emotion was gone. Death had, in an irrevocable instant, drained her synapses. Her intellect and learning now evaporated, her voice forever lost. It was the most profound thing he had ever witnessed. Here it was: the end. Everyone's destiny. She'd taken the final leap across the great divide, freed forever from the pain and joy of mortality. Her life was done and could never be resurrected.

It was his first ever dead body but seeing her somehow left him feeling calm. However she had died, whatever had caused it, surrender to the big sleep seemed the most natural of things.

He stood up as Jeff re-entered the room.

'Is she dead? Is she dead?' he said with rising panic. He knelt down in front of her and took her hands. 'C'mon Susan, wake up. It's alright, there's an ambulance on its way. C'mon,' he said, gently shaking her as though she was a sleeping child.

Nick didn't know what to say. He patted him on the back.

'It's no use Jeff. She's gone. Bless her.'

'What?! Why?! Why has this happened? She's just an old lady, a clever old lady living a quiet life. I don't understand. She wasn't that old. What's happened? What's happened?' His voice was choked with emotion.

'I don't know, man...probably a heart attack or something.'

Nick retreated to the doorway, got out his camera phone and took a picture of the scene. Then he took a shot of the body.

'What the hell are you doing?' said Jeff, getting up and advancing towards him, pushing him in the chest.

'We don't know what happened here. I want to have a record of it.'

Jeff was astonished.

'What the fuck? She's dead! Have a bit of respect! What the fuck?!'

'Look, it's no use going crazy at me. Yes she's dead, but it's not like we can upset her now. You getting angry won't change the fact she's dead. We need to keep calm and analyse this.'

'Piss off. Who do you think you are, bloody Hercule Poirot? Don't be so bloody heartless,' he shouted. He tried to look at her body again but clearly couldn't face it and left the room in tears. Susan lay there, motionless, a silent witness to his upset.

Nick was glad to see him leave as this was no time for crippling emotion. The police and ambulance wouldn't be far away. He looked around. There was a book on the table, it was The Queen of the Tees by Diane Edwards, and it was open at the front page. It had been signed by the author with the inscription 'To Susan - without you, none of this would have been possible'. He took a picture.

A tray with a single empty teacup and a silver teapot stood on a coffee table. He took a photo of that, too, and then touched the pot. It was tepid. The cup had a thin trace of tea at the bottom. It felt warm, as though it had held tea within the last 20 minutes. It was 10.40am. He'd been there less than 5 minutes. She really must have died in the last ten or 15 minutes, 20 at the most.

He went through to the kitchen. It was neat and tidy. Blue willow-patterned plates sat on racks and cups hung on mug trees. The back door was slightly ajar, resting on the Yale latch but not properly closed. That seemed odd - the front and back door had both been left open...no-one sits in a house with both doors open, especially not in October.

The sirens were approaching so he went back to look at Susan. There was no sign of any injury to her, but the position of her body was odd, perhaps as though she had collapsed while getting up from her chair. There was certainly no sign she'd been assaulted and the house looked untouched by robbery, so much so that her purse was still on the kitchen table.

The wooden coffee table was the largest of a nest of three tables, the other two being tucked against a wall. He got down onto his knees to look - there was a gouge in the wood at one end of the table. He ran his index finger over it. It felt rough and raw. He took a photo and was about to go outside when he noticed a chip of wood near the door and picked it up. It was sharp. Returning to the coffee table, it was obvious this was where it had come from. He turned the small piece of wood until it fitted perfectly in the hole. It looked as though it had been gouged out very recently, the wound in the wood fresh, raw and clean. After one last photo he went outside to meet the ambulance.

Jeff was sitting on a low wall that formed part of a small garden feature. He had his head in his hands and had clearly shed tears. He'd never seen Jeff cry. Then again, he'd never seen him with a dead relation before. He patted him on the back.

'Take it easy. I'll handle everything, big man,' he said.

A police car pulled up with blue lights flashing and an ambulance wasn't far behind.

Two policemen got out and came over. Nick explained what they'd found. Paramedics went into the house but emerged within minutes shaking their heads. Eventually, after much police procedure, the body was taken out in a black zip-up bag. At that moment, Nick felt an unusually strong tinge of melancholy for her. It seemed an undignified end for a woman who had been the model of middle-class respectability. She'd have hated all this fuss in the first place and then to leave the house for the last time in an anonymous big plastic bag...it was very sad and almost vulgar. That day at the car boot when she'd touched his face, kindly, emotionally, empathizing with him almost, now it felt like a gift she'd left with him; an abiding memory. 'Keep love in your life', she'd said. He looked around the room, she'd had a love of archaeology and history, that much was sure, but what about people?

The drive back to Harrogate was a difficult one. Nick still didn't know what to say to Jeff, who in turn had nothing to say. It had left them both numb and tired.

Nick parked up outside Jeff's flat.

'At least we've got the awards thing on Wednesday. We can have a good big free piss-up at that. Forget about all this. We'll fucking need it, eh,' said Nick, trying to appeal to one of Jeff's pleasures in life. Life went on. That was the most obvious thing. Susan's life now had a full stop but the world turned on and on and her death, though significant to those who knew her, was nothing to humanity. Just another death in a day of deaths. 250,000 or more happened every day on earth, every one of them someone's son or daughter with a trail of life stretching out behind them in an endless parade of mortality. Death was the final unifier which brought together the rich, the poor, the young, the old. No-one here gets out alive.

Jeff nodded slowly. 'You know, I've never seen a dead body before. They never let me see my dad when he passed away. It's fucking horrible. I don't think it'll ever leave me, the image of her lying there. People say it's just like they're sleeping but it's not. It looks totally different.' Nick hadn't actually found it horrible. In fact, he'd found it closer to fascinating.

'Yeah, it's my first time too. With my dad going, it's a second death this year for me. One thing does occur to me though, you know - we saw the ex-husband just before we went in. Surely he must have been there to see Susan. Why hadn't he seen her body? The door was open. If he did see it, he didn't raise the alarm. He could have gone in if no-one answered the door. I mean, it's weird, isn't it?'

'Yeah...yeah, that's right. I forgot all about seeing him. It is weird, and too much of a coincidence if you ask me.'

'Could his being there have caused her death, somehow? Maybe she got upset and had a heart attack or something.'

'Yeah, maybe. I'll get in touch with him and find out what he was doing there. I've got his number somewhere - he gave it to me at the car boot the other day, remember?'

'Yeah, it'd be good to know what he saw, if anything at all. If she'd...err...y'know...if she'd died when he was there, he'd have called an ambulance, wouldn't he?'

Jeff nodded. 'Yeah, yeah, of course, he's alright, is Martin. Smooth, but he's not a bastard. He'd have done what was necessary, like. I'm sure he would. Maybe he wasn't even at Susan's.'

'Aye...he might have a friend in the road from the old days,' said Nick.

'I'll ring him tomorrow, then.'

'Look, you'll be alright, Jeff, you'll get over this. There's no changing things now, I mean, there's nothing we can do to bring her back, no point in beating yourself up about it,' said Nick, then knew he had probably judged those words badly. Too harsh.

'I know that,' said Jeff, looking out of the window, frowning, 'but I'll really miss her. She was good to me, she was a really nice person and there's not many nice people around, is there? She treated me right when no-one else did. When my mam was on the piss, when my dad was dead, when school suspended me, when all that shit happened, she was patient and kind.' His voice broke with emotion.

What could you say? You can't comfort someone after a loss because it's exactly that, a loss, and there's no altering the fact. Words won't help. He wondered whether he should say that to Jeff but just couldn't tell if it was the right or wrong thing to say and didn't want to risk upsetting him even more.

'Alright, big man. I'll call you tomorrow.'

When he got home he loaded the images from his phone onto his computer. Looking at the body again through the computer screen made him realise just how much such images fail to capture. The stillness, the lifelessness that was the very definition of that scene was missing from the picture. It looked like a staged photograph instead of the reality of an ended life.

By the time he got to bed he was dog tired and slept solidly until 10am.

As soon as he woke up, he felt it. Shit. Fuck. A dark mood had infected him the way a virus silently corrupts you from the inside. He knew what it meant. He sat up in bed, let out a low moan and lay back down and didn't even feel like getting up. His instinct was to crawl away and hide from the world. It was like wearing a hermetically sealed helmet, as though a layer of something dense and smothering had been applied to his head. It made his mind impenetrably foggy, so much so that even organising his thoughts was hard work.

He had no control over these depressive episodes. Indeed, the helplessness when they came upon him was one of the most troubling and upsetting aspects. It was like someone else came to live inside your skin without invitation and you couldn't make them leave, you just had to wait until they wanted to go. It made him feel aggressive towards himself, wishing he could beat it out of him. 'What the fuck are you like this for?' he said out loud as he dragged himself out of bed miserably, hitting himself on the head with the palms of his hands. This was what he'd tried to explain to Marc Lewis but there were no words that could truly describe how this felt. It was everything and yet nothing, like being engulfed by an emotional black hole where the joy and the pleasure in anything is sucked out of you and replaced with a gaping void within which nothing at all can exist. Life simply seemed pointless now.

He stood looking out across The Stray feeling worried and yet somehow useless then squatted on his haunches and briefly held his head in his hands as though to better hide from the world. From there he sat on his sofa and stared into the middle distance for half an hour, thinking, mulling things over and yet not really thinking at all. He should eat but he didn't feel hungry. The day drifted miserable, shapeless and heavy in his head and as the time passed he could feel himself sinking further and further into his shell, the defensive layers painted over his psyche. All he really wanted to do was to be quiet and alone and not have any stress or responsibility. It was hard to cope with anything or anyone but he knew he'd promised to call Jeff, yet he hated using a phone when he felt like this. Any form of communication was difficult and the actual phone was physically intimidating. He had to pluck up a lot of courage to even pick up the handset.

'Hello, mate. How are you this morning?' he said, digging his nails into the palm of his hand as he did so, digging them right in, holding them there, pressing hard into the flesh, so much that it first stung, then burned and hurt. The pain calmed him.

'I came into work. I thought it was the only thing to do and I've got loads of sorting out to do here so I'm getting into that while blasting out some Sabbath. Seemed to make as much sense as anything.'

'Yeah, good idea, right.'

'I tried calling Martin but got his voicemail. I left a message.'

'Right. Okay.'

Jeff didn't say anything else. That was his chance to get out of talking. He spotted it and grabbed it. 'Okay then, I'll leave you be. I'll ring you before the thing on Wednesday.'

'Aye. Thanks for calling.'

He went for a long walk around the outskirts of Harrogate onto the edge of the countryside, feeling only half alive. It was like looking out at the world through thick glass and it was hard to feel the joy in anything, not in green grass or a sunny afternoon or a dog running with a stick or some tasty bacon. Nothing. Everything was just fucking rubbish and felt like it always would be forever and ever.

But he wanted to fight it. This was where therapy at £85 an hour was supposed to help but he didn't feel like he'd made enough progress to cope. This mood or chemical imbalance or whatever it was could affect him for the next few days or longer. It could twist him up inside and make Wednesday's awards night just impossible. Yet it wasn't something it seemed possible to fight or resist. You can't wrestle something that you can't grasp.

So he kept walking, hoping that the endorphins from the exercise would help and he kept digging his nails into his hand until finally he broke the skin on his palm and a trickle of blood ran down his fingers. It was too profound, too powerful. It would only go away when it was done with him. The black dog had control. It really did feel like an independent, malevolent force possessing him.

Back at home he sat with the lights off as the light faded from the sky over the Pennines. Talk about it, Marc Lewis had said, and don't dwell on things on your own. Pull it out of yourself and acknowledge it, it'll help, he'd said. It'll help to puncture the balloon of depression. Don't swallow it down and suffer it alone. Share it. But he didn't want to share it, he didn't want to curse anyone else with it, he didn't even want to admit to its existence. His instinct was to suffer on his own and not admit to anyone else what was happening. He felt it was a self-indulgent depressive siege which he didn't want to taint anyone else with. But he knew he had to try. Even without his grief, Jeff wasn't a candidate to talk to. There really was only one person to whom he could turn. He hoped it was the right thing to do. It was a big test. He'd avoided doing this every time he'd been depressed in the last six months. Every time because this was what had killed their relationship. But there was no running from it forever; he had to try and climb over it and towards her. So he called Julie.

'Hello there, lovely Mr Nick,' she said, in her lovely, sing-song voice.

'Hello, beautiful Julie,' he said on hearing her voice, suddenly feeling tearful. He could hear the smile on her face as she spoke.

'Aw, that's nice,' she said, and he could see her turquoise blue eyes. 'And to what do I owe this pleasure?'

He sighed and swallowed down his emotion. 'Oh I just...err...I just wanted to hear you, err, you know...talk to someone...' he said, immediately regretting calling her and wanting to stop. He beat his fist hard against his hip, digging his nails into the wounds on the palm of his hand again to distract his brain from the urge to put down the phone.

'Are you alright?' she said, concern now in her voice. He could never hide anything from her for long. 'You're not, are you?'

'I'm OK...well...no...no I'm not...I woke up depressed...or whatever it is...you know...Marc, the therapist, said I should talk about it when it starts, he's always going on about not suffering it alone...and I woke up with it today and...sorry...I shouldn't have disturbed you...it's selfish of me.'

She interrupted his scattered thoughts.

'No no, it's fine. You can always talk to me about anything, any time. I want to help,' she said, without judgement. This was different. When they'd lived together she had lacked sympathy, not that Nick thought sympathy was appropriate. Who could live with this? He didn't bloody want to.

He walked slowly around the apartment, looking at his feet but not saying anything more, feeling even more strongly that he wanted to put down the phone.

'Are you still there?' said Julie.

'Yeah.'

'So what's brought this on do you think?' she said calmly.

'Dunno.' He went silent again. 'It's just...on me. I hate it.'

'It must be horrible. Talk to me about what you've been up to.'

'Err...well...we went to Susan Rutherford's yesterday to show her this thing we found at Jeff's, but she had just died. So we were...'

'What? Susan?! Susan Rutherford, you mean? From Durham Uni?!'

'Yeah. We don't know why or how. I found her dead on the floor in her house. We called the police and everything. We were there for hours.'

He knew this would be shocking news, he really did know that, but he really couldn't care about saying it politely.

'Oh, poor Susan! Oh, god...god bless her.'

There was a hiccup of tears in Julie's voice. It did her credit. He didn't feel like crying for anyone except himself and he didn't think he was worth shedding tears over.

'God, man, to think we only saw her at that Boudica Society meeting the other day. She didn't look well though. The poor, poor lady. And you found her?'

'Yeah.'

'You poor lad. That must have been upsetting.'

'No, it wasn't. She was dead. There was nothing we could do.'

'Well...all the same...it's not nice for anyone to see. Maybe that's what...'

He knew what she was going to say and butted into the conversation bluntly.

'It's not that. I mean, I can cope with that, I mean, I didn't know her really, and I'm not bothered, or rather, I don't mean I'm not bothered, I mean, it's not that, OK? So don't say it is. It's not her fault. It's my fault. It...it just comes over me and I really, really fucking hate it. I'm so sick of it. It makes me wish I was dead as well. It fucking feels like being fucking dead. I shouldn't have called you, it's selfish of me. Susan's died and all I can talk about is myself.' He felt disgusted with himself and now he was being aggressive and sharp towards Julie. He'd taken enough of her time and was about to put the phone down.

'Don't hang up, Nick...don't go yet. I'm worried about you. Look, I'm going to come down to see you to make sure you're OK. It won't take me long. I'll be there in an hour or so. Don't worry about anything. We'll sort it out together. I'll stay with you until it's over. You can talk if you want but you don't have to. I'll just be there, alright?'

Nick felt so awkward and his overwhelming desire was to turn down her help. This is certainly what he would have done in the past: be self-sufficient, survive everything on your own, don't let anything leak in or leak out. It was embarrassing to be like this in public. But he needed help.

'You don't have to.'

'I know, but I want to.'

'But I'm not worth it. Not like this.'

'Of course you are. Just try and relax and I'll be there soon.'

Despite feeling disgusted with himself, he accepted her help. He let out a sigh. 'I won't be any fun and I might be a real bastard and I don't want you to have to suffer that.'

'I understand that. I'll cope. Right, I'll set off now.'

He put the phone down and sat at his kitchen table, staring into the middle distance.

An hour later, Julie pressed his intercom. He hadn't moved an inch since putting down the phone. Nick knew she still had a key so she had used the buzzer out of politeness or respect. She hadn't been back to the flat since she'd moved out 18 months ago. He buzzed her in, unlocked his door and went to put on the kettle.

She put her head around the open door. 'Hiya!' she called out, typically cheerfully.

He came out of the kitchen.

'Hello,' he said, forcing a smile. She was wearing a soft, cream-coloured wool sweater and khaki cargo pants, and stood, head on one side, smiling but clearly looking at him with a degree of suspicion, unsure what she was going to find.

'Now then, how's my favourite loony?' she said with obvious kindness in her eyes.

'I'm urggh bluergh. There are no words for it.'

She shut the door behind her, put her a shoulder bag down and kicked off her baseball boots.

'I was just making some tea,' he said, and she followed him into the kitchen.

She'd had some blonde streaks and loose curls put into her usually straight hair since Saturday.

'You've had your hair done,' he said as the kettle boiled.

She played with one of the loose curls.

'Well spotted. I just freshened it up a bit. I get a 20 per cent discount as student at this place in Durham.'

'It looks really good. Suits you.'

She smiled. He couldn't.

'Ta. So what about you, then?'

He shrugged.

'I was going fine, looking forward to Wednesday, then I woke up this morning and bam...it's like I've got a different head on. You know I realised today I'm actually embarrassed about it, embarrassed in front of you and in front of myself, even. I feel like a twat. I hate myself for being so dysfunctional. I really do...I hate myself. I'm so shit.'

She frowned and shook her head. 'You can't help it, it's not your fault and there's no need to be embarrassed. Millions of people have depression. I never realised it was so commonplace until I did some reading up.'

'Hmm. I dunno,' he said, finding it hard to look at her while talking about it. He went quiet and turned to pour water onto the tea. As he did so, she came up behind him and hugged him, putting her arms around his waist, rubbing his tummy and briefly kissing him on the neck. 'You don't have to talk about it. We can just watch some telly or listen to the radio, if you like,' she said, 'or I brought a book with me if you just want to sit, or you can play with yourself while I watch if you want. I used to like that.'

She gave a little laugh. He knew he should laugh at her joke but he had no humour in him.

'Thanks, Jules.'

He wrapped his arms around her and hugged her tightly to him for a full minute, feeling her belly breathing in and out against his, trying to suck some positive energy from her into him. She felt warm and soft and suddenly, out of the blue, he felt really emotional, tears melting at the corner of his eyes. What was wrong with him? He didn't usually cry and it made him feel so awkward in his own skin. These bursts of emotion had started happening in the spring when he was sorting his dad's estate out and had kept happening.

While she was looking away, he wiped the moisture from his eyes with a finger and carried the tea into the living room. The TV was on.

She looked around.

'You know, I don't think this place has changed at all since I moved out. I thought you might have redecorated or something,' she said, pulling her feet up under her on the old brown leather sofa.

Nick sank down next to her.

'I always liked what you'd done to the place, so I just left it.'

'It's a great flat. Very art nouveau. Stylish, like.'

They sat and watched a documentary in silence. Julie leaned into him, hooking her arm around his and resting her head on his shoulder. He kept letting out involuntary tense sighs as though his body was trying to calm his stress. Every time he did it, she gently squeezed his arm to comfort him. There was no need to talk, thank god, because he had nothing at all to say.

The distraction of the TV, the stillness, the quiet and the warmth of her against him eventually began to thaw the dark, icy tension in him.

The quiet companionship of simply being with her on the sofa began to feel relaxing and warm and eventually not embarrassing or awkward. He dropped off to sleep.

Later, well after midnight, when she got up to go to the toilet, he stirred. When she came back, she stood in front of him smiling.

'Now then dozy, shall we have a little nightcap? A glass of something? Have you got anything in?'

'There's a bottle of Barolo red wine on the wine rack in the kitchen, if you fancy that.'

She poured two glasses, set them down on the coffee table and got back on the sofa, sitting with her legs across his lap. He took hold of her feet and rubbed them, something she had always liked.

'These are bonny socks,' he said, pointing at the rainbow-coloured stripes and yawning.

'Nice, aren't they? I got them from Benetton for a fiver.'

Nick took a drink of the powerful, velvety wine. As he did so he felt now brighter, sharper and less introverted. Oh, thank fuck. How could this thing just come and go, wash in and out like a tide? He looked at the wounds on his palm and winced, not at the scars but at the emotions which had driven him to make them.

'Giz a look at ya,' she said, leaning forward and taking his hand. 'Did you do that to yourself?'

He held up his hands, palms facing towards her. 'These are my depression stigmata.'

She looked at him, frowned and shook her head, not knowing what to say. What could anyone say?

'They look sore, do you want something on them?'

'No. It's OK.'

'You shouldn't hurt yourself like that, y'know... not unless the Boro are playing, anyway. Then I'd understand it, obviously.'

He managed a smile. 'Sorry, Jules. Thing is, I look at what I've done and even now it feels like a different man did that to me. It...it frightens me.'

'That's understandable. But you do look different now. There's a light back in your eyes again.'

He smiled. 'Yeah, it's like coming back to life. Hard to explain or describe. I used to think it was just a mood, but when you think about it, what is a mood? It's a chemical thing in your brain, isn't it?'

She held his right hand in hers as she talked, lightly stroking the puncture wounds with her thumb. It was a simple, gentle act that made tears rise in his throat again.

'When you feel like that it looks like someone has turned off your battery, you almost look physically different. I was doing some research and I think you might have some kind of bipolar depression. There's loads of different types, it's not all very high and very low, y'know, not all that classic manic behaviour.'

'I might try going to a different doctor, just to see what they say. The therapist thinks it's all to do with my childhood. We were talking about my mother in the last session. He puts a lot of my problems down to her being ill and dad being useless when I was in my teens.'

She nodded. 'That makes sense. You know, I was very impressed with you for even trying therapy.' She stroked his thigh with her foot as a sign of her approval.

He shrugged. 'Well, I don't really like the bloke that much 'cos he's a bit smooth but in fairness he might have helped me put it into some sort of context, though it's not stopped me getting depressed. Not yet anyway. At least I could ask you for help and I've never done that before. Not that I wanted to. You've no idea how hard it was to make that call to you.'

He pulled her socks up and stroked her legs as they lay across his lap.

'Thanks for coming down and doing your guardian angel thing. I don't think it made the depression lift because it seems to have a life of its own and I didn't really want to see you, if I'm being honest. That's nothing against you or anything; it's just that I wouldn't wish Dirtbag Nick on anyone, especially you. But it's really nice to have you here now.'

She leaned forward and stroked his face and ear. 'Anytime. I mean that, darlin'. I hope I'm starting to understand it all a bit more. It's so difficult for someone like me who doesn't suffer from depression to really grasp it. It almost seems like you're making it all up, putting it on, like. I think I used to half believe that's what you were doing when we lived together.'

'I used to think that about my mam when she was ill.'

'While you were napping I took a look at your notes about poor Susan's death,' she said, nodding at the pad on the table. 'How's Jeff?'

'Very upset. I think that'd describe it. Understandably.'

'But you don't think that could have caused your depression today?'

'I don't know. Maybe it's stress or something but I don't think so.'

'Well it must be upsetting seeing a dead body. '

'You'd think so but I found it more fascinating than frightening. That probably sounds a bit sick. There didn't seem any point in feeling sorry for her because she wasn't actually there any more. Does that make sense? The woman we'd talked to on Saturday night was gone and it was that facet of her that was important, not the flesh and blood. But poor Jeff was in tears and I've not seen him like that before.'

'I suppose being a cold-hearted dysfunctional head case has its advantages sometimes, eh, mister. Well, let's not dwell on it just at the moment. Like you say, there's nothing we can do for her now. It's hard to believe though, isn't it? There she was, shouting the odds on Saturday and now she can't shout any more.'

'Yeah, the on-off nature of existence is hard to comprehend. You're either alive or you're not.'

They sat in silence for a few minutes with the rumble of the traffic from the road below as a soundtrack.

'Ooh, there's something I want to show you, this might cheer you up some more. Have you got two grapes?'

'No it's just the way I'm sitting,' he said, pulling a face. She slapped at him good-naturedly, got up, went into the kitchen and came back with a small yellow tomato and a small red one.

'Just watch this,' she said. 'Now, you take the red tomato and I'll keep the other one, see?' She held it up at him. 'Right, now you show me yours.'

'That's what you say to all the boys.'

He opened up his palm. Julie took the red tomato. 'Oh that's a lovely tomato,' she said, picking it up and looking at it before pressing it back into his hand and closing his fingers over it.

'Okay, so what was that all about?' asked Nick.

'Look at the tomato in your hand,' she said, grinning.

He looked. It was yellow. She was holding his red one.

'Bloody hell. That was good, Jules. I never spotted you switching them.'

'Class, eh? My brother Terry taught me how to palm something but I forgot all about it until he reminded me this week when I went to visit him in Durham jail.'

'Ah, right, you don't normally visit him, do you?'

She shook her head. 'No, but he gets out soon so I thought I should see how he is, as I'm in town every day, like. It's a horrible place, Durham jail. I don't know how anyone can stand it. It stinks of disinfectant and despair. '

'And how is he?'

'Full of good intentions but then I've heard all that before. He says he's going to get a flat in Roseworth. He's in his late 20s now, it's time he got his act together and gave up this stupid and frankly rubbish career as a thief. It's not like he's even any good at it.'

'Show me that trick again and I'll see if I can spot you changing them.'

She went through the routine but he still couldn't see her sleight of hand.

Nick laughed at this new skill. She gave him a silly grin and wobbled her head.

'Is there no end to your talents?'

'You should see what I can do with a ping-pong ball!'

'Ha ha. A talent acquired when working as an exotic dancer in Bangkok, I assume.'

'I can actually do that, you know,' she said laughing, putting her hair back behind her ears.

'What? Fire a ping-pong ball out of your...you know what?'

She nodded. 'Yeah, I came home drunk one night and someone had been talking about it in the pub and I happened to have a ping-pong ball in the flat so I tried it, on my own, like, not for anyone else's entertainment. One of these days, if you're a very good boy, I'll give you an exhibition of my talent.'

He rubbed his hands together. 'I'll look forward to that. You're a loss to the Jim Rose circus. Maybe I should pick up weights with my bollocks. We could go into business as a freak show double act.'

She pulled a face and laughed. 'That's got to hurt though, hasn't it?! Weights on your balls, like. Ouch!'

'You'd think so. I don't believe a gentleman's reproductive organs are especially well designed for the lifting of heavy weights.'

'Ha ha...no...and it's not like you need your dangly bits stretching, is it?'

'Certainly not if it involves heavy lifting.'

They finished their wine and he made them a ham and cheese supper.

'You seem back to full power now,' said Julie as they finished their food.

'Yup, I am.'

'Good, because I need to raise the tricky matter of the sleeping arrangements. Is it OK if we share your bed?' she asked, raising her arched eyebrows in a mock authoritarian manner.

'Of course, there's a gale blowing outside, I'm not sleeping on this draughty floor and I wouldn't dream of asking you to.'

'Good. But are we agreed there'll be no...' she made a circle with her thumb and forefinger on her right hand and pushed her left-hand index finger in and out while pursing her lips.

'Neither rumpy nor pumpy,' nodded Nick, now feeling totally relaxed and at ease for the first time since he'd woken up that morning.

'Not even if we really, really want to?' she said, wrinkling her nose as she kissed his hand.

'Not even if we really, really want to,' he replied, wagging a finger.

She nodded and smiled as she went towards the bedroom. 'It'll be just like old times in here then, eh!'

He laughed out loud.

'But Jules...' he said as she stopped and turned around at the bedroom door, taking him by both hands and leaning back, '...are we doing the right thing, do you think...about ...you know...all that? Me and you...y'know...it's really nice...I'd like to...but...I still worry about us if we do...y'know...I don't want it to all go wrong if I'm not right in the head, and I know I'm not right in the head.'

She grinned in a girlish way she sometimes had. 'Hopefully we've got years ahead of us to have proper super-spunky, drippy orgasmic sex, so there's no hurry, is there? We're just rebuilding things. It's nice. It won't harm to go slowly.'

She gave him a kiss on the lips. 'So we won't have any actual proper sex, not just now - soon maybe, but not just yet. Not if it makes you feel uneasy.'

'It does, a bit. Isn't that incredibly wussy? Sometimes I think I'm not a real man at all.'

'You're a real man, believe me,' she said as Nick checked the door was locked, turned out the lights and then followed her into the big bedroom.

'I just hope your sheets aren't too crusty,' she said, pulling back the covers of the king-sized bed they'd bought together.

'I just changed them actually...the old ones are still leaning against the wall in the bathroom.'

'Aw, and you're wearing PJs, too,' she said, pulling them out of the bed and subjecting them to close inspection.'Very clean, too.'

'I like to maintain standards,' he said. He pulled off his t-shirt.

'What's the etiquette as regards nudity?' he said, as Julie took out a toilet bag from her shoulder bag. 'Do we undress in front of each other? Or do we do it in the bathroom like we're strangers?'

'Oh, just get your kit off, lad, I've not seen a naked man since...well, since the last time I was in this room, actually. I could do with a thrill, couldn't you? The only naked women you've had in here since I left have been on your computer.'

'True...well actually, not true. I haven't even bothered with that.'

'Gettaway. Have you not?'

'Nah. You know porn makes me feel uncomfortable, always has done. The politics of it bothers me and the aesthetics of it even more so. And isn't watching people having it off actually a bit boring?'

She laughed. 'You don't have to pretend on my account to try and be PC about it.'

'I'm not. I like a dirty story in a book. Words are my thing. I don't really want to see horny naked blokes or some sort of gynaecological inspection. It's all a bit too icky and embarrassing for me.'

'I'm no connoisseur but I'd much rather be doing it than watching it, that's for sure. Mind, men are usually more visually stimulated by such things than women.'

'Well, I'd make someone a lovely woman, then,' he said as he took his clothes off.

'Eeee, well from where I'm stood, I'm not so sure about that, kidda. Blimey, look at you, Mr Muscle. Is that from lifting those weights in the corner?'

He flexed his biceps.

'Yeah, that and the diet,' he said, looking for his pyjama bottoms, feeling a bit shy under her scrutiny.

'Your body shape hasn't half changed. You're triangular instead of apple-shaped.'

'Yeah well it needed to change, didn't it?' He pulled on the pyjama bottoms and went into the bathroom to wash and brush his teeth, hoping she wouldn't undress while he was in there.

As he went back into the bedroom she was in the middle of pulling off her sweater. He stood and looked at her for a second, admiring her round breasts held in a black, sheer bra through which he could see her pink nipples.

'I can see through this you know, dirty boy,' she said from inside the jumper.

He laughed and jumped into bed.

She pulled open a drawer, found an old t-shirt and took off her bra. He didn't know where to put his eyes so it didn't look like he was obviously ogling her. He picked a book off the bedside cabinet and skimmed through it, distracted.

Julie burst out giggling. 'You can look at me if you want. It's not illegal. You've not seen the over-40 Julie naked. Everything is slowly slipping southwards. Anyway, I looked at your naughty bits so it's only fair you cop an eyeful of mine.'

'Were they up to the required standard?'

'Well, I've not brought a ruler with me but you'll do, aye,' she said, grinning to herself. 'It's funny that you're still so shy with me.'

'Sorry.'

'Don't apologise...it's nice.'

She unbuttoned her cargo pants and let them fall to the carpet.

'You're in good nick, Jules. Gorgeous, in fact.'

She did a little twirl in the old white t-shirt and black knickers.

'Stopping eating wheat and playing some sport seems to have melted some of my lard. My arse is sagging, though.' She lifted her buttocks up and down, then took off her rainbow socks and climbed into bed beside him.

'I've actually started getting grey pubic hairs,' he said, trying to be nonchalant about her being so close to him with so little on.

She looked over at him.

'Hello!' she said cheerfully as though they were strangers who had just accidentally ended up in the same bed. She looked around. 'It's funny, it's so familiar being here, only now it feels nice. It didn't always used to.'

'I can't believe you're in my bed. I'm not sure I ever thought that would happen again.'

She leaned over, put her hand on his bare chest and kissed him lightly on the lips.

'I never quite gave up hoping, big boy.'

He put the light out. It was strange having her there, feeling her body heat and hearing her breathing. As he lay flat on his back he felt her hand unbutton his pyjamas, peel them back and, with a light hand, stroke his penis up and down a couple of times. He was already hard and his heart pounding. Thank god she'd decided to seduce him.

'Just checking it's still in good working order,' she said with mock innocence, giggling a little. 'I think it'll pass the MOT.'

He responded by doing likewise, resting his hand between her legs. She parted them a little and gently pushed herself up onto his fingers. It was a lovely, intimate move. He moved his hand up and down a couple of times, feeling inside her a little through her underwear.

'Yes, all that seems to be in order, Ms Wells. I can confirm you have a top-quality vagina there,' he said.

'Thank you, doctor.'

They turned their heads so that they were face to face. She kissed him on the lips lightly and they lay breathing in each other's air for a minute, the sexual tension between them electric, both lusty and aroused, both enjoying the presence of the other.

'I'd forgotten how much I like this,' she said softly. 'When I moved out, you know what I missed about you most?'

She kissed him gently on the lips again.

'What?'

'It sounds daft but I missed your smell.'

'Funny. What do I smell of?'

She kissed him again. 'Male...you smell of male...in a nice way, like.'

'That doesn't sound that nice.'

'You wouldn't say that if you were a horny woman,' she said, laughing a low, rumbling laugh.

She kissed him again, rubbing his chest, a finger circling one of his nipples.

'And what does this man smell like?' he said, his heart pounding as he pretended to be calm.

She nuzzled into his neck and sniffed at him, her soft, shampoo-scented hair tickling his chest. 'I'm getting notes of soap, spicy beef and err...oooh...black pepper. Mmm, very sexy.'

'You're making me hungry in more ways than one.'

She began to rub his belly and chest slowly with the flat palm of her hand. He felt like he would burst.

'Bloody hell, I can feel your abs.' She traced them with her fingertips. 'They're very firm,' she said into his ear, pressing on his stomach muscles.

'They're not the only thing that's firm,' said Nick, licking his dry lips. He laughed a little and she laughed a little. He could see her in the street light that shone through the curtains.

'And would you like me to do something about that for you?' she said, a laugh lingering in her voice.

'Of course I would. But we said we wouldn't, didn't we?'

She leaned on an elbow and looked at him.

'Well, to bring some of my legal background into the bedroom for a moment, technically we said no proper sex,' she said as she continued to rub him in slow circles, the circle getting wider until she brushed his erection.

He took her soft hand from his chest and rested it on top of his penis. Instinctively she grasped him and began to slowly rub him up and down. He wasn't sure he was going to last long - he was so horny and it had been so long.

'Oooh, you're such a big randy sod, c'mon, let's make each other come,' she said. It was all he wanted to do.

She rolled over onto him, straddling his left leg and grinding her crotch on his thigh. He firmed up the muscle to give her something harder to push down onto and pulled her knickers down so he could feel her smooth, warm, round buttocks.

'Y'see, we said we'd not have sex...' she said, pulling away from a kiss but continuing to slowly push up and down on his leg, his hands pushing at her arse in rhythm with her thrusts, '...and this isn't sex...'

'It isn't?' he said while they pushed on each other, their breath intermingling as they kissed with wet tongues. Her saliva tasted familiar, sweet and fabulously erotic.

'It isn't sex unless you put your cock inside me,' she said, pulling him up and down in time with her own movements on his tensed leg.

'I didn't know that.'

'No. This isn't sex. This is just heavy petting,' she said, letting out a little moan as she pressed herself on his leg.

They moved together slowly, breathing hard in each other's ears. She began to push harder and faster and he knew instinctively she was almost there and pushed his hands up inside her t-shirt to lightly brush her breasts with his fingers. Her nipples were tight and hard, he touched them tenderly between thumb and forefinger and she let out a noise that was somewhere between a groan and a scream, pushing harder and faster as she cried out.

Her whole body tensed into a shudder as she came. She let out another animal noise and kept on pushing hard, coming once, then twice, then three times in a rolling orgasm, her whole body dedicated to the pleasure.

Her body was hot and soft and electric and he had to tense his pelvis to stop himself from coming as she rode him.

'Oh fuck, fuck fuck,' she said breathlessly as the pleasure waves subsided and she kissed him on the mouth and neck before sliding down the bed. He watched as she took his erection between her hands and licked at him long and slowly like he was an ice cream. 'Fucking hell, your hard cock is massive,' she whispered hoarsely, as though to herself, though it was for his pleasure. This was more stimulation than he could resist; he closed his eyes, arched his back and came with an intensity and power that was so overwhelming it almost hurt.

With an irrepressible howl, he ejaculated in the haze of orgasm. Time slid sideways for a few seconds and his brain went into neutral as he felt himself turn inside out.

As he came down, he watched her kneel between his open legs, rubbing him between her hands and grinning wickedly.

'That wasn't bad considering it wasn't actually sex,' he said, panting like he'd been running.

She pushed her hair from her eyes. 'That was a bit nice, eh,' she said, getting out of bed and putting on the bedside lamp. She went into the bathroom and came back with a box of tissues.

'Were you going for some sort of record?' she laughed and pointed at the wall. He looked up - there were two streaks of come on the wall about six feet above the bed and a trail all the way back down. She dabbed at it with a tissue. 'You must have had a full tank, lad, it's everywhere.'

'Christ, that is some sort of record, isn't it?' he said, in awe of his own powers of ejaculation.

'Have I got it in my hair?'

'Yeah there's a few blobs - hold on, I'll mop them up for you...there you go. Sorry about that, I am not in control of my own sperm.'

He got out of bed to clean himself up in the bathroom. When he came back in she was back in bed, her face flushed pink.

'You have a post-coital glow about you, Ms Wells,' he said, getting back in and putting his arm around her as he did so. She cuddled into him, putting her arm across his middle.

'Mmmm, that was lovely.'

'You've lost none of your talents.' She grinned up at him and played gently with his now-soft cock and balls. 'I've missed seeing and feeling you all hard and horny.' She kissed him on the lips. 'And you went off like Vesuvius. I've missed that as well.' She played with him as she talked. 'It's lovely to give you some pleasure, mister.' He kissed her and rolled her onto her back, running his hands all over her body.

'You feel fantastic.'

She laughed a low laugh as he put his hand firmly between her legs and she pressed up against him.

'You still know what to do to make me come,' she said.

She felt soft like cotton wool.

'And it really wasn't sex?'

'No. I told you. It's not sex until you put this in me,' she pulled at him. 'That's what my mam taught me.'

'She really taught you that?'

'It was her way of telling me not to get pregnant when I was a teenager. She said, you can do anything with a lad as long he doesn't put his willy in you. So it's not proper sex unless you do.'

He kissed her again.

'Oooh, you're all hard again. How did that happen so quickly?'

'Not having any sex for years might have something to do with it.'

'Oh god, yeah. Okay, horny...let's see what you've got left in you, then.'

They fell asleep wrapped around each other.

When he woke up, Julie was drying herself after a shower. There was a cup of green tea on his bedside table. Bliss.

'Morning,' she said, waving at him comically while wrapping herself in a towel. She did a little naked wriggling dance in front of him and got some clean underwear out of her bag.

'Hey, missus.' He propped himself up in bed. 'Wow, this is a great thing to see in the morning. It's never too early to see a beautiful naked woman. Thanks for last night, Jules. It was bloody brilliant.'

She pulled on her cargo pants, sat down on the edge of the bed next to him and pushed his hair off his forehead, 'You don't need to thank me, man, it wasn't a service I was selling. But yeah, it was great to share a bit of Percy Filth with you. I wasn't going to be able to keep my hands off you forever. To be honest, I don't know how I held out this long. I've been relying on my memories of you for ages and they're not as good as the real thing.'

'I know just what you mean.'

She kissed him on the lips. 'And I really think we can cope with a little bit of strokey-pokey now and again without it messing up our...you know...our relationship, we've just got to be grown up about it. I know we said it might make things emotionally difficult...but maybe we've both grown up a bit since the big split, like...we can do a bit of intimacy now and again, can't we? Even if it's not The Proper Sex just yet. We're only human and let's face it, we do still fancy the arse off each other and it's nice to make each other feel good.'

He laughed loudly. 'You're not wrong. I'm surprised your arse is actually still on you, I fancy it off you so much, and I love the expression "strokey-pokey" too. Did you make it up?'

'One from my sordid teenage past, I'm afraid.'

She kissed his lips again and rubbed his crotch through the duvet. 'Eeee god, ready for action again? You'll be shooting feathers, lad.'

'I'll be what?' he laughed.

'As much as I'd love to oblige your massive throbbing manhood you'll have to take such matters into your own hands 'cos I've got to go into college this afternoon and I need to get going without smelling of your sex gravy.'

'Ha ha. Sex gravy?! Okay, cool. I'll see you tomorrow afternoon anyway.' He got out of bed to see her off.

'Put it away, you big horny monkey,' she said, putting his erection back into his pyjamas, laughing as she did so. They embraced for a moment. Nick gave her a big squeeze around her waist, lifted her up off the ground and swung her around.

'Thank you, Ms Julie Wells of Norton, for coming over and saving me from myself.'

'You're welcome, Crazy Nick, thank you for coming over me and everything else!'

CHAPTER 4

After she'd gone, he washed the dishes and went to make the bed, picking up the pillow she'd been sleeping on to remind himself of her. It was heavy with her smell. The t-shirt she'd worn echoed of last night's lust. He felt happy, really happy and that was the rarest, candy-sweet emotion - certainly rare in his life. He was sometimes content or at least not miserable, but rarely actually properly happy. But in that moment he was and it was Julie who had made him happy and that was no small achievement. It wasn't just the sex endorphins; it was the intimacy, the affection, the loving - they were the priceless, life-enhancing and elusive things that he'd missed. It fed his soul and he didn't realise how much he'd really needed that until he'd tasted it again. He'd shut down that side of himself in order to survive being on his own but now it was wide open again. The scary thing was he couldn't get that kind of happy without being vulnerable.

He felt like a different person to the one he'd been the day before. Strong, able to cope, sharp witted and, importantly, like he had someone on his side in life: he wasn't alone.

Around 5pm, Jeff called.

'How you doing, big man?' said Nick.

'Alright. I just had a strange phone call.'

'Oh yeah? Who from?'

'Malton coppers. '

'Oh, right. About Susan?'

'Yeah. They asked me if I knew what her state of mind was recently.'

'Weird. I wonder why?'

'I don't know. I said she'd seemed a bit tired but had been her usual self. That's right, isn't it?'

'Yeah, she was tired and a bit upset after that Boudica Society meeting, especially. Did they say anything else?'

'They asked if I was surprised by her death. I said I was. Of course I was. Then they said did I know of any reason she might have wanted to take her own life. Obviously, I said no. Then did I know if anyone had a grudge against her, which obviously I didn't. I think they were just box ticking, really.'

'Well, they've probably got to go through all the possible options, haven't they? Mind, those Boudica kids were not over fond of her, I'll tell you that. Talking of which, it's funny that no-one has tried to rob you again, isn't it? I'm sure I saw the lass that broke into your shop up at Durham, you know. It keeps coming back to me.'

'You can't have done, man. Maybe they worked out I had nothing worth robbing. Also, Martin James just called me back. I had to break the bad news to him.'

'Oh god, yeah. I suppose he couldn't have known. How did he take it?'

'Hard to say on the phone, isn't it? He was surprised but he didn't break down weeping or owt like that. Like I said the other day, there's not much love lost between them.'

'Did you say we saw him?'

'Aye, it was like you said, he was visiting a neighbour opposite who he's still mates with. Now he wishes he'd looked in on Susan but he thought he shouldn't, not after she'd been so short with him at the car boot. She didn't like him just popping in, like. It was appointments only.'

'Even so, you'd think, well, he's there and needs a box of papers or whatever. It'd be easier just to let him in and take them, wouldn't it?'

'Aye, it's odd, isn't it? But I think there's a lot of bad blood between them.'

'Do you know why they broke up?'

'Not really. No-one said anything back then and I've never felt I could ask her. Doesn't seem right...well, it didn't seem right. That's going to take some getting used to. I tell you what though...I never said this to the police...'

'What?'

'...that Susan's death seems odd to me.'

'Odd? In what way?'

'I was reading up on what someone who dies of a heart attack looks like just afterwards.'

'Bloody hell Jeff, that's a bit macabre.'

'And she didn't look like that.'

'Well, maybe it was something else.'

'Yeah. I think it was. The coroner should be able to tell us soon. She hadn't been ill, though, and she stood out in the cold at the car boots every week. I never knew her to even get a cold. She was small boned but I always thought she was very strong. And there wasn't an ounce of fat on her, either.'

'Well, it's hard to tell if someone is ill on the inside, isn't it?'

'Hmmm, I dunno about that,' said Jeff. Nick could tell he was in conspiracy mode but didn't want to indulge him.

'Okay man, well, get your drinking trousers on for tomorrow. It's going to be a big thrash.'

'Can't bloody wait.'

For the rest of the day Nick happily wrote and played albums. At just after 8pm, an e-mail from Julie dropped into his inbox.

'Just a little gift for you attached. Stand well back and don't make a big mess on your computer! Thanks for the red-hot lovin'! See you tomorrow, big boy.'

He opened the attachment. It was a photo of herself in black underwear taken in her bedroom, lying on her back on the bed. She knew what he liked. He printed it out and headed straight for the bathroom.

After lunch on Wednesday, Nick went down to Sid's Scissors and got his shaggy mane trimmed so it looked a little more artfully scruffy. He trimmed his beard stubble and then dressed in his new shirt, tie, suit and shoes.

He hung the jacket on a hanger in the back of his old BMW and set off to pick up Jeff.

'Bloody hell, look at you, it's Brad Pitt's more fashionable sister,' said Jeff as he emerged from his flat and took a look at Nick, flicking at the black silk tie.

'I look bloody great and you know it,' said Nick, dismissively.

'Oh yes, luv, you do...you're done up like a pox doctor's clerk.'

'Were pox doctors clerks especially well dressed?' asked Nick.

'I have no idea. Were there actually pox doctors? Specialists, like?'

'Maybe they had revolving bow ties or something to distract the punters as they drew the disease out of the patient's wang with some instrument of torture.'

'Oh, please, no dirty talk at this time of day,' laughed Jeff.

Nick took the A66 east off the A1 and hit heavy, rush-hour traffic, eventually arriving at the Teesside International Hotel, just off Darlington Back Lane. It was an imposing Georgian building with a classical, columned entrance and extensive grounds and had been a large, rambling country house owned by an aristocratic family until the 1970s when it had been converted into a hotel. Recently it had been bought by a major chain and renovated again to host conferences and other large events.

He pulled into the large, gravelled car park and handed Jeff his invitation.

'They should have your name down. They'll probably put you on the friends and colleagues tables. Me and Jules will be on the journos and WAGS tables...so I might not see you for a while.'

'Don't worry about me, I'll have the nosebag on all night,' said Jeff. 'If I don't see you beforehand, good luck with the award. I shall be cheering you on, probably in a socially unacceptable manner.'

'I wouldn't have it any other way,' Nick said, slapping him on the shoulder. 'Have a bloody good time, big man.'

'And we're crashing at Julie's place later, right?'

'Yup. We'll be riding the sofa and the floor,' said Nick.

'I bring my own padding with me,' he said, patting his belly. 'Right, here we go...rock and fucking roll!'

Driving back to the A66, he headed east again, turning off into Stockton-on-Tees and through to Norton, where he arrived just before six. They still had an hour spare. He parked just off Norton Green, right outside her flat, put on the jacket and smoothed it out as he rang Julie's bell.

She buzzed him in and he went up the stairs two at a time. She was standing in the doorway putting on her shoes as he arrived and broke into a huge smile when she saw him.

'Aye aye, what's all this? Look at you! You never said you'd bought this posh clobber!'

He held his arms out wide.

'I wanted it to be a surprise. Will I do?'

'Oooh, come here and I'll let you know,' she said, pulling him in for a hug.

'You feel all nice,' said Nick, running his hands over her back and buttocks. 'You're all silky and soft.'

She looked at him again and shook her head in disbelief, pulling open the jacket and inspecting the Armani label on the inside.

'It's class, man, really class,' she said, lapsing into broad Teesside.

'I went to David Watts in town. Cost a bit but I thought it was worth the effort for an awards do. For what it's worth, I feel great in it...you were right all along.'

'What? When I said clothes can make you feel more confident? And you told me that was - and I think this is an exact quote - "women's magazine shite".'

'Sorry. I was wrong. About that and so many other things. Sorry.' He meant it from his heart.

She smiled and gave him a quick kiss. 'Apology accepted. You look a million dollars, kid. What about me?'

'Give us a twirl.'

The vintage 1920s dress was made from unstructured black silk and chiffon with long, lacy black sleeves and open, bare shoulders. The silk was enhanced by black embroidery and black sequins. The look was completed by shiny black shoes with a low heel. 'You look like a 20s flapper crossed with the original Morticia Addams, and this is a very good thing in my book. Is it an original?'

'Yup. I got it locally at a vintage clothes place. Cost a lot less than a designer dress. It was originally floor length but I had it shortened to below the knee so I could actually walk properly. I'm wearing it with some vintage black silk stockings.' She lifted the dress up to her thigh.

'Oh baby, you are talking my language! Have we got time for a bit of...you know...we don't have to get naked?'

He felt excited and horny and happy and put his arms around her waist, his hands rubbing her backside.

'We probably have, but we're not going to because you'll only get your love juice all over our nice clothes. You'll be full up again by now so god knows where it'd all go.'

'That's true. A crusty Armani suit is probably a bit of a social faux pas, isn't it?'

'Not as a big a social faux pas as having spunk all over your best dress,' she said, pecking him on the lips and gently squeezing his crotch. 'Save it for later, lad.'

The Northern Football Writers Awards had been a massive event every year since its inception in 1960. Given that northern meant anyone who wrote for a publication that was based or sold north of a notional line drawn at Sheffield, it was a big catchment area.

The short list for the awards used to be solely decided by a self-appointed and self-defined committee of movers and shakers in the press and publishing industry in the north. More recently it had incorporated a public vote run in all the local newspapers and now online. An audience of 500 had been invited and local TV cameras also turned up to film 30-second clips and vox pops for the next day's news reports.

As the cab dropped off Nick and Julie at the entrance to the grand lobby of the hotel, the place was abuzz with people in evening wear and staff in white shirts, black pants and waistcoats.

Nick showed his invitations to a man dressed in top hat and tails at the door.

'Good evening, Mr Guymer, Ms Wells,' he said, with a small bow to each of them in turn. 'You'll be shown to your table in the ballroom. If you'd like to go into the bar area, drinks are being served.'

'I could get used to that level of respect,' Nick said. It was a very noisy bar - it seemed everyone was simply shouting at each other, as opposed to merely talking. It was typical of his industry; so many people were more interested in hearing themselves above anyone else.

Waiters were circling with silver trays of wine and champagne. Nick took two flutes and handed one to Julie. He held his glass up to hers.

'Here's to you and me Jules, and lots of good stuff.'

She clinked her glass on his.'To having a good time, all the time.'

As they drank, Nick was approached by a large robust-looking man.

Trevor Goulding had been his boss many years ago on the Northern Echo. A larger-than-life figure now in his mid-70s, he was a throwback to another era when newspapers were all about long liquid lunches and cigars.

'Nick, my boy!' he boomed, advancing towards him with arm outstretched.

'Hello Trevor, long time no see, how are you?'

He gripped Nick's hand powerfully for a man of his age.

'Splendid, splendid! You look in fine fettle. And who is this delightful young lady?' he said, turning to Julie.

'This is my partner, Julie, said Nick, instinctively. It was out of his mouth before he could stop it. Was that OK? They were partners, weren't they? He glanced at her but she didn't return the look; instead, she shook the older man's hand with a smile on her lips.

'I'm neither young nor a lady but I'll take delightful,' she said. Trevor Goulding boomed out a laugh. 'And delightful you are my dear...splendid! I must tell you, I voted for you for writer of the year, old boy. Yes, yes. Tremendous work, especially covering the fine and august working-class institution that is Middlesbrough Football Club.'

'Thanks, Trevor. Well, it was a hell of a season for Boro, wasn't it? Getting to a European final...I don't think any of us ever thought we'd see the day that happened.'

'Indeed, indeed. Well, I do hope you're successful Nicholas, then I can tell everyone that I gave you your first break and your success is all down to me! Ha ha! Pleasure to see you and meet the very, very delightful Julie, too.'

As he moved away, Julie turned to Nick. 'So I'm your partner now, am I?' she said, looking over her glass of champagne as she drank.

'Was that wrong? It just came out. I couldn't say "girlfriend", it sounds too teenage, and yet "friend" sounds too cold. Mind you, "partner" does make it sound like we're in a same-sex marriage.'

She wobbled her head from side to side as though trying to find her place. 'I feel more like a girlfriend, I think. I quite like that, it makes it seem like we're young lovers. So you're my boyfriend from now on, right?' she said, smiling. Nick gave her hand a squeeze. As he did so he saw a familiar face.

Coming towards them was Stevie Salmon, known to everyone simply as Big Fish. At 6'2" and nearly 20 stone he was a big presence in most rooms. His shaven head and stuffing-exploding-out-of-a-cushion beard only added to his impact.

Big Fish was a well-known comedian in the northeast and beyond. Although he was considered too blue and un-PC for television, this didn't stop his live shows being very popular. He could sell out a 2,000-seat hall as quickly as more well-known comedians. Those who liked him saw a man who was kicking back against perceived injustices on behalf of the common man, someone who wouldn't take the PC bullshit and would call a spade a fucking shit shovel if he must. Those who disliked him saw a boorish bully who picked on easy targets and used the language of misogyny and intolerance. It had made him a lot of money and he was very popular on the after-dinner circuit and at awards ceremonies such as these. He was so popular that he even had his own catchphrase - 'Talk to the beard' - which he deployed as a kind of challenge to anyone who disagreed with his viewpoint. His biggest fans would shout it out like it was a mantra to disaffection.

'Oh god, I can't stand him,' said Julie in Nick's ear.

'Too late, he's seen me.'

He held out his hand. 'Big Fish! How goes it, man?'

'Not bad at all,' he replied as his fat hand almost crushed Nick's.

'This is my girlfriend, Julie.'

'You're a lucky man, then; hello, Julie. From round here, are you?'

She nodded. 'Norton.'

'Ah, the old homeland, as I like to call it. Well, you caught a tasty one here, Nick. Better than some of those old boilers you used to date at the Echo. You should've seen them, Julie. Dear me, he went out with some right munters.'

'I'm sure they were nice people,' said Julie, already annoyed by his tone.

'I'm sure...and let's face, it you don't look at the chimney while you're poking the fire do you, eh? Ha ha!'

Julie set her jaw against him.

Stevie Salmon's father was a big landowner on Teesside and

Durham, having inherited a large estate from his own father, an estate that Stevie would eventually inherit himself as the oldest son. It had been built on the money earned by Jobriath Salmon, who set up one of the first steelworks in the area at the start of the industrial revolution and subsequently successfully invested by his son, Henry, who set up a merchant bank in the late Victorian era. While a few dissolute relations had made a good attempt at drinking, whoring and gambling away the estate's money, none had quite managed it and the main asset, the land, remained undiminished. Apart from farming, they could also boast a well-established and successful stables with horses running most weeks of the year.

Stevie Salmon had enjoyed a life of luxury and privilege, which made his oppressed common man routines sound very hollow. Nick had first met him nearly 25 years earlier when he'd started work on the Northern Echo, where Stevie's father had engineered a job for him after he'd left school. They'd worked on the same desk for 18 months before Salmon started his comedy career and had run into each other several times over the years.

'Julie lives in Norton...your family own some of that land just north of Norton, don't they?' said Nick, keen to change the subject away from his past, misogyny or talking to beards.

'The Blakeston estate, yeah, that's ours. Everything east of the golf course.'

'When did your dad sell the land for the golf course?'

'Must have been 1988 or 1989 I reckon.' He pulled at his beard, which was evenly flecked with ginger, grey and brown hairs. 'Not sure it was the best use of the land but there you go, what do I know? I'm just a jokesmith. So I hear you're joint favourite in the betting tonight, Nick.'

'Am I? That's good to hear, but I've never won anything in my life and I doubt I'll start now.'

'Nah, c'mon man, like Eric and Ernie said, good strong positive thinking, good strong positive drinking!'

He was joined by a skinny woman in a tight little black dress. She was at least 20 years younger than Big Fish.

'Kerry, this is Nick Guymer, we used to work together on the

Echo...'

Nick saluted her.

'...and this is...sorry pet, I've forgotten your name,' he said to Julie.

'Julie.'

'Hiya,' said Kerry who appeared to be chewing gum while drinking something that was fluorescent orange. How could you do that?

'So are you handing out the gongs?' said Nick.

'Aye, and I'm doing a short set after everyone's had their dinner and a few drinks. Won't be that long. Just a few beard jokes.'

'Has anyone told you who's won what yet?' said Kerry, in an accent born in Middlesbrough, the word 'told' being stretched out to become 'toe-ald'.

'Not a dicky bird, no. It's all top secret. I won't know until I open the envelope. It's like Miss World only for balding middle-aged journos,' he said, breaking into a laugh which was high-pitched and at odds with his bulk.

'I hope they have avocado in there, I love avocado,' said Kerry, apropos of nothing, her accent doubling the length of the word to 'aaav-ohhh-caaar-doah'.

'I'm sure they will,' said Salmon, making a 'women, huh' raised-eyebrows look at Nick as though he would empathise. He didn't, and he also knew that sort of casual sexism infuriated Julie.

'That's a very brightly coloured drink you've got,' said Julie. 'What is it?'

Kerry looked at it. 'Orange,' she said, looking back with blank eyes.

'Nothing gets past you Kerry, does it?' said Salmon, sarcastically.

'Normally I like purple drinks,' she added, pronouncing purple in the classic Teesside manner as, 'pear-pull'.

'Purple is good, like,' said Julie. Nick had to swallow a laugh along with a mouthful of wine.

'Right, come on Kerry, we'd better go and mingle with the management. Nice to see you again, Nick. I'll probably see you at the Boro Xmas do, won't I?'

'Ta ra,' said Kerry following Big Fish across the sea of people.

When they were out of earshot, Julie said, 'Fizzin' hell, the fuse box has blown on that one.'

'He makes me feel uncomfortable, it's like he's always one sentence away from some appalling racist or sexist outburst,' said Nick.

'Girls like that hanging off the arm of a rich man really aren't helping the sisterhood either.'

'Yeah, but you can see why she does. It's probably her only way off the estate she's grown up on,' said Nick.

'I know, but that's a cop out though, isn't it? You can get educated and move out and up. I know it's difficult and not fair and you have to work twice as hard as someone born into middle-class money but you can still do it. You don't have to just get your tits out for some rich man,' said Julie.

'Somehow I don't think she's going to be going to college, do you?'

She shook her head and laughed. 'Not unless it's to study the colour of drinks. She seemed well read on that subject, poor lass.'

The PA system crackled and a voice announced, 'Ladies and gentlemen, please take your seats in the ballroom.'

Everyone began to shuffle out of the bar.

The Teesside International ballroom was originally a Georgian ballroom where the great and good of the north of England were entertained by the former owner, Manny Benwell, a local industrialist. It was huge and lit by several massive chandeliers. Fifty tables were laid out with 10 places on each. At the far end, there was a small stage with a microphone on a lectern.

A member of staff showed Nick and Julie to their seats. They were at the front and to the left of the stage.

'Ooh, we're near the front, that must mean you've won something,' said Julie, squeezing his arm.

The place soon filled up. Nick stood up and spotted Jeff right at the back with a glass of red wine. He raised his hand to acknowledge him and Jeff responded by raising a glass with a grin. He was already probably fairly pissed. Good on him. Hopefully he was enjoying himself.

Four other journalists and their wives were seated at Nick's and Julie's table, all from regional newspapers. He didn't know any of them but some seemed to know his work. As he'd never been very good at networking and had been a freelance for most of his working life, he rarely knew many people at these kinds of events. Julie chatted easily with a tweedy Tory-looking woman who was the wife of a man from the Hexham Courant as her husband looked on.

They got through a three-course dinner starting with goats' cheese salad and moving on to some succulent rump steak. Nick avoided the bread and potatoes and amused the table by eating big spoonfuls of butter, then passed on the dessert and opted for some cheese and celery instead. It was all very nice, more like good pub food than top restaurant fare, but it was free so there was nothing to complain about.

His default mode in such social circumstances was to talk about football. Football was a universal language and meant he didn't have to think too hard to say something. So that's what he did with his neighbour, a man called Robin who worked at the Press Association in Hull and supported the Tigers. As Nick had been born in Hull, he sympathised.

After the cheese he got up to find the toilet, weaving a little unsteadily through the tables, the wine having gone to his head a little. As he was leaving the ballroom, he spotted Jeff coming towards him.

'Ah there you are. Everything going OK?' he said.

'Aye, bloody, bloody and a third bloody great. Luxury for me, this. I must thank you again old boy. I'm on my second bottle of cheap Cabernet Sauvignon and all my pain is fading away. Cheering me up no end after this week's bollocks. Having a bit of a laugh with a tabloid hack on my table...bloke can hold drink like the Pacific Ocean and he's got some cracking stories about footballers, mostly involving blondes and cocaine.'

'Good, I'm glad you're enjoying yourself.'

'Aye, well, I'm using it as a private celebration of Susan's life as well, like. My way of thanking the old girl.'

'That's nice Jeff. Count me in on that, too. She was a lovely old bird.'

'Yeah, though I have to say, the more I've been thinking about it, the more I think there was something really odd about her death.'

'Odd?'

'Yeah. Why was the front door open when we arrived? That's odd. No-one sits in the house with the front door open. Her legs were odd as well...like they'd melted under her. If she'd had a heart attack, she'd just have been lying on the floor or in a chair or in the bed. It looked like she'd just dropped dead and sank straight down. And like I said, she'd never had a day off with illness in her life.'

'Well, there'll be the coroner's report soon, won't there? That should give us a proper idea about the cause of death.'

'Yeah, that'll make interesting reading but I'll tell you this,' he swayed a little and pointed at Nick, 'it wouldn't surprise me at all if there was foul play involved or if she was actually murdered. Seriously. I've got a feeling in my water.'

Nick shrugged. Jeff loved a conspiracy at the best of times.

'Well, we'll just see what the report says.'

Jeff nodded and then said, 'Hey, hey... I tell you what, though, Julie looks stunning tonight, man. A bit of Hollywood on Teesside! You're well in there.' He slapped Nick on the back.

'Thanks, man. She does look amazing. Dunno what she's doing with me.'

Jeff slapped him on the back again. 'I can tell you why...' he said, pointing down at Nick's trousers, 'the lady loves a bit of the old Whitesnake.'

He slapped him on the back again and strode back to his table with a ruthlessly quick stride.

The toilets were all gold and marble and were possibly the only male toilets in the north without the merest whiff of stale piss. He was making his way to his table when the lights went down in preparation for the start of the awards ceremony.

He squeezed in next to Julie. 'I just saw Jeff.'

'Oh aye, is he pissed?'

'Yeah, but he deserves a good night on the lash after Monday, doesn't he?'

She nodded. 'Not that he's ever really needed an excuse to get rat-arsed, like.'

'Hey, and I'll tell you what, he said you looked fantastic - like something from Hollywood!'

She burst out laughing, 'Christ, he must be pissed!'

A screen dropped from the roof and highlights of the northeast football year were shown. Mostly this was Middlesbrough's triumphant march through the UEFA Cup in the spring. Massimo Maccarone's winning goal against Steaua Bucharest still sent a prickle up and down his spine and Julie turned to grin at him, fist clenched, mouthing 'get in'. What an incredible thing to have happened to a small, unfashionable club like Boro.

Stevie Salmon came on stage. He'd changed into a bright green suit with a jarringly bright purple shirt and odd socks coloured yellow and green.

'Wacky colours, wacky guy,' said Nick into Julie's ear.

'Kerry will like his pearpull sherrt, though,' said Julie, making him splutter.

Big Fish made a few quips, one a rather tired one about mushy peas and guacamole which ended with his trademark 'Talk to the beard', another with a punch line involving a naked Polish cleaner and third about why drunk men are better lovers. The audience, now a few drinks in, laughed politely but without much enthusiasm. He'd cleaned up his act a little for his audience and managed not to say the F or C words once, which for Big Fish was damn close to being a career move into family entertainment. His fan base was mostly pissed, working-class lads under the age of 40 who found rape jokes funny. This wasn't his core audience, so he moved on quickly to start the awards.

'The first award of the night is for Young Northern Journalist of the Year. Open to writers under the age of 23.'

He read out three names and announced that a chap called Gary Richards had won. Gary got up on stage wearing a cheap suit that fitted someone, but not him. He peered out of it like a small creature looking out of a cave. Everyone applauded as he took his trophy - a pen set into a plank of wood. He held it up modestly.

The next award was for top cricket writer, then top rugby writer. Nick hadn't heard of any of them. That was followed by something called 'other sports' which was won by a woman called Gillian Ochs for, as far as he could tell, reporting on badminton and bowls in

Billingham, perhaps out of sympathy as much as anything else. Still, good luck to her. Someone had to do it.

'And now we come to one of the big awards of the night; the "Northern Sports Writers Award" sponsored by East Coast Ales,' said Stevie, tearing open an envelope and arranging the trophy on the lectern in front of him.

Julie patted him on the back.

'The nominations are as follows: Mark Siddon, Evening Gazette; Harry Jenkinson, Sheffield Star; Nick Guymer, freelance; and Roger Smith, also a freelance.'

The palms of his hand were sweating. He hadn't expected to win, nor even really had a strong desire to win, but now, on the verge of the announcement of the result, he discovered he really bloody did want to win. C'mon. Just one bit of luck, one time.

As Stevie tore open the envelope, a few voices from the floor shouted for their favourites, including Jeff's booming voice.

'And the winner is...Mark Siddon of the Evening Gazette.'

Nick's heart sank. Fuck.

'Aw, hard luck. But at least you're still in it for the top award,' said Julie as they applauded.

'That was probably a fix for the sponsors. Siddon has drunk so much of their beer, it's their way of rewarding him,' said Nick. He knew Mark Siddon a little - he was the sort of small-minded, right-wing idiot that he hated but who was popular on phone-ins where he could attract an audience of equally small minds. He didn't like foreigners, didn't like anyone really, especially himself, and was fond of beer the way leeches are fond of blood.

A lifetime achievement award was given to a chap who seemed to have been editor of every northern newspaper since 1945 at some point or other. He was at least 90 and looked older. That was followed by an award for photography.

'And now the big, big, big one of the night...who is 2006's "Northern Football Writer of the Year"?' said Big Fish.

He turned to receive the new trophy from a woman in a tiny black dress who was presumably taking a night off from the darts circuit. The trophy was, in essence, the same as the others but bigger: a silver pen stuck into a slab of marble instead of wood and with a silver plaque.

'It was a tough decision for the judges to make this year with many great writers from the region making an impact on both the local and national stage. The four candidates are Nick Guymer, freelance; John McIntyre, Manchester Evening News; David Carey, freelance; and Francis Ngog, Liverpool Echo.'

Salmon tore open the envelope. 'And the winner is...'

Nick had resigned himself to not winning; he had nowhere to put a big ugly pen on a plinth anyway.

'Ah, I know this fella; the winner is...Nick Guymer!'

Julie shot up to her feet punching the air as though the Boro had just scored the League cup final winner again. 'Yes! Get in!' she yelled, letting out a big whoop, clapping and slapping him on his back while jumping up and down excitedly.

'Well done, Nick. Much deserved. He's a great writer, this fella! I actually worked with him on the Northern Echo back before The Beard came out to play. I always thought he was destined for big things. C'mon up, Nick.'

He was stunned. What did he do now? He got to his feet. People were all standing up at the other tables applauding. The ripple of applause filled the room. All for him. A spotlight picked him out at the table. He'd seen everyone else do it, now it was his turn. Julie was still bouncing up and down clapping.

Laughing seemed the only sensible response. It was surreal. He spent most of his life sitting in front of a computer on his own going anywhere from a little to lot crazy and here were all his peers applauding him for that work. It felt unnatural and strange but good, fantastic even.

'Well done, you clever cunt,' said Stevie, grinning at him and handing him the trophy.

Nick instinctively thrust it one-handed above his head as though it was the FA Cup. It was what everyone did with a trophy, wasn't it?

Like all other winners he was ushered to the microphone to say a few words. He placed the pen and marble thing on the lectern and cleared his throat. The applause died down. His heart raced. The ballroom looked huge from the stage. All eyes were on him, the massed audience of suits and dresses murmuring to each other about him, agreeing, disagreeing and no doubt asking, who the hell is he? But it wasn't like having to talk one to one with someone, this was somehow easier. He just leaned into the microphone, opened his mind and let it speak.

'Well well, this is a very nice surprise. Thank you,' he cleared his throat. 'It's been an amazing year for me on many levels, not least as a Middlesbrough fan. When you're a writer it sometimes feels as if you're shouting in the dark to no-one in particular. We get limitless abuse on the internet and have to accept it as part of the job. And for it to be a northern award is so much more special. The north means so much to me - its people, its landscape and its history. It's in my bones and in my blood, the spirit of the north is a special thing that people from other places don't quite understand but which I know we all feel in our hearts and in our souls. So to be "Northern Football Writer of the Year" really means so much to me.

'I'd like to thank a couple of people - Trevor from the Northern Echo for giving me my break 25 years ago, my best mate Jeff for putting up with my endless moaning about almost everything...'

Jeff shouted, 'Get on with it Nick, the bar's about to close,' and got a big laugh.

'Ha ha...OK, big man.' Something popped into his mind and he said it without thinking. 'A friend of mine who died recently, Susan Rutherford, she once told me to "try and keep love in your life" and that was really good advice. So this is for her as well.' He raised the trophy and looked to the sky. 'Thanks Susan. And I must also thank my girlfriend Julie for being her lovely self. Wow, well, I'm glad I bought this new suit now! Thanks again...'

His last line brought a big laugh and a round of loud applause. He took a bow and then, with a surge of exhilaration, punched the air in triumph yelling, 'Yes! Get in! C'mon!'

Julie was waiting for him with open arms, and gave another whoop as he lifted her up in a big bear hug.

'Who's a clever boy then?' she said, eyes sparkling.

'Me, I'm very big and very clever!' he laughed.

He'd never won anything in his life. Writing about football rarely even got you a kind word - quite the opposite, in fact. It all scarcely seemed real. A surge of excitement and adrenalin shot through him again.

And that was the end of the event. The organisers were quick to let everyone know by putting on the lights. No more wine, no more food. Empty your glasses and get out. Waiters began clearing away plates.

The TV crew came over for a quick interview for the next day's evening news and a few people shook his hand and congratulated him on his victory. Jeff came over holding a bottle of wine in one hand and a glass in the other with a big grin on his face. 'Nice work, lad,' he said, 'I never doubted that you'd win...'

'Bollocks,' laughed Nick.

'Nice of you to mention Susan as well. That surprised me.'

'Yeah, me too' said Julie. 'What was it she said, again?'

'It was at a car boot. I'd said about going to see my therapist about depression and that and she put her hand on my cheek and said, try and keep love in your life. It just came back to me up there and I thought, yeah, you know, love of football, love of life, love of a good woman. She was right.' He put his arm around Julie.

'Brilliant,' said Jeff, nodding and emptying the bottle into the glass.

'How sweet of her. What a nice woman she was. God rest her soul,' said Julie.

They paused for a moment to remember her.

'You look very glamorous tonight, Jules, too glamorous for Worzel Gummidge here,' said Jeff.

'Aw, he looks class, I reckon. And he's a very, very clever boy!' She jumped up and down on the spot excitedly again. 'I'm so proud of him.'

'Aye, well, rightly so, and he does look very hunky. I almost fancy him myself. I think I missed my vocation as a promiscuous gay bloke. I'd be great at it.'

'Trust me Jeff, you didn't!' said Nick, laughing. 'Come on, let's go to the bar. I'll buy you a glass of something. I don't know if they do Brasso here, though.'

'I'll have a Mr Sheen if they don't. Mmmm. Sweet, delicious polish,' said Jeff, licking his beard as they walked out of the ballroom laughing uproariously.

'Mind, Big Fish stank the place out, didn't he?' said Jeff as they moved through the crowds.

'Terrible,' said Nick. 'I'd rather abuse myself with a Toilet Duck than watch him for an hour and a half.'

'And that would actually be funnier,' added Julie.

The bar was packed. As they walked in, some people turned to look at him and a small round of applause broke out, which eventually became a room full of applause. He was embarrassed but took the accolade by clapping his hands back at them and punching the air. What was the right way to react? He didn't know but it didn't really matter on this occasion. Overwhelmed by the support and the attention, his mind was a blur of emotions. Jeff went off to the bar.

'Eeee, it's like being out with a star,' said Julie, her arm around his waist. Something made him pull her into him and kiss her on the lips passionately. Someone called out, 'Get in there, lad!' For a second, it was the only thing that made sense to him: kissing her, tasting her, feeling her breath inside him. It was the only thing that seemed real.

'Come on now, no porno please, there are depraved, fat bearded men present,' said Jeff, arriving with three drinks in his hand.

They pulled apart, laughing. 'Sorry Jeff, I feel a bit like a love-struck teenager tonight,' Nick said, holding onto Julie's hips.

'I'm a rock 'n' roll doctor, as you know, and I can tell you without fear of contraception that a skinful of drink and a good-looking lass will do that for you,' said Jeff, handing out glasses of wine.

'I don't know what's come over me,' said Julie, pushing her hair back, wafting air in front of her face with her right hand and then smoothing out her dress.

'He will be in a minute if he doesn't calm down,' said Jeff. She slapped him on the arm.

'He'd better not; I don't want to have to send this dress for dry cleaning!'

'Look, can we stop talking about my sperm, please. My sperm is a private matter!'

Some people overheard him and burst out laughing.

The evening turned into a monumental piss-up. It was no surprise since the Northern journalistic brethren is, at the best of times, fuelled by an industrial consumption of booze.

They spilled out of the Teesside International at 1am and got into one of many taxis queuing for business outside the front entrance. Nick's head was spinning. Every time he tried to focus on something, it slipped from left to right. This wasn't a good sign. A spinning room invariably led to vomiting. Julie held onto his arm, her head on his shoulder. She was almost asleep. Jeff, on the other hand, was full of life.

'Pity we had to stop at one, I was up for an all-nighter there. By four I might even have started to cut a rug on the dance floor. The dawn death dance. Yeah...and as you know, Jeff don't dance dude, not until the fourth bottle of wine kicks in anyway.'

'How are you not comeytie...combovertoes... err...whatever the fuck,' said Nick, unable to control his ability to speak.

'He's not human,' said Julie, eyes closed.

'I am 28 per cent dustbin, never forget that. You can put anything in me - except hot ashes,' he said, laughing all the way back to Julie's flat while drumming out a beat on his legs.

Nick went up the stairs on his hands and knees for fear of falling over backwards. Once inside the flat, Julie pulled out a sleeping bag for Jeff and pulled the cushions off the sofa.

'You're coming in here with me,' she said, taking Nick by the hand into her bedroom. He left Jeff with a wave. She closed the door behind them.

'I am absolutely wankered,' said Nick, collapsing on the bed. The walls moved from left to right.

'Me, too,' said Julie, putting on her bathroom light and sitting down in front of a big mirror to remove her make-up, but unable to focus properly, she gave up and turned out the light.

The need to become unconscious was too great to resist. He pulled off his clothes and got into her double bed, vaguely aware of a lovely sandalwood smell and the cool, smooth linen sheets before the alcohol put him to sleep.

By the time he stirred back into consciousness, light was coming in through the window and its half-drawn curtains. His mouth had dried up totally and felt like it had been laminated with plastic. A wet patch of drool was on the pillow. As he picked a crust out of his eye, he looked up at the ceiling and tried to assess how he felt. Julie had got up and he could hear her clattering around in the kitchen. He got up to use the toilet and rinsed his mouth out with some water. As he was getting back into bed, Julie came in wearing a white towelling dressing gown and carrying two mugs of green tea.

'Arghh! There's a naked man in my room...' she said in mock horror, '...and how does the naked man feel?'

'Like I have been shit out of an elephant's arse...but surprisingly, I haven't got a splitting headache. I do seem to have acquired some bruises, though. I wasn't fighting at any point was I? Or wrestling?'

'I think Jeff might have lifted you above his head at one point, or at least tried to,' she said, climbing back into bed herself.

'Christ. That might explain it. How are you? You put away a skinful of wine. Very impressive. Glad to see you haven't lost your drinking trousers.'

'I'm alright, a bit fuzzy,' she said. 'I seem to recall you were a morning puker.'

'Yeah, I've always been one to unload the drink after sleeping it off rather than before. Stupid really, but I think I'll be alright today, probably because we had a good feed and I wolfed down all the butter.'

'They all thought you were trying to commit death by cholesterol poisoning. I had to explain to that wife of the Hexham Courant man about your high-fat, low-carb diet.'

'It lines your stomach, does butter. Great tip to avoid getting wasted quickly. Slows everything down.'

They sat in silence next to each other, drinking the hot tea.

'Is Jeff up?'

'No. He looks like road kill. I made him some coffee and left him on the floor. He stinks. It's like having a massive wet, smelly dog in the house. I don't know what he's been doing in there...I had to open a window.'

'He is a bit of animal...though quite which bit, I'm not too sure. Did

I tell you he was saying last night that he reckons Susan's death might be murder?'

'Gerraway. He's just like that though, isn't he? Paranoid, like. She had a heart attack or something, surely'

'That was what I said. But he thinks there's something odd about how she died.'

'When is the coroner's report due then?'

'A week or two, I think. That'll clear it all up, I'm sure.'

She rubbed her face.

'Just as well I don't have any lectures until this afternoon. I had a feeling it would end up a bit messy,' she said.

Nick looked around her bedroom. It was the first time he'd ever been in there, let alone slept. It was all gold and wine coloured, simple and plain but rich. The bed was covered in an antique silk quilt, the curtains were red velvet covered in gold and green embroidery and the whole room smelled of sandalwood.

'I miss your taste,' Nick said, sipping his tea.

'My taste? Do you want to lick me? This sounds promising.'

'No, I mean your taste in décor. You know how to make a place look nice.' He looked at her for a few seconds.

'What are you looking at?' she asked, without turning his way.

'You.'

'...and?...'

'...and nowt. I was just thinking how nice it was to wake up next to you for the second time in three mornings.'

She smiled at him, leaned over and gave him a kiss on the cheek.

'You were very, very frisky last night. I never saw the like. Kissing me in the bar like that. A public show of emotion, that's very un-Guymer-esque. It must be your therapy or something,' she said, twirling a strand of hair around her finger.

'Sorry. I was a bit carried away by it all. You in that dress, the award, everyone being so nice to me,' he laughed and looked at the trophy which was sitting on a bedside table. 'What a mental night.'

'You don't have to apologise for kissing me, I'm officially your girlfriend now, remember? I'm not letting you get out of it.'

He took her hand, squeezed it and laughed. 'I'm happy to sign up for that gig, lady. I shall do my ablutions in a minute and then I'll cook us all some breakfast like a good, well-trained boyfriend.'

'Yay food!' she said, waving her hands in the air in an unselfconsciously silly fashion.

He finished his tea, swung his legs out of bed and went for a shower. She watched him go.

He had just got the water to the right temperature when Julie pulled the cubicle door open. She was naked. Very naked.

'You don't mind if I share with you, do you?' she said with a suggestive look in her eyes.

He wasn't about to say no.

She squeezed in beside him and let the water fall down her back, taking a bar of soap and handing it to him.

'Do my back, will you?' she said, turning around.

He soaped her from the back of her neck to her thighs, running his hands in circles on her firm buttocks.

'Now the front, there's a good boy,' she said, turning around, holding him with a hand on each of his hips.

'Ah, the more detailed and pointy side of the female body,' he said, with a smile, sliding the soap over her round breasts and her now-hard, pink nipples. His hand was shaking a little and he dropped the soap, so she bent down, picked it up and returned the soapy favour, making his cock as slippery as it was hard.

She kissed him under the water as he ran his hands over her back and between her legs. She sighed and pressed into him. 'Remember, I'm not on the pill, so be careful not to put your big, hard cock into me,' she whispered in his ear, taking hold of him firmly. That did it for him. Words were his thing. Her words.

His heart pounded in his chest as she stroked him up and down and caressed his balls. He couldn't control himself for more than a few seconds. His orgasm was molten and intense and so pleasurable that he went weak at the knees. He let out a cry of pleasure as she pulled and pulled on him, her tongue wrapping around his, her hand massaging the small of his back as the water fell over them. He slid his hand between her legs, his fingertips exploring her. She played with his fingers as he stroked her.

'Ooh, there's no time for this now and I don't want Jeff to hear me having an orgasm,' she said, gurgling a laugh as she pushed herself onto his fingers. 'Let's save it for another time when we're alone.' She kissed him on the lips. 'I just wanted to show you how much I love waking up with you too...' she looked down at his softening erection, '...and it's nice to see you again too, Big Pink.' It was an old affectionate name of theirs from when they'd first met, derived from their mutual love of The Band's album, Music from Big Pink.

Nick was still very horny as they got out of the shower and he pulled her into him for a big hug, pushing himself up against her.

'Aren't you the horny toad?' she said, feeling him hard and pressing against her again.

'Sorry.'

'There's no need to keep saying sorry. Being randy is allowed, but I've really got to get ready for college.'

She had a big smile on her lips as they got dry.

'Are you sure you're going to be able to get that back in your pants?'

'I think you've caused a permanent redistribution of blood. I'm stuck like this now.'

'Permanently priapic? I'd better get some fitness training done, then. You'll be wearing me out.'

Dressed again, he held his arms out wide for her and they hugged.

'I don't want to know what you were doing in there but I'd like you to know I think it's disgusting and quite probably illegal,' said Jeff, as they emerged from the bedroom and walked into the kitchen. He was cooking bacon and eggs for them all.

'Look at this - it's the Galloping Gourmet,' Nick said, slapping his friend on the back. 'How are you, man?'

'I'm actually still pissed but that is not something to be sad about on a Thursday morning, is it?'

'You had an absolute bloody skinful last night,' said Nick. 'In fact, you had the skins of several people.'

'I had a lot to drink off my mind, didn't I?'

'And did it work?' asked Julie.

He snorted. 'Even I know you can never drink something off your mind but it's like Harry Hippy here said the other day about Susan;

there's no changing the fact she's died. No amount of crying is going to change it. I've just got to accept it and get on with life.'

'Life is for the living - it's a terrible cliché, but it's right,' said Nick, surprised to hear Jeff so philosophical.

'You are allowed to be upset, though, Jeff. She was an important person in your life,' said Julie.

'No, I don't want to be upset...it doesn't achieve anything. I'll feel better once we've had the coroner's report and they've explained how she died. Right, the food is ready. Where's the bread, Julie?'

'There isn't any. I've given up wheat.'

'Bloody hell, you've been hanging around with Low-carb Larry here for too long.'

She laughed. 'I like it and I feel better for it. Like that song says, you've just gotta roll with the changes.'

'Don't bring your evil Adult Orientated Rock ways into this. It is no time to be quoting REO bloody Speedwagon and I'd be grateful if you'd refrain from doing so in the future!'

CHAPTER 5

A couple of weeks later, after a night out at a blues bar with Jeff which had seen both of them drinking into the small hours of the night, Nick suffered another depressive episode. It was the worst he'd ever had; deep and black and impenetrable. He woke up feeling down and it got worse throughout the day. By the afternoon he wasn't just in low spirits, he was darkly depressed and angry with himself, angry with the world. He knew he should call Julie again or maybe Marc Lewis but this time it was so psychologically subterranean and airless that he just couldn't face it. He doubted he could even talk to anyone and just had to hide instead. A silent, private rage built up inside him. Even though she'd been so supportive, he couldn't let Julie see him like this. It was the worst feeling he'd ever had; even breathing air seemed devoid of meaning.

Isolated and alone, he felt like hitting his head against the wall to pound the depression out of his brain with sheer physical aggression. As darkness fell he began to scare himself. Why not kill yourself? It didn't really matter. Just another minute-long news story on the TV, a line in the local paper. Another life gone. Life was disposable. He opened a sash window and looked at the road 50 or 60 feet below with ceaseless traffic rolling by. The cold air blew in. He could just jump into the road below in front of a bus. It would be soon done. Kill yourself. Go on. Susan Rutherford looked at peace when she was dead. He imagined himself similarly deceased. Lying down there on the road, gone from the world and away from this shit. Not much was stopping him as he swayed in front of the wide open space; only the thought of Julie's face when she heard what he'd done, of how much it would hurt her and how upset she'd be; only that put a brake on his actions. He'd have stained her life again but then she would be better off without him in the long run. She'd get over it. One small step was all it would take. Just lean forward and let gravity do its thing. Someone was walking along The Stray holding a small boy's hand. They stopped and looked up at him, possibly wondering what he was doing. He slammed the sash shut and broke down into floods of tears. He couldn't spoil that boy's life by letting him see him jump, could he? Stop being so selfish. Try and keep love in your life. But all the happy hours of life, all the nice days, all the fun, it all now seemed so distant, inaccessible and impossible; a vague recollection of something now utterly alien.

He tried to write about it but couldn't see the bloody point. What was the fucking point in anything? What if this wasn't a passing mood but was actually how life was going to be from now on? There really was no going on if that was the case. It was intolerable. He went to bed at seven and thankfully fell into a long sleep from which he didn't properly awake until six the next morning.

As he sat in bed drinking tea, the darkness and misery was still with him so he stayed there all day, not eating, just lying, dozing, scared that it would just never go away, scared to get out and face the world. Around six in the evening, he felt it start to lift by small degrees, very slowly at first but by midnight, the black void of existence started to let in light. He slept for another 10 hours and awoke feeling like there was hope after all. The intensity of this depression was frightening and emotionally exhausting. It felt like you were breaking up with yourself. While he really didn't want to go to the doctor, where else could you go? He made an appointment for the following morning and spent the rest of the day looking through his diary, searching again for a depression trigger.

The only constant factor he could find was booze. He drank every single day and it had been that way for as long as he could recall, stretching back to when he was 15. He didn't get wasted very often but almost every single day in the last 30 years he'd had a drink buzz on him and had always used alcohol as self-medication to boost his mood. Sometimes he'd known only being very drunk would shake him out of a depression. To that extent, the booze was like a medicine. Maybe drinking was part of the problem then. He'd felt for a long time that he should try and be sober for a while. He looked around his kitchen. There was a little tequila left in a bottle of Cuervo Gold but no other booze in the house. He poured it away and resolved not to buy any more and to take a break to see if it helped. It wouldn't be easy. It was such an ingrained habit, such a part of British culture and one he really enjoyed. But feeling like you wanted die was so bloody scary that he was prepared to make the sacrifice.

The next morning he went for his doctor's appointment. The health centre was a characterless purpose-built unit with a reception counter at its heart, behind which women in white and blue nurse-style smocks sat and looked at computers. Behind them were acres of files on shelves with doctors coming in and out with various notes and cards.

It was always women who worked as doctors' receptionists. Were men not allowed to do the job? He couldn't ever remember seeing a man in the role of doctor's gatekeeper. If it had been the other way around, he'd have suspected it was a form of discrimination at work. Surely some bloke would want and could do this job?

The receptionist had a face that looked like it had been lived in by squatters. He went to sit in the waiting room with all the other sick people.

Being there made you feel weak and needy. Everything about it was horrible, from the junk gossip magazines on the table to the beige-plastered walls covered in posters warning of various diseases or addictions, not to mention the screaming children of exhausted-looking women. Depressing. All of it. What was he even doing there? You couldn't even explain anything in your 10-minute allocation of time. He contemplated walking out but as the thought crossed his mind, his name boomed from a PA system set to stun for the one hard-of-hearing person that would be in there all day. It was like being told by god to go and see Dr Harrison.

He trudged off down a corridor, knocked on the depressingly cheap, plain plywood door of Dr Harrison and went in. She was in her late 20s or early 30s, a skinny woman with a large fleshy backside which seemed to spill out of her padded chair . The contrast to the first doctor he'd seen when he left home in 1979 could not have been greater. Sidney Leith was a massive fat Geordie who chain-smoked and had an upturned wheel hub as an ashtray on his desk. He had once treated him for tennis elbow with a cortisone injection by sticking the needle in and saying, 'Just tell me when it hurts like fuck kidda and that's where this stuff needs to go'. Fantastic. Treated him like a man and not a silly child. He needed Sidney now. A big man.

There was no chance of Dr Harrison being like that. These were different days. They had to pretend to respect you even while ignoring everything you said and they were so simpering; more like Junior School teachers with children.

'Hello,' she said with a trained smile. 'How can I help you today?'

Nick sat down on the chair beside her desk and faced the opposite wall. He felt like a little kid who had been called into the headmaster's office.

'Put simply, I'm going mad,' he said.

She gave a polite laugh. 'OK. In what way?'

He tried to explain about his depressive episodes and how they affected him.

'Have you had suicidal thoughts?'

'I did recently, yes, and not idly. If it had happened, I wouldn't have cared. I nearly did it.'

'Do you sleep well?'

'I can sleep for 12 hours straight when I'm depressed. When I'm unwell I feel foggy-headed and stupid. I can't think straight and feel knackered. I also get short-tempered and angry.'

'Do you hurt yourself?'

'Sometimes. Yes.'

She nodded, glancing at her screen every so often. Then she took his blood pressure - it was 113/78.

Nick noticed the blood pressure machine had a Lipitor logo. 'Did Lipitor give you this?' said Nick, pointing at the machine.

She glanced over from her screen. 'They come through the reps, I think.'

'Why do you think Lipitor give you free gear? It's not out of altruism, is it? That's the biggest-selling statin on earth. It's all part of their marketing campaigns, you know.'

She ignored him.

'Have you considered antidepressants?' she said.

Nick looked at an imaginary watch. 'Blimey, that didn't take you long to get the prescription pad out.'

'People do find them to be helpful.'

'No, they don't. Some people sometimes do, that'd be a more

accurate use of words. I've done research and only 30 per cent of people who take them report long-term improvement and 3 in 10 is a rubbish result in my book. If you had a 30 per cent win ratio as a football manager, you'd get the sack sooner than later, and how would you know which one to give me anyway?'

She obviously wasn't used to anyone asking her questions and flushed slightly.

'We find that Fluoxetine can be effective over time.'

'That's Prozac, isn't it? Okay and how would you know if that was the right one for me, because there are lot of different antidepressants, aren't there?'

'We'd monitor your response to them on a regular basis, of course. If they didn't help, we'd take you off them and try another.'

Nick frowned and looked at her. 'So what you're telling me is you'll just keep trying different drugs until one works regardless of the fact that taking the wrong one might have really bad consequences.'

'Well...yes,' she said. She didn't seem to think anything was wrong with that plan.

'How long did you go to medical school for?' he asked.

'Five years,' she said with a puzzled shake of her head.

'Okay and after five years of learning, this is the best solution you could come up with? I don't mean to be rude but I could sit there with no qualifications in medicine at all and say the exact same things as you. Saying "I've a list of drugs for this so just take them until one works", well, come on, that isn't exactly top-notch science, is it? If some sort of quack said that, you'd be rightly cynical. Anyway, what if I kill myself after a bad reaction because it was the wrong drug for my condition?'

She sat back and smiled in that 'I'm being patient' corporate way that doctors have. 'So how would you like me to help you today?'

Nick recognised this as the 'move the smart-arse on' manoeuvre.

'Can't you do tests on me to see if my serotonin or dopamine levels are too low? If you give me an antidepressant that raises the wrong one, I'll likely as not go manic or worse, so why not try and find out first and then treat the condition with the correct drugs rather than blindly throwing the dart at the board and hoping to score a bullseye?'

It didn't seem like the most unreasonable idea.

'Did you read that on the internet?' she asked.

'Yes, of course I did; should I not have done that? Should I not try and get better by doing research?'

'It really isn't that simple, Mr Guymer...'

'Fair enough, I'm sure it isn't, but just trying drugs randomly is as simple a solution as is possible. That's my exact point. I just want to have my health looked at in more specific detail.'

She ploughed on with the other default responses.

'There are other non-drug treatments, such as Cognitive Behavioural Therapy.'

'But clearly, my issue is chemical or maybe hormonal. It's a physical thing that's wrong with my brain chemistry. Just sitting in a room talking to a bunch of depressed people won't change that. The root of it is some imbalance in my brain, that's what I want you to help me with. I already have a therapist for the psychological stuff.'

'Well, I'm not sure how I can help you today. We can refer you to a specialist but they will want to try similar remedies, at least initially.'

'Well, I'm sure as hell not going to take such powerful drugs speculatively and I don't think you should be suggesting I do.'

He stood up; clearly they'd reached an impasse.

'It seems odd to me that I can't buy more than two packets of painkillers from a shop but you'll hand out these strong narcotics within five minutes of me saying a few words to you. I just thought you might be able to help me but I'll just have to sort this out myself. I always knew I'd have to. I genuinely don't think you know what you're doing, do you? You're as in the dark as I am even with your training because if you weren't in the dark, you'd have a better solution than just to try some drugs until one works, wouldn't you? I suggest you reflect on how good you really are at your job when you go home tonight. You really should be doing better than this.'

He was pleased. There's nothing more satisfying than some well-expressed righteous indignation. She didn't say anything but looked red-faced and somewhat annoyed. Maybe nobody had ever walked out on her before. Well, there's a first time for everything, baby. He closed the door behind him feeling quite liberated. He hoped it made her question herself but doubted it would. It was in everyone's interest that people like him remained sick. Everyone made money; thousands of people kept their jobs; whole sections of the economy relied on the profits from real or imagined illness. Hanging on in quiet desperation was a great money spinner. If everyone got well, there would be a global economic depression.

He left the office feeling quite upbeat, having articulated his point as well as he could. Maybe having a row with doctors could actually be prescribed on the NHS. Just shouting 'you're a fucking useless wanker' at a doctor would probably lift the entire nation's spirits.

As he was leaving, he saw a familiar face coming towards him from the other side of the surgery. It was Jeff's mother, Jean. She was in her late 60s and an energetic, bustling woman. She wore a multi-coloured silk scarf around her head and a long red coat. Nick had met her back in the late 70s but still never knew whether he should call her Mrs Evans or Jean so usually he avoided doing either.

'Hello there,' he said.

'Oh, hello, Nick,' she said, as she pulled on a pair of gloves.

What could you say to someone coming out of the doctors'? What's wrong with you, then?

'I haven't seen you for ages,' said Jean as they left the building. 'I've never had chance to thank you for comforting Jeff after Susan's passing. I'm sure he appreciates it. He was very fond of my sister.'

Nick smiled but didn't know what to say. Should he offer words of comfort for her loss or was it too late?

'Well, it was all a bit sad really,' said Nick, instantly feeling that wasn't quite the right thing to say.

'I'm only sorry you both had to find her like that,' she said, putting her hand on his arm as though it would be a comfort.

She rummaged in a bag for cigarettes as they stood in the health centre car park.

'You don't smoke, do you?' She lit up a Marlboro. 'The coroner's report is due in the next few days, so we'll know what happened and maybe we can all move on but...I don't know...I have a bad feeling about it.'

'What do you mean?'

'Oh I don't know, Nick. She was a complex person, was Susan. They say still waters run deep, don't they? Well, that was very true of her.'

She stopped and looked at the pavement.

'Are you OK?' said Nick, putting his arm on her shoulder then taking it off, panicking that he was being far too presumptuous or intimate.

She didn't say anything but nodded. 'After the inquest has been heard, they'll read the will,' she pulled heavily on the cigarette, 'and I'm afraid a lot of things are going to be made public that have been...have been kept quiet for a long time now.'

She stubbed out the cigarette with her foot.

'What sort of things like? About her research, you mean?'

She shook her head again as they walked on. 'No. No, I mean things from much further back than that. There's a lot that has gone unspoken about in our family. A lot has been swallowed down and tried to be forgotten and I'm worried sick about it. I'm worried for our Jeff as well.'

'Jeff? Why?' If he was a more sympathetic man he might have been able to find the right words to coax more out of her.

She shook her head. 'I dare say you'll find out soon enough, Nick. I'll see you.'

'Suicide?!' said Nick, nearly dropping the phone.

'Suicide, yeah. The coroner's verdict is that it was suicide and the cops say it was suicide as well,' said Jeff, slightly breathlessly. 'It's total bullshit, man. She did not kill herself. Why would she do that?'

'How...err...what...err...' Nick was confused.

'How did she "kill herself"? Poisoning with potassium cyanide, apparently. Biggest bunch of bullshit I ever heard. She was murdered. She was murdered Nick, I'm certain of it.'

'Poisoning? Bloody hell. I...I can't believe it. Where the hell do you get cyanide from?' asked Nick, shocked to think that someone like Susan could have died like that.

He could hear Jeff walking out of the coroners in York.

'Fucked if I know. I was the only one there, you know. The two sons

119

didn't bother to come back from Singapore and Germany, Martin didn't turn up either. No-one was there to hear the verdict except me and the detective who's on the case, a bloke called Kowalski. He's a prick. Just wants the paperwork done and off his desk, I can tell. He even said that she might have got the idea from Boudica because she was supposed to have topped herself with poison. Arsehole.'

'Wow, this is all really weird shit, Jeff. We need to think about it. Get back over here and I'll buy us some dinner and we'll go over it all.'

An hour later they were sitting down to a steak dinner in the Yorkshire Steak House in Harrogate. Nick had brought his notes.

'So what was it like?' said Nick, after they'd each ordered a sirloin steak.

'Quite formal. It's in public, like, but I comprised the whole of the public. There was Kowalski, a court reporter, oh and another copper called DC Paul, but no-one else.'

'It's always confusing when someone has a surname that's a first name,' said Nick.

'Anyway, he's called Steve Paul who, as probably only you and I know, founded the Blue Sky label, managed Johnny Winter and ran the famous Scene club in New York.'

'Did you tell him that?'

'Of course I did. He wasn't bothered. Fucking philistine.'

'So how come they came to the conclusion it was suicide? It's not like we found her with her head in the oven.'

Jeff crossed his arms, sat back and said, 'He reckons they found an entry in her diary.'

'A suicide note?'

'Not exactly. Though they reckon it's evidence of her intention.'

'What did it say?'

'I don't know exactly, but he reckoned it was all "I can't go on like this" and that sort of stuff. But that wasn't the whole story - she'd ordered the poison herself from some place in the Far East. They found her card payment and a receipt, and there was no evidence of a struggle.'

Nick nodded. It sounded like quite a reasonable conclusion. 'What about any visitors she'd had that morning?'

Jeff shook his head and sneered. 'They found no evidence of anyone having visited her that day. But we found the front and back door open, remember? And we saw Martin James in the street. He could have popped in. The poison was in the tea: a massive dose. She'd have passed out within 15 or 20 seconds and then be dead within a minute or two. It's really quick. You saw her at that Boudica Society thing, she wasn't depressed or anything, was she?'

'Well, I know all too well that it's hard to know what is going on in someone's head and let's face facts, no-one buys potassium cyanide for a good reason, do they? So if she bought it...well, I dunno...it's weird.' He backed away from stating the obvious fact that Susan had indeed meant to kill herself.

'Buying it and taking it are two different things, though, and anyway we don't know that she did buy it, not for sure. The cops said they found a receipt on her computer. That still doesn't mean she bought it for herself or that someone didn't use her computer to do it. Maybe she was hacked. Nope, I'm not having it. There's no way a woman like Susan would kill herself. I reckon someone broke in there or was invited in and they put the cyanide in her tea to murder her.'

Nick wondered if he wasn't just clinging to the idea that she hadn't taken her own life to somehow insulate himself from the grief; after all, who would want to kill a semi-retired academic?

'So what happens now?'

'I dunno. There'll be a funeral at some point, I suppose. She had a lawyer in York and she's handling it all. It doesn't seem like her family are even that bothered. I'd like to find out what went on in those last hours because something feels wrong.'

Nick sympathised but really, what was he likely to discover?' The police might not be perfect but if there was any evidence of foul play they wouldn't have just let it lie. Maybe it would be better to somehow distract Jeff from her death and his theories while the truth sank in.

'We were going to Susan's to show her that old badge-type thing we found in your cupboard. It'd still be nice to know if was worth something and why people were trying to steal it from you.'

Jeff nodded. 'Yeah, I've not paid it much thought since. Who can we show it to, then?'

Nick was looking through his notes. He pointed to the name "Diane Edwards".

'We should take it to her at Durham University. She'll point us in the right direction if she doesn't have any idea herself. She's an expert in archaeology. Actually, I wonder how she took Susan's death. They were colleagues, well, actually more like rivals. She must have been really shocked.'

Jeff pointed at him. 'Shocked or delighted. Y'see, that's a better idea than you know Batman because, I'll tell you what, I was thinking about what you said about her and I reckon she should be the prime murder suspect.'

'Really Jeff?' said Nick incredulously. Jeff waved away his cynicism.

'I'm telling you man, Susan did not kill herself. And if she didn't kill herself, that means someone else did. Someone else murdered her. So who would do that? Think about it. Diane Edwards was her big rival and we know they were at each other's throats from what you saw at that meeting. I've thought about this...she's got to be the prime suspect. She stood to gain most from her death.'

'You've made a lot of leaps of imagination there, man.'

He held up a fat forefinger to indicate he had another theory.

'And about this thing we found, let's say it's not mega-valuable, 'cos I don't think it can be. Even if it was 24 carat gold, which it isn't, it'd not be worth a huge amount, so that means someone wants it for another reason. What other reasons are there? Who the hell left it in the bags and why did they do that? If it's not valuable then it's significant to somebody. Or it was. Now something has changed and that's why they're not interested any more. And I'll tell you another thing, you said you saw the lass who robbed the shop at the Boudica Society meeting, didn't you?'

'I thought I did, yeah.'

'Right...hmm...' He tapped his teeth on the glass of beer. 'I can't think why she'd be down here or how she'd be interested in my shopping...I'll have to work on that.'

'Look, I'm going up to see Boro play Liverpool with Julie on Saturday, I could try and arrange to see Diane Edwards in the morning at Durham.'

'I'd like to come up with you and see her, if that's possible, like. I want to get a feel of her...not like that...not in gropey way...though if she's a looker...'

Nick laughed. 'She's quite attractive, actually. A bit weird, though. Yeah OK, I'll get you a ticket for the game if you want.'

'Aye, go on then. I've not been for a while. It'll be nil bloody nil now, you watch.'

'Well, we've seen the last three home games and we've won every one. We must be good luck or something. Either that or we're suffering from some kind of collective hallucination.'

Jeff sank the remains of a pint of lager.

'I went bike shopping again, y'know?'

'See anything you liked?'

'Plenty I liked; nothing I could afford. I've only got two and a half grand to spend.'

'Christ, you might have to buy a chopper bike with a sewing machine engine strapped onto it for that sort of money.'

'Tell me about it...it's just a matter of waiting until the right machine crops up at the right price,' said Jeff, cutting into his steak.

'Julie used to have a bike when she was 18...or maybe it was her brother's. I forget. She came off it outside the Mitre.'

'Ah, rite of passage, that. I bet she looks good in leather.'

'Even better out of it.'

Jeff grunted a laugh. 'How's that all going?'

'What?'

'You know - with Julie and that.'

'It's, err...it's going well. Dunno what to say. I just don't want us to go down the same route as before with the same ending, so we're still trying to keep it on a loose sort of footing, like we're dating or whatever.'

'You've been up there a few times this past month, like.'

'Aye, but really just for the football. We're being careful with it. I've not stayed over, not since the awards do, I mean. Just...y'know...going slow, not getting too heavy.'

Jeff picked at his fries.

'If that means you're not having sex then you must have some bloody self-control, son. Christ...don't look at me like that...she was bloody gorgeous when I saw her at the awards...it can't have escaped your attention. How the fuck could you keep your filthy paws off her? It's a crime against manliness!'

'Well, we've not exactly been celibate but not exactly, whatever the opposite of celibate is either, if you know what I mean.'

He ran his hands through his hair, feeling a little embarrassed.

Jeff looked at him blankly

'What does that mean? Just hand jobs, not actual wang dang sweet poontang?'

'Wang dang sweet poontang?!'

'Aye, y'know, a bit of the old wang dang doodle.'

'Does all your knowledge about sex come from Ted Nugent songs?'

'Pretty much, yeah, though technically 'Wang Dang Doodle' is originally a Willie Dixon number.'

Nick laughed and shook his head in disbelief at his depth of music knowledge.

'Well yeah, it's something like that, yeah, I can't talk about it. It makes me feel awkward. I dunno why. But it does.'

'Eh? Why? You've known me since you were 15. You told me quick enough when you'd put your hands down that lass's knickers in the sixth-form smoking room. '

'Yvonne Riley. She was nice her. Hairy downstairs, too. I liked that. Yeah, that was different...you know Julie...it's not right...if you didn't know her, then it'd be fine. I'd tell you everything. But...nah...not when you know her. It's off-limits, all of that. Got to be. Always has been and still is. No details.'

He drew an imaginary line in the air.

'Christ, what are you doing, like? Badger sex, is it? You're both having sex with badgers, aren't you?'

'Don't judge us harshly. It's just a different kind of love.'

'It's got a nice arse, has a badger. But covered in fleas and a tad rough on your dangly bits, I'd imagine.'

'You've got to coat them in goose fat first.'

'Ah, of course. Greasy Badger - sounds like a 70s prog rock band.'

Nick finished his steak and eggs, pushed his plate away and changed the subject.

'Julie's loving University though.'

'What's she studying? Roman history, wasn't it?'

'Yup, more specifically the Romans in Northern Britain. She's been going to Vindolanda this week, out by Corbridge.'

'Hadrian's Wall and all that eh...draughty place to live in a skirt. Can you imagine, they must've thought they'd got the shitty end of the stick. You leave opulent, balmy Rome and end up in the wilds of Northumberland with a load of riotous Geordies and rebellious Scots trying to stick a pike staff up your arse.'

'Hadrian was gay, apparently.'

'Presumably that's what happens if you wear a leather skirt for long enough.'

'Maybe I should ask Jules to wear a leather skirt.'

'What? To turn her gay? Nice idea. I'd pay money to see her in a lesbian romp.'

They laughed and then Jeff got serious.

'Okay, well, if you can arrange this with the Diane woman for Saturday morning, why don't we drive up there in your car - my van doesn't like to make that sort of exertion - like me, it's anti-exercise. You two can have a drink in the Bridge, we'll go to the match and then I'll drive us home if you're not staying at Julie's for the full poontang doodle business.'

'That sounds like a good day to me,' said Nick. 'We might quiz her a bit about Susan. I wonder if she thinks the death was suspicious, too.'

Jeff took a drink, stared at the table and blew out air.

'Yeah, I really feel like I have to do right by Susan. She was so good to me, like, all through my life, so I can't just let this go, not until I'm happy that the verdict was correct. She wasn't the sort of woman to kill herself, I'm sure she wasn't and like I said, I'm just not convinced the police have done enough or any work on it.'

Nick sympathised. 'She was nice to me as well. I'd like to make sure this has all been handled properly. I'll find Diane's number when I get home and see if I can set up a meeting. I saw your mam a few days ago, by the way. She was coming out of the doctors'.'

'Oh, aye. She's got gout, y'know. If anyone in our family should have gout it's me.'

'How's she been over the whole Susan thing? Can't be easy losing a sister.'

'She was upset, like, but they were never very tight, not buddy-buddy close. Susan moved away from Teesside when she was 18 and never came back, so until mam moved here a few years ago, they'd only had a Christmas and birthday card sort of relationship.'

Later that day Nick called the archaeology professor.

'Diane. Hello, this is Nick Guymer. You don't know me but I saw you last month at the Boudica Society meeting. I came with my girlfriend, Julie Wells, she's doing her History MA at Durham.'

'Oh, yes. I remember that meeting all too well.'

'Yes, it was very err...well, lively. Anyway, I'm not calling about that. My friend Jeff Evans has found an old artefact and he was going to show it to Susan Rutherford...but...'

'...Oh, Jeff...Susan's nephew? Oh, I know your name now, Nick Guymer, Nick...yes...you were with Jeff when he found Susan, were you not? Is that right? I saw the news in the paper.'

'Yeah, Jeff's very upset about it. He was very fond of the old girl, as indeed was I.'

Her tone was harsh and unsympathetic. 'I read about it in the newspaper. It came as a shock to all of us. We all thought she was in good health. She hadn't been ill as far as I know.'

'Well, the inquest report was filed yesterday and its verdict was suicide,' said Nick.

She went totally silent. He listened for a few seconds. 'Are you there, Diane?'

There was no reply.

'Diane?'

Still nothing.

He listened intently. She must have left her office.

He was about to hang up when he heard some noise on the line.

'Hello, Mr Guymer?'

'Hi there.'

'Sorry, I was just called away there. How can I help you, anyway?'

She cleared her throat. Nick was no expert on reading feelings in people's voices but she sounded different now. Had she been crying? Or maybe she just had a cold. It was hard to tell, but on balance he was sure she was trying to hide some emotion or other.

'Well, I was hoping you could help me identify this thing we found. I think it might be very old, Roman possibly, but obviously I know almost nothing about this sort of stuff. It's three pieces which make up something, maybe a fastening or a brooch or something. I wasn't sure who to show it to, but as Julie's at Durham Uni and we'd come to the Boudica meeting, I thought of your good self.'

She exhaled into the phone, her breath undulating as she did so.

'Is it very old?'

'I think so, yes.'

'Well, I'm quite busy and I don't usually do this but I'd be happy to give you a quick assessment. Where did you find it?'

'It was Jeff, her nephew, who found it...err...at a car boot of all places, in a bag of potatoes.'

'A bag of what?

'...of potatoes?'

'A bag of potatoes?'

'Yes.'

'Goodness me...and who found it, did you say?'

'Jeff. He's my best mate. We'll be in Durham on Saturday morning anyway, would that be convenient?'

'Jeff. Okay, yes...err...I have a class to take but I'll be free at 11.15 or so. I'll be in my office in the department building until around noon.'

'That's very kind of you, Diane.'

He put the phone down and looked out of his window across The Stray. The news of Susan's death being suicide sounded like a shock to Diane, a shock or possibly a relief. It was hard to tell.

It was raining and windy when Nick parked in Durham on Saturday morning. He, Julie and Jeff made their way against a headwind to the archaeology department. Jeff had the three pieces in his donkey jacket

127

pocket.

Nick knocked on Diane's office door on the first floor.

'Come in,' she called.

Her office looked like a small library. Diane Edwards was more soberly dressed than when they'd seen her at the Boudica Society meeting, Now in a three-piece suit of wool tweed, she looked every inch the top academic, with a pair of owlish half-framed glasses perched on her nose and a Celtic printed scarf tied around her neck. Her dark green-blue eyes looked up from a large pile of essay papers .

'Hello, hello. Do come in. How nice to see you,' she said, smiling and getting up to shake their hands.

'Do take your coats off; this place is always overheated even in winter. So Julie, are you enjoying your MA work? What are you studying?'

Julie took off her black wool coat and hung it on a stand in the corner.

'I'm doing Northern Romano-Britain: the politics and administration of ruling in the first century - to give it its full title, like. I love it. I've spent this week at Vindolanda. Amazing place.'

'Splendid. Yes, absolutely fascinating. We all keep learning, that's the important thing.'

She turned to Jeff.

'And you must be Susan's nephew. I'm sorry for your loss. Susan was...err...well, she was an old friend and colleague. She was a brilliant academic. It came as a great shock to all of us to hear what happened. Nick told me the coroner said it was suicide.'

Her face was set into a frown, her eyes flicking up and down, looking at him.

'I'm not sure it was suicide, to be frank with you,' said Jeff, smoothing down his beard.

Diane sat forward. 'Really? What are you saying?' She looked surprised and maybe a little frightened. When she moved her unsteady hand off her desk, Nick could see she'd left a sweaty imprint.

'I'm saying it wasn't suicide. Something else happened. I don't know what but I'm going to find out. I think she may have been killed, poisoned, y'know?'

Diane sat back in her chair and stared at him as though she was trying to assess if he was serious, her face still set in a deep frown, the crow's feet around her eyes scored deeply into her weathered skin.

'So you're Susan's sister Jean's son, is that right, Jeff?'

He put his thumb up and nodded. She nodded slowly and looked away from him, still nodding.

'Did you go to college?'

'Aye, I went to what is now pretentiously called Northumbria University but which we were proud to call Newcastle Poly back in '79 - a fine academic home for those of us who didn't need to go to a university in order to be a smart arse.'

Diane gave a small laugh and nodded. 'What's in a name? It's all marketing. It's the education that matters, not the institution's name.'

'Me and Jeff went up there together,' said Nick.

'Ah, right, right. I see. 1979, you say? Gosh, doesn't that seem a long time ago?'

'I'd like to point out that I was just an innocent 14-year-old when you two went to college,' said Julie. 'I'm the youngster here.'

'So you two were both 18 back then...isn't it funny how four years seems so many when one is 18 but now, it seems like nothing at all,' said Diane. 'And incidentally, I think 18 is far too young for many people to be going to University. It'd help a lot of people to take some time away from education, in my opinion.'

'We both spent most of our three years at college away from education, ironically enough, mostly drinking and taking mushrooms,' said Jeff.

'And you are not alone in that,' said Diane with a small smile.

'I seem to recall I gave you a big bag of magic mushrooms for your 19th birthday,' said Nick. 'Picked by my own fair hand, I do believe.'

'Ah, yes, I took them at the first Monsters of Rock festival, Castle Donington, 16th of August 1980. I remember it like it was yesterday.'

'I'm afraid these two are rock music fanatics - they know literally everything about the history of rock music...like you wouldn't believe,' said Julie, rolling her eyes at Diane.

'Rainbow headlined that year, didn't they?' said Nick.

129

'Yep. Rainbow headlined. First on were a band called Touch, don't remember anything about them, then Riot, then Saxon, April Wine, Scorps, Priest and then Blackmore's mob. I really liked April Wine, they wore red spandex I think, but then I was on drugs.'

'See what I mean?' said Julie.

Diane laughed. 'It's nice to have an interest in life, whatever it is...now shall we get on?'

'Sorry, I was getting distracted by thoughts of my youth. I was going to show Susan this before she died,' said Jeff. 'I found it in my potatoes.'

He took out the three pieces wrapped in tissue paper and handed them to her.

She put it on her desk and undid the wrapping. 'Okay, let's see what we have here.'

She pulled the tissue open and froze in mid-action as though she had seen a ghost. The colour drained from her previously rather flushed cheeks and she stared open-mouthed at the three pieces.

'Is anything wrong, Diane?' asked Julie, sitting forward.

Nick sat back and watched Diane's face, trying to discern what was going through her brain. She just stared at the pieces without touching them for half a minute, her eyes glazed over as though she could no longer see anyone else in the room.

'Wh...wh...where did you get this?' she said, still not looking at them.

'I just told you, I found them in my potatoes,' said Jeff.

'Where?!'

'In my potatoes.'

'In your what?'

'They were in my bags of potatoes; I can't say it any more clearly than that.'

'Good god. In potatoes! This is hard to believe.'

She blew out her cheeks as she tried to collect her thoughts.

'Can you tell how old it is?' said Julie. 'I thought it looked very old...it looks like some Roman finds I was looking at in Vindolanda.'

Diane didn't reply. She took out an eyeglass, held up the largest piece and peered closely. She then did the same with the other two pieces. Her hands were shaking a little as she did so. Nobody said anything. Nick looked at Julie, who made an excited face back at him. Every emotion from exhilaration to fear to bewilderment passed across Diane's face like storm clouds blowing at speed across the sky.

After a minute, she put them down carefully on the tissue again, swallowed and looked up.

'This is a first-century brooch. Now it's very important that you tell me everything you know about this.' Her breath had become short and wavering.

'I've told you everything...I found it in my potatoes,' said Jeff, his arms folded, sitting back impassively, now somewhat annoyed by her attitude.

Diane was distracted and staring into the middle distance as though trying to hear some far away, barely audible sound. Her lips were moving as she conducted a silent conversation with someone in her head. She was visibly upset, tears in the pink corners of her eyes. The sensibly dressed, tweedy professor seemed to have been replaced by someone very different, someone emotionally raw and vulnerable. It was a remarkable change and not a healthy one. She looked on the verge of breaking down altogether.

'Are you OK?' asked Julie again. 'You seem upset.'

She just got up unsteadily and walked out of the room, leaving the pieces on her desk.

They sat looking at each other.

'Did someone fart?' said Jeff.

'Stop being a dick, Jeff. Should I go after her?' said Julie to Nick.

Nick had no idea but he trusted her instincts more than his own. 'Maybe, yeah. Maybe this brought back some bad memories or something. It's a weird reaction to an old bit of metal.'

Julie left the room in pursuit of her.

'Or alternatively, she's just a bit mad...' said Jeff, getting up and looking around the office. 'Look at this photo. She's a witch if you ask me.'

Nick got up and looked at the 8 x 10 photo of a group of women. It had to be the Boudica Society. They were all dressed in clothes straight from ancient Britain and stood at the edge of a forest. A couple even had shields and swords. He recognised Florence Farrell front and centre with her spiky red hair.

Jeff peered at it. 'Playing at Romans and English in the woods by the look of it. Mad.'

'Lots of people do historical re-enactments, it's very popular,' said Nick.

'Waste of bloody time,' said Jeff, sitting down again.

'I thought she was giving you the full once-over when we came in,' said Nick.

'Yeah I noticed that, largely because I'm not used to any woman's eyes lingering on me for any amount of time. Usually it's a quick glance, a look of fear and then the sound of running.'

Diane opened the door and came back in with a tissue, wiping her nose, followed by Julie. She rolled her eyes at Nick.

'I do apologise for that. I'm sorry to take up so much of your time,' she said.

'That's OK. Can I ask why you were so upset?' said Nick.

'It's err...well, it's complicated,' she said and then had to compose herself again. 'There are some things you wait your whole life to see and think you may never see and...well, I think this may be one of those things. Would you object to my keeping this in order to do some tests? It will, of course, be fully documented and returned to you once we have finished our work.'

'I suppose so,' said Jeff. 'Why do you think it's so important?'

She held the largest piece between her thumb and forefinger and pointed to the latticework.

'This symbol - look closely, it's like a funny-shaped letter B, isn't it?'

She traced the latticework with her finger. It certainly could have been a capital B, though it hadn't been obvious before she'd pointed it out.

'This is Boudica's insignia,' she said with her eyes wide.

'Bloody hell,' said Julie, and put her hand over her mouth.

'You're not saying it was Boudica's though, are you? Not hers personally,' said Nick.

'I can't say that, no, at least not without knowing exactly where it was found. I'm pretty certain that we have no other examples of this insignia - a logo to put it in modern parlance - but there are references to something like this in various texts and it has long been speculated that Boudica's army would have had some common insignia, but we have had no hard evidence. This could be that evidence. We know she branded the leaders of her army, giving them her own insignia to wear. We may be able to tell from the gold used - I'm assuming it is gold - where it may have been made. I just wish we had a record of the context it was found in.'

'Would you say it's valuable?' asked Jeff.

She took off her glasses and carefully rubbed her eyes. She looked and sounded very tense, her voice shaking a little as she spoke.

'Well that depends. As it is, unassigned to a context, it's hard to think it would raise a lot of money. But if it is a Boudica army or tribal piece from this region and if we could prove it was worn by someone close to her or in her family, which I think it must have been because it is such a special piece - it may even be grave goods, well in that case, it would be of worldwide significance. If it was unearthed in the northeast, it would be the absolute proof I need to justify all of my theories about Boudica. It's, it's...it's momentous.'

She filled with tears again and dabbed at her eyes, apologising as she did so.

'Wow...this is incredible,' said Julie, her hand over her mouth. 'Have you no idea at all where it came from, Jeff?'

'I've said haven't I? It was in the...'

'Yes, yes, potatoes,' said Julie, turning back to Diane.

'I've never seen anything from that period as good as this - nothing as high status. We have nothing comparable. If this is first century, I can't tell you how important this is. There's even a chance this did belong to the great queen Boudica herself. A chance. To think she may have touched this...' she visibly shivered, 'I would love to know who owned this before you, Jeff, and how on earth it ended up in your potatoes.'

'So would I,' said Jeff, 'and I've never heard the word potatoes more in such a short space of time.'

'I'd very much like to have these pieces thoroughly tested and analysed. Would you mind? I'll give you all the proper documentation.'

'Yeah, I suppose that's fine.'

'Thank you very much for bringing it in for me...you have no idea...'

They stood up to say their goodbyes. As Nick shook her hand he looked in her eyes. She took his hand weakly and her eyes betrayed someone now vulnerable and nervous. The confidence that she'd shown at the Boudica Society meeting had gone; she looked half the person. Maybe Susan's death had hit her hard. There was an air of shock and incomprehension about her.

She gave Jeff a receipt and Nick took a photo of his friend holding the artefact.

Jeff drove them from Durham straight to Middlesbrough and they went into the Bridge for a pre-match drink.

'I reckon that Diane Edwards is a whack job. No-one who isn't at least a bit strange runs around with their students dressed up like it's 2,000 years ago,' said Jeff.

'I don't think that's fair,' said Julie. 'Lots of people do historical re-enactments.'

'Yeah, but not with students who are 40 years younger. Those kids loved her. She was like their leader or their guru or something. That red-headed girl, Florence, she was like her general, conducting her army. They listened to Diane like some people listen to priests,' said Nick. 'I'm not saying she's mad, but there's something odd about her.'

'Mark my words...she's a whack job,' said Jeff again. 'And a murderer.'

The game was a poor 0-0 with Boro rarely threatening the Liverpool goal. It was the sort of game that you saw a lot at Middlesbrough. After about 50 minutes you began to wonder if there really wasn't something better you could be doing with your life. Afterwards, Jeff dropped off Julie and drove them both home to Harrogate.

Nick wrote some notes about their meeting with Diane before going to bed, while it was fresh in his mind. She'd had a disconcerting habit of talking to herself under her breath, her lips moving but no sound coming out, yet in front of the students at the Boudica Society meeting she was an entirely different person. Strident and confident.

But that was before Susan had died. Perhaps that had changed her. Could Jeff be right? Just maybe she had killed Susan and it was slowly but surely driving her crazy.

CHAPTER 6

A thick hoar frost covered The Stray as the first light of the day broke over Harrogate on Tuesday morning. Nick looked out of his window at the transformed ice world. Every bare branch or twig was coated in a thick sugar frosting. Footprints from early walkers made a random, weaving pattern on the white and green carpet. Frozen air hung heavy and still over the town like an ice-cream smog. Would there really be a car boot in Starbeck on a morning this cold and if there was, would anyone go? It had always surprised him just how deep into winter car boots would still be held. Only persistent heavy rain seemed to put people off, no matter what the time of year.

After a breakfast of scrambled eggs and thick slices of bacon, he set off to walk the two miles down Knaresborough Road, wearing a wool hat pulled down over his ears and a heavyweight leather coat to keep out the frost. It was a proper bloody northern morning. The cold air felt cleansing to the body and soul.

As he approached the car boot, held in a field next to the golf club, there was already a queue of cars to get in and set up. A burger van was already on site dishing up fried meat and hot coffee. There was something unpretentious and invigorating about the scene. It was common in a good way, being of the people and community. He knew Jeff wouldn't have eaten so early, so stood in line and bought him a large coffee and a big, fatty bacon roll. Wisps of steam drifted into the cold morning air as he watched the ever-changing scene unfold, the sellers followed by the punters, some of them huddling around newly arrived cars and vans to watch and judge goods being disgorged from vehicles. Harrogate was a very wealthy town, but here were people from the other side of the economic tracks, picking over old clothes to buy their kids for little more than pennies.

In the middle of an economic boom when many people seemed to have unlimited credit to buy more and more new things to chase an illusion of greater status and happiness, the car boot mentality seemed the saner one. It soaked up the underappreciated and never used; it picked up the throw-away society's detritus and found use for it. Or, in his case, it hoovered up vinyl records that had lain unplayed for perhaps three or more decades.

Jeff soon arrived in his van. He took his usual spot in the far corner next to the golf club. It was funny how regular sellers always occupied the same spots, as though it was their unit on the high street, and other sellers seemed to respect this unofficial and unspoken arrangement, not wanting to tread on someone else's pitch. He was wearing a huge green army parka with a big furry hood.

'Bloody hell, look at you, it's Nanook of the North!' said Nick, approaching the table where Jeff was laying out his boxes of albums.

'Is that a bacon roll I see before me, its greasy fat turned toward me shouting "come hither" unto my cake hole?' Jeff said, beckoning the food towards him.

'Err...yeah...and there's coffee too, Lady Macbeth.'

'Bloody hell, you'll make someone a lovely wife someday, if you'd only do yourself up pretty and put on pantyhose,' he said, taking them off him gratefully. 'Bollock-freezing morning, isn't it?'

'Aye, it's a real northern winter morning. Proper.'

'Winter? This is summer weather in Middlesbrough, son. You're getting soft down south.'

Nick gave him a hand with the boxes, if only to keep warm, and then went for a walk around the field in search of something interesting, but a box full of awful 80s pop albums was the only vinyl on sale. Disappointing, and it was sad not to see Susan there. Normally she'd have been laying out her books and he'd have had a look through in search of volumes of 1960s beat poetry, but now she was gone.

As he walked back to Jeff's corner he noticed something he'd never noticed before. Right behind his stall was a tall pole, maybe 20 feet high, and on top the pole was a CCTV camera, presumably as part of the golf club's security system.

He stood and looked. As he watched, slowly it moved in a 180-degree arc, covering the golf club car park on one side of the wooden fence and the car boot field on the other.

'Hey, big boy. Seen that?' he pointed at the camera.

Jeff looked up and raised his eyebrows. 'Ah ha, Big Brother is watching us. Hopefully he's looking out for copies of The Best of

Bread, volumes one and two.' He waved a copy of each album at the camera. 'Come and buy these, oh great oppressor.'

Nick had a thought that sent a charge of electricity up his spine.

'You remember when you bought those bags of potatoes and vegetables...the ones with the old brooch in? Were you selling here that day, in this same spot?'

'Yup. I'm always here, give or take a few feet either side. Ah...' he held up his finger. 'I see what you're getting at here Batman. Yes, yes. I like it...if someone put that brooch in those bags, they will have been caught on film.'

'Exactly. Do you suppose the golf club will let us view their CCTV footage?'

Jeff laughed a big steamy laugh. 'Do I hell as, like. I imagine they'd be more inclined to tell us to sod off and never darken their Tory golf jumper hell again.'

Nick rubbed his face with his gloved hands. 'Yeah, it does seem a bit of a long shot. Especially as neither of us is exactly Prince Charming.'

'You're a good liar, though. Can't you just make up some shit and get in there? Make out it's to do with security at the car boot - all about catching East Europeans on the rob...y'know...appeal to their right wing Daily Mail bigotries.'

'I could give it a go. Hang on, let's work out the right time and date.'

Jeff got out his phone and flipped through the calendar. 'It was the 10th of October. Now, I got those bags of veg towards the end of the boot, when it was pretty quiet. So that'd have been somewhere between 11.45 and 12, maybe quarter-past 12 at the latest.'

Nick wrote it down. 'What colour were the bags?'

'They were just regular Tesco bags. White with blue stripes. Three of them and they were on the right-hand side of the stall.'

'Right. Okay, I'll nip round there when it opens up. '

The lights went on in the golf club at just after 8.30, though surely no-one would want to play on such a cold morning. Nick gave it until nine before walking round. He pulled open the clubhouse door and went into the warm. His feet hurt with the cold. It was a pleasure to feel some heat.

'Good morning, sir,' said a grey-haired man in a navy roll-neck sweater and what could only be called golf slacks in a white, black and red hounds-tooth check.

'Ah, hello,' said Nick, consciously speaking more posh. 'I wonder if you can help me, I'm investigating some thefts from the car boot next door and I noticed you have a CCTV camera out the front on the edge of the car park...'

'Oh yes...?'

'Yes, would it be possible to have a look at the footage from a specific day last month? It's asking a lot, I know but really, we'd like to catch these...err...' he nearly said blighters but that would have been OTT, '...these criminals. We think they're eastern Europeans...you know...we have problems with them.'

'Yes. Well. I was never in favour of them holding that particular gathering in the field, a magnet for the criminal classes, if you ask me. It doesn't surprise me at all, this country is becoming Polish!'

Nick felt a twinge of annoyance. The Poles were only trying to improve their lives by coming over here, you couldn't take against someone for that. But this was no time to lecture the man on politics.

'I'll get Nicole, she'll be able to help you,' he said.

A minute later, an authoritarian-looking woman appeared. She was in her early 30s and was dressed in the kind of golf slacks that a 70-year-old woman might have worn in the 1970s, acrylic and with a garish check. Was this 'dress up weird' day? Her badge said Club Admin. He ran the story past her.

She was very keen to help, nodding appreciatively. She didn't even bother to ask if he was the police; perhaps it was just assumed anyone looking at CCTV footage must be from some sort of government agency. Who else would be interested, after all?

The CCTV footage was stored for a couple of months on site and so she led him to a small, dark room. Inside was a short, fat man whose job seemed to be to look at camera pictures of the outside world like some sort of golfing voyeur or an electronic mole living an underground life, his only experiences coming vicariously through the slightly overexposed and fuzzy images on his 12 CCTV camera angles.

'I'll leave you with Mick,' said Nicole, 'he should be able to help you.'

Mick stood up. Nick towered over him. He was probably just five foot tall and about the same wide. He smelled of sweat and cheap aftershave.

'Now then,' he said in a broad West Yorkshire accent, ' 'ow can I 'elp you?'

Nick explained.

'Oh aye, I can find that date. What hours do you want?'

Nick told him 11.45 to 12.15.

Mick opened a cupboard and pulled out a rack of silver DVDs on which the footage was stored. He located the date and the correct time period.

As he put it into a DVD player hooked up to a TV, he said, 'From Harrogate police, are you?'

Nick didn't flinch. He'd thought this through. 'No, I'm with the security team that looks after the car boot. We've been getting some serious thefts and noticed your camera might have filmed one that happened in this corner.'

Mick looked puzzled. 'But it's only old car boot crap, in't it? Does it matter if old crap like that gets nicked?'

'You'd be surprised. There are people trading gold and silver over there.'

'Is tha? Well, I never. 'Ere you go. 11.45. You can just sit 'ere and watch it if you want. Skid it forward with that button there.'

'Do you spend all day in here?' said Nick, slightly incredulously.

'Don't be bloody daft - I'm security as well. I just set these up every morning.'

'Ah, right, thanks Mick.'

He settled in front of the screen. The camera was focused on the car park at the golf club and every 20 seconds or so, it moved from left to right and back again. That was far from ideal because it could easily have missed the crucial moment. He kept an eye on the timer and noted that it took just over a minute to get from one side of its arc to the other and another minute to come back. As it reached the car boot field he paused it. He could make out Jeff as clear as anything - his long hair and huge hulk made him easily identifiable. He didn't seem to be doing much, just wandering up and down behind his stall with his hands thrust in his pockets. There were no Tesco bags on the floor.

He skidded it forward to the next pass. No change. He spooled it on two more minutes, no change. He got past midday and although half a dozen people had wandered past the stall, no-one had so much as bought a record, let alone done anything with a brooch. But at 12.02, Jeff had gone. He must have gone to the vegetable stall. Nick let it run through to 12.04, he still wasn't back. But by 12.06 the camera showed him wandering back, holding two bags in his right hand and one in his left. He was yawning. If there was one thing this CCTV showed it was how boring it was to stand at a record stall for nearly five hours. As it panned away from him, he was putting the bags down beside his tables. By 12.08 he was sitting with his backside resting on the front of the table, talking to man Nick recognised from Jack & Danny's, another record collector. The Tesco bags were down beside the right-hand side of the stall. Nick could see them clearly. He stopped the tape.

'Seen anything?' said Mick.

'Not yet.'

'You can zoom in a bit if you want. Freeze it and press that button on the right. Yep, that's it. It just blows it up a bit but it might help.'

Nick tried. He could now see quite clearly that two bags were full of Kerr's Pink potatoes and one of carrots, onions and a cabbage. It was a funny feeling looking someone else's mundane day-to-day reality.

There was still nothing much to see. Not even anyone walking around now. At 12.10 Jeff was looking through some records a youngish lad had brought. Jeff was shaking his head and handing them back. As he did so, someone ran past the stall. Nick stopped the playback, hit rewind and re-watched it. It was just some kid or teenager. They had on blue jeans and a hat...no...it was a beret. Who wears a beret? He rewound it again. Their head was turned away from the camera but as the figure came backwards into view, he realised it looked familiar. He blew the picture up again; poking out of the black beret was some red hair. That triggered something. It wasn't a kid. It was a girl. It was Florence bloody Farrell, he could tell by her unusually long legs, strong thighs and broad shoulders. But she certainly hadn't put anything in Jeff's bag. She was too far away but it was bizarre that she was there at all.

He wound it forward to 12.12. As the camera panned from left to right, the stall came into view again. Jeff was starting to pack up. He had a box in his arms and was loading it into the back of his van. The camera moved on further to the right. Then the Tesco bags came into view, still sitting there beside the stall. Still nothing. Still nothing. It stopped at the end of its arc and started to go back the other way.

At 12.13 and 20 seconds he slammed the pause button hard. His heart rose up into the throat with one gigantic leap. His mouth went dry. 'Spotted summat?' said Mick, getting up from his desk and looking over his shoulder.

Nick stared at the frozen frame.

It clearly showed Susan and it clearly showed her with her hand over one of the bags of potatoes. She was dressed in a long, dark coat, her grey hair spilling down her back. He blew up the image.

'What's she got in 'er 'and then?' said Mick.

'Something very valuable,' said Nick. 'Can I get a screen print of this?'

Somewhere in the darkness, a printer whirred into life.

He let the playback move forward at one-second intervals. Susan leant over the bag, looked at Jeff, who was facing in the opposite direction, bent her knees slightly and opened her hand. He froze it again. There were the three pieces falling but now suspended in mid-air.

He watched it back in real time - it all took no more than five seconds from her arrival to her departure. She walked away from the stall. Jeff hadn't even seen her do it.

'Right, that's all I need to see, thanks Mick.'

'Are you sure? That old woman? She was who you wanted to catch? Is she some sort of ringleader? She doesn't even look Polish.'

Nick got up, nodded and took the printout. 'Thanks Mick. You've been a big help.'

'There's another camera if you want to see it,' said Mick, pulling out a DVD from a box. 'It's at the back of the clubhouse but it overlooks the field. It's supposed to be focused on the boundary of the course to check that no-one gets in without paying green fees but it's been blown to one side...needs fixing. But you can see more of the field from it. Here...'

He put in the DVD from the same day and ran it forward to 11.45am.

Nick settled down and took in the scene. From this view, Jeff's stall was on the right of the field. Stalls were all lined up around the perimeter. It was a more distant shot but sharper quality. He ran it back quickly and then played it forwards at normal speed. It showed a different scene. One he couldn't have seen from the other camera. It showed Florence come into the field through the farm gate, she stood, looked around and then marched over to Susan's stall. She didn't stand in front the way a customer would, but instead walked behind the wooden tables and straight in to Susan. Even though the pictures were distantly shot, there was no mistaking the aggression that Florence showed towards her. The older woman took a step backwards only to find herself advanced upon by the tall girl. Florence leaned in, jabbing a finger in her face. Susan slapped the finger away. Florence put her hand on her shoulder, Susan shook her head, and Florence pushed her hard, making Susan step backwards twice. There was no other stall holder to Susan's right and the next one along was 10 feet or so away, so probably didn't notice what was going on. Finally Florence leaned into Susan again, holding her by her shoulders, speaking nose to nose, clearly intimidating her. Then she pulled away and strode off and around the field, passing by Jeff's stall and being captured by the other CCTV camera.

Florence Farrell, Nick thought, you're a bloody nasty bit of work, aren't you? Pushing around an old woman - yeah, very brave.

After Florence had left, he watched as Susan rubbed her face with her hands. Even at a distance it was clear she was agitated, poor old girl, she walked to and fro behind the tables fiddling with her hair. Then she left her stall and did the drop at Jeff's. Clearly, Florence's bullying had made up her mind to dispose of the brooch. But she must have been seen, maybe by her or one of the other Boudica Society kids that he couldn't identify and that's why Jeff was targeted for the break-ins. Susan had panicked, and hadn't been careful enough not to be seen. It was hard to watch her distress.

'Thanks for letting me see this,' said Nick, getting up. 'It's been very useful.' He was out the door and gone before he had to answer any more questions.

Jeff was drinking more coffee when he returned.

'Ah, here he is, you've been away long enough. I take it you talked your way behind enemy lines? And you're not even wearing a V-neck Pringle sweater and garish trousers.'

'It worked like a dream. There's bloke in there that runs a CCTV room. They've got cameras all over the place.'

'Paranoid tendencies, that sort,' said Jeff, making a wild face. 'So what did you see? Anything?'

'Oh yeah, I saw exactly what happened,' he said, holding up the printout.

Jeff looked, did a double take and took it from him, staring in disbelief.

'Yes, it's her,' said Nick.

Jeff stared at him with a frown. 'Bugger me, I don't understand why she gave me this but I do know that she must have had a bloody good reason. All she had to do was tell me and I'd have looked after it for her. Why all the secrecy?'

'The only reason she'd just dump this in your bag is to get rid of it quickly. She can't have planned it. She just panicked. But for some reason Susan didn't want to have to tell you about it.'

Nick sat on the edge of the van and pondered things.

'It means she was giving you that to keep it safe or to keep it out of someone else's hands. The thing is, I saw a lass on the CCTV who was at that Boudica Society meeting. There was another camera angle and I could see she'd been bullying Susan just before she dropped the brooch in your potatoes. Her name's Florence Farrell and she's one of the leaders of the Boudica Society. You saw her in one of those photos in Diane's office. She was clearly being aggressive towards Susan. Giving her a hard time, like. I think she was trying to get it off her.'

Jeff nodded, his lips pursed. 'This is all coming together. Think about it - the girl you saw up there who robbed my shop, this Florence lass and Diane Edwards. They're all in this together. This Farrell girl is probably doing Diane's bidding, which is why Diane looked like she'd shit herself when she saw the brooch. Here was something she'd always needed to prove her theories, something she'd sent the kid out to get for her and it's just given to her out of the blue by this big hairy sod...'

'...and which, if it's a Boudica artefact from the north, would effectively make her the top dog in her field. Susan was the old ruler and this evidence deposes her in a kind of academic defenestration,' said Nick.

'Don't be a posh wordy twat, Guymer.'

'It means it throws all the past ideas out of the window and introduces a new orthodoxy.'

'Oh, right, I'm glad you simplified it for me,' he said, with a typically heavy dose of sarcasm.

'No, but don't you see? This could be a way into understanding Susan's death. Think about it. Susan had this old brooch somehow, probably as a result of the undocumented dig that Diane accused her of doing. Susan must have known that it proved Diane was right all along but didn't want to go public with it. Maybe she thought it was all going to come out and that someone was going to steal it from her and she couldn't face the humiliation or being overtaken and so she took the poison,' said Nick.

Jeff raised his index finger to interrupt him.

'Or alternatively, Diane killed her to try and get her hands on it. She'd never have given it to her. They searched the house but couldn't find it because by then she'd already got rid of it to me.'

Nick opened his arms out wide. 'Could be, could be that, easy, yeah.'

'Aye, so maybe this Florence Farrell bird was saying "We know you've got some good stuff, give us it you rat bag", that sort of thing.'

'Or they wanted details of this supposed dig she'd done so they could go there and explore it themselves. But what do we do now?

Go to the cops?'

'The cops don't care. It's all done and dusted for them. The one I saw was a paperwork jockey, more interested in clearing his desk. We've got to do it.'

'We?'

'I'll do it on my own if you don't want to but I've just got to do what's right. It's fucking well eating away at me, man. Something just isn't right about all this. Susan was being hassled big time, you've just seen that - and that won't have been the first time. Why would she kill herself? She had her retirement to look forward to, probably on a good pension. She loved doing the books at car boots and she had a nice house. There was no reason for her to kill herself. I'm sure she was murdered, someone killed her, Nick. Bollocks to what the police say. Maybe it was Diane Edwards or maybe that kid or someone else did it for her but someone, somewhere is guilty of killing her.'

Nick looked at the ground and then up at the big hairy man and slapped him on the arm. 'You can count on me, man. You can count on me. I want to see her done right by as well.'

'Thanks man. Right, we'll reconvene at Jack & Danny's tonight and plan what we're going to do when hopefully some of my body will have thawed out.'

But it didn't get much warmer and as the sun went down, the night was bringing more frost. Nick looked out at the gloaming from his flat, the last rays of gold and pink illuminating the sky over the distant Pennines. It was the time of the day he enjoyed most; the transition from day into night always has a mystery and romance.

As the last rays of light gave up the fight against the navy blue night, his phone rang. It was Julie.

'Hey, Jules.'

'Hiya. How are we?'

'Just thawing out after getting frozen at the car boot this morning. Enough to wither a man's vitals.'

'Oh, I hope yours aren't too withered, I was thinking of coming down to see you next week.'

'If they are, I'm sure they'll perk up again when they see you.'

'I shall bring that ruler to make sure they're up to the full size.'

'Size me up, baby. I'm all yours.'

'Here's a fizzin' funny thing. I saw Diane today on campus and we got talking a bit. She's invited me round to her house for a coffee tomorrow morning. She lives by the cathedral. I got talking to her about Vindolanda and the Romans and she was very friendly and said she had some books that would be helpful.'

'Ah right, well, that's good because we found out loads of very interesting stuff today.'

He explained what the CCTV had revealed.

She let out a small yelp of surprise when he said it had shown Susan putting the brooch in the bag.

'Jeff's still convinced it wasn't suicide but I can't tell whether it's really good perception on his part or just a delusion he wants to believe. So I've said I'll try to help him find out. It bothers me that she was being given so much grief by Florence and I can't help but think that Diane was encouraging that at the very least. Anything you can find out from Diane would be useful. See if you can get a grasp of the state of her relationship with Susan - have they always been at each other's throats? How long has this dispute between them been going on? I find it hard to believe Diane or Florence or any of that Boudica Society lot actually went round there and poisoned her though, I really do.'

'It is hard to believe, but that might just be naïvety on our part - what does a killer looks like? It's almost always someone who is known to the victim. And, frankly, from what we've seen, these women are very driven and totally overfocused on Boudica. There's a herd mentality about them. We saw them go after her that night. Not all of them were wound up, but enough were to make me wonder about them.'

'So it wouldn't surprise you if they did kill her?'

'Well...sort of...but no...no it wouldn't. It'd be shocking but not surprising. I'll see what I can get out of Diane when I go round there. You should try and talk to that Florence Farrell. Don't give away that you've seen her on the CCTV, mind.'

'Yeah that's on my "to do" list. Whoever told you the Boudica Society people are loons wasn't far wrong.'

'Hey, do you know if a lawyer's handling Susan's estate, like Leslie West did for your dad's?'

'Jeff did say she had one, yeah. What I can't work out is why Susan's family haven't come home to sort all this out or to arrange a funeral or anything. There's two kids both in their late 30s, early 40s and an ex-husband.'

'Uh, families, who knows? Could have been a big rift. She seems to have been a bit of a loner but I imagine that's not unusual for a dedicated academic. They're sort of married to the work, aren't they?'

'Aye. The thing is that even though Jeff doesn't want to accept it, the evidence absolutely does point to suicide. She did buy the cyanide and the police say they found a suicidal type of note. I know Jeff might not want to accept it but, y'know, we should keep that in mind. If we could prove she didn't buy it, well, that'd be different.'

'Yeah, I'm not big on conspiracy theories. Life is always more cock-up than conspiracy.'

'I'll resist making an obvious cock-up joke.'

'Okay, I'll see if I can milk Diane for info on Susan and the bonkers Boudica birds.'

'Call me once you've met with her. Oh, I've got one other thing to tell you.'

'What's that?'

'I've stopped drinking.'

She paused for a moment in surprise.

'You've not, have you? Really?' He cleared his throat.

'I didn't tell you at the weekend but I had a couple of really bad days last week. I didn't tell you because I couldn't face talking to anyone about it.'

'A depression?'

'Uh uh. A bad one.' He let out a low groan. 'Like, really bad. I mean suicide bad, Jules. I'm sorry.'

'Oh my god, Nick, please don't talk like that. It's frightening.'

'I'm just telling you the truth. It has really scared me. I went to the doctor but she was useless - just gave me the "try all these drugs until one works" thing...which seems so stupid to me. People kill themselves on badly prescribed antidepressants but it seems to make

148

no difference to how these idiot doctors work, so I didn't get any tablets.'

'Oh god. Poor you. Are you alright now?'

'I'm fine now, but it I went through my diaries and I'm always boozing. I've barely been totally totally sober for a single day in the last 30 years. So I thought I'd stop boozing to see if it made any difference to my brain. I've always drank to lift my spirits but anything that can make your moods go up and down can't be good for someone prone to depression, can it? So I'm dry from now on. I dunno if I can stick to it, mind. I have to try something, though. '

'I'll support you in this. You know I will. Shit man, I worry about you. I wish you'd tell me when you're having problems. I know I didn't used to want to know and I know I used to walk away from it but I want to be able to help you now, or at least look after you and protect you.'

'That's nice, but honest, sometimes I just can't be around anyone. It's crippling and I'm just not able to. It's not possible. In fact, being with strangers would be easier, weirdly. Sorry.'

'Poor kid. If it happens again you can just text me if you can't talk about it and I can come over or even if I don't do that, at least I'd know and I can keep an eye on you, pull you out from under the train or whatever.'

'Yeah, OK. I'll text. I could probably do that. But I hate to even have to admit it. I feel so fucking useless and humiliated. Hopefully it won't happen again like that, but if it does I'll text you to let you know.'

'Good.'

'Anyway, I'll speak to you after you've been to Diane's.'

'Okay. Love you, mister Nick.'

It caught him totally by surprise, this casual declaration of love. He stuttered a stupid response. 'Oh, err...thanks Jules.'

He put the phone down with a smile. What did it mean? A slip of the tongue? Was she just being nice? They hadn't really properly said the L word to each other in six months or so. It was a pressure word.

He got into Jack & Danny's before Jeff, bought a pint of Stella for him and a fizzy water for himself and took a sofa by the window. Ten minutes later, a massive hairy bulk appeared at the door and came over, still wearing the huge parka. He pulled the hood back and made his usual face.

'Hello my bony-arsed friend. Ah, lager. Nice. And you're not having a Gay Mexican, decided to join the men of the world and drink something less camp?'

Nick told him he'd made a definite decision to quit drinking, though without telling him of his suicidal thoughts. He couldn't share that. By the end, Jeff had a look of horror on his face.

'Not drinking? You'll never last, man. You've been drinking since you were 15.'

'Maybe that's the problem. It's time I gave it a break. Don't go moody on me about it and don't try and talk me into having a drink, either. I've got to do something to stop these depressions or at least try. Right?'

Jeff looked doubtful. 'You'll never keep it up.'

'Stop being so negative.'

'I'm not being negative.'

'Ah ha! See...I'm not being negative...see...you're being negative!'

'Hang on...that's mental. If I say I'm not being negative, I'm being negative, but if I say I am being negative, that means I'm being negative as well. So basically, there's nothing I can say to prove I'm not being negative. You've got me stitched right up.'

'I'm just saying, I need support in this.'

'Alright son, if you think it'll help you, I won't force drink down your throat.'

'Now, onto other more interesting matters, do you know the name of the lawyer handling Susan's estate?'

'Not off hand but I've got it at home. I took note of it at the coroner's. She's in York, I remember that much. She should have the police's summary of the case. I got the impression they'd worked together with the coroner so when the inquest was completed they could close the case.'

Nick nodded. 'It'd be interesting to find out just how much work the police did. Did they ever come around and interview you?'

He shook his head.

'Not after the day when we found her, which was odd because, as far as I know, I'm her only living relation in the country unless you count the ex-husband. They rang me that once and asked half a dozen questions but that was it.'

'They've not even done that much with me.'

'See, I think they just shut it all down too quickly. Found their story and didn't look any further. There wasn't a single mention of the Boudica Society, for example.'

'Let's go over there tomorrow and get what we can out of the lawyer. Then I'd like to have a look around the house in Malton. Is there any way we could do that? The lawyer must have keys.'

'She probably does, but then so have I!' He produced a set of Yale keys from his pocket. 'I took these before we left there that day. I thought I'd need to get back in sometime.'

'Well done, big boy. The lawyer will doubtless have the so-called suicide note, too. We need to review all the evidence that the cops said proved she'd killed herself. Once Jules has done slavering up to Diane we might have a better idea what she really thought of Susan.'

'I know I keep saying this but I really don't trust her. She had a funny look in her eye if you ask me, a bit Herbert Lom in that "Pink Panther" movie. Anyone who is so fixated on something like she is with Boudica, who knows what they might do? I would love to talk to that Florence Farrell lass you were talking about as well, especially if she is a sort of Boudica ringleader. Plus, I like a tall lass. They're sort of exotic, aren't they? Not many of them around so when you meet one it's always a bit special, especially for a massive fucker like me.'

'Yeah, Julie said I should speak to her as well. Talking of Jules, she's coming over to stay with me next week.'

Nick rubbed his hands together, then looked at them and didn't know why or what this represented.

'Nice one. Look...' Jeff coughed and traced pattern on the table with his finger. 'I know I take the piss about you and her and that...and me and her haven't always seen eye to eye, like...probably because I can be a bit of a tosspot...but just to say, I'm really pleased you're getting on with her, getting back together, like. Seeing youse together it's pretty bloody obvious you're daft about each other, so...y'know...it's all good, really, and I hope it works out right for you. Now...don't expect me to come over all New Man with you again, right? We shall never speak of these things called feelings again shall we? Right?'

Nick laughed, got up to buy a drink and slapped him on the back.

'That was very awkward son, so no, let's never speak of them again.'

CHAPTER 7

Annabelle Proctor was a serious, middle-aged country lawyer with ruddy cheeks and dry, exploding black and grey hair only just kept in check with a hair band. It gave her the appearance of a Herdwick sheep. She sat opposite Jeff and Nick in her office in York shuffling through files of papers.

'Is it your intention to appeal the verdict of the coroner, Mr Evans?'

Jeff wobbled his leg nervously. 'It might be.'

'Do you have any reason to believe it is an incorrect verdict?'

'Something isn't right about it. I've got a hunch.'

'Sadly Mr Evans, a hunch that something isn't right is not in and of itself a good reason to overturn a coroner's verdict which, in this case, has been reached after a post mortem and a police investigation.'

She looked over her glasses at him with unflinching eyes.

'Can I see the police report?' said Jeff.

She gave him a copy and read from it.

'They speculate, based on stomach contents analysis, that the cyanide was taken with black tea and that there was no sign of trauma or coercion. No bruising to suggest she was forced to drink it. It concludes that she had a massively fatal dose - probably as much as a teaspoon - and that she would have been unconscious within 10 to 20 seconds. Death would have occurred soon after. There was no evidence of visitors who might have witnessed or caused this. They also say they found a payment receipt for the cyanide on her computer and on her credit card. There was also a diary entry which suggested strongly she intended, if you'll forgive me, Mr Evans, to kill herself.'

She was making a pretty good case, even if Nick had his doubts about some of the points.

Jeff interrupted her.

'But surely, a teaspoon of cyanide could have been put into her tea and she could have drunk it without realising. We found her collapsed onto her own legs which, to me, suggests she stood up after drinking it, maybe feeling sick or panicking as it entered her bloodstream, and she collapsed there and then.'

The lawyer looked over her glasses at him nodding, her lips pursed together, clearly not convinced.

'Do you have a copy of the suicide note?' asked Jeff.

She passed him a sheet of paper on which the note had been transcribed.

'This isn't a suicide note; it's a diary entry for the previous day,' said Jeff.

'Yes however, if you read it, it does make her intentions more than clear.' She allowed Jeff to read it and he grunted in response. Nick sat in silence in the overheated office. Should he speak? Should he make small talk with the lawyer? Should he talk about the case? He didn't know, so he said nothing, staring at his hands, the floor or out of the window, anywhere he didn't have to meet the stern Mrs Proctor's eyes.

Jeff finished reading the diary entry before putting it in a folder without comment.

'Can you tell me who the investigating officers were and give me contact details for them? I'd like to talk to them.'

She wrote two names down for him. They were both based in Malton police station.

'What's the situation with her will?' asked Jeff.

'I am the executor. It will be read and the beneficiaries notified.'

'But it's not been read yet?'

'No. I plan to do it early next week now that we have the inquest results. Now, if that is all?'

'It seems to me that everyone has made up their minds about this,' said Jeff.

'Well, to be fair, Mr Evans, it would have been hard for the police to construct a case for anything else.'

'Based on the small amount of evidence they considered, yes,' he said, standing up. 'C'mon Nick, let's get out of here. We shall meet again, Mrs Proctor, and when we do, it'll be with evidence to prove this was not a suicide at all.'

'Well, do keep me informed. I shall see you again once I start work on the will.'

Nick nodded at the lawyer and followed Jeff out of the office and out onto Mickelgate.

'C'mon, we're going up to her house,' Jeff said.

They drove up to Malton and stopped outside the large Victorian villa.

A man was cutting his front lawn at the house opposite Susan's as he got out of the car. They crossed the road and gestured to him. The man cut his lawnmower engine and came over.

'Sorry to bother you,' said Nick.

He was a tall man with square shoulders, probably in his early 60s, possibly ex-army. He had a certain bearing.

'Can I help?' he asked.

'Yeah, I'm Nick Guymer and this is Jeff Evans. Jeff is Susan Rutherford's nephew.'

'Oh, I'm sorry...Susan's...err...you do know...' he hesitated, clearly thinking he was going to have to break the news of Susan's death to them.

'It's OK, we know she passed away. It was us who found her, actually.'

'Ah, I see, I see. Yes, very sad. We saw the coroner's verdict in the local paper. So sad. My condolences. One always feels that one could or should have done something to stop someone taking their own life when it's so close to home. I'm afraid, well...I simply never imagined. Susan was always so steady and sensible. I'm Harry Thomas, by the way.'

He was well spoken, very middle class, a hint of a Yorkshire vowel to his voice. Another member of the conservative, solid citizenry of the north.

'Thanks, mate,' said Jeff, nodding in appreciation. 'It was a shock to everyone.'

'Thinking back to that day, did you see anyone visit Susan that morning, by any chance?' asked Nick. 'I know it must be a bit hard to see from your house.'

He swept his white hair off his forehead.

'Well yes, I did, actually. I didn't realise it until I was talking to Sally - that's my wife - when I read the verdict in the paper. That was the morning I saw Martin.'

'Martin - her ex-husband?' said Jeff.

'Yes. I had a brief word with him. I had just nipped out to chase a cat away when I saw him coming out of Susan's...'

'Coming out of Susan's?' said Nick. 'Are you sure he was coming out?'

'Yes, he came out of her driveway and I waved at him and he came over for a brief chat. He said he was just picking up some papers. It was a while since I'd seen him but he was in a hurry so we didn't get long to chat.'

'He was in a hurry?' said Nick.

'Yes, very much so.'

'Did he have any papers on him?' asked Jeff. 'Because we actually saw him when he was getting into his Porsche and he didn't have any papers with him then.'

'No, he wasn't carrying anything. I...I didn't think of that. Why? Is it important? Martin was a friend of mine when he lived here. We went to the golf club together. He's a fine chap.'

'Did you see anyone else that morning?'

'No, but I went straight in after speaking to him and I was at the back of the house so I wouldn't have been able to see anyone else. I didn't see you two arrive. Then the next thing I heard was the ambulances and police. It was quite a shock, I can tell you.'

'Do you have any idea why Martin and Susan split up?' said Nick.

'Well...it was a long time ago.'

'Even so...' said Nick, sensing he did know.

'Well...it was personal. They...they went in different directions, drifted apart. He didn't talk much about it to me. Our generation...we don't talk about our feelings much.'

More Northern repression. It wasn't always a good thing.

'Was he bitter toward Susan?' said Nick.

'No, not bitter. Upset, perhaps. I think he lost himself in his work to compensate.'

'Did he remarry?' asked Nick.

'No. No he didn't. I'm afraid we tried to stay in touch but as usually happens, we drifted apart when he moved away in the late 80s. We've always kept in touch, but infrequently.'

'Okay, thanks for your help,' said Nick.

'Is everything OK? Is there a doubt about Susan's death?'

'Thanks again,' said Nick, not wanting to comment any further.

They crossed the road and walked up to Susan's house.

'So Martin James is a liar, then,' said Jeff. 'He was so casual on the phone to me, too - butter wouldn't melt - he was a bloody good liar. Almost as good as you.'

'Aye, but why would he do that?'

'I'm coming up with the obvious reason...because he killed her. He poisoned her and then legged it, which is when we saw him.'

'Okay, well we'll think about that later. So what are we looking for now?' asked Nick as Jeff unlocked the front door with the Yale key.

'A big bit of paper which says Diane or Martin killed me on it, or whoever. Nice and easy, just like that. Failing that, anything to do with the brooch, anything to suggest she was under threat or pressure. Anything that'll tell us who were the last people to see her alive that morning, evidence of visitors. Any proof that Martin or Florence Farrell was giving her grief. Hang on, remember when we turned up that morning?'

'Yeah?'

'Well, the door was open, wasn't it? We stood here on the step and pushed open the door - it was ajar.'

'Oh yeah, I keep forgetting that. You're right. I thought that was odd at the time.'

'Why would that door be open? The only explanation is that the door was open because someone else had just come in or just left.'

'Or because Susan forgot to close it.'

'No. She was an efficient, well-organised woman. She wouldn't leave the front door open in cold weather. And she'd certainly shut it if she was going to kill herself so she wouldn't be disturbed. She'd have it all planned out and she wouldn't want anybody walking in. That's what she was like. So either way, the door being open is wrong.'

It was an excellent point.

'And I'll tell you another thing,' said Nick. 'Remember I said the back door was open, too. I closed it when I went into the kitchen when I was taking photographs. It had been just resting on the latch.'

'Both doors open is very weird and proves something was going on here that morning. I think it suggests somebody left in a hurry. They came in the front, left the door ajar by mistake. Then they left by the back door in a rush - maybe when someone, possibly even us, arrived at the front.'

'Jeff. I think you're onto something there,' said Nick, slapping him on the back.

They went inside. The house had a still, airless quality similar to his dad's house just after his death earlier that year. It seemed that when life departed, a house went into a form of stasis and became a void or vacuum waiting to be reactivated by new life. Without humans all of the inanimate objects in the house, up to and including the bricks and mortar, had no meaning or purpose. Susan's lifetime of possessions evoked scenes from a life now absent. It was eerie and ghostly.

He went into the room where he'd found Susan. The paramedics had moved furniture around and the teapot and cup were missing, presumably taken by forensics. Diane's book was now sitting closed on a low, small bookshelf.

There was a telephone sat on a table beside the television. Nick picked it up and dialled 1471 to find the last number that had been called. He noted it down. It had an 0191 prefix to denote Durham or Newcastle. He pressed the redial function to see the last number she had dialled. It was marked in her address book on the phone as 'Carol'. He noted down the number.

The tea table had been put against a wall and the other two smaller tables slid underneath it. The dislodged chip he'd found was still in place on the top.

'What do you think of this, Jeff?'

The big man peered over his shoulder.

'What, like?'

'See this...' he picked out the chip of wood and showed it to him. 'I found this on the floor and fitted it back in here.' He replaced it. Jeff ran his thick forefinger over it, squinted and peered closely.

'That's been done with a sharp point. Look...it goes in here at the top. It must have been done with a sharp, pointed knife. It's gone in here and pulled backward, splintering the wood.'

'But Susan wasn't stabbed...so it can't be anything to do with her death, can it?'

Nick went into the kitchen and took a look around. On the drainer stood one white china mug. On a small shelf was a packet of Sencha green tea, the same brand he used. But Susan had told him she didn't like green tea the last time he'd seen her. He turned out the tea bags on the kitchen table and counted them - there were 23 and the packet contained 24.

'Susan didn't like green tea, did she?' asked Nick as Jeff looked into the kitchen.

'Your hippy stuff? No. She drank Twinings English Breakfast. '

He pointed at a packet on the same shelf as the green tea.

They went through the hall and up the stairs to the first floor and into Susan's bedroom. 'This feels proper spooky,' said Jeff. 'It's like she's still in here, somehow.'

'I'll take a look around if you don't fancy it,' said Nick.

'You're OK...I'll just take a look around the other rooms on the next floor up.'

The bedroom was simple and plain. White cotton duvet and pristine white linen pillows. Simple plain pine furniture, everything neat and tidy and well-organised. What could give a clue about Susan's state of mind?

There were no photos of family members but there was a small pile of books on a stripped pine bedside table, mostly historical novels.

He went into the bathroom next door and straight to the medicine cabinet, always a great place to nosey around. There wasn't much except a small jar of zinc cream, an old tube of sun lotion and a packet of tablets, Atorvastatin, a statin to reduce cholesterol. Doctors gave them out to everyone like Smarties. He looked inside. She'd had the good sense not to take any. The label was dated 2005, so she'd obviously been prescribed them but then abstained, probably after doing her own research.

Jeff came in. 'Hey, there's an office on the top floor - we may have hit pay dirt, baby. All her papers are in there but it's in a right mess.'

Nick followed him up the stairs to the top floor of the house. As he reached the landing, he noticed an inset square in the ceiling.

'Jeff,' he said, pointing his finger.

'Ah ha, the loft. The traditional place to hide anything valuable...well, don't look at me, son. I'm too big for that small hole, as the actress said, et cetera et cetera.'

Nick got a wooden chair, stood on it and pushed the loft lid to one side. A cold blast of air fell out of it like cold water. He hoisted himself up and sat on the edge of the space, his legs dangling back into the house as he felt around for a light switch, eventually finding it attached to a wooden joist. 'What's it like up there?'

'Cold and empty,' said Nick, taking a look round. It wasn't much of a space and not even tall enough to stand up in. 'There's a small pile of newspapers here from 1972. Do you want them?'

'Deffo aye, there might be old tour dates or page-sized ads for albums that I can frame up and sell. Why did she leave them up there?'

'Dunno, maybe they just got left. Trouble with this investigation lark is we think there's got to be a reason for everything when half the things I bloody well do are for no obvious reason at all. Just accidental or whimsical.'

Nick held the papers over the space. 'Get ready to catch these, then.'

He dropped them in a flutter of yellowed paper then crawled on his hands and knees along the joists which ran the length of the house, probably 30 feet in total at its widest point. There was nothing at all in the whole of the space except large cobwebs and thick dust. He crossed over to the corner that was furthest away and sat on his haunches looking back. That's when he saw it. Taped to the top of a diagonal joist that led up to the cross-beam was an A4 brown envelope. It was impossible to see it from the loft entrance because it had been right above his head.

He scuttled across the joists around the perimeter of the loft until he was alongside it.

'I've found something! An envelope stuck to a beam.'

'What's in it, like?'

He tore the envelope away from the peeling brown parcel tape that held it in place and looked inside. There was nothing inside it at all.

He looked once and then twice to make sure something small wasn't lurking in the corner.

'Nowt. There's nowt in it. Here, take a look,' said Nick, dropping it and lowering himself down onto the chair.

'I thought that was going to be something interesting,' he said, brushing himself down.

'Aye, well, you were not wrong,' said Jeff.

'What do you mean, like? There's nothing in it.'

'Au contraire, my unshaven friend.' He held out his thick index finger. 'See that?'

Nick peered closely.

'Green dust? What's that?'

'You're pretty stupid sometimes for a clever get. It's not green dust, it's oxidised metal. Remember, the brooch in my potatoes?'

'How could I forget?'

'Those pieces of metal shed a green dust-like stuff like...like spores, almost...I'd bet a pound to a penny that the brooch was in here at some point.'

He looked at the brown envelope.

'See how old this is. It's been up there for ages. It's gone all soft and furry.'

'Ah yeah, I see what you're saying. She's put this up there to hide the brooch...'

'And took it out recently...maybe to keep it on her. Yes, yes...' he looked into the middle distance his finger aloft, nodding. 'Yes, yes...how about this...recently she's feared someone breaking in and finding it, so she took to keeping it on her instead. Then when that got too dangerous she put it in my bags. She knew she could trust me and felt she couldn't trust anyone else. Even if I didn't find them and threw them out or lost them, at least no-one else would have them. And that's not all. Come in here,' he said, leading Nick into her office.

It was a large room with a big leather-topped desk at the window and a view north towards open country and, in the distance, the dark purple, brooding North York Moors. Shelves messily stacked with box files, arch files and folders occupied one wall and other books and stationary another. There was a dust mark on the desk which showed where a computer had sat until it was taken away by police.

'Look at this place...it's so untidy. There are boxes and files all over the place,' said Jeff, looking around. 'This just makes me think that someone was having a root around in here to find something. The rest of the house is so neat and tidy. She wouldn't have an untidy office.'

'Maybe the police did it?'

'The police? Nah. There's no mention in any of their reports that they searched the office for anything. Her diary was in her bedroom. Maybe it was Martin? He was after something that morning. We know he wanted to come round to pick some papers up, that's what he said at the car boot, and we know he was here around the time she died. That's not a coincidence. It can't be.'

'Maybe not. But why would he have left the front and back door open? Susan would have shut it after him. He wouldn't have just left and not closed the door.'

'Hmmm, good point. You only leave a door open if you're in a hurry and he obviously wasn't in a hurry when Harry across the road saw him, was he?'

'Nope and he wasn't when I saw him getting into the Porsche either. He wasn't running or doing anything in a rush.'

Nick looked around. It certainly didn't feel right. Jeff was right. The whole house was so tidy, so why would this room be so unkempt?

'This has definitely been turned over, man,' he said. 'No-one has a messy office and a tidy house. It looks like everything was well-organised but has just been pulled out and rifled through.'

He took down two box files marked 'Correspondence'. The top letter was dated 1996 and was an inter-faculty request for a book. Talk about keeping everything. There were loads of pointlessly kept papers that were mere administrative documents. He took out the whole sheaf of papers and looked at the earliest one, dating back to 1985. The second box dated back to 1978. Everything was still in chronological order but had clearly been disturbed.

As they looked though the filing cabinets and folders, it looked like the same story time and again. No papers were out of order but almost everything had been opened, pulled out and not put back neatly.

There was file after file of documents relating to archaeological digs. They dated back to the late 60s and were mostly located in the north ,from York to Berwick in the east and up in the Pennines at Alston, all perfectly organised and documented in the same way he organised and documented his record collection.

'See, if the police had done this, though...they'd have taken papers out and looked through them and more than likely pulled out some sheets but they've not...nothing is out of order at all. And it's only the box files and drawers that have been opened. All the regular A4 binders and files are untouched. '

'In other words, it was someone looking for something - not papers but an object - maybe an object such as a brooch which could be hidden in a box file or drawer but not in a regular binder file.'

'Exactly,' said Jeff, scanning a random sheet of paper from the box of correspondence.

'Fucking hell! Whoo! Get in!'

'What?' said Nick.

'Fuck me...now we've got something...fucking hell...this is dynamite...you thought I was crazy saying Diane killed her but listen to this...'

He sat down on a swivel chair and pushed his hair behind his ears, his eyes scanning the paper back and forth

'What?' said Nick, hands on hips.

'It's a letter from Diane Edwards dated March 3rd, 1978. Listen, listen...it says, "Susan, my love, I will always hold you dear in my heart but it is so difficult to love another woman in the northeast of England in 1977. We both know that. The pressure to keep our lives secret is more than I can stand. I can't live like this, Susan. We must try and put this time behind us. We must try not to feel what we both know we do feel for it will do neither of us any good in the long run. It is a fight I cannot undertake even if you feel you can. This last year has been wonderful but now our relationship must become platonic and purely academic. I'm sorry, truly I am, but I shall not change my mind." How about that, eh?' Jeff looked up at him in astonishment. 'Well...bloody hell! Susan was a pipe-smoker,' he said. 'Christ almighty, you think you know someone...that never, ever occurred to

163

me. She'd been married and had kids. I'd never have guessed...you couldn't have guessed. Never even occurred to me. I bet...I'm sure she wasn't...y'know...active, like. We'd have noticed if she had...err...what do you call them...girlfriends. Aw, man...this is just too weird.'

'They don't all wear it like a tattoo, man, especially not your old-school lady-likers. Anyway, maybe she swung both ways, though she may just as likely have been in denial and was trying to live a "normal" life, hence the husband and kids.'

'Aye, yeah...maybe she liked both ends of the stick...can't blame her for that. Shortens your odds on the pull, doesn't it? Often wished I could have had the slightest inclination to have sex with men, if only for that reason.' He scratched at his beard contemplatively.

'You're the least gay bloke I know, Jeff. So I don't reckon that was ever an option for you.'

'What about you? Ever fancied it?'

'Not with you, no, but I might have given it a go when I was a teenager just to see what it was like. But the opportunity never arose and anyway, lasses clearly gave me the horn from an early age, so it was never really in doubt which set of genitals was going to get my attention.'

Jeff looked at the letter again, reading it through while shaking his head. 'So from this it sounds like they were together for a year. How old would they have been back then?'

'We know that Susan was 64 from the coroner's report and this is 29 years ago...so, err...35...Diane is a bit younger I reckon, maybe 59 or 60, so she'd have been in her early 30s.'

'Hmm, so they were well established in their careers by then and Susan was married to Martin.'

'At some point love turned to hate because Diane was going at Susan at that Boudica thing like a feral dog at a sheep's throat. She tore into her. There was no sisterly love there. I suppose 29 years is a long time to get over someone. What it tells me is that there's a whole world of unhappiness in Susan's history and also possibly the reason for her divorce.'

'Like I said, Diane's a proper weirdo. She's just got this look about her and now we know they had a relationship, that only strengthens my case that she's a potential murderer. Maybe they were still having an affair - maybe they were still lovers until recently. Good lovin' gone bad, that's a classic motivation for murder.'

'Diane is very intense. I bet she was a good-looking young woman, though, very magnetic. She's got those bright bluey-green eyes. It feels like she looks right into you. '

'And she's all but the leader of a cult if what you say is right about that Boudica Society.'

'They're not a cult but they're...well, they're something...I don't know what exactly. The word bonkers comes to mind.'

Jeff put the letter back in the file and put it on the shelf. 'I wonder what will happen to all this stuff?' he said.

'It might be thrown out by the company that clears out the house. You know what, you should keep it all - the university might want the research stuff - all these boxes here...' he pointed to a shelf unit with files recording archaeological digs.

'Good idea. We'll box them up and I'll take them home. I'm not having some auction rooms just binning everything. Why the fuck doesn't the family get involved, though? It's like the two kids and the ex-husband don't want anything to do with her. Maybe because of all this.' He tapped the sheet of paper with his thumb. 'Families fall apart - look at mine. But I wouldn't mind betting that the divorce was linked to her relationship with Diane.'

Jeff filled several large cardboard boxes with academic papers dated until 1995 - after which they were presumably written and stored on computers - and they carried them downstairs.

Nick pulled open the hall cupboard; it was full of coats, a Dyson vacuum and some yellow dusters. The top coat was a green quilted jacket, the sort country people wore. He felt in the pockets. There was a tissue but nothing else. Underneath was the long, heavy wool coat that she wore at the car boots. It was the one she'd worn on the CCTV images. He reached into the inside pockets, found nothing in the right-hand one, but reached into the left and felt a small pocket book. It was a black slimline diary.

Interesting. He turned to the day she had died. In pencil she had written 9am and underneath was a capital letter D. She had circled it many times until the paper had started to tear a little. She might have meant to kill herself at nine, but she was still alive until around 10.30am. So what was due to happen at nine and did the D mean Diane? Or Death, maybe? If anything deserved a capital letter it was death. If it was a meeting, had she arranged it here at the house or somewhere else?

He had an idea. He got out his phone and called Julie. She answered on the third ring.

'Jules, have you met Diane yet?'

'I'm just about to set off there, why?'

'We're at Susan's house. We've got her appointments diary. Can you try and find out where she says she was when Susan died? There's a note in Susan's diary that might refer to meeting her that morning.'

'Right. Do you really think she killed her, though?'

'She might have done...so be careful, right?'

'Don't worry about me; I could snap her in two with one hand if she tried anything.'

'We've also found out that her ex-husband was here around the time she died. A neighbour saw him coming out of the house and had a chat with him, but he'd lied to Jeff about that when he rang him.'

'Eeee, the lyin' toe-rag. That's suspicious. Very suspicious.'

'Yeah, it is. So can you see if Diane knows much about him?'

'Okay, will do. He wouldn't be the first ex-husband to kill his ex-wife.'

'There's another thing.'

'What, like?'

'Check to see if she drinks green tea and if so, what sort.'

'Green tea? Weird. Okay, got it.'

'Do you have Diane's home phone number, by any chance?'

'Yeah, she gave it to me in case I needed to cancel.'

'What is it?'

She read it out and he checked it against the one he'd noted from the phone. It was the same as the last call Susan had received.

'And there's just one more thing...'

'You sound like bloody Columbo.'

'...she's gay.'

'She's gay?! She's not, is she? How do you know that?'

'Not only is she gay but her and Susan had an affair in the 70s for a year. We found a letter.'

'Fizzin' hell! Eeee god!'

'So you might want to probe her a bit.'

'Probe her? I'll do anything for love, but I won't do that!'

'Well obviously, an act of lesbian love isn't strictly necessary but if you fancy it, I won't be judgemental, especially if it helps us find out more about her relationship with Susan.'

'I do like cats and k.d. lang, so that might help.'

'I wouldn't bank on it.'

'Okay. I'll try and get as much juice out of her as a straight girl can. Love ya.'

There it was again. She loves you yeah, yeah, yeah.

'See ya, Jules.'

He rang off. 'Right, Julie's off to Diane's now.'

'She might turn her!' laughed Jeff.

'Nah. Julie is even more heterosexual than me, I reckon. Never had even so much as a passing consideration for girl-on-girl thoughts. She digs dudes too much. Always has.'

'Pity.'

'Right, come on, you, we're going to see if we can meet those police officers who handled Susan's case. Just don't argue with them...'

'Okay, I shall refrain from punching them or vomiting on them, which are my two traditional responses to the police.'

They got into the BMW and Nick drove the half mile to the police headquarters on Old Malton Road. As they sat at some traffic lights, Jeff read through some of the papers the lawyer had given him.

'You know, this so-called suicide note that has been typed up from her diary entry...'

'Yeah?'

'Reading it now, after reading her notes in the house...it's really different.'

'What do you mean?'

'The style, the expression of her writing is very different to how it is in other documents I've seen.'

'Well the way people write changes.'

'Hmm, maybe. Or maybe this is forged.'

Nick looked at him; he was in conspiracy mode again, one finger held aloft.

'Yes, yes, that's it...this was forged! Forged to make her seem suicidal when she wasn't. Y'see, this is much less formal and I can't imagine her speaking like this. She never swore for a start, but here she says, "I'm absolutely sodding exhausted by living like this. I've lived a lie for so long. The pressure is too great to bear any more. Thank god it all ends tomorrow". She would never say sodding and she'd not write it, either.'

'Does she say what the lie is?' asked Nick.

'No. But it must the gay thing, mustn't it?'

'But it could equally mean the whole Boudica thing as well, couldn't it?'

'It might, but then it might be someone faking it to make it read like that.'

'Well, that's just a typed-up copy of the diary, isn't it? We need to see the original to make sure it's her handwriting.'

'Good thinking.'

He pulled into the police car park and they sat in the car.

'Does it say in there which website she bought the cyanide off?' said Nick.

'Hmm, yeah, it's in Singapore, it's just a string of letters and numbers - www.geqqz423we.sg. They must have got that off her computer. I'd like that computer back too. It was a packet of 12 pills; the coroner reckoned the amount in her blood suggested she'd taken 6.'

'Did she take the capsules or the powder in them? Does it say?' asked Nick.

Jeff looked through the coroner's report. 'No it just mentions the level of potassium cyanide in her body.'

'Makes a big difference, that. If it's tablets you'd assume she'd taken them herself because forcing someone to swallow six capsules would be hard. But powder can be put into tea and the damage done before you know.' He realised he was only adding to Jeff's conspiracy theories.

Jeff liked the idea and slapped him on the leg. 'You're quite clever for a bimbo, you.'

They got out of the car and went to the front desk. Jeff explained who they were and asked to see Detectives Foreman or Kowalski. As they explained, a tall, gaunt man came into the station jingling a set of keys.

'There's DC Foreman now,' said the desk sergeant. He turned and looked towards them at the mention of his name. He was in his mid 40s.

'Can I help you?' he said in a west of Scotland accent.

'I understand you worked on the Susan Rutherford suicide,' said Nick, not wanting to give Jeff a chance to be arsey.

'Yeah, that's right. Sad case.'

'Yeah, very sad. I'm Nick Guymer and this large man here is her nephew, Jeff Evans. We were wondering if it would be possible to have a quick chat about the case.'

He looked at his watch. 'I've got 10 minutes, tops. Come through.'

He punched a code into a door and led them to an empty interview room painted in two shades of slate grey with blue lino on the floor. Behind his back, Nick made a finger over lips gesture to Jeff and pointed at himself, hoping he'd understand it meant, leave the talking to me. He couldn't trust Jeff not to get angry.

'You two guys found her body, didn't you?' asked Foreman.

'Yeah, we did,' said Nick.

'So how can I help you?' he asked, pulling out two chairs on one side of a brown Formica table and sitting opposite them.

'Obviously, Susan's case is now closed following the coroner's report. We just came from the lawyer who's handling this, Annabelle Proctor. She didn't have some of the stuff that was taken from Susan's house in the investigation. We just wondered if you still had it and could release it to us.'

He sat up, seemingly surprised at the request.

'Oh ,yeah, if we've still got anything, but it should've all gone to the lawyer.'

'Well, it it didn't. Her diary wasn't returned and nor was the computer,' said Nick.

He frowned. 'That's odd. It really should have been. Hold on, I'll see if I can find where they are.'

He got up, scraping the chair across the floor noisily.

'Weird being in a police cell as a free man, isn't it?' said Jeff once they were alone.

'Aye, I was arrested once for stealing a car, remember?' said Nick.

'Aye, you couldn't even drive at the time,' snorted Jeff.

'And I was interviewed over a murder just because I was walking down a road two miles from the crime scene with a bloody scythe in my hand!'

'You got away with that one, killer.'

They waited for 10 minutes before Foreman returned.

'Sorry to keep you. I thought this would be a simple thing to sort but it isnae. You're Jeff Evans and Nicholas Guymer, yeah?'

They nodded.

'Yeah, yeah, I was given copies of your statements. I just spoke to Annabelle but the fact is we don't have any evidence here from the case. Everything we had was all boxed up and taken around to her offices in in the marketplace.'

Jeff held up his index finger. 'That means some evidence has gone missing, Mr Foreman. Why would that happen?'

The Scotsman wore a blue shirt with damp armpit stains. He shrugged and looked from side to side. 'As of this minute, I really don't know. Administrative, I'm sure. Someone will have put it somewhere it wasn't supposed to be. Leave it with me and I'll track it down.'

'Can I ask you why you were so convinced it was suicide?' said Nick, thinking this was a good chance to get his perspective on the evidence.

'Sure, well, everything pointed that way from the start. There was no evidence of any foul play. Once we discovered the payment to the website for the poison and the diary confession, and no evidence of any other involvement whatsoever, it was an easy conclusion to draw and the coroner agreed.'

He interlocked his fingers as though to illustrate the watertight coming-together of the facts.

'Was there any evidence of Susan having had visitors before she killed herself?' asked Nick. Jeff sat back in his chair, stroked his beard and stared at the detective.

'No. She seemed to live a quite solitary home life.'

'So she was on her own all that morning before we arrived?'

'That's what we concluded. We had no evidence to the contrary. It's a sad thing. We don't see many suicides in Rydale - not outside of the farming community, anyway.'

'So tell me this, where did the missing cyanide capsules go?' asked Jeff, his arms crossed over his chest.

'Missing capsules?'

Jeff leaned forward. 'She bought a packet of 12, the coroner says she'd taken 6, so what happened to the other 6? Did you find them?'

'No...err...no, we didn't. In fairness, when we did the first search of the property, we didn't know anything about the pills, so we didn't know they were missing.'

Jeff chewed at his lip and looked at the cop, unconvinced.

'Whatever, it doesn't affect the verdict. She might have just flushed them. There's strong evidence for suicide and no evidence for anything else.'

Nick left their contact numbers with him. Foreman promised to call with an update on the missing evidence as soon as he could.

As soon as they were back in the car, Jeff said, 'Something is so wrong about this. It's either incompetent or malicious.' He thumped the side of the door in frustration. 'He wasn't the one I saw at the coroner's; that was Kowalski. He was worse than Foreman. He'd stitched it all up with the coroner so that it could all be put to bed.'

'So you think. You can't be sure.'

'Whose side are you on?' said Jeff, looking at him indignantly.

'Yours, but I'm just trying to keep a perspective, y'know. We can't just assume everything is proof of a conspiracy. We need hard evidence.'

He drove back to Harrogate and stopped outside Jeff's flat while they carried in the boxes of Susan's research files.

'I'll let you know what Julie says about her meeting with Diane,' said Nick. 'I'm going to go through these papers and see if I find anything about this Boudica dispute between her and Diane and what it all stems from.'

'Okay, man. Good luck, I'll see you later.'

Nick was glad to get home. He put in a small chicken to roast and sat down to write his notes of the day's investigation while it was still fresh in his mind.

To take a break from all the thinking, he went to his record collection and put on 70s prog rock band Gentle Giant's album, Octopus, put his feet up on the sofa and watched the TV news on mute. He was just about to doze off when the phone rang. He looked at the display - it was Julie.

'Hey, Jules.'

'Hello, mister.'

'You sound perky.'

'Man, I've had a real heart-to-heart with Diane. I've got so much to tell you. I might write it all down and email it to you later.'

'Cool. How long were you there for?'

'Over three hours. She sort of poured her heart out to me...or some of her heart, anyway She's definitely one fucked-up lady. '

'In what way?'

'She's so focused on her work and on Boudica, it's like nothing else in the world exists to her. Her emotions were very close to the surface the whole time as well. She's totally devastated by Susan's death, totally messed up by it. Their relationship was on and off for over 30 years, every time they were getting it together, one or both of them did something to ruin it...then there was the Boudica controversy...' she let out big sigh, '...and she's convinced Susan has taken the details of an undocumented dig to her grave. She thinks Susan knew where Boudica's burial location was and that she hid it because it proved her theories wrong and Diane's right.'

'Bloody hell, that sounds like a heavy and complicated relationship. Did you tell her about the CCTV footage of Susan?'

'No. I thought it best not. She might have freaked out.'

'Good. When was this dig supposed to have taken place?'

'About 10 years ago. Man, it's so complicated. I am exhausted by it all. It makes you and me seem like a smooth ride.'

'Did she say where she was when Susan died?'

'She says she was at home and didn't know anything about it until she went into the university later that day when the police turned up to search Susan's office.'

'Did you believe her?'

'Yeah, well...no...I mean, it's hard to tell, isn't it? Especially when you don't really know someone that well. She seemed sincere.'

'See, that's very interesting because we found a letter D in Susan's appointment diary for that morning.'

'Really? That's almost proof then, isn't it?'

'Almost, but it might not be.'

'Well she definitely drinks green tea. You said to look for that.'

'Ah, what sort, did you notice?'

'Clearspring Sencha. I only know because it's what you buy. We had two pots.'

'Y'see, that's exactly what Susan had in her kitchen. But we know Susan didn't drink green tea. So she was getting it in for someone and who might she have known apart from Diane who drinks Sencha green tea? One bag had been used.'

'I doubt if many do - but then - it's almost proof but not quite, isn't it? I tell you what, though, she is very charismatic and attractive. I can see she has something almost magnetic about her. You end up wanting her approval somehow. I'm sure when I was 20 I would have had a bit of a girl crush on her.'

'Did you discuss Martin James?'

'Yeah, a bit. She really doesn't like him. She went as far as to say he was a bigot.'

'A bigot?'

'That's what she said.'

'A bigot against what?'

'Gay people.'

'Ah. Right. So Susan came out as gay to him and he freaked out.'

'To cut a long story short, yeah. She paints him in a very unflattering light. She said he was unsympathetic and didn't really accept it. He thought there was more to it and that she was just pretending to be gay to get a divorce.'

'Well...that doesn't make him a bigot, does it? Though why she'd do that...I mean...that's crazy.'

'Reading between the lines, I think he was disparaging about gay people and lesbians in particular but I didn't want to go into details because I didn't want her to get upset and blow up on me. She was snide about him, saying he does seem to like his young students, implying he has affairs with the girls. Mind, that happened all the time at Newcastle Uni when I was 18.'

'Yeah, at the Poly, too. Do you think that's a bit weird, though?'

'What, older lecturer shags 18- or 19-year-old student? Nothing men do surprises me, but yeah, it's a bit of a creepy power trip.'

'Yeah, I never thought anything of it at the time but now I'm the age some of the lecturers were, it feels sort of wrong. I mean, 18-year-old kids are so young...childish in some ways...and you know they're vulnerable because they're away from home for the first time and all that.'

'Like I said, it's taking advantage. At best he sounds a bit of a creep.'

'Interesting. So, any idea if Diane expected Susan to do this - to kill herself?'

Julie hummed for a second. 'Well, I have a feeling she wasn't that surprised. She said Susan was an intense woman and felt things quietly but deeply and she kept her private life very quiet.'

'So she'd never told anyone about being gay?'

'Only a few people knew, according to Diane, which is awful, isn't it? I really feel for her.'

'Really, why?'

'Nick!' she said indignantly. 'Try and think about it for a minute. She had to hide her own feelings - she couldn't be open and honest about it. That's a basic human right, or it should be. Poor woman. The children didn't want anything to do with her after that - maybe they sided with their dad. There seems to have been a lot of angst in their family about it all. That's all very upsetting stuff for anyone to have to go through.'

'Oh yeah. Of course it is. Sorry. So you got on well with her, then?'

'Yeah. I do like her, but I felt like I had to be very careful not to upset her. I mean, she was fine and everything, but I got the feeling that she could break into tears or have a big screaming fit at any moment.'

'So does she have a partner?'

'No. She lives alone. I didn't ask but I got the impression she's not had a long-term relationship at all or at least, not for a long time, maybe not since Susan.'

'And she never got married or had kids?'

'Nick - she's gay.'

'Yeah, but that doesn't stop some women. Susan was gay but she got married and had kids.'

'I think Susan tried to pretend she was straight for a while.'

'Well, the letter Jeff found was from 1978.'

'Like I said, it'd been on and off since they were at college together but I think they were still close in some ways. But it was that so-called undocumented dig in '96 which she just kept going on and on about, and how it had really come between them and it had all come to a head with the publication of The Queen of the Tees.'

'Well if that's the case, inviting Diane around to her house is an odd thing to do, isn't it? They were at each other's throats at the Boudica meeting. Why would she invite her that morning?'

'I don't know. Like I said, she claims not to have been there at all. Diane was also pretty cagey about the Boudica Society when I asked. I said how odd we'd thought it all was with that "tribes" business. But she just said it was little more than a history club and she changed the subject pretty quickly. That was the only part of the conversation where I felt she did a proper body swerve. I tried to ask about Florence but she totally steered me away from her and, like I say, I felt if I'd pressed her, she'd have become difficult.'

'It looked like more than a history club to me - to some of the people there, anyway. Do you think she could have poisoned Susan, murdered her in a fit of rage?'

She went quiet, thinking it over. 'I don't want to say yes because it's a terrible thing to say about anyone...but...you know what...I really think she could have.'

'Really?'

'The balance of her mind is not healthy at all. When someone is in that state, they could do anything, especially when it's just putting powder in some tea. She could have done it, run off and not even seen her die. I know she says she wasn't there but...I don't know...she's got something on her mind, something's bothering her. She's so distracted mentally, her eyes drift off as though she can't shake a memory or a problem.'

'The last person to call Susan was Diane the night before she died, maybe to confirm the meeting in the diary. The last person she rang was someone called Carol. I'm going to call her and have a chat.'

'Right, OK, Diane said she'll have the results of the analysis on the brooch in a day or two. It'll be interesting to know what that reveals. Look, I've got to go; I've got a badminton match. Did I tell you I joined the Uni club? First game is tonight. It'll knacker me.'

Later, he got an email from her with notes about her meeting with Diane. He wrote them into his own notes and sat back to read through it all. A picture was finally emerging. Susan was obviously conflicted for most of her adult life. She had a confused, fractured private life with an estranged husband and children as well as a lesbian lover and, on top of all that, her life's work could be overturned and superseded by the only person she'd really loved. She was certainly being bullied to give up her findings or that brooch. It was a recipe for unhappiness and maybe even a recipe for suicide. Clearly, killing yourself is the most extreme thing to do, but maybe she'd just got to the end of her tether. Was life likely to get any better or any happier? Probably not. So why not end it quickly?

His own suicidal thoughts during his last depression showed him just how quickly and suddenly you could lose your grip and perspective on life, even when you were familiar with feeling depressed. Suddenly it could get a lot worse. When that dull, blank void of nothingness descended on you, everything was pointless. Everything devoid of meaning. Life itself seemed alien. It wasn't hard to see how intolerable it might become. Not hard at all. He felt he could understand what she might have been going through. That void was something that was hard to endure and the thought of relieving yourself of it was very attractive. Yet the outside world might never guess you felt like that. Outwardly you probably didn't look any different, but inside you just wanted to fucking die.

When he and Julie had met her after the Boudica Society meeting, she'd seemed tired but now, thinking about it, she was in fact depressed. Poor old girl.

He noted down the last number she had dialled - the number for the mystery Carol. It was a mobile. It rang four times and then a woman answered.

'Hello?'

'Oh hi, is that Carol?'

'Yes.'

'Hi Carol. You don't know me, my name is Nick Guymer...'

'...the football writer?' she said, interrupting him.

What? No-one had ever heard of him.

'Err...yes that's right. I didn't realise I was that famous.'

'I used to do work for the Press Association on the sports desk, so I've seen your name a lot one way or another over the years. How can I help you?'

He explained how he and Jeff had found Susan that day. As he talked she made little sympathetic noises and said how sad she'd been to hear of Susan's death and that she was a good friend to her.

'Can I ask how you knew her?' said Nick

She laughed a little. 'You can ask but it's rather complicated.'

'Where are you based, Carol? Could we meet up to talk about it?...it's quite important...we think Susan may not have committed suicide but might have been killed instead.'

'Good god. Seriously? Yes of course. I'm in Beverley. Do you know where that is?'

'Oh god yeah, I was born in Hull, actually. I'm only in Harrogate so it's not far. Great, well, I'll come down to see you tomorrow morning if that's OK.'

They agreed to meet outside Beverley Minster.

He was just making himself some hot milk to drink in bed when the phone rang, making him jump. It was Jeff. Should he pick up? It was already after 11pm. He deliberated but he wouldn't be ringing unless it was something important.

'Alright, Jeff.'

'I've just found the Holy Grail,' he said in a monotone voice.

'I'm very pleased for you but I was just about to go to bed.'

'Bed, granddad? It's only 11! Bloody hell. Look, I've just been looking through all those papers. There's so much, but I've come across some stuff which was in a plain sealed envelope. It'd have been easy to miss it. I opened it on the off chance and inside are a few papers and what looks like a map of a trench she dug in 1996 just near Norton.'

'Okay, but why the excitement?'

'It's titled "Boudica's Burial Site?" With a question mark mind, like she wasn't sure.'

'Fuck!'

'Exactly. This must be the secret dig that Diane was going on about, the one she denied had ever happened.'

'Christ, she was so adamant that dig was a figment of Diane's imagination. She was a sodding good liar, I'll give her that. She stood up at that Boudica Society meeting and swore blind she hadn't done that dig. We spoke to her afterwards and she denied it again.'

'There are loads of notes and sketches but I can't find any of the brooch and I can't find any mention of it being found. There's a conclusion in which she says "a more detailed dig would reveal the full range of grave goods and, most important of all, Boudica's remains". There are drawings of a small trench in the ground and photos of half-buried bits of stuff that look a bit like the brooch but are crusted up with mud. There's some other jargon I don't understand, and a map. It's just north of Norton. You know the golf club?'

'Really? Bloody hell. Oh yeah, I used to play there when I had a brief flirtation with golf just before I discovered drinking.'

'Well it's just east of there, on top of a small slope. I looked it up on a map, it's just a copse of yew trees surrounded by arable land now, no sign of anything else, but this really is the Holy Grail for Diane and her mob, isn't it?'

'Totally, yeah. So Boudica really is the Queen of the Tees. Christ, I mean, wow...that's amazing when you think about it and the implications for the region and everything.'

'Yeah, but what the hell do we do with this information now?'

'It's late. We go to bed and we think about it. But I'll tell you something...'

'What?'

'This is all much more fucked up than even you thought.'

CHAPTER 8

The next morning he parked his BMW on Highgate near Beverley Minster, a grand, medieval Gothic building which dated back to the 13th century. Beverley was a smart little town, like a mini-version of York.

Carol had said she'd be wearing a blue denim jacket and black polo-neck sweater. They were due to meet outside the main entrance on the north side. As he walked up no-one was around, but within a minute a woman wearing exactly those clothes came up the lane towards him.

'Are you Nick?' she asked as she got near.

'Yes. You must be Carol.'

She nodded and held out her hand. She was unexpectedly glamorous, with a large pile of crow-black curly hair, bright red lipstick, black eyeliner and lashes and a tan that you didn't get in East Yorkshire. Her clothes looked expensive and her teeth iridescent white.

They shook hands.

'Nice to meet you. Shall we get a coffee and get out of this cold wind?' she said.

They walked off down a cobbled street.

'It's a lovely town, Beverley. We used to come here from Hull when I was a kid. Have you lived here long?' said Nick.

'I grew up here, all my family are here, too, but I spend half the year in California these days.'

'That sounds very sensible. Do you work out there?'

'Sort of, I'm a writer. So I write while I'm out there but I write here, too. My pen name is Violet Reddy, you might have heard of me.'

It hit him like a ton of lead.

'Is it really? Good grief.'

She laughed.

'I didn't expect to be meeting a best-selling novelist this morning.'

'Oh, I like being anonymous. I'm not interested in being famous. I'm here researching my next book, actually. It's set in York and Beverley in the late 19th century.'

'I won't pretend I've read any of your books - historical romance has never been my kind of thing - but I imagine you have to do a lot of research. It's not like making up any old story.'

They went into a café housed in what was originally a medieval cottage.

'It's all in the research for me. All of it. As I'm fond of saying in interviews, history is the best storyteller; I just allow the stories to breathe a little.'

'Fact is always stranger than fiction. Not a day goes by without me thinking that, even though I write mostly about football. I should try and branch out but it's a furrow I seem to enjoy ploughing.'

'And you just won the "Northern Football Writer of the Year" award. I looked you up. So you must be at the top of your game.'

'Yeah, well, that was very unexpected.'

'As I said on the phone, I remembered your name from my days working for the PA in Howden. That was, ooooh, 10 or more years ago. You used to do reports from Hull City - who I still support by the way, even from California. Come on, you Tigers!'

She ordered black coffee and, as they didn't have green tea, Nick ordered Earl Grey.

'So you've been researching Susan's death, then?' said Carol.

'Yeah, me and my best friend, Jeff. He's Susan's nephew and had a massive soft spot for her. It's all very odd. The coroner reached a suicide verdict but the police seem to have badly investigated the case. Did anyone speak to you about it?'

'No. Not at all. Which is odd given what you told me. I was very shocked when I heard about Susan's death and even more when I heard it was suicide. I wouldn't have known at all if I hadn't read the Yorkshire Post online from California.'

'Well - as I said over the phone - you were the last person she rang. Did she seem OK?'

'When you said that, I went back to my dairies and looked to see if I'd made a note of anything odd.'

She reached into her shoulder bag and took out a black hardback notebook.

'I keep a ridiculously detailed diary, I'm afraid. It's an affliction...takes me half an hour to write every night. She called me at just after 3pm, so that'd have been after 11pm here. '

'Where you in regular touch?'

'Oh, yes,' she smiled a pearly white smile. 'Susan was very good to me...sorry, you won't know what happened. I'll give you the synopsis. I was at York University 20 years ago, studying history, and her husband at the time, Martin James, was my course tutor. In what was not my finest hour, I had an affair with him. I was 18 or 19 and I thought I knew everything, as any 18 or 19-year-old does. Then I got pregnant with Rory, who is now 20 and has just started at University in Santa Barbara.'

'Good grief. That's almost a book right there.'

'Oh, it's too boring for a book. All standard stuff: student gets seduced by her tutor, blah blah...it's all same old, same old.'

'It's an unusual plot twist that you're friends with his wife, though.'

'True. She was an amazing woman, really. I didn't know what she was going through at the time - not until she told me years later.'

'...about her sexuality?'

'You know about all that? She was very protective about it. It wasn't something she felt comfortable talking about even after all these years.'

'We had no idea. We just found her letters.'

'When Martin found out about her affair with Diane he went crazy. In fact, the way Susan tells it, he just thought she was putting it on to get a divorce. That's how respectful he was...or wasn't.'

'So Susan was married to him when she fell for Diane?'

'Yes, they'd been married for four years and she'd already had the two kids. She'd tried to be the wife and mother but it wasn't her really. But she kept quiet about it. I think she would have kept quiet for her whole life if Martin hadn't found out, then it all went crazy.'

'He was angry?'

'Furious in the way that only a man who is already having affairs himself can be. Of course, I was one of those affairs and stupidly I got pregnant but I never told Martin it was his child. I quickly woke up to the fact he was a sleazeball and wanted nothing more to do with him. So he thought it was someone else's child, but Susan knew. She used to come to York from Durham as a visiting professor and so we got talking after a class and she told me she knew who the father of my child was. She'd found out about his affairs - I was just one of many - but she was totally cool about it. She understood why, as a young woman, I'd made this big mistake. She blamed Martin for exploiting me for sex. Although she might have looked like a fusty academic, she was really a very cool lady. Hip in her own sort of way, y'know and very supportive to me in so many ways. Eventually, of course, they got divorced but by then I was good friends with Susan and we always stayed in touch even when I was living 6,000 miles away.'

'So when she called you that last time it was a routine call?'

'No, it wasn't. She'd called me to tell me that Martin was trying to get my number and address, trying to find out what had happened to me. In a row with him over some academic papers he wanted, I think, she'd made an oblique reference to his "fatherless children" and he'd put two and two together and now wanted to meet his child. He'd been calling around the house a lot apparently, putting pressure on her.'

'So he knew that she knew you?'

'Well, it wasn't just me, Susan was friends with a lot of Martin's cast-offs.'

'A lot? How many affairs did he have?'

'Oh, quite a few. I don't know for sure. He was always at it, especially with each new intake. He probably still is. And then when Susan finally had enough and asked for a divorce, after telling him about her relationship with Diane, he acted like the injured party. He's one serious egotistical freak, that man.'

'So Susan was a sort of mother hen to all these girls?'

'Yes. That's a nice expression for her though not one she would have enjoyed hearing. She wouldn't tell him anything about where I was or who I was. He doesn't know anything about me and I'd be grateful, if you do see him, not to tell him. I'm not frightened of him or anything, it's just a load of hassle I don't need or want. He's irrelevant to my life. Rory can contact him in due course if he wants to. He's not interested at the moment.'

'So would you say Martin is a dangerous man at all? Could he have harmed Susan?'

She replied without hesitation. 'Oh yes. He has a nasty temper; or rather, 20 years ago, he did. I doubt that he's changed. He seems very urbane but he can change just like that.' She clicked her fingers.

'Did he ever hit you?'

She nodded firmly. 'Yes, he did. He slapped me across the face during a row and punched me in the arm and if I hadn't walked away, he'd have done it again and worse, I'm sure. This was the mid 80s and no-one ever complained if a man did that to you. Today, I'd have reported him, of course I would, but back then it was all different and I was young. But looking back with experience, I can see exactly the sort of man he was or is. Charming but nasty and vain and in that respect exactly the sort of man naïve girls with self-esteem issues might fall for.'

'Jeff thinks Susan was murdered. And we know that Martin lied about not being at the house the morning she died.'

'Really? Well before you even say it, I am absolutely of the view that he could have killed Susan. Yes.'

'Are you sure?'

'Yes. I'm not saying he did, because I don't know, but I'm saying he could and if he did he'd have been cowardly about it because that's what he is at heart, a coward. He would have poisoned her because it wouldn't be messy. He'd not have to touch her or do anything except put the cyanide in her tea and then leave. Nice and clean. He wouldn't even have had to be there to watch her die.'

Nick drank his tea.

'Wow. That's very interesting. Well, that's about all I need to know. You've told me so much.'

'I hope you get to the bottom of this. Susan was always kind to me, sometimes when nobody else was. If I can help in any way at all, just call me. I only wish I'd known before now that there was any doubt about her death, but of course that wasn't in the newspaper.'

'Well, to be fair, officially there isn't. Jeff thinks she wouldn't have killed herself but he bases that on conjecture and speculation, not hard facts. I'm trying to help him get some hard facts if there are any hard facts to get.'

'Sometimes hunches are all we have to go on in life,' she said and smiled.

They paid their bill and left.

'Thanks again for your help,' said Nick, shaking her small, soft hand.

'Not at all. It's nice to meet you. Do stay in touch. Good luck with everything.'

She handed him a small business card with her contact details and walked away with the confident stride of a multi-millionaire.

When he got home he wrote Julie an email outlining all the new information. He had an appointment with Marc Lewis at 2.30pm. It was a dry, overcast but milder afternoon, so he pulled on a grey sweatshirt and an old pair of jeans and made the five-minute walk to the therapist's offices.

'Before we get started today Marc, I'd like to talk about something that started happening this week. Not a bad thing. But I'm not sure how to deal with it.'

'Of course Nick.'

'Julie has started ending phone calls by saying "love ya" or "love you".'

Marc Lewis smiled. 'And that makes you feel uncomfortable?'

'A bit, yeah.'

'Why is that, do you think?'

'Because as soon as love, the big L word, comes into it, everything gets heavier and serious and I'm worried it'll put pressure on the relationship to work.'

He paused and Marc Lewis interjected, 'You've always said she's a much more emotionally literate person than you...'

'Yes, she is, much more.'

'...so maybe she's just saying what she feels. She feels love for you.'

Was he totally stupid?

'Well, yes, I assumed that was the case and that's great. I mean, it's not that I don't want to hear it. My issue with it is how to react. Whether to respond in kind or whether to act as a kind of brake on the relationship.'

'You see what you're doing there, Nick, is you're trying to apply intellect to emotions. I have little doubt from everything you've told

185

me that Julie is very important to you above anyone else.'

'If I have ever loved anyone it's only ever been her. She's the only one. But y'see that's it, the fact that my first instinct is to rationalise it rather than embrace it or just respond naturally with what is in my heart...shows how messed up I am, doesn't it? Normal people would be able to just say it, wouldn't they? How do I free myself from that instinct to rationalise it?'

'Have you told Julie you love her recently?'

He paused and thought for a moment. 'Not for a few months, no.'

The therapist nodded and smiled in his sickly manner again. 'Don't be too hung up on what is normal. There is no normal. What concerns me more is that you are unhappy with yourself, with your own instincts, perhaps. This is a recurring theme that we often return to, part of what you feel is your general emotional disconnect from people. You need to free yourself from these worries.'

Nick leaned forward, hands between his knees. This was doing no good. This bloke had no solutions. 'And I had a bloody terrible depressive mood recently. For a while I felt that dying was no big deal and might actually be a good thing. I nearly threw myself out of my window. It's scared me. I went to the doctor but she was useless.'

'I'm sorry to hear that. You don't deserve to suffer.'

'I've stopped drinking to see if it makes a difference.'

'Good. It's healthy to be proactive and try to take control. I hope you find it helpful. Can I also suggest that you just tell Julie what her words mean to you. Don't hide from it. Just be honest. She'll want you to be honest. Just tell her what you feel.'

'With all respect Marc, I could say this shit you're saying without any training. It's not exactly rocket science, is it? You know, I can't help but feel that if you really knew what I should do about all these problems, you'd have said so by now. You don't know, do you?'

He shook his head. 'It's not about me knowing what you should do but rather you discovering what will work for you. I'm here to guide you towards that but I can't magically produce a solution that will change you into a different person. It has to come from within.'

Nick sat back and folded his arms across his chest and said nothing else while the other man wrote some notes. As he wrote he talked.

'I'm sensing some hostility, Nick.'

'I'm not being hostile. If I was being hostile, you'd know about it.'

'Some passive aggressive behaviour, then.'

'I'm just wondering if I'm not just wasting my money here.'

Infuriatingly, Marc Lewis replied: 'I can't answer that for you...'

'I know you bloody can't...I wasn't asking you to, it was rhetorical. You can be really bloody annoying, sometimes.'

'Okay, OK, let's just calm down.'

Nick got up and paced around the room. 'Calm down? What if I think not calming down would be rather bloody good for my mental health? What if it helped me? Maybe I need to let some rage out.'

But as much as he was annoyed at the therapist, he was more annoyed at himself for getting annoyed. It wouldn't do any good. Still, Marc did look briefly concerned that he was going to thump him in the face and that felt like a small success, somehow. There had to be some grit to make any pearl and he was too smooth and creamy.

'Ironically, I was going to say to you today that I thought you had made so much progress in the last couple of months. You're re-establishing your relationship with Julie. You're starting to have a more positive outlook more often. Okay you've had a setback or two, that's inevitable, but by and large this is all good and you are making progress. I'm not just saying this for effect. You are opening up and getting healthier, I've no doubt about that, these depressions apart. I do feel you may need medical help with those.'

'They're getting worse, though, and that's one of the things I wanted to stop, that's why I came here. Sorry if I was...err...rude, or whatever. I just can't do this any more. I think I'm done with seeing you, Marc.'

'Nick. Just a moment before you go.'

'What?'

'I don't blame you for doubting me. This is an imprecise art. But ask Julie and Jeff if you've changed. You trust their views. I think you'll be surprised. And I'll still be here if you need me.'

At £85 per hour, I'm sure you will, thought Nick as he walked away.

He took out his phone as he walked across The Stray. A dog came running up to him, a shaggy-looking mutt that he liked to call a tripe hound. He gave it a ruffle of the ears as the owner called it back.

He hit the first number in his address book.

Julie answered after three rings. 'Hey, you,' she said. She sounded like she was walking.

'Hi, Jules.'

'What's up? You sound cross,' she said after he paused for a second too long.

'Yeah I am a bit, I'm just...I've just been to the therapist...'

'Oh yeah? Any good?'

'Not really. I think it might be a waste of money now. He just doesn't really understand me. He hasn't got any answers for anything.'

'What's brought this on? You didn't hit him, did you?' She was only half joking.

'No...I dunno Jules...I don't feel like I'm getting anywhere with it and I've been going for six months now.'

She paused and he could hear her breathing.

'Maybe you don't want to hear this but I think it's been doing you a lot of good.'

'You don't, do you? He said to ask you.'

'Totally, yeah. I've not said because I didn't want to put any pressure on you. You're really not so wrapped up in yourself as you were six months ago and that's made you less selfish and introspective. You've opened out. A lot. Even when I've seen you with Jeff, you've been more...I dunno...sort of touchy-feely with him. You still have your moments, but you're much better.'

'Really? Have I? It doesn't feel like that. Sometimes I feel like I can't get out from under myself.'

'And what does Marc say about that?'

'He thinks I'm harsh on myself and worry too much about what I do and don't feel. That I'm too obsessed with it and that overthinking these things makes me worry more than I should.'

She gave a snort. 'Well he's not totally stupid, then.'

He stopped on The Stray and looked around. In the distance, traffic moved slowly down York Place past his apartment in the Dales Mansion.

'I've got to be honest with you, Jules. I was talking to him about the fact that you'd started saying "love you" at the end of our chats on the phone...and I was stressing about the fact that I was consciously thinking about the right way to respond to you saying that...'

'Oh Nick!' she said, incredulous at this confession.

'I'm sorry. I know it's fucked up, but you're supposed to be able to talk to a therapist about anything, aren't you? I probably shouldn't have talked about us...but you see, this is what I mean, I'm still messed up and I start overthinking everything and he doesn't know or can't know or he hasn't got anything to say about it really...except...' He began talking fast and garbling his words.

'Shhh! Just be quiet for a minute,' said Julie, firmly. 'Of course you can talk to your therapist about our relationship, that's what he's there for. I don't mind at all. But you are thinking far too much about this. If I say "love you" or something at the end of the phone conversation it's not some big thing. It's just a nice way to say goodbye. You are thinking about it way too much.'

'Am I? Yes, obviously, I am.' He felt embarrassed now.

'Yes, you are. But look...I don't say "love you" to anyone else and I never meant it when I did say it to anyone else, not like I mean it with you. But that doesn't mean you have to analyse everything I say.'

'Okay. Yeah, maybe he was right, then. He said I should ask you and Jeff if therapy has helped.'

'Well, I think he's good for you and you should think carefully before kicking him into touch. Just because everything isn't perfect doesn't mean you have to get rid of him.'

He sighed. 'I didn't think you'd say that.'

He walked on a bit and stopped again. 'You do know I love you, don't you? I know I've not said it since after all that business over my dad's estate, but I really do.' The confession even caught him by surprise. He just had to say how it was from his heart; he had to uncork the bottle.

'You're a daft bugger.'

'Why am I a daft bugger?'

'I'm not blind.'

'What do you mean?'

'I know you love me. I can see it in your eyes. You can't hide it. That's changed as well. You never used to be so transparent, but it's nice to hear it as well.'

He laughed a little, feeling relieved.

'Who was it that sang, 'Love Hurts'?' she said.

'It's an old country song. The Everly Brothers did it, Gram Parsons too, and Nazareth,' said Nick.

'I knew you'd know; well, that song is very true of our past. We've both taken a lot of pain...I mean we've caused each other a lot of pain...'

'Yeah. I wish that wasn't true, but it really is.'

'...but hopefully that's in the past now, so here's a nice thought, why don't you fill me with the full extent of your love when I come to stay next week? I think it's time we gave it a go, if you're alright with that?'

'You mean properly...?'

'Yeah, properly, with a capital F...but look, I'm going to see you tomorrow, anyway. I saw Diane today and the results on the brooch are due back in tomorrow morning. I said you and Jeff would come up for 10.30 - is that OK?'

'Yeah. Did you get my e-mail?'

'About Jeff's discovery? Yeah, totally amazing. The plot thickens, eh? Susan was a bloody good liar. I never for one moment doubted what she said was the truth. How did it go with the woman called Carol?'

'Well that was amazing, as well. She's actually Violet Reddy. The author. '

She let out a cry. 'Fizz me. She's not, is she? The Duchess Disappears and all that.'

'Yup. That's her, aye.'

'Tell me about her later, I'd better go, I've got a lecture about to start. Love you. Now don't go dwelling on that!'

He hung up feeling happy and in love.

He walked around to Jeff's shop. 'Dance on a Volcano' by Genesis from the Seconds Out live album was blasting out of the shop speakers.

'Nice choice,' he shouted above the music as he went in.

Jeff was looking at a map spread out on his counter.

'Here, look at this.'

He spun it round so Nick could see. It was an Ordnance Survey map of Stockton-on-Tees.

'The co-ordinates Susan has recorded are here,' he said, pointing to a pencil mark he'd made just to the north of Norton, east of the golf course on open farmland. 'You know whose land that is, don't you?

'How could I know that?' asked Nick.

'Think about it, pillock, all this land is owned by Brian Salmon - they own all this land and further north and west up into Durham.'

'Shit, yeah, that's the Blakeston Estate, isn't it? So Boudica is buried on his land? Christ, as if they aren't rich enough already. They'll clean up if this all turned into a tourist or heritage spot.'

Jeff shook his head. 'Some people just fall arse backwards into money. Mind you, no amount of money will make me like Stevie Salmon and his excuse for a comedy turn.'

Nick looked at the neatly handwritten notes Susan had made.

'Does it say if she dug it alone?' he asked.

'No, but neither does it say who else was on the dig, like all the official ones do. I think she did it on her own. I don't know, but looking at her notes of other digs, I think this was only a small thing, more like an exploratory look, really.'

Nick sat down to read the whole thing. She had such small, neat and precise handwriting.

Reading her notes, one thing immediately became clear - her motivation for the dig was stated very baldly as 'a previous find'. In fact, in comparison to the official dig documents, this was little more than a brief sketch, an outline.

'What do you reckon to this idea?' asked Jeff. 'We get some archaeologists to dig this site properly and see if there's anything else there. If it is Boudica's grave, it will go down as Susan's find and will be a tribute...or memorial to her.'

'Yeah but that's what she didn't want - she could have gone legit with this at the start but she didn't because it proves what Diane was saying all along. Boudica is the Queen of the Tees.'

Jeff scratched his beard. 'Aye, but it doesn't seem right. If she found it, she should be remembered for that. The brooch is public knowledge now. She can't take offence, anyway, can she? It'll be her name that goes down in the history books. '

'But it'd be Diane Edwards who would organise it. It's her turf, isn't it?'

'Aye well, maybe. We'll have to see, won't we? If we've got her nicked for murder by then she won't be doing any work for 30 years or more.'

'I dunno, Jeff. Is she really a killer? It seems more likely to me that it's Martin or someone he knows,' said Nick. 'Carol was pretty sure he was a bit of a twat.'

'Firstly, I note that you've already come round to my point of view that she was murdered and that the suicide verdict is wrong. And for that I'd like to pause and say "I told you so". Secondly, what was Carol like?'

'Wealthy and successful and glamorous. Have you heard of Violet Reddy?'

'Violet Reddy? No. Sounds like someone who would play the fiddle in a folk rock band.'

'She's a very successful historical novelist, but she didn't have any airs and graces. Her Yorkshire roots seem to have kept her feet on the ground.'

'Ah, shame. There's no point in having massive success if you don't go woo-woo-woo and freak out. You owe it to the rest of us nine-to-fivers to live life on the edge of lunacy. I hate sensible celebrities.'

'She's hardly a celebrity. I doubt most people could put a face to her name. I'd heard of Violet Reddy but hadn't a clue she was from around here. She doesn't really do much publicity so she's got the best of it, if you ask me. All the money but you don't have to put up with the public taking pictures of you on their phones all day. The key thing is, in her view, given her experience of him, she thinks Martin could kill.'

Jeff raised his eyebrows and nodded. 'Does she now? Interesting. I'd like to meet our friend Martin and confront him about lying to me about visiting Susan. Are you up for that? His lying is making me feel like he's guilty of something.'

'Okay, where does he live?'

'I don't know but he's a lecturer at Teesside Poly. I still can't call it a university. We could go up there and talk to him tomorrow.'

The phone rang.

'33AndAThird,' said Jeff. 'Yes it's...hello...yes...have you? Really? Err...yes, I'll drive over later today. Aye, cheers.'

He opened his eyes wide at Nick. 'That was Malton coppers. They've found Susan's computer and diary in Leeds.'

Nick nodded, glad that was a Jeff conspiracy theory laid to rest. 'Good, that's good isn't it? You can have a look through them, see if you can find out anything. You can check that diary entry to see if it was forged.'

'I know what you're thinking. But just because that turned out to not be nicked doesn't mean I'm wrong about everything. In fact, it proves the police are sloppy and negligent. They should've known where the evidence was.'

That was true. Nick had to give him that.

'Diane told Julie she reckons the brooch will be back from being analysed tomorrow so it might turn out to be from the 14th century or something, which will shake things up a bit. By the sounds of it Diane is already convinced it's 1st century.'

'Of course she is. She's desperate for it to be first century, especially with The Queen of the Tees just coming out. It'll make her the big star, won't it? She'll be like the Led Zep of first-century archaeology.'

He took the record off the turntable, put it back in the sleeve and selected another record from a pile he was inspecting for scratches, this time opting for a copy of Canned Heat's Cookbook. He held it up to Nick. 'Got this?'

'Yeah, their début record's not there, is it? I've always wanted that.'

Jeff looked through the pile, pulled out a record and held it up to show Nick with a look of genuine surprise on his face. 'Your luck is in, Canned Heat's début and it's a UK copy on Liberty, too.'

He slid it out of its sleeve and inspected the vinyl.

'Bit scuffed but playable on your deck. Should go out for 20 quid.'

'I want it. Here's the money,' said Nick with the familiar, excited flutter in his belly that he always got when he found a record he wanted. He put a crisp 20-pound note on the counter.

Jeff took it, put it in the till and gave him a tenner back. 'Half price for mates.'

'Cheers, man. I love this cover - even though it's pretty straight electric blues it's still been psyched up in 1967 style.'

Jeff had his nose in his reference book. 'It came out in July 1967. Didn't chart. '

'Right, I'm off, I've got work to do. We'll nip up to Teesside and Durham in the morning then, OK?'

'Okay, cool. Are you up for a brain-changer or three tonight in Jack & Danny's?'

'Yup, I'll see you in there but I won't be changing my brain. I'm sober, remember?'

'Oh aye, I forgot you've become a monk, fuck me...not drinking...you'll be surrendering your Northern passport next.'

'Hey, Jeff. Do you think I've changed in the last six months?'

'Changed? What? Changed your clothes?'

'No, my personality.'

He stroked his beard. 'Oh god, you're not on this trip again, are you? No, not really. Is that what you want to hear? Is this something to do with your shrink?'

'Yeah. I'm actually supposed to have changed.'

Jeff put down a copy of the Byrd's Sweetheart of the Rodeo and looked at him. 'Ah well in that case, I was taking the piss; yes, you've changed quite a bit.'

'Fuck off. You're kidding me now.'

He shook his head. 'Nope, straight up. You're much less arsy and you buy me food and drink without me asking. I know that's not much but I really appreciate it. And you look me in the eyes more when you talk to me - you never used to do that. I don't care though like, I mean, if you didn't do any of those things, I was happy enough with you how you were. I thought it was down to the fragrant Julie. Now, can I stop talking about it? It's embarrassing. You'll be wanting me to wear panties and a bra next.'

'Ha. Fuck me. I genuinely didn't know that.'

'See, those neurotic Yanks were onto something with this therapy lark.'

Nick left the store and walked back up Commercial Street and was approaching the station when he saw someone he recognised in front of him. Her spiked red hair was so distinctive - it was Florence Farrell. She was dressed in black leggings and a long, loose, plain, rust-red wool sweater. What the hell was she doing here? He followed her at a distance.

She strode at a quick pace. He followed her down Station Parade and to the junction with York Place. As she passed the entrance to the car park at the front of the Dales Mansion, she crossed the road and walked on The Stray heading south.

Because she stood out from a good distance, it wasn't hard to keep her in view. She got onto the Leeds Road, headed out of town for two miles and walked through Pannal to a village psychedelically called Spacey Houses, eventually stopping outside of a pair of semi-detached old farm cottages, now almost derelict. Filthy grey net curtains hung at the windows and looked like they had done for 50 years. The place was abandoned. She walked down a rutted muddy track towards more derelict buildings from a long-gone farm and went out of view.

He walked down a public footpath past the old farm and along a tall hedge into open countryside. After 250 yards there was a semi-derelict farmhouse with an old picnic table at the front. Florence came out of the old front door and sat down at the table with a white and blue enamel mug of coffee or tea. She was joined by two other women, dressed similarly. Nick recognised both of them from the Boudica Society meeting. A more delicate-looking blonde girl who had been on the front row, and whose name Nick recalled was Sophie, was there as well as an older woman, maybe about 30 years old with close-cropped hair. Even in passing he could see it was obviously a squat. Wood smoke from the chimney filled the air.

Out of sight of the farmhouse he rested on a tree stump in case he'd been seen. After five minutes he walked slowly back up the path towards the road. As he passed the farmhouse, he heard a cracking noise, turned and saw that Florence had an old metal sword and was fighting with the older woman, who had what looked like a thick broom shank.

Florence was swinging the sword from her shoulder but being parried by her opponent. He turned and looked as he neared the road. Florence took a big swing but was blocked and, with a piercing yell, her opponent swung back hard with the pole, knocking the sword out of Florence's hands and sending it clattering to the ground.

It was all a bit odd, to say the least. Okay, students were skint, but living in a broken-down farmhouse in the North Yorkshire countryside was a bit extreme, though Nick could see the attraction, fighting aside. Maybe they wanted to live in old wattle-and-daub huts and this was the next best thing. Maybe it was a modern version of the old hippy 'back to the land' thing, living simply and primitively, getting away from 21st-century bullshit. Fair enough, but sword fighting?

He walked home wondering about Florence. If she was capable of bullying a woman in her 60s, she had to have a really nasty side, one that seeing her fighting with a sword hadn't done much to dispel. Could she be responsible for Susan's death? Did she have some sort of vendetta against her which had led to her murder? It didn't seem that unlikely.

When he reached home, he reread Susan's notes about the dig on the Blakeston estate and kept coming back to a single reference to 'previous finds' as the motivation behind the dig. That had to mean the brooch. Had she found that at an earlier date on or near the site? If so maybe there were other similar finds made there. On the off chance, he went to Stevie Salmon's website, found a contact e-mail address and wrote him a quick message.

'Stevie, good to see you at the awards do - I always really needed a pen stuck into a lump of marble. Wondering if you can help me? Julie - you met her the other night - is doing some research into the Roman history of Teesside and was wondering if you'd ever had anything that old dug up on your Teesside land? Any old pots, metal or Roman porno mags? Cheers, Nick Guymer.'

That evening he went into Jack & Danny's and bought a small bottle of fizzy water and a pint of Stella. Jeff looked up from his copy of Classic Rock with contempt as Nick poured the water into a glass. 'Men everywhere are ever so slightly neutered by you drinking that;

you know that, don't you? You are significantly reducing the overall level of masculinity of the nation.'

Nick ignored him. 'Did you pick up the computer and diary?'

Jeff put the magazine down and nodded.

'Yup. And it's all very interesting. I booted it up and looked at her Outlook. There's not much else on the computer really, just some academic stuff, papers prepared for lectures and that. She's incredibly well-organised. Everything is in well-named folders. She had one called "Purchases", so I looked in there and there's an e-mail from that company in Singapore that sold the cyanide.'

'Christ...so she did buy it, then?'

'Maybe. The cops obviously thought that was enough proof but they didn't look close enough. First up, it was ordered in mid September and was supposed to take four days to arrive. But there were actually two e-mails. One confirmed the order and money paid and that's what they looked at judging by the date and time it was last opened. But there was a second e-mail which was sent out when the pills were dispatched the next day. It was in her "Deleted" folder so she probably never even noticed it. It looks like every drug spam e-mail you ever get, so she probably just deleted it without looking. It hadn't even been opened. So I looked at it. That receipt confirmed the delivery address and the delivery address on the receipt was not to Middlecave Road in Malton, it was to a PO box in...you'll never guess where...'

'Where?'

Jeff sat back and folded his arms across his checked shirt.

'Here. In Harrogate. I can tell the cops never opened it so they don't even know this. Proof of how slapdash they were.'

'What? Harrogate? This gets weirder and weirder.'

'I know it was paid for on her card - the police have got proof it was - but was the order actually placed by her? So then I thought, if she's bought a PO box in Harrogate for some reason, she'll have a record of it. But she didn't. Nothing by e-mail, anyway.'

'Maybe she did it the old analogue way in a post office. '

'I think someone did, yes, but she did everything else online. She shopped online, bought groceries, paid tax, did everything online. If she was going to buy a PO box, she'd have almost certainly done it on the Royal Mail website, even if it was just to download the forms to print out, complete and take in, but she didn't even do that. There are no downloads and the Royal Mail site isn't even in her browsing history.'

'So what are you saying?'

'I think someone else used her computer and card to buy the pills, had them delivered to a PO box they had set up under her name using forms from the post office and then used them that morning to poison her tea. They killed her but tried to make it look like suicide.'

Nick sat back and blew out air. He must have looked doubtful.

'Alright, alright, I know you don't believe me, but ask yourself this...' he raised his index finger in the air, '...why would she do that? Why would she have a PO box here? There's no reason at all.'

Nick wrestled with it in his mind.

'I don't know, Jeff. The thing is, you may be right, I know that, but maybe there is a reason, a mad reason, but a reason nonetheless why she did. Just because we can't think of one doesn't mean one doesn't exist. It's all too easy to start fitting every bit of information into your theory. It's like diagnosing yourself on the internet - soon enough you find your simple headache has turned into every disease from a dose of Oldfield's Bells to a severe case of Nugents Stranglehold.'

'Rock diseases. I like it.'

'But I'll tell you something weird that I saw this afternoon just after I left you.'

He was about to explain what he'd seen out in Spacey Houses when a thin lad with long hair came in, nodded at Jeff and came over.

'Alright there,' he said.

'Now then, Luke, I suppose as your new boss I should buy you a pint...here, take it out of that.' He tossed a 20 at him.

'Cheers Jeff,' Luke said and went to the bar.

'He's the new help; I'm just starting him this week.'

Luke sat down opposite Nick with a pint of lager. He had a pale face detailed with blemishes ranging in colour from pale pink to angry red and capped with an occasional ruby of dried blood. He was the very definition of scruffy and exactly the sort of lad you might find in any second-hand record store anywhere in the country, a new generation inheriting the great unselfconsciously unkempt traditions of the vinyl-hunter. It was oddly reassuring.

'Now see this one...this one is trouble,' said Jeff, pointing at Nick. 'When he comes into the shop you've got to call the police. He's insane.'

'He don't look that insane,' said the lad in a broad Yorkshire accent.

'I'll tell you how mad he is, he likes jazz fusion! Al Di Meola and all that widdly nonsense.'

'To be fair, that is pretty bloody mad stuff,' said the lad, who had long straight hair over his shoulders, the beginnings of a beard and a cannabis leaf earring.

'Don't listen to him. I bet he hasn't showed you his easy listening records, has he?' said Nick.

'No.'

'Oh aye, he likes all that - the Swingle Singers, Herb Alpert, all of that!'

'Bollocks,' said Jeff. 'This is Nick, by the way.'

Nick held out his hand. 'Alright, mate,' he said and shook his long spidery fingers. 'What bands are you into?'

'Rock mostly. Foo Fighters, Chili Peppers, that sort of stuff. What about you?'

'I love blues rock, late 60s west coast, prog, jazz-rock, folk rock, too...some soul...basically anything recorded before 1976.'

'He's got a massive collection, mostly vinyl,' said Jeff. 'I thought Luke would be useful when we get modern rock stuff in - I know sod all about most of it.'

'I like the Chili Peppers, Frusciante is a hell of a guitarist,' said Nick.

Luke nodded enthusiastically. 'It's great to work in an old-school vinyl record shop, there's not many around.'

'See, I like to employ discerning staff with taste,' said Jeff.

'It's a bit intimidating trying to learn it all, though. So many bands and that...I've got my head in Record Collector most of the time. Though I don't reckon I'll ever know as much as him.'

Jeff patted Luke on the head like he was a dog.

'Nobody knows more about records than Jeff. I know a lot, but he knows everything,' said Luke.

'I'm a bit crap on anything recorded after 1998 though, plus I know sod all about early jazz. After you've spent a week looking at the condition of Beatles singles and taking Jim Reeves records to the tip, we'll see if you're so enthusiastic, Luke. Anyway, what were you saying about seeing something weird, Nick?'

'I saw that Florence Farrell lass just after I left your shop earlier and I followed her out to the edge of town. I think she's living in a squat out there, out in the country, old-school hippy style.'

'Nice, I like that. Better than becoming a thrusting corporate type,' said Jeff, 'there's enough of them in world already.'

'Is she, like, really tall and got spiky red hair?' said Luke.

'Aye that's right,' said Nick. 'Do you know her?'

'God aye, I know her. She went to my school and then up to Durham Uni.'

'Is she local then, Lukey?' asked Jeff.

'Yeah, her mam and dad are both lecturers at Leeds University. She used to live up Cold Bath Road way. I fancied her. I did English with her in sixth form. She's got massive tits.' He grinned and held his hands away from his chest.

'Good observation skills, Lukey. I like the sound of her a lot,' said Jeff enthusiastically.

'What's she like? Huge breasts aside?' asked Nick.

'Brainy. She got straight As without even trying that 'ard. She were odd though - played rugby and liked folk music...'

'...bloody hell, that's a terrible combo, there's no call for that,' said Jeff disparagingly.

'Bloody sexy, though,' said Luke. 'She only went out with brainy older lads, crusties mostly, the sort of lads who liked the Levellers and that. Dope smokers, most of them.'

Jeff patted him on the back. 'That's quality work Lukey - identifying people's characters by the bands they like saves us all so many words. I'm glad I took you on, now.'

Luke laughed.

'So she's what, 19 years old?' asked Nick.

'Twenty. She's the same age as me. Must be in her second year at Durham now.'

'She actually looks older than that,' said Nick.

'Aye she does, like. How do you know her, then?' said Luke.

'It's a long story. I don't really know her. She's in this Boudica Society thing at Durham which me and my girlfriend went to see. They do historical re-enactments and stuff. They're all mad about Boudica, she's a sort of role model for them.'

'Oh aye, I think her mam and dad were into all that an' all. Fighting old battles in fields dressed like knights. They teach history, so it's probably a family thing.'

'Well, I reckon they're squatting out there. They had fires going. Hey, is it legal to fight with an actual metal sword? It doesn't sound legal,' said Nick

'It's only legal if you live in Hardwick or do it with consenting adults in an officially approved boozer,' said Jeff. 'Why do you ask?'

'That's what she was doing with another lass. She had a big sword. Very distinctive-looking kid; tall, broad, long legs, red hair, she was striding through the streets like she was some kind of ancient tribal leader.'

'She's always been like that. Always had weird hair and tats,' said Luke. 'Since she was about 14 or 15 anyway.'

Jeff belched. 'That's all bit bloody fanciful, that, isn't it? Tribal leader? You're only saying that because you know she's in that society thing. If you didn't know that it'd just seem like she was some sort of hippy, back-to-the-earth, Mother Nature type, the sort of lass who used to go and watch Hawkwind at a free festival in the 70s and get her tits out, Stacia-style. That was always where you got the pagans and white witches and lasses who painted their entire body with woad to worship the god Pan or something. Then they'd go home and resume their life in the civil service. Weekend hippies we used to call 'em, if you remember.'

He had a point. Maybe he was just letting his imagination run away with him. Then again, maybe not.

Jeff rummaged in his bag and brought out a hardbacked navy blue book.

'This is Susan's diary. I've bookmarked the last entry...see what you make of it.'

He handed over the book. The last entry was written in a shaky-looking hand. Letters were badly formed and occasionally fell off the lines.

'I am sodding well tired and sick of life. I have lived a lie for my whole life and I can't go on living a lie any more. Everything is wrong. Everyone is against me. Nothing is right. I just can't face my decline. Queen Boudica shows us the way. To die is not to end, it is to start again. That must be better than more of...this.' The last word was written with such pressure that the paper was slightly torn by the pen.

Nick read it and then flicked back to previous entries. That final entry was in a different style of writing, much more untidy, much sloppier and far scruffier. Previous entries were usually neat and precise. But that being said, there were similarities in how letters were shaped and formed.

Jeff pointed at the diary. 'That last entry...that was written by someone else...someone other than Susan wrote the so-called suicide note. You can't tell me that was written by the same person and like I said before, it's not her sort of words.'

Nick flicked back and forth between the entries. Most striking was the lack of coherence in the last entry. It looked as though it had been difficult to write, as though done in little bursts. The last word hadn't just been written with a heavy pressure, it has been traced over and over, wearing out the paper with the blue ink.

'I'm totally convinced that someone is trying to make this look like suicide,' said Jeff. 'It's different handwriting.'

Nick wasn't so sure. It looked more like a disturbed version of the same style.

'We should go and see Martin James,' he said. 'I know you think this is all about Diane, but we know he lied about not being on Middlecave Road that day. I'd like him to know that we know he lied and find out why he didn't tell you the truth.'

'Maybe he was in league with Diane. Maybe they worked together to kill her. Suits them both, doesn't it?'

'Maybe, or maybe he did it all on his own. I think if it's anyone, it's him.'

Nick got up to get a round of drinks, deep in thought. That last entry might have been done in a different hand - that wasn't the most outrageous theory Jeff had ever had - but given that the balance of Susan's mind must have been severely disturbed, perhaps that explained the unusual handwriting. If he'd had to write about his own feelings during his last depression it would have been really difficult both physically and emotionally. If he'd been able to do it at all, his writing would not have looked the same as usual. It would definitely have been more chaotic, messy and disrupted, especially if done when he was feeling bitter and angry.

The last entry was so final. All the subsequent pages were blank. The life she could have lived was unwritten. Blank didn't mean unrecorded, blank meant dead. He ran his fingers over the indentations that she'd left by pressing so hard on the last entry page, feeling really sorry for her.

'So is Julie still coming down next week?' said Jeff.

'Yeah. I was just talking to her on the phone before.'

'Look at you. Soppy twat.'

'What?'

'You've gone all gooey-eyed just at the mention of her name! How old are you, again?'

'Yer bollocks, I have.'

'I'm not knocking it man, not really, like.' He winked at Luke. 'Here's an idea, why don't you two get married?'

'Married?!'

'Married.'

'Why would we do that?'

'Because it's exactly what you would never have done before. It's the opposite of what you both used to want, so that's why you do it. To prove it's 100 per cent different this time.'

He turned to Luke. 'He used to live with this lass Julie, a right bloody stunner she is, bit old for a lad like you, mind; they broke up a year and a half ago and now they're trying to get back together. He's a bit bloody love-struck all over again.'

'Sounds like bit of a soap opera,' said Luke.

'That's right, it bloody is. No bodies under the patio, though...not yet, anyway,' said Jeff. 'See, if you get married it means the rest of us will get to have massive piss-up at your wedding. I can play records and then cop off with a bridesmaid or drunken auntie. It's my only chance of sex and it's frankly very selfish of you to deny me that opportunity. Go on, make her Mrs Guymer.'

Nick laughed. 'Julie would never become a Guymer. She's old-school feminist about such things and rightly so. It's all bollocks, that.'

He finished his water and got up to go.

'Right, don't get too wasted, I'll be round to pick you up around half-past eight. After we've seen Diane, we'll go over to Teesside Uni to see Martin James as well, right?'

'I'm with you, Batman.'

Nick got home at just after 11pm. It was very unusual not be drunk after a night out. He took a shower, made himself something to eat and sat down to check his e-mails before bed. In amongst the spam was an almost totally unpunctuated email from Stevie Salmon.

'Now then Nick I asked dad for you he says they've ploughed up loads of stuff over the years especially on the Blakeston he's still got most of it if your Julie wants to have a look shes a cracker by the way mate. Cheers BigFish'

He stood naked in front of his bathroom mirror and looked at himself. Sober. Bloody sober.

CHAPTER 9

They pulled into the Department of Archaeology car park on a bright, sunny, windy morning.

'I'm excited to know what the history of that thing is,' said Nick as they walked in.

'I don't mind as long as I don't have to say I found it in my potatoes again,' said Jeff, his long hair blowing sideways in the wind. 'And remember, we're talking to a killer.'

They went up a flight of stairs to the first floor where Diane's office was situated. Nick peered through the glass panel in the door.

'No-one is home. We'll just park ourselves here, eh?'

They sat on a couple of chairs in the corridor. A door slammed and Julie came running in.

She broke into a big smile as she saw him.

'Sorry I'm late,' she said. He got up and gave her a hug.

'Hello, gorgeous,' she whispered in his ear. 'Hiya, Jeff.'

Jeff saluted. 'Now then, Julie. I dig the long multi-coloured scarf. Very Tom Baker-style Doctor Who.'

She waved it around. 'Very student, isn't it? I knitted it myself from old bits of wool I got off Stockton market. I can only do plain stitch and can't shape anything so this is the full extent of my craft talents.'

As she spoke, Diane came in wearing her long, dark-green velvet coat with the gold lining.

'Ah, there you are!' She was red-faced and windswept. 'It's good news, good news indeed,' she said unlocking her office door. She smiled and nodded at Julie. 'Ah ha...long scarf...very colourful...yes, indeed.'

She flung a file of papers down onto her desk and pulled open the blinds to let in bright sunshine, took off her coat and then sank onto her swivel chair, her greying brown hair blown all over the place. She looked at each of them individually and clapped her hands together. She was hyper, her eyes flitting between each of them in turn.

There was a look in her eye that Nick recognised from his mother's mental illness, a manic distance to her expression as though she was simultaneously intensely in the now but also gone from the world. It was very disturbing.

'Righty ho and off we go,' she said, taking out the three pieces of the brooch, laying them on the desk and launching into a speech which fell out of her mouth with barely a pause.

'I can confirm that this is almost certainly first-century gold and it's not a stolen museum piece. This latticework into which the letter B has been woven is very similar to one described by the Roman historian Cassius in his description of Boudica, in which he also tells us she wore a large gold torc, which is a sort of necklace - how lovely it would be to find that. Without the burial context we can't know who this was made for and whether it was worn by a follower of Boudica, someone honouring her, someone remembering her, someone influenced by her or indeed, most tantalising of all, Queen Boudica herself. We simply cannot know and as much as we would like to speculate, it will remain exactly that. Context is almost everything in archaeology.'

She spoke quickly and then looked at them again.

'That's all pretty much what we thought,' said Nick. He turned to his left where Jeff was sitting, raised an eyebrow at him and nodded.

'Jeff's been doing a bit of investigation of his own, Diane. Haven't you, Jeff?'

Jeff opened up a shoulder bag and took out a copy of Atomic Rooster's début album. 'It's nothing to do with this, obviously. I take it you're not an Atomic Rooster fan.'

Diane laughed - something she didn't seem to do often. 'Ah, yes, I remember them - "The Devil's Answer"!' she suddenly said. 'I remember that from my student days. It was a hit record, I think. Splendid keyboard music, I always rather liked...what was their name now...they were German I think...'

Jeff pointed at her. 'Tangerine Dream?'

'Yes! Yes that was their name. Marvellous, floaty music, very popular with the marijuana smokers as I recall, not that I was one myself...I never inhaled Mr President! Well, only once or twice, perhaps...oh dear...a long time ago...too long...' she seemed overcome by a moment of sadness just as they were laughing politely.

'Well this is possibly more interesting even than Tangerine Dream and Atomic Rooster combined,' said Jeff, producing the file that was marked 'Boudica Dig July 22 1996'. 'I found this in a plain sealed envelope in Susan's office amongst her other academic papers.'

He passed it to her. Diane put on her glasses and as soon as she opened the envelope, her mouth dropped open.

'Oh my good god!' she exclaimed, her eyes immediately filling with tears again, just had she had when they'd first showed her the brooch. Her pale, blue-veined hands quivered as she held the paper. The shock of seeing this seemed to spread like an earthquake through her body. Her breath became staccato and shaky.

'Oh you silly, silly girl' said Diane quietly, almost under her breath. 'You silly thing...why...why?'

She looked through the papers, tears now rolling down her cheeks. Julie got up, squatted alongside Diane's chair and put her arm around her. 'Is it hard to believe after all these years?'

She nodded her head silently.

'It doesn't say she found the brooch there, though...not as far as I can tell...I don't know where that came from...though she says there were other things still in the ground and there are photos of them, too,' said Jeff.

Diane looked at him, her eyes raking him from top to bottom as though she was trying to compute the information.

'So...so... let me get this right...err...hmm...the brooch was actually hers? Was Susan's? And then she gave it to you? Is that what you're telling me now? You said you didn't know how it came into your possession.'

'We found out that she hid it in my potatoes, yes. We've got her on CCTV doing it,' said Jeff.

'My good god...what on earth...that wasn't...hell fire...no,' she muttered words under her breath as though conducting an argument with herself or someone else. Her eyes radiated a mixture of great worry and extreme upset. 'Silly girl,' she said again, quietly. It really did look like she was going to have some sort of breakdown. How did you help someone who was so emotionally disturbed? Her lips moved as she mouthed silent words to herself or to Susan. Then she suddenly shouted, 'We must dig!'

She looked out of her window and then searched for a tissue. Julie gave her one from her own bag. She dabbed at her cheeks. 'We must dig for Boudica and for my Susan!'

Now she seemed in a daze, her hands shaking a little. Should they get her a doctor?

'Do all those notes make sense to you?' said Jeff. 'I could read the map but the rest of it was a bit difficult for the layperson. There are drawings of the trench or hole...'

'It's a sort of test pit...of course it is...a test pit...it's what we do...it's not detailed but it will be enough to get us started.'

She looked through the papers again, tracing the words with her index finger. 'She found something else...more jewellery, this photo looks like a fragment of...of...good god, fragments of a torc...that could be Boudica's torc! That's what I just mentioned! Good god. By Christ...it could be...it looks...look, there's a curve...my word...my my my...'

She spoke to herself again, lost in a reverie, running her fingers through her tangled hair, her hands shaking badly now while they fiddled with the tightly tangled strands.

'Thank you for this. Thank you...everything I have worked towards...everything that is in this book.' She picked up the copy of The Queen of the Tees that lay on her desk. 'This is exactly where one of my options for Boudica's burial was. It's a yew copse, the only remaining sign that it was ever a place of burial and worship, but I have long believed it was a holy place for the Brigante tribe despite what Susan said.'

'Why were you so sure she'd done this unofficial dig?' asked Julie.

'Well...there had always been rumours in the department. Someone claims to have seen her working there but she always denied it. Martin, her ex, said she had too. Florence Farrell said Susan had shown her a sketch when Flo was about 12 or 13, a very impressionable age, and said she thought it was Boudica's personal symbol. She wanted to inspire her, make her interested in archaeology...now I realise it was probably a sketch of this brooch.'

'But, like I say, it doesn't mention the brooch in there,' said Jeff.

She rifled through the papers again.

'Hmm, no...no it doesn't. Strange.'

She put her hand over her mouth once more and tears came again. This time she couldn't even support her weight and she sank into her chair, her face wet, her whole body shuddering with sobs. She had lost it totally. Nick made a 'what shall we do?' face at Julie.

She reached forward again, took Diane's hand to comfort her and gestured to Nick and Jeff to leave the office and give them some space.

Nick let out a gasp of air as he closed the office door.

'Pffff...that was heavy stuff, eh?'

'Aye, she wasn't faking that,' said Jeff. 'Interesting. My question is this...' up went his index finger, '...was she crying because Susan wouldn't give her the brooch for all those years or because she actually killed her because she wouldn't give it to her? If Susan was still alive and in possession of the brooch, none of this comes out, remember. Diane remains in her shadow. Her tears don't mean she didn't kill her - it might have sent her mad but...y'know...she could have done it...it's just as we said, she's the one who benefits most from it.'

'Jeff, man, I'm sure she's not a killer. She just isn't. Look at her in there.'

'Don't be fooled by the tears. I think she is. I think she's weeping because she knows she killed her and she's remorseful or it's sent her mad. She wanted to share this whole Boudica thing with her and she can't because she put that cyanide into her tea. She did it. I'm sure of it. Just put the drug in the tea and stood well back. It's not like having to cut someone's throat.'

'Aye well, she looks certifiably bonkers to me. I've seen people have breakdowns, my mam for one, and that is a stone-cold certifiable, woo-woo window-licking breakdown right there.'

'Well, we have to find out. A lot of evidence points to her. We know she was there - the appointments diary tells us that.'

'Julie says that she says she wasn't at the house that morning. How do we prove she's lying? We don't have any hard evidence. That diary entry with the D doesn't actually prove anything."

Jeff rubbed his face with his hands and looked out of the faculty window building. Nick continued in hush tones so he wouldn't be overheard.

'The police didn't conclude it was suicide for no reason, Jeff. I know we thought they might have been sloppy or worse, but maybe they were right and it was suicide. You've got to entertain that as a possibility, that's all I'm saying. Anyway, we'll see what Martin James has got to say later.'

But Jeff had stopped listening and was looking outside. 'Come here, is this your mad swordswoman, by any chance?'

Nick went to the window and followed his gaze. Walking along the road towards the department building was indeed Florence Farrell.

'Aye, that's her. She's got the same clothes on as she wore yesterday.'

'Has she? Oooh lovely. I like an unkempt, dirty woman.'

'She's distinctive, isn't she?'

'She's bloody fantastic. I love that hair. She looks wild and musky. Oh man. What a woman.'

'Musky!?'

'Aye, musky, like a wild animal. She's coming in here; stand by your beds.'

The door to the first floor was flung open and crashed against the rubber door jam. She strode in, didn't even take a side glance, didn't even notice them. Just as she reached Diane's office door, it opened and Julie came out, walking straight into Florence.

'Ooh, I'm sorry,' said Julie, side-stepping her.

She said nothing and pushed past Julie, slamming the door shut behind her.

'What a rude girl,' said Julie, coming over to Nick, pushing her hair behind her ears.

'Didn't you see who it was?' asked Nick.

Julie looked around. 'No, who was it?'

'Florence Farrell.'

'Oh, yeah, of course, I didn't really look at her. Big Flo eh, she smelled a bit odd,' said Julie.

'Musky by any chance?' asked Jeff.

'Musky? No, it was patchouli I think, though I suppose that is a bit musky. Diane's calmed down a little. I think she should see a doctor but she won't listen to me and I can't make her, can I?'

As she spoke, there were raised voices from Diane's office.

'Sounds like red Flo is a bit cross,' said Jeff.

There was a weird, warbling banshee fox yelp emanating from the office.

'I wonder if she makes that noise when she has an orgasm?' wondered Jeff.

Julie slapped him on his arm. 'Stop thinking about strange young girls having orgasms.'

'I was just wondering the same thing, actually,' said Nick with a laugh.

She punched him on the arm too.

The office door was flung open, Florence emerged and then turned, looking back into the office. 'The tribes are celebrating our success. When I killed her, I knew her death meant victory was ours!' she said triumphantly and slammed the office door behind her.

The three of them stood and looked at each other with eyes wide.

She stormed out without looking at them, wrapped up in her emotions, her pale face flushed pink, her red hair glowing, crashing the door again.

'Did you hear that?' Did you?' asked Jeff, his voice at a high pitch.

'Steady on,' said Nick, 'that wasn't anything...'

'...the fuck it wasn't!' said Jeff and stormed towards the office and yanked open the door with Nick and Julie in pursuit.

'What did she mean?' Jeff boomed. 'When I killed her? When I killed her? She killed Susan for you, didn't she? Didn't she?!' He was yelling at the top of his voice.

Nick entered the office behind him. Diane was puce faced, her eyes red and swollen and shocked by the sudden intrusion. Jeff was an intimidating presence at the best of times, but when angry he was downright scary.

'What? What? I don't know you're talking about...what?' She began shaking again.

Jeff pointed in the direction Florence had gone.

'She killed Susan didn't she? Tell me! She just confessed it.'

Diane was flustered and confused. 'But, but...no...Jeff...no...she's in the Brigantes, they re-enact battles. She was talking about the last one they did. It's all a game they play. It's a hobby. A club. She wasn't...no...no...Julie, you understand, please...please...Florence hasn't killed anyone. It's all mock battle...'

Julie stood behind her. 'It did sound a bit weird, Diane. Jeff thinks Susan was murdered, he doesn't think it was suicide, and then she storms out saying she's killed her. I'm sorry. I know it's upsetting.'

She put her arm around Diane's shoulders to try and calm her but it was no good, she was sobbing and shaking and then with a howl of furious indignation she flew into a rage. Screaming loudly, spittle flying out of her mouth, she ran at Jeff and began to beat him with her small tight fists.

'You stupid overgrown child! Get out! Don't you dare come here with such heinous accusations. What are you saying, man? That I killed Susan or Florence did? Or someone else? You are mad! You fool! Out! Get out! I will not stand for such slander, such a gross insult to Susan and to her memory, you are a bloody fool. A bloody fool! Get out now before you make an even bigger fool of yourself!'

She began pushing him, beating him on the chest and slapping him with the flat of her hand. As he was a foot taller than her and probably 12 stone heavier, it was like watching a child trying to push a large car. Jeff looked down at her with bemusement and didn't move. In response to his indifference she pulled her arm back and whacked him across the face with the full palm of her right hand. It was a good hit and it rocked him back on his heels. He retreated, holding up his hands.

'All of you! Out now!'

It was a spectacular freak out. It was one thing to be annoyed or insulted by Jeff's accusation but this was a full-scale meltdown.

They left the office to the sound of the door being slammed shut.

'If that isn't a guilty reaction, I don't know what is,' said Jeff as they walked towards the door.

'Oh, bloody well shut up, Jeff!' said Julie. 'You don't know what you're talking about. Just shut it. You've already dropped a massive bollock today, don't say anything else!'

Nick patted him on the back to endorse her comments. It was time to cool off and calm down. They got outside and into the bright, cold air. Julie looked at her watch.

'I'm worried about the state she's in. I'll check on her later but I've got to go to lectures now and then I've got badminton. I'll see you later,' she said and kissed Nick on the cheek, crossed over the road and headed north towards the cathedral to the history department.

'Come on, son, we'll go to Middlesbrough and I'll buy you a lager as long as you don't upset any more crazy women,' said Nick.

'At last, someone is talking sense.'

Forty minutes later they parked off Linthorpe Road and walked to Teesside University.

'Can you tell me where Martin James's office is, he's a history professor?' said Nick to a man who looked old enough to be a lecturer.

'Straight up to the top floor,' he said.

Nick thanked him and they went up the stairs.

'Now don't go losing your rag again, right?'

'Okay. I'll play nice and I'll smile a lot.'

Each office had its occupier's name in a metal slot. The last one said Martin James. Through a small glass strip, they could see he was studying some papers. Nick knocked.

'Come in.'

'Hello, Martin,' said Nick.

'Hello, again,' said Jeff, standing beside Nick and doing a big slow wave with his right hand.

Martin was surprised to see them, that much was obvious.

'Remind me who you are again,' he said.

'Nick Guymer. You remember Jeff Evans, Susan Rutherford's nephew?

'Oh, right...what can I do for you two?' he asked, taking off some expensive-looking silver-framed glasses.

'Well the thing is Martin, we're still err...well...looking into Susan's death...' said Nick.

'Just trying to sort a few things out, like,' said Jeff, casually.

'Oh, OK, is there a problem?' asked Martin.

'Yeah, it's this, on the phone you told Jeff that you had been visiting an old friend on the morning Susan died, didn't you?'

'Yes, that's right - Harry Thomas across the road.'

His grey eyes flicked between them.

'Hmmm, well we know that's not true Martin. We spoke to him and he says he saw you coming out of Susan's house, he waved you over and you had a brief chat,' said Nick.

'Yeah, so we just wanted to know why you lied about that,' said Jeff, smiling wider than he would normally do under any circumstances. It made him look oddly intimidating.

A look of apprehension spread across Martin James's face. 'Well...err...he must be mistaken.'

'He wasn't mistaken. He was quite clear,' said Nick, taking a seat away from the wall and sitting down. Jeff did likewise.

'What were you doing at Susan's and when did you arrive that morning?'

He drummed his fingers on the desk and then looked out of the window.

'I really don't see why I should say anything to you. You're not the police. It's nothing to do with you what I was or wasn't doing,' he said rather pompously.

'That's true, Martin...but they will be talking to you if you don't tell us,' said Jeff, pulling his big, wide smile again and looking far more insane than encouraging.

Martin James shook his head and stood up. 'No no no...I won't tolerate this. You two, come on...out!' He said it like they were schoolboys and gestured with his hand for them to leave.

Nick looked at Jeff.

'Is he talking to us, Jeff?'

'Nah, can't be us, Nick. We're grown ups. You wouldn't address two adults like that. Especially not two blokes as big as us.'

He stood up and took a step towards his victim, towering over him by six or seven inches.

'Now you sit down like a good little boy Martin, and answer our questions.'

'You don't scare me.'

'Good. I'm not trying to scare you. Not yet, anyway,' said Jeff.

'Get out my office! I shall call security.'

Nick was still seated. 'We're not going anywhere; sit down Martin. We just want you to answer our questions. If you don't, we'll just get a man in a blue uniform to do it instead. Now, tell us why you were at Susan's that morning.'

He sat down, adjusted his glasses, placed his hands on his lap and turned to face Nick.

'Alright, if you must know I was there to collect some academic papers. When your friend here told me that Susan had died, obviously I didn't want to mention it as it might have seemed...well, odd. But I'd just called round to pick up some papers, that's all. There's nothing more to it than that.'

'You didn't have any papers when I saw you getting in the car,' said Nick.

'No. Susan seemed to be in a hurry.'

'A hurry?'

'Yes she said, "What are you doing here? I've no time for all that now. Go away". I think those were her words.'

'What time was this?' asked Nick.

'About 10.15 or so, I think.'

'Where do you live, Martin?' asked Jeff.

'Stokesley. You know where that is?'

'Very well, yeah. So you'd driven down to Malton from Stokesley across the North York Moors early on a dark autumn morning just on the off chance that Susan would let you in to look for some academic papers?' asked Nick.

'No. No I was already in the area. I'd stayed with a friend.'

'A girlfriend?' said Nick.

'It's none of your business.'

'We heard you're a bit of a ladies' man. A bit of a pork swordsman, like,' said Jeff, nodding and smiling oddly again.

Martin shook his head and laughed bitterly.

'Alright gentleman, that's enough fun and games, now I have work to do.'

'No I don't think we're done yet, are we, Jeff?'

'Oh no, Prof. We're not going yet.'

'Y'see we know about Carol Charles, too. We know all about that.'

'Tut tut, Marty...you were a bad boy,' said Jeff, shaking his head.

'Carol Charles? When did you see her?' he said, now clearly annoyed.

'Recently.'

'Where?'

'I'm not going to tell you that. Just like Susan wouldn't tell you. It's why the last call she made before she died was to Carol to warn her that you were trying to find her again. Y'see, Susan was loyal to her friends and stuck by them even when they'd made mistakes.'

'And that means you've just lied to us again when you said that you wanted to pick up some academic papers. Bollocks...you were there to get Susan to tell you where Carol was.'

'Fuck you!' shouted Martin James and got up to leave the office, knocking over his chair on the way.

Jeff stood up, reached out and grabbed him by the arm, holding him back like a fly trapped on sticky paper. But with more strength than seemed possible, Martin swung around with a clenched fist and connected with Jeff's chin, knocking his head backwards. He did it again, harder this time, but Jeff didn't release his grip on his arm. Instead he pushed him so hard that he stumbled back against the wall. Then he pinned him back with his left hand around his neck and, with his right shaped to punch him in the face. Martin groaned and shouted, 'No, please!'

Jeff turned to Nick.

'Can I hit him? Just one good hard one? He's hit me. It's only fair.'

'No. Best not. He looks like he'll shit himself if you do. We don't want him to make a mess of this nice clean floor or of your best Doc Martens.'

'Aw, go on.'

'What do you think, Martin? Should I let him hit you?' asked Nick, rather enjoying himself.

Martin James was gasping for air under the pressure of Jeff's grip around his neck.

'Tell him...tell him to stop. I'll tell you. I'll tell you anything you want to know...' Nick gestured to Jeff to loosen his grip on the history professor.

'Alright...yes...I admit it...I was at Susan's to get Carol's address or phone number.'

He rubbed his neck. 'I'd heard that she might have had my child and I just wanted to see them. That's not so weird, is it?'

'Oddly enough, slapping women around and making threats tends to alienate them. I mean, I've just threatened you with violence and bruised your neck and you've not fallen in love with me yet, have you? Carol probably feels the same way,' said Jeff.

Nick laughed. 'That was very good, man, the way you connected those two things together.'

'I know, I was pleased with it, too. I like this bullying middle-class wimpy blokes gig. I missed my vocation, I reckon.'

Martin James didn't appreciate their humour.

'Okay, so I don't live up to your moral standards, but so what? I didn't kill Susan if that's what all this is about. She was as alive as you or me when I left that morning. I had no idea what she was about to do. But if I'd said I was there, with my history, I thought it might look bad. I didn't think it through. That's why I lied to you. Nothing more than that. I had nothing to gain from killing Susan and anyway, the police and the coroner said it was suicide, not murder...so that's good enough, isn't it? You've got to believe me.'

They looked at him. Red faced, his eyes flicked nervously between them. He was scared and he didn't seem to be lying now.

'With your history?'

'Eh?'

'You said, "with my history". What did you mean by that?' asked Nick.

He ran his hands through his cropped grey hair.

'I was...err...I was arrested on assault charges a couple of times. Lot of fuss about nothing.'

'And I bet it was assaulting women too, wasn't it?' said Jeff.

He nodded while looking down at his desk.

'What the fuck is wrong with you?' asked Jeff.

'Piss off. I won't be judged by you...look at you...look at the size of you...you're a bloody disgrace.'

'The only person I abuse is myself. I don't think that's a claim you could make is it, son?' said Jeff.

'Okay Martin, we're going. We know where to find you if we have any other questions.'

'Aye, remember that,' added Jeff, pointing a thick finger at him as he got up.

They walked away from Teesside University feeling rather pleased with themselves.

'There's a career for us in loan sharking, I reckon. You play the nice guy and I'll do the menacing and actual bodily harm,' said Jeff, rubbing his bruised chin. 'He had a decent right hook on him, though.'

'Aye, I think we got the truth out of him eventually, though, don't you?'

'Aye, definitely. I think he was just there on the off chance...I still think it's Diane who's our killer. '

Later that afternoon, Nick dropped Jeff off at his shop and went home to have something to eat. Over a plate of pork ribs he studied his notes again. The potassium cyanide capsules had been sent to a Harrogate PO box. He couldn't get past that. If he could find out who collected them, it would give a pretty good indication who killed her, wouldn't it? If it was Susan, he'd know for sure it was suicide. He went to the Royal Mail website and checked the Ts & Cs for a PO box. As she lived outside the area, she'd have to collect the mail rather than have it sent on.

He sat and thought, doodling on a piece of paper, then called Jeff.

'Jeff, what's the name of your postman?'

'Geoff Lee? I call him Geddy, obviously. Why?'

'Geddy. That's it...he's a mate of yours, isn't he?'

'Yeah. Well, he's not a proper mate but he comes in here and buys records. He's a big UFO fan. Loves Schenker. Not Rush though, sadly.'

Nick outlined his thoughts about the PO box. 'If we could find out who collected the capsules, it would prove to you once and for all if she was murdered or not.'

'I like your thinking. But Ged can't do that. He's just a humble foot soldier tasked with sticking stuff through letterboxes and stealing anything that looks interesting.'

'Yeah, but he works out of the main sorting office, doesn't he? He must do because he's the postie for both of us and we live in the centre of town. And that's where Susan's PO box number would have been held because the postcode on the address is HG1. It says here on the Royal Mail website that to collect your mail you have to have a Royal Mail identity card. You show that and they hand over your mail.'

'So we get the CCTV film of them doing that and we've got our killer?

'That's what I thought at first, but we don't actually need to do that. We just need to find out who applied and paid for the PO box. More likely than not it was created just for this delivery. I mean, Susan had no other need for a PO box number, did she?'

'I don't think so. No. Certainly not one in Harrogate.'

'And since you can only buy the service for 6 or 12 months, it might still be active. Your Geddy Lee bloke will be able to ask his manager for that information. We could tell the police and let them look into it...'

'...no we couldn't, we're going to do it. I don't trust them to do anything. Hold on, I've got his number somewhere on my phone. He likes me to call him if any rare UFO-related stuff comes in. What shall I ask him?'

'Have you got a note of the PO box number?'

'Yeah.'

'Ask him if he can find out who set it up and who is authorised to collect the mail. He might not be allowed though; it might be above his pay grade.'

'I shall resort to bribery if necessary. They get paid sod all at Royal Mail so a bit of wedge or some free records might help things. I'll get on to him now.'

Nick then did a directory of enquiries search for the name Farrell in Harrogate. There were only two - one in an outlying village and one on Harlow Terrace, just off Cold Bath Road about 10 minutes' walk from his apartment. That seemed the most likely to be Florence's parents.

He put on a black jacket, jeans and a blue polo shirt to look as smart as possible. It still wasn't that smart but it made him appear a little more respectable. After smoothing his hair down, he knocked on the door of a large Victorian terrace. A woman opened up. She was about the same age as Nick, wore jeans, a stripy rainbow-coloured wool sweater and a Celtic-print scarf around her hair.

'Hello!' said Nick, doing his best I'm-a-decent-member-of-society-and-not-at-all-a-weirdo shtick. 'Is it Mrs Farrell?' he asked.

She half-smiled and nodded without saying anything, presumably thinking he was selling something.

'Ah, good. I was looking for Florence. Is she in?'

'No. She...she err...' she said, clearly hesitant to say anything at all. 'I can give her a message when I next see her. Who shall I say called?'

'My name's Nick Guymer, I'm a writer and I live in the Dales Mansion just on York Place and I'm interested in the Boudica Society. I went to one of their meetings up in Durham. From what people have told me, Florence is one of the leading lights of the society so I just wanted to talk to her and find out what it was all about. I'm writing a novel about that period and basically, I'm just looking for inspiration. I hope you don't mind me just knocking on your door like this out of the blue. '

'Well, it's not really convenient. Florence leads her own life these days, you'll have to ask her,' she said, starting to close the door.

'That's what I'd like to do.'

'Well, she'll be at Durham University.'

'Could I just have a quick word, Mrs Farrell? I'm really interested in that period of history and it's important research for my book.'

'Well, I don't know.'

'I didn't know how to get in touch with her, y'see, but a friend of mine knows a lad who went to school with her in Harrogate, so I looked up the name on the BT website. '

'Well, we don't see her here much. She's got a flat in Durham but she comes down here and...' she folded her arms across her chest and looked up the street as though looking out for anyone who could hear her, 'just step in for a moment.'

He went up the steps and into a beautifully carpeted hallway and was shown into a front room, not dissimilar to Susan's except it was more thickly carpeted and lavishly furnished.

'Florence is a worry to me,' she said, brushing her hair of her face distractedly.

'She's a striking woman. Very powerful in her own way.'

Her mother snorted and smiled wearily. She seemed a little more at ease with him now.

'I'll pop the kettle on. My name is Jane, by the way,' she said, shaking his hand..

Nick took a seat on a reproduction Victorian armchair upholstered in a tapestry-style fabric featuring Latin words. There was clearly good money in academia.

She returned and sat opposite him.

'Florence is a bit of an enigma these days. As I say, we don't see a lot of her. The truth is that when she's in Harrogate she prefers to stay at an old derelict farmhouse on the outskirts of town.'

She looked at him with embarrassed eyes.

He smiled at her and nodded as though this was all normal stuff.

'She says she likes to live a simple rustic life when she can.'

'Well, there's nothing wrong with that. I was a bit of a hippy when I was her age. Back to nature, all of that, y'know.'

'Yes, well as you say, she's very caught up in the whole Boudica thing. We always encouraged her to have an active interest in history - myself and Peter are both history professors at Leeds University.'

She got up at the click of the kettle, went to make tea and returned with two mugs. Nick sipped at it - he never drank black tea. It tasted treacly, bitter and strong.

'The Boudica Society is a bit odd, though. They all take an identity based on the pre-Roman tribes and I found that very bizarre.'

Jane Farrell smiled. 'Yes, I've heard about that. It must seem very odd from the outside. They do it as a way to subsume themselves into their roles, I think. It's silly really but perhaps no more silly than any other people who re-enact history. '

Nicked nodded. 'I had the impression that they see Boudica as a kind of role model. A strong, powerful woman hell bent on righting wrongs.'

'That's the part of it all that concerns both me and Peter. We worry about Florence because she seems so obsessed with Boudica that her coursework is suffering.'

'My friend Jeff's auntie was Susan Rutherford. Did you know her?'

She nodded and turned her mouth down. 'That was such a tragic thing. I had known Susan for oooh, what, maybe 25 years. Not as a friend but as an academic colleague. We met many times at conferences. I was sad to hear of her death. Academics often go under the radar as suicide risks but it's not as uncommon as people think. They are often highly intelligent, highly strung people whose whole life has been given up to research. Sometimes, when they reach an impasse or their work is devalued or worse still, ignored, it drives them over the edge.'

'Do you know her husband, Martin?'

'Err...well, yes, I do a little, though I haven't seen him since he moved to Teesside five or six years ago. I know they divorced a long while ago now.'

'What did you make of him?'

'Well...I don't wish to cast aspersions but, in my view, he was a little unpleasant or rather, I never took to him and I wasn't alone in that.'

'Why was that?'

'Just not my type,' she said, being polite in that very middle-class manner.

'Did you ever see him being aggressive?'

She grasped her hands together and looked away.

'Well...yes...that's what I meant. Not violent as such but aggressive. He liked to argue his case very forcefully. I never took to that style and there were rumours...'

'Go on.'

'...gossip really, perhaps, that he could be a bit of a bully. I don't know if that was true, though. I thought Susan was right to divorce him, that I will say.'

'Did Florence know Susan?'

'Yes. Since she was about 10 or 11.'

'So she knew her quite well?'

'Oh, yes. Even as a girl she would accompany me to various history gatherings and sometimes Susan was there, too. I think Susan had retired a year two before Florence went up to Durham, though.'

'She's still a visiting professor.'

'Yes well, she had so many years of experience. She was very learned on Boudica and Roman Britain. She inspired Florence's interest in history as a young teenager.'

'She inspired her?'

'Yes. She was very good to Flo. Lent her books and such. Susan had such a passion for her subject and there was nothing she liked more than to inspire youngsters with an interest in history.'

Nick nodded. This was all very interesting.

'I got the impression that Florence and her friends were all of the view that Boudica was from Teesside - I'm sure you're aware of that debate - it went against Susan's ideas.'

'Yes of course; it's a controversial view and not one that everyone agrees with. Florence likes it because it's the most exciting - the shock of the new, I suppose, which is understandable but not something an academic should really be influenced by.'

'Did she mention anything to you about a Boudica brooch that Susan had?'

She shook her head. She was a confident, articulate Yorkshirewoman, hardly ever pausing for an 'err' or a 'y'know', quite like Susan in some ways: plain and reliable, a good person and another member of the solid citizenry of the North. He liked her, though suspected that life in their house was a bit dull and lacking in rock 'n' roll, which may well have explained how Florence had turned out.

'So if I wanted to have a chat with her, where would be the best place to find her?'

'What is it you're writing?'

'A historical novel about the early years of the Roman empire in the north of England. My girlfriend is doing her MA on a similar topic, actually, also at Durham. She got a first from Newcastle in the 80s and she's just returned this year to pick up her studies.'

'How fantastic. It must be very exciting for her. If you want to speak to Florence she usually spends a day or two every weekend at this old farmhouse near a village called Spacey Houses so you might try her there. Or I have her address in Durham, though how often she's there, I can't say. She might look a bit fierce but she's a nice girl really, if a little immature and unworldly in some ways.'

She wrote down an address on South Street, across the river from the Cathedral.

'What does she plan to do after she leaves University?' asked Nick, putting the address in his jacket pocket.

'Oh, lord knows. She's a brilliant girl. Very intelligent. She would be a great loss to academia but I have a feeling she wants to do something that is more exciting. Though what that is, neither she nor I know.'

'Well, she's still young and has plenty of time to decide what her focus is going to be.'

'I do worry about her, though. She seems to live in her head a lot, if that makes any sense.'

It made a lot of sense. It was often the best place to live.

'Well, thanks for all your help, Jane. I'll see if I can track her down and have chat about all things Brigante.'

Despite her initial suspicions, she seemed to have been glad to talk to someone about her daughter.

'I'm sure she'd like that. By the sounds of it, you're from the northeast, the heart of Brigante land, so she'll probably take to you.'

He must have given her a slightly incredulous look.

'I know, I know...it's silly. But it's where her head is at right now.'

As Nick walked home, Jeff called back.

'Well?' said Nick, eager to hear the news.

'This is some heavy shit, man,' said Jeff. 'The PO box was paid for by Susan, or at least it was charged to her debit card. And she's the one who's authorised to collect the mail. No-one else. She set it up in late September and it's due to expire in March.'

So it was Susan. She'd arranged it for herself. She had killed herself.

Jeff continued, 'But I've got a copy of the form she filled out here...Geddy did a great job, actually. But the thing is, and this is the heavy shit, she's signed it at the bottom but her signature is nothing like her real signature.'

He gave a nervous laugh. 'I know you'll think this is just my conspiracy tendencies again but this hasn't been signed by her, I'm telling you. I've seen her signature a lot in the last few days. Look, I'll see you in Jack & Danny's in 20 minutes.'

Nick didn't know what to make of it. Was Jeff just being paranoid? Had someone assumed her identity? He had downloaded the application documents from the Royal Mail website and all you needed was proof of address from two recent utility bills. No photo ID. So if you had access to two bills, you could easily set up a PO box under someone else's name and collect it under that assumed identity. He walked down to Jack & Danny's and ordered a glass of mineral water

Jeff came bustling in and sat down at a table with a pint of lager.

'Look, this is her signature on a recent document.'

It was a flowing, looped signature with the middle s of 'Susan' written as though it was a small capital letter rather than a cursive s. 'Rutherford' was written in a flowing, unbroken style. 'And this is the signature on the Royal Mail form.'

He pushed the photocopy over to Nick.

He was right; the signature was totally different and clearly done by a different hand. This was more broken and didn't flow at all, despite it being written in a more traditional cursive writing style. You couldn't mistake one for the other. In fact, although all the writing on the form was printed in black capitals, none if it looked like Susan's writing.

'Shit, we're no further forward then,' said Nick, folding the copy and putting it into his back pocket.

Jeff raised his index finger. 'Not true, Batman, not true at all. We now know one very important thing.'

'What's that?'

'We know that Susan didn't set up the PO box. So Susan couldn't have ordered some cyanide to be delivered to a PO box she knew nothing about, could she? '

Nick sipped at the water. 'True...but...but we don't actually know that she didn't know about the PO box, do we? We just know she didn't sign the form. That's not quite the same thing and that's all that we actually do know.'

Jeff sat back in his seat and folded his arms across his chest.

'Fucking hell, can you stop nit picking at the detail? Okay, but realistically, it's much less likely she killed herself now we know this. Not impossible, I'll grant you that, but much less likely. Who gets someone else to sign a PO box form for them? No-one. Why would you do that?'

'I can't think why anyone would do that. It does seem really unlikely.'

'There's only one reason why - someone else set it up so they could order the cyanide on Susan's card without it being sent to Susan. They've collected the stuff and then used it to poison Susan and make it look like suicide.'

It made perfect sense. He was right. He had to be right.

Later that evening, Nick was watching football on TV when Julie called.

'Now then, beautiful,' he said.

'Hiya, it's just a quick call 'cos I've got some work to do. You know I went to play badminton?'

'Yeah, any good?'

'Rubbish. I'm a bit of a chuffing old bag compared to the perky-bosomed 20-year-old lasses. God, they make me feel old and I know they think I'm an ancient old goat. Anyway, I was getting showered afterwards and that girl Florence came in with some other girls. She'd been playing rugby, I think.'

'Really?'

'And you should have seen her!'

'Does she look good naked?'

Julie laughed. 'Don't start getting the horn, lad. She's certainly a big girl. Her tits will be down to her waist when she's my age. Anyway, she's got a huge tattoo across her back. Across her shoulders and down to the small of her back.'

'I'm guessing it's something to do with Boudica.'

'You're ahead of me...across her shoulders is written "Brigante"...'

'...I bet it was written in a Celtic font.'

'You guessed right about that as well. But more interesting than that, she had the Boudica army B tattooed below it and it was exactly the same as the design on the brooch.'

'Are you sure it wasn't just a general Celtic-type design?'

'I'm sure. I saw and it and I thought, "god, fizzin' hell, look at that", and I was trying not to get caught looking at her...I mean, she doesn't know me and might have thought it was weird. She must have had it done from the sketch Diane said Susan had shown to her.'

'I just found out from her mam that Florence knew Susan well when she was younger...so it's entirely possible that she even showed her the brooch at some point. They all knew each other well. Are you sure it was the same and not just in the same style?'

'It was identical but much, much bigger. It wasn't a fresh tattoo either; it must be at least a year old.' Nick sat forward on the sofa, thought for a moment and then told her about the PO box. 'I really thought it was going to be Susan who had set up the PO box, y'know...that Jeff was just off on one about it being murder...but now it really looks like someone set up that PO box just to get the cyanide delivered to it. I reckon he's been right all along.'

'Why set it up in Harrogate, though? Why not nearer to Malton? If someone was trying to pass it off as Susan's, it looks odd being in a town away from where she lives.'

'Because there was a risk someone would have known Susan if it was locally. She's lived there for so long, it might have been mentioned by the local postie or something. And if someone had gone in to collect the mail pretending to be her, they might have been spotted as an imposter. She had good connections with Harrogate, she went there most weeks to do the car boots.'

'If that's true, it had to be a woman. Couldn't have been a man collecting mail under her name.'

'Of course, yeah. Jeff is more certain than ever it's Diane.'

'I can see why, but I think he's out of order. There's no way she'd have done anything to hurt Susan. In fact, in some ways I think she still loved her,' said Julie. 'I went back after badminton to see if she was OK but she'd gone. I'm worried about her. My auntie Edith had a nervous breakdown at our house when I was about 15. I'll never forget it. She was behaving like Diane - she was uncontrollably emotional and went from being over affectionate to being desperate and paranoid. I remember I took her a cup of tea in for her and she burst out crying saying what a nice thing it was to do for her.'

'What happened to her?'

'One day I came in from school and she was fighting my mam. Well, she was throwing punches at her, at any rate. They called a doctor and eventually sectioned her. Poor Edith. She did make a recovery, mind. I'll call Diane tomorrow to see if she's any better. If she isn't, we really should get her a doctor regardless.'

'But you see...that could point to her having killed her. It's disturbed her mind. It's like she was detached from reality. Maybe when you're in that state you'd be able to poison someone. I suppose it's different to stabbing them. There's no blood. You lace their tea with poison, stand back and let it do its work. When I'm depressed I reckon I could do that, y'know. I know it makes me look bad but you get so distanced from every day life that the usual rules don't seem to apply any more. I can imagine it, at least.'

'Mmm, it's so horrible. It's hard to even think about it without getting the shivers. Well, it is for me, anyway.'

'I was looking at the notes I made after I came home from that morning, and when I found her she was still warm. The report that the coroner gave Jeff said death had occurred between 10 and 10.30am. I found her at around 10.35am, so it obviously happened just before we arrived. Very frustrating, that. If I'd driven quicker on the A64 we might have been able to stop it happening.'

'C'mon...you can't beat yourself up about that. You should have a closer look at the photos you took in there again. See if you've missed anything.'

'Yeah, I might go over there tomorrow and ask around to see if anyone saw anything apart from that neighbour. I know it's over a month ago now but you never know. The police don't seem to have asked anyone. They assumed it was suicide from the start. I'm still not happy about Martin James, either. I think me and Jeff got the truth out of him but he's a devious conniving sod, that one.'

'The only thing that stops me thinking he killed her is that he really had nothing to gain - it would have to be out of sheer anger - like a gunshot or something - but this was much more calculated than that - it was premeditated...buying cyanide, setting up the PO box and all of that. Right, I'm off to bed. I'm knackered. This physical exercise is killing me. All the muscles in my legs are sore and in my shoulders and arms, and belly and neck...I'm a physical wreck.'

'I'll give a massage when you come down here.'

'No you bloody won't. Not unless you've learned how to do it since a few years ago. It was like getting probed by aliens.'

'I've never been so insulted. These are healing hands.'

'You can't be blessed at everything...you have other talents, darling, which I might just go to bed and contemplate. Night night.'

'Night Jules.'

He loaded the photos onto his computer and arranged them so all six were displayed on his screen. The image of Susan collapsed with her head on the fire surround was still powerful. Her pose, slumped forward and to one side, with her legs under her, still made it look for all the world as though she had got up from the chair but the cyanide had taken her down and out before she could get anywhere. He stroked the beard growth on his chin. Surely, if she'd committed suicide she'd have just drank the tea, sat back and waited for the Great Beyond. It took a maximum of 20 seconds to render you unconscious, so it wouldn't have been a long wait. A terrible thought occurred to him. Maybe she had taken it, realised she didn't want to die and then got up in a panic just as its toxicity took effect. Jesus. Poor Susan. She'd been a canny old soul and kind, too - she'd thoughtfully put that Ferlinghetti book aside for him. Emotion suddenly rose up in him and a single tear covered his right eye. He swallowed it down and carried on his scrutiny of the photos.

The room was so neat and tidy, everything in its place. The photo of the table with the teapot and the cup which had delivered the deadly liquid seemed especially poignant. He looked at the closeup of the table and the dislodged chip of wood but it didn't seem significant. But the photo he'd taken of Diane's book lying open on the table was quite the opposite. He increased the picture size. The book was open at the first page and signed. He blew it up as big as he could before it broke into pixels and read the inscription: 'To Susan - without you, none of this would have been possible'. It was signed 'Diane' with two kisses.

A little frisson of excitement fluttered in his stomach. This was Diane's handwriting. If she had set up the PO box in Susan's name, as Jeff had suggested, now was the chance to find out. He took out the copy of the Royal Mail form from his back pocket and laid it out on the table. The photo of the book was taken from an angle that made the letters look compressed so he held the form beside the computer screen at the same angle, flicking his eyes from screen to paper, comparing the line 'To Susan' in the book to the 'Susan Rutherford' signature on the application form.

They were identical.

The large, expressive S and the flattened cursive middle s. The inscription in the book was more flowing but obviously done with the same hand. She had signed Susan's name on the form. Good grief. This was proper evidence and it put Diane Edwards right at the heart of Susan's death. She had to have set up and signed the PO box application form and, given her on/off relationship with Susan, presumably at some point she had access to her computer, and to her credit card, too. So she could have bought the pills, had them delivered to the PO box and then administered them. Sure, it looked like suicide, but in reality, she really was behind it all. It was just like Jeff said, killing her old friend and lover had sent her crazy. It seemed incredible but it was true. Diane Edwards had murdered Susan Rutherford.

As he looked in disbelief, comparing the writing on the form to the book, another surprise was waiting for him. The rest of it really didn't look like Diane's writing at all. The name at the top of the form, the address, none of it was in Diane's handwriting. The letters were all formed differently. But the signature most certainly was her handwriting. She had either signed a PO box form for Susan that she hadn't actually filled out, or could it be that the handwriting in The Queen of the Tees wasn't Diane's? But if it wasn't, who the hell's handwriting was it? Surely Susan hadn't inscribed the book herself? Or was there someone else involved in all of this?

CHAPTER 10

It dawned a still, grey and cold morning. The brisk wind of the previous few days had dropped so it didn't feel too bitter as Nick took his morning walk, this time heading out to Spacey Houses dressed in his leather jacket and a black roll-neck sweater.

As he got to the village, he could see there was smoke rising from behind the old derelict buildings. It looked like someone was home. He walked down the muddy track, picking his way between puddles, past the two ruined houses towards the old farmhouse. There was no glass left in the windows and tiles were missing from the roof. It was a hell of place to live rough when your mam and dad had a nice big house a couple of miles away but then it was a classic middle-class kid thing to do. After a comfortable upbringing, here was her chance to emerge from the insulation of that life, to feel cold at night and perhaps feel more alive. A solid middle-class upbringing, for all its virtues, could be a stifling, claustrophobic existence protected from the harshness of life, well padded and comfortable. It was natural that any kid would want to feel what life was like on the less-pampered side of the tracks.

As he approached, the familiar small blonde girl, Sophie, emerged from the building wearing old black trousers and drowning in a garish purple charity shop wool coat that looked like it had recently belonged to a 75-year-old woman called Doris.

'Hi, there,' said Nick.

'What do you want?' said Sophie, defensively.

'I just wanted to have a word with Florence if she's around.'

She was around. She emerged from behind the big old paint-flaked door as he spoke.

'Hey, Florence,' he said and held out his hand. She looked at it and then decided to shake it with a firm grip. She wore a long hand-knitted rough brown wool jumper that went down to her thighs, a purple silk scarf, spiked-up red hair and the same black lipstick she'd worn at the meeting in Durham. It all combined to make her look like a hippy punk crossed with a zombie. She had big hands and feet and was a couple of inches taller than him. She coughed up some phlegm and spat it out to one side like a teenage boy trying to look tough.

'What do you want to talk to me for? Who are you?' she asked. She took a long knife from her waistband and jammed its point into the table. It was about a foot long, came to a sharp point and had a brass-coloured hilt. It looked like something from medieval times. He looked down. Was this supposed to be some sort of threatening gesture?

'I'm Nick Guymer, I'm a writer, I live locally and I'm interested in talking to you about Boudica for research I'm doing for a new novel I'm writing,' he said. As he spoke, the knife fell over, the weight of the handle tippling it onto its side. The point hadn't been jammed into the wood hard enough and it lifted up a splinter of wood as it fell.

'How do you even know about me and my interest in Boudica?'

'I saw you in Durham at a Boudica Society meeting and then I saw you in town, so I looked up your name in the phone book and went around to your parents' house. Your mam said you might be out here.'

She gave a wry smile and a shrug.

'Sounds a bit like having a stalker, that,' she said. But he could tell she was, if not flattered, then interested in being interested in. She adopted a voice that was obviously more working class than her natural voice. She was trying to be much more Yorkshire.

'I was fascinated by your passion for Boudica and you seemed to be the leader of that group so I thought you would be the ideal person to talk to.'

While he was speaking, he looked at the knife again. The splinter it had lifted from the table was exactly like the one at Susan's. He ran his finger over the hole made by the point of the knife.

'She is our leader,' said the other girl, clearly the proud subordinate in the relationship.

'Shut up, Soph. I'm no such thing. Diane is our leader. You know that. Go put some water on for a brew,' said Florence like a teacher talking to a student.

Like a lot of 20-year-old kids, Florence had plenty of confidence and clearly thought of herself as a grown up without realising quite how big a streak of immature childishness still ran through her.

She gestured at the seats by the old bleached wooden table.

'What sort of novel are you writing?'

This was an easy lie for Nick.

'It's a novel set in AD 61 in the north of England. It's a combination of imagination and historical fact. I wanted to imagine how people would have reacted to the news of Boudica taking on the Romans. It inspired some folk I bet but Cartimandua was pro-Roman so...'

Florence jumped in with puppyish enthusiasm.

'Can you imagine that? It must have been a huge rift. She had her court at Stanwick Hill, which is near modern-day Darlington,' she said, leaning forward. 'I believe Boudica was born a Brigante and was from that area, from modern-day Teesside. Professor Diane Edwards at Durham University has written a brilliant book about it and now she thinks we have the proof that our queen was buried on Teesside. The whole accepted history of Boudica is about to change. It's totally revolutionary.'

'Wow, well, that's where I'm from originally, Teesside, like. Yeah, that is very exciting and, like I said, I saw your debate. Susan Rutherford opposed that view, didn't she?'

Florence avoided eye contact him for the first time since his arrival, looking at her boots.

'She's dead now and we have new proof,' she said, taking out a roll-up and lighting it with an expensive-looking silver lighter.

'Yeah I saw that in the papers. She killed herself. That's awful.'

'Her views were outdated,' she said, trying to be hard but failing; her eyes gave away an echo of upset. She still wouldn't look at him. Sophie brought two mugs of black coffee made from water boiled in a camping stove kettle.

'We don't have any sugar.'

'That's OK, I don't take sugar,' said Nick. 'Did you know Susan Rutherford?'

'Yes. Since I was young, actually. She was a colleague of my mother's,' she said, slipping back into her middle-class voice.

'Why was there such a division between the two camps during that Boudica Society meeting, do you think? It really surprised me. The strength of feeling was astonishing.'

'It's because Boudica is ours. She is a Brigante and not an Iceni.

She's been stolen from us by the likes of Susan. We want her back. These lands should be her lands.'

Now she looked right at him, staring into his eyes.

She spoke with a real passion, her eyes shining. She was unconventional looking, with big features and a strong jaw, but her passion made her very attractive. She had a spark, there was no denying it and it was easy to see why she might emerge from any group as a leader. There was a wild look to her a bright, challenging face and real presence. And Jeff would be pleased to know she did give off a slightly musky odour, probably a mixture of patchouli, wood smoke and henna. Passion is always an attractive quality and she was very attractive and, it had to be said, also felt a little dangerous.

Nick nodded keenly. 'Well, I'm a Brigante too, so I can see where you're coming from.'

'Brigantes rule!' said Sophie, punching the air with a small fist. 'Flo won't even go out with someone who isn't a Brigante.'

'Shut up, Soph, I just think who you are and where your ancestors are from is important,' she said as Nick grinned and nodded.

'I've always felt this sort of mystical connection to the northern lands. I love being a Teessider. It's not just where I grew up; it's part of who I am. It's weird, really. I can't explain it properly but it's in my DNA. I love being Northern, even just saying it gives me a thrill. There's something heroic about it to me, something epic. Does that make sense?' He was speaking from the heart but knowing it would resonate with her. She was nodding vigorously as he spoke and gave him an irrepressible broad smile.

'I feel exactly like that,' she said and bounced up and down a little as she sat, like a child. 'It's as though it comes from the sky or out of the ground. It must be because these have been our lands for generations - we have a spiritual as well as cultural connection to the land.'

He nodded in return. 'And if you're not from the North, you just don't get it. Have you noticed that? People pay lip service to it if they come from London or something but you know they don't really understand what being Northern actually means. But we all know absolutely implicitly what it means and we carry it with us wherever we go in the world.'

He was warming to his theme and could tell she was warming to him in return.

'Yes. You can take the girl out of the Brigante lands but you can't take the Brigante lands out of the girl.'

They all laughed a little, but with a tinge of embarrassment

'I often think I should get a tattoo with something that expresses the Northern spirit,' said Nick.

'She's got a massive one,' said Sophie, keen to show off on behalf of her friend. 'It's brilliant.'

'Really? Where?' asked Nick, knowing the answer already.

'Across my back and shoulders, but don't ask me to show you,' she said with a grin. 'It says "Brigante" and I have a Boudica army insignia as well.'

'Brilliant. Sounds great. I've never seen that insignia, what book did you get it from?' asked Nick, thinking this was all too easy.

'Oh it's not in any book. It was from a sketch of a Boudica brooch. It took 10 hours to do. Hurt like hell.'

Nick smiled to himself again. He took a chance.

'It was Susan Rutherford's brooch, wasn't it?'

She shot him a quick, nervous glance but tried to remain cool. 'What?'

'Too late, Flo. You've given the game away with your expression,' he said, bluffing. 'You know what I'm talking about, the one you've been trying to get her to give you.'

'Eh? I don't know what you're talking about, mate,' she said, reverting to her version of a working-class Yorkshire accent, clearly as a defence measure.

'Aye, you do,' he said quietly. 'I'm sure Diane has told you about it. About the brooch we took to her.'

'That was you?'

'Yup. Susan put it in my mate Jeff's potatoes.'

'In his potatoes?' she said a little too incredulously.

'Yeah, in his potatoes.'

'Why in his potatoes?'

'She wanted to get rid of it because you were hassling her. Bullying her. Let's not pretend anymore. You were bullying her. I know you were. I saw you on the CCTV and you or a friend of yours saw her drop the brooch in Jeff's bag, didn't you?'

He could see her trying to compute all this information and come up with a response. She frowned at him and he knew he'd hit a nerve. She took out a packet of tobacco and a pack of Rizlas and began rolling a cigarette. Why did middle-class students like roll-ups so much?

'Jeff is her nephew, and is also a Brigante from Teesside, by the way. He's very upset by her suicide and wants to know why she took her own life. Have you any ideas?'

'We weren't bullying her,' said Sophie, coming back to the table after walking around in a circle. 'We just wanted her to help our cause and she wouldn't, stupid cow. She wouldn't give in no matter what we did.'

'Shut it!' barked Florence towards her friend. She turned to Nick.

'Look, I never wanted any harm to come to Susan but she was dishonest. She found Boudica's grave and then she denied it when she knew there was a movement to relocate Boudica to the north. She didn't want to lose her...her...pre-eminence as an expert. She had been the authority on the subject and had got it all wrong and she knew it. She knew it! That's totally dishonest. I couldn't let that go.'

'So that's why you broke into Jeff's shop and flat and car to try and get the brooch because you obviously saw what she'd done at the car boot that day. No point in denying it Flo, I saw you there. I've got you on film.'

'I didn't break in anywhere,' said Florence defensively, sucking on the roll-up but not actually inhaling the smoke, blowing it out straight away. She was so obviously a new smoker.

'No, you didn't, but someone in the Boudica Society did, I saw her at the meeting,' said Nick. 'But you stopped after Susan's death. Presumably the police investigation scared you off.'

'Look, I feel sorry about Susan, she was a nice woman really, just stuck in her ways. In the end she took her own life because of the lies she'd told for so long. It's sad but it's not my fault.'

'Were you at her house the morning she died?' asked Nick. 'What happened that morning?'

He looked from Sophie to Florence. They glanced at each other. It was like being a headmaster and having a couple of sixth-form kids in your office.

'I don't know what you're talking about,' said Florence. 'I wasn't there. As far as I know, she died alone.'

Nick grabbed the knife. 'So how come this knife had just left a fresh hole in her table? I found it Flo...and it had just been done. It was fresh. Was it just part of your bullying? A tactic to scare her the way you just tried to scare me with it when I arrived. The thing is Flo, I'm a hard 46-year-old Northern bloke not a 64-year-old woman and you don't scare me.'

'You're talking bullshit,' she said, getting up. 'Give me the knife.'

'No. I'm taking this as evidence. I'm going to match it to that hole. I'm sure it's a perfect fit and I can tell by the look in your eyes that I'm right.'

'Give me it!' she shouted, lunging at him.

He pushed her away, the palm of his right hand connecting with her large left breast, and she staggered backwards.

'The thing is, Jeff thinks that it wasn't suicide, he thinks that she was murdered and he won't rest until he's found out what happened that day. Did you kill her with the poison? Was it you, or was it Diane, or Martin James? Eh?'

'She didn't do anything,' said Sophie, now in tears.

'You better go now. Please. Just go,' said Florence, more composed than her friend. 'I've nothing more to say to you.'

Nick nodded, turned and began to walk away, putting the knife into his pocket, convinced that Florence Farrell was edgy, passionate and dangerous.

The following morning he went to Jeff's house and got the key for Susan's house.

'I just want to have a long, quiet look around. I've got a few ideas. Oh, and I met Florence Farrell yesterday.'

'Oh aye, what's she like?'

He didn't want to go into detail in case he was wrong.

'Interesting. Very interesting, a bit scary, attractive and definitely musky.'

'Get in. I knew it!'

Forty-five minutes later Nick parked the car on Middlecave Road outside Susan's house and walked down the right-hand side of the house towards the back garden. It wasn't a big space, just a patch of grass and some mature shrubs. Very low maintenance. At the back were some tall hedges that defined the border of the garden. Beyond was an open ploughed field and in the far distance to the north and east, the North York Moors. He strode around the perimeter of beech hedges on a fringe of grass. They were dense and covered in dry, copper-coloured dead leaves. As he reached the far corner, there was a worn patch of grass to and from a narrow gap in the hedge. He squeezed through and emerged on the edge of the grassy field which stretched eastwards. A clear footpath could be made out around the field. Looking back towards the house, it was perfectly possible to make a quick escape out of the back door, push through the gap in the hedge and follow the path. It was a well-worn dog walkers' route and was probably one that Susan herself took regularly.

He and Jeff had arrived that day at about half-past 10; it was now 10.25, almost the same time of day, but there was no-one out and about as he walked around the outskirts of the field. Walking on, he turned right and headed across the full length of the field. About 60 yards from the house, there was a white box. It had been blown under a blackthorn and hawthorn hedge and stood out bright white against the dark wood. There was black Chinese writing on the box and in bold were the letters KCN and the number 12, the amount of capsules it contained. He had been rubbish at chemistry but remembered K was potassium while CN could easily mean cyanide. The box had a red triangle with black skull and crossbones and more writing underneath along with some exclamation marks. It was empty but he pocketed it and walked back to the house.

As he got to the back door, he took a close look around. Everything was so tidy. Susan had put the garden to bed for winter, a line of rose bushes were pruned and stark against the soil. Rose bushes - bloody things always burst your football. He turned to go in the house but stopped and turned round again, his eye distracted by something. Something untidy. There beside the last rose bush, 10 yards from the door, was some litter. He walked up the garden path and squatted down to pick it up. It was a tea bag. Now half decomposed, it almost blended into the soil and was easy to miss. He tore the remains of it open and looked at the leaves and recognized them immediately as green tea. Was this the tea bag missing from the pack of 24? It had to be.

He was about to go back and look at the box of tea bags when he noticed a man coming out of the side door of the neighbouring house. It was a three-storey Victorian villa. He was a tall, distinguished-looking with a beard, probably in his early 60s. Nick sprinted to the road and caught up with him.

'Excuse me,' he said as he reached the man's shoulder.

He turned and looked at him with surprise and a little fear.

'I'm sorry to bother you. Do you live next door to Susan Rutherford's house?'

'Err...yes...yes I do...though she's sadly passed away recently...'

'Oh yes, I know. It was me and her nephew Jeff that found her that day. My name's Nick Guymer.' He held out his hand. The man gripped it with a dry cold hand and looked at him with a serious expression.

'Ah I see. Yes it was all quite a shock to us. I'm Daniel Yarrow.'

'Did you know her well?'

'Well, yes. We've lived next to each other for 20 years. Though I have to say, the suicide verdict took me and Janet...that is, my wife...took us both by surprise. She didn't seem...well...then again...who does?'

He spoke with reliable, flat vowels and seemed to be an old-fashioned, polite man. Another solid citizen of the north lands; another Brigante.

'Did the police interview you after she was found dead?'

He shook his head. 'No, no they didn't. Should they have done?'

Nick scratched his head. 'I'm not sure...maybe. There's some doubt about whether it was a suicide.'

He widened his baggy, creased eyes. 'Really?'

'Well, not by the police. But Jeff certainly thinks so. I know it's a long time ago now but did you see anyone visiting Susan on the morning we found her? Or did you see anything unusual at all?'

'This is what I said to Janet. Yes, we both did.'

'Do you know who it was?'

'Yes of course. Just after nine in the morning I saw the dark-haired woman visit, I forget what she's called now. Very nice woman, she's a professor I think.'

'Diane Edwards?' He nodded. 'The name sounds familiar.'

'Did you see her leave?'

'No, but I wasn't standing at the window. I could have easily missed her. About an hour later I saw Martin, her ex-husband, arrive. I was surprised because we hadn't seen him for a long time really, but it was certainly him. I saw him from the front room where I was reading the morning paper.'

'What time was that?'

'Around 10 past 10. Ten minutes later I saw him have a quick chat with Harry across the road and then walk off down the street. A few minutes after that, two girls arrived. That's not unusual, they come to see Susan regularly, or they have done recently. A tall red-headed girl and a smaller blonde girl. They look like students. They usually come with the older dark-haired woman, actually.'

Diane was at the scene with the girls. She'd lied to Julie. She was covering up her involvement in her death. She had to be.

'Did you see them leave?'

'No I didn't. I must have missed them, I suppose. Then you and the big chap arrived.'

'Jeff.'

'Yes, Jeff. I've seen him occasionally before. I thought, "Oh, there must be a meeting going on or something". She sometimes had academics round. So I thought nothing more about it. By then Janet was ready and we went straight off to Scarborough.'

'So you missed all the action with the ambulances and police.'

'Yes, it was all over when we came back and in fact we didn't learn anything about it until I spoke to Harry the next afternoon. I could hardly believe what had been going on while we were away. It still shocks me to think about it.'

Nick thanked him and gave him his mobile number should he remember anything. What he had told him surely discounted Martin James from being involved in her killing. If Diane or Florence and Sophie had arrived and found her dead, surely they'd have reported it. It pointed to only one outcome because all of them had lied about not being there. One of them must have poisoned her and then left via the back door when he and Jeff had arrived. They'd taken off with the packet of remaining cyanide capsules, dumping the box as they escaped across the field.

He walked back into Susan's house. A thin layer of dust had now settled on all surfaces. It felt as though the building had gone into hibernation, like entering a vacuum from which the vibrant, lively air of human life had been sucked out. It was unnerving, as though at any moment it might awake from its stasis and become animated again. He took out Florence's knife and went into the back room to the wooden table. The gouged bit of wood was still in place. He placed its point at an angle into an indentation at the front of the loose piece of wood. It's shape fitted perfectly. It was possible to see where it had gone in, and then fallen backwards to lift out the shard. You didn't need a forensics team to see that Florence had jammed this into the table, probably to try and scare Susan into giving up the brooch.

In the kitchen the white china mug still stood on the drainer. He checked the green tea bags. Only one missing. The one in the back garden, surely.

Upstairs in her office, as he stood in the doorway, it struck him again just how untidy and messy the room was. It had clearly been searched by someone other than Susan. Maybe it was the police or maybe it was Diane or the girls looking for evidence of her unofficial dig. That D in her diary at nine obviously had meant Diane. But she'd not died until around 10.30, so she'd had a last hour and a half with Diane.

Rather than randomly pull out draws and look in cupboards for god knows what, he just stood there quietly and tried to imagine Susan in there.

'Come on Susan, give me a message,' he said out loud. 'Tell me what happened that morning. Did Diane come here and poison you or was it Martin or Florence, or even little Sophie?' Suddenly out of the still silence came a noise - a soft thud and then a low rumble from downstairs. He stood stock still. Every hair on his body felt like it was shocked upright. He listened and listened, trying to detect movement downstairs. Was someone there? He crept silently downstairs. As he reached the hallway he heard it again, louder this time. Then it struck him. Of course. It was the gas boiler. It ignited with a little boom and then purred like a cat as it heated the water. The central heating had been turned off but here it was still gamely keeping the water to a preset temperature. Machines don't know when the humans they were created to serve have long since gone. They keep on keeping on.

A potent mixture of relief and upset washed across him as the tension left. The boiler setting was an echo of her life; a symbol of her existence in the house which lived on after her death as a mechanical embodiment of her spirit. Oh, god. He wiped tears away from his eyes. What was the matter with him? This kept happening. Were these surges of emotion something to do with the therapy? Was this what it was like being in touch with his feelings?

Returning to her office, he sat down at the desk and looked around. The desk had two drawers so he pulled open the top one and looked in. It was full of stationary but on the top was an A4 writing pad. He flipped it open but it was blank. Half of the pad had been torn out. He ran his finger down the spine where a few tears of paper were still anchored by glue and then picked up the pad and held it to the light that shone in through the west-facing window. He could see a messy pattern of indentations made by a pen pressing on the last sheet of paper but angling the paper towards the light didn't really make them readable. On an off chance and remembering an old trick he'd learned in childhood from Enid Blyton's Famous Five books, he took out a soft 2B pencil from a pot on the desk and, turning it on its side, began to lightly rub across the indentations. The graphite darkened the paper and left the indentations white and more clearly visible. A quick comparison with Susan's handwriting on other documents clearly showed it was her handwriting. He squinted and it quickly became obvious that she must have torn out the last sheet of paper and then written on it at an angle because the writing fell outside the boundaries of the lined paper and sometimes fell off the edge. It looked like the final page of a letter as it ended after a dozen or so lines and was signed by Susan.

He looked closely at the pencil rubbing to make out the impression of the text. At the top it was clearly addressed to Diane:

'It is with some pleasure to me that as you read this, I will be dead or dying. But be assured, if I am able to haunt you, I damn well will.' Christ almighty. What a thing to say.

The next section was overwritten several times as she had moved the sheet of paper around but much of it was still readable.

'I have no use for life anymore. It has become a worthless experience, so much so that I feel those who do not share this feeling are merely deluding themselves out of fear of death. I no longer have that fear. My life has been one of pretence and quiet disillusion. For years I pretended that I was normal. But I wasn't. My family rejected me not because of anything I had done but because of who I was. My work was all I had and you have sought to undermine even that because of the nature our relationship about which I know you have never forgiven me. But no more. I can tolerate no more of you and your followers' aggression, no more unpleasantness and stupidity. The time to end all the pain and hurt has arrived. Maybe I am weak but like Boudica, I would rather die than suffer any more at the hands of my enemies and I include you as number one on that list.

'My lasting hope is that when you see me die in front of you today, the sight of me in my death throes will damn well haunt you for all eternity. If it does, I will have had my revenge from beyond the grave and that at least, will be something. As I know all too well, life is not just about the choices you make but about the consequences of those choices. This final choice to die is the best I have ever made.'

She had signed her name in full at the bottom of the page. The writing was messy, just like her last diary entry which had presumably been done the evening before she died. It was her final message and there was no disguising her bleak bitterness.

The thought of Susan, a regular, quiet, middle-class person, being torn up so badly by life that death was preferable, was profoundly upsetting. Seeing her words there on the page, written by her hand as a manifestation of her emotions and intellect, made him feel ice cold. It felt like he was witnessing her suicide there on the page. Here were her last written words, her last contribution to life. She had used her death as revenge against the people or person who, rightly or wrongly, she saw as her enemy. And in losing, she felt she had won. She must have given Diane this letter, probably just after taking the cyanide, in the seconds before the poison worked its mortal magic. That was why her legs had folded under her. She had stood up to give her the letter and had been going to sit back down to meet her death when the poison had rendered her unconscious and she had collapsed. She had deliberately cursed Diane and accidentally, Florence and Sophie too, with the sight of her death. She surely intended to haunt Diane with the most profound and cruellest of all images; that of someone actually dying.

He tore the sheet out of the notepad with a heavy heart, feeling like crying but also knowing this was too big and it had been going on too long for mere tears to wash it away. It made his soul feel heavy to think of a life so ripped up. This had seemed to be all about Boudica but now he could see, sitting in her house, inside her life, that it wasn't. It was about her and her life and her relationships and the lies about her life and her work that she'd lived with and what they had done to her over the decades; how a few wrong or hard choices had irrevocably altered everything.

Sitting there in the stillness of her after-life, he now understood just how depressed she had been. How utterly desperate to the bottom of her soul she had been and how the outside world could have no idea of the depths of that depression. It was just a short step from being alive to being dead. A very small step indeed. We cling to life so tenaciously precisely because it is fragile and death is always near. When your grip on life loosens, just letting go gets easier and easier and finally, irresistible. He knew that now. Murder might have seemed more likely or almost more understandable but it wasn't murder, it really was suicide. She had been profoundly depressed and was alone and unreachable, shut down inside herself with all the joy of life extinguished. Her last hope was to communicate this to the people she saw as the root of the torment. But they weren't the root, not really; the root lay in her own life and in her own psyche.

He went back down to her bedroom and sat down at her small, modest dressing table. She probably sat there at the start and end of every day. She had sat there that last morning, that deep, dark hole in her soul about to swallow her life up. There was a hairbrush complete with strands of hair, a last echo of Susan's presence; a picture from a gone world.

He looked upward and spoke out loud, tears now rolling down his face.

'I wish you could have taken your own advice and kept love in your life, Susan. I wish I'd known or had guessed or could have helped you. Rest in peace.'

When he got home he made a beef stew, put it in the oven and went for a shower to wash off the dust from Susan's house and, more poignantly, to wash away the whole mess. It was over. He changed into a loose pair of khaki pants and a black t-shirt and then left a message on Julie's voicemail. She called him back as soon as she was out of lectures.

'Hey, baby,' she said in a faux American accent

'Hey, Jules. I had a really amazing morning. I think I've found out everything about Susan's death. I know what happened.' He explained what he had discovered in the house. She listened without interruption.

When he'd finished she said, 'You know what? I think that's even more shocking to hear than if you'd found out she'd been murdered. It's so sad and then such a horrible thing to do to kill yourself in front of someone. You know, all the time I was at Diane's house and every time I've met her I felt she had her mind on something, you know that feeling you get that someone is almost subconsciously distracted by their own thoughts or running something in front of their inner eye. Now I know what it was.'

'Why do you think they all ran off and pretended they hadn't been there?'

The line went quiet as Julie pondered his question.

'They must have been worried that they'd have been incriminated in her death - administered the poison, just as Jeff said, especially when their bullying was revealed. They weren't thinking straight. And don't forget, Diane signed that PO box form...'

'Oh god, yeah. Susan must have somehow asked her to sign it. Just given her the form or whatever. That was a deliberate act...'

'...maybe she actually tried to frame Diane. Made it seem as though she might have killed her. Even if it wasn't enough to convict her, it would be enough to have her dragged over the coals. It was all more revenge for Susan. She was so twisted up,' said Julie.

'She really was and I don't think Florence and Sophie are in a very good place over it all, either. The fact they were hassling Susan for months clearly contributed to her decision to kill herself. They got caught up in this Queen of the Tees thing to a ridiculous extent. I mean, you wouldn't want that on your conscience, would you?'

'When you're that age you can get so absorbed in things, you think you're all grown up and sensible but really you're just having a sort of crush.'

'I just wish I'd understood more about my own depression earlier. Looking back on it now, I can see Susan was stuck in the depths of a very deep, airless, dark black hole. I can easily imagine how she felt and why she decided to kill herself, why it looked like a good or the only way out. In judging her choices you have to cast that light on her.'

'Do you think she could have been reached, though?'

'We'll never know now, but judging by her medicine cabinet, she wasn't on any medication for depression. Maybe, like me, she just didn't even think it was the thing called depression that everyone talks about, she just thought that this was just how her life was and would always be.'

'I never realised that when people behave weird, or badly or are irresponsible in some way, it could be down to their mental health. You just think they're bad people or whatever.'

'Can you imagine how destructive that Boudica Society meeting was to her? I think it really broke her and set her mind to end her life that night. Remember when we saw her afterwards she said she had to go home to "make some plans". We know what those plans were now.'

'Oh god, poor Susan.'

'Yeah, poor old girl. I don't mind saying I shed a few tears for her inside her house.'

They paused and went quiet for a few moments before Nick spoke again.

'But, y'know...what's done is done and as sad as it is, nothing will change it now. She's gone. But she may yet have a Boudica legacy. From her unofficial dig it looks like Boudica's burial site really is on the Salmons' Blakeston estate. I e-mailed Stevie the other day and he said his dad had found a lot of old stuff on the land over the years and still had most of it. I was wondering if any of it was Boudica-related stuff. It might have been ploughed up over the years. If so, maybe we can get a big dig organized there to finally unearth Boudica. Although Susan clearly couldn't bear the thought of Diane being proven right, she was still the first to discover the burial site. She should be honoured for that.'

'Great idea. I think Diane would actually like that, as well. It might help her deal with Susan's death. Would Brian show us his finds, do you think?'

'Yeah, I think he would. I said to Stevie it was all part of your MA research.'

'Okay, well, to keep that story going, why don't I ring old man Salmon up and arrange to go over there and take a look?'

Within 10 minutes she called him back. 'It's all sorted for tomorrow morning - 10am at the farmhouse. He's given me the address. He sounded nice, Brian Salmon. Nicer than his vulgar son, anyway.'

'Right. I'll pick you up at 9.30.'

'Love you.'

'Love you too ,Jules.' It had never, ever been easier to say.

There was one last big job to do. Tell Jeff. He had been right to be suspicious about his aunt's death but had put two and two together and made 22 instead of four.

He went to the shop, put the kettle on, sat down on a stool behind the counter and began to explain it all to the big man.

Jeff sat impassively sorting through records as he spoke, slipping the vinyl out of the sleeve, checking its condition and placing the record on a yes, no or maybe pile. Nick gave him the sheet of paper with the impressions of her last letter on. He went over it all point by point, explaining what he'd found in her house.

Jeff nodded and flicked his hair over his shoulders, letting out an occasional grunt and groan. 'For her to do this she must have been under a lot of pressure or had totally cracked. She was a nice woman, or at least, she had a really nice side to her - maybe that's the only side I saw - but I can't see her just doing this out of casual spite or anger. Nobody kills themselves on a whim, do they? This was all seriously premeditated, the culmination of many things, like.'

'I was just saying to Jules, that last Boudica Society meeting must have been the breaking point for her. She was shouted at, abused and laughed at by Diane and by everyone else there. It was nasty and personal. On top of the bullying from Florence, she'd just had enough and was emotionally crushed by the whole thing. She wanted it to all stop but wanted to somehow get back at Diane and the rest of them who had spent so long attacking her, but I also think she was angry at herself for pretending she knew nothing about Boudica being from Teesside. She just wouldn't give them the pleasure of the truth and knew killing herself in front of them would stay with them for life. She'd given you the brooch so knew they wouldn't get their hands on it. It was ironic that Martin was there just beforehand. I wonder if she contemplated keeping him there to torture him with the image of her dying, too.'

'No, she seems to have dismissed him straight away. She didn't want her plans to be interrupted. As much as she disliked him by the end, the pain of her suicide was only for Diane - the D in the diary - but I reckon the two girls turned up unexpectedly and so they got both barrels as well. It was them who left the front door open,' said Jeff, who then raised an index finger. 'I don't think she'd made up her mind to kill herself when she dropped the brooch in my bags. I think she dumped it on me with the full intention of coming around and getting it back. But once she'd decided to end it all, there was no point and she probably just assumed I'd bin it as piece of junk that had fallen in the bag which, to be fair, is probably what I would have done, if I'd found it at all. The important thing though, like you said, is that Diane didn't get it.'

He began filing records alphabetically in his racks. 'I tell you what, though, it explains why I felt all along that something was wrong. I fucked up on who did what, but I always knew it wasn't right in some way. Poor old bird though, eh, Susan I mean. She must have been really sick of life and bloody angry. Weird though because, I dunno, you can't tell, can you? I mean, we saw her, what, most weeks, didn't we? And you'd not have known she was so depressed or desperate, would you? I wouldn't, anyway.'

'No but then did you realise I was suicidal the last time I was depressed? I nearly jumped out of my window.'

Jeff stood and looked at him with his mouth open. His eyes wide. 'Really? Fucking hell, Nick. Don't go doing that, man.'

'I don't want to. Not now. But I did.'

'Fuck, This is all new to me. Who would I talk to about live albums recorded at the Fillmore East if you snuffed it?'

'You've got Luke now.'

'Oh yeah. I forgot. OK then, go ahead. No no...I don't mean that, obviously.'

'One thing I've learned from all the therapy sessions is that we're all alone in our own heads and if you want to change the way your brain is, you have to do a lot of work. It isn't just something you flick a switch and alter.'

'We're all alone in our own heads...sounds like a Doors lyric, that,' said Jeff, putting a copy of their Strange Days album into the rack. 'So that's the mystery solved, as it were, and what lesson have we learned?'

'What's that line from 'Jack and Diane'?

'Oh, god, don't look to John Cougar Mellencamp for philosophy, I beg of you.'

'Something about life still goes on even when you're sick of it.'

'Much like his records.'

'Me and Jules are going to see Brian Salmon tomorrow morning to look at the stuff he's dug out of his fields if you want to come along.'

'I can't go tomorrow - I've got a dentist appointment. He's going to drill me a filling or three. So why are you doing that?'

'See if we can find any more Boudica stuff. Although there's been so much shit around the whole thing, I'd actually love to see her relocated to Teesside. It'd be a big thing for the region, wouldn't it? Jules would as well. It'd be a legacy for Susan.'

'Definitely. Not convinced your man on the street is overbothered with 2,000-year-old warrior queens, mind. They're more vexed over the price of drink and petrol...especially if they drink petrol.'

'Aye, you might be right. Jules is mad keen on it all, though.'

'Are you going to do anything special when she comes down next week?'

Nick laughed. 'Aye, you might say that.'

Jeff shook his head. 'You're like a couple of kids, you two.'

'Sorry big man, I'll try to keep the public displays of affection down to a minimum.'

'Quite bloody right...remember what I said about having a wedding an' all, I could do with another free piss up. That awards do was a classic - so if you're not going to get hitched, hurry up and win something else, eh!'

He laughed and began to walk out of the shop. 'I'll see what I can do. I'm sure Julie will be prepared to get wed just to give you a big party.'

'Seems fair enough to me,' said Jeff. He held up an album by A Band Called O, a mid-70s group who did a proggy sort of rock. 'What the hell do I file that under? A, B or O?'

Nick squinted. 'You've got to go with O, not least because they changed their name to The O Band later and you want to have that in the same place, don't you?'

'Aye, I'm tempted to go with A but O makes sense. See all the problems I have to sort out? People think this job is a piece of piss but it's dead hard, really.'

'I'll see you later, Hairy Boy.'

He walked out of the shop but Jeff called him back.

'Hey Nick! Seriously though...she's the one isn't she? Julie, I mean, not A Band Called O.'

'If she's not the one then no-one is,' he said with a smile.

'Well, there you go, then. The job's a good 'un. Make sure you get in some Stella for the wedding reception and not that overpriced cider stuff. What's it called again? Ah, yeah, champagne. I'll do the disco for you and at a discounted rate too, that'll be your wedding prezzie!'

Nick laughed and walked off up Commercial Street.

CHAPTER 11

The following morning he drove to Norton and collected Julie. She bounded out of the house in chunky cream Arran sweater and old blue jeans.

'Morning, gorgeous,' he said, grinning.

'Hello, sexy,' she said, slapping him on the thigh, excitedly.

He handed her a printout from Google maps.

'It's not far to the Salmon farmhouse. Tell me when we get to the turn off from Junction Road,' he said, driving away from her flat.

'I'm excited about being a part of this Queen of the Tees thing,' said Julie.

'Yeah, I really hope she was a Teessider now. It'd be awful if it was all a massive mistake after all the heartache it's caused. I can't believe we got to the bottom of it all. Pleased we have, mind, even if the outcome is basically really bloody awful. There's no happy ending, is there?'

'No. It's horrible,' said Julie, 'you did really well to find it all out, though.' They went quiet for a couple of minutes.

'Have you ever met this Brian Salmon bloke?' she asked.

'I might have done way back in the early 80s when I was at the Northern Echo with Big Fish but if I did, I don't remember. I tend not to mix with millionaire landowners much.'

'He sounded nice on the phone. I think he was surprised that no-one had ever asked him to dig around on his land. He'd watched Time Team on the telly and said history had always interested him.'

'Well, we should take anything that looks as old as the brooch to Diane to identify,' he said. 'She'll be in charge of the project to dig the site I would think, if she's well enough.'

'I called her office yesterday but there was no reply. I'm hoping she's sought medical help. Take a right here at Blakeston Lane.'

Soon they were driving out into the countryside and surrounded by farmland on all sides. It actually felt like they were a long, long way out of town when they were little more than a mile or two from Norton.

'Take a left here.'

They swung onto a single-track road that headed up a slope towards a large old farmhouse, pulling onto a long sweep of gravel before turning off the engine.

'This is very grand,' said Julie, looking up at the house.

'Must be one of the finest old Georgian houses in the area. Cracking view, as well.'

They got out and stood for a moment, taking in the scene. It was quiet. Crows cackled to the east, flapping above the copse of yew trees that Susan had identified as the Boudica burial site, a few hundred yards down a sloping field. The air was fresh with the smell of ploughed soil and horse muck.

'Do you fancy living in the countryside?' asked Nick as they walked up to a large side door. Beyond were rows of stables - a couple of horses stuck out their heads and took a look at them.

'Yeah, I'd love it. I'd live round here in a heartbeat,' she said without hesitation.

'Yeah I think it might be time to move out of town sometime soon. We should make a life in the countryside.'

'We?'

'What?'

'You said "we".'

'Well, we're going to live together again, aren't we? I'm not letting you get away from me again.'

She grinned and nodded, ramming her hands in her pockets to keep them warm,

'I think it's a fantastic idea, though I don't know how we'll manage it given our current circumstances.'

'We'll work something out somehow, Jules, where there's a will and all that. We need somewhere with big open fires. We'll get snowed up in the winter and drive a Land Rover.'

She hooked her arm into his.

'And we'll have dogs and cats.'

'Definitely. Lots of them.'

He kissed her on the forehead.

'Some peace and quiet will be a pleasant change from the A61 running outside my flat.'

She patted him on the backside as he rapped on the back door using its large iron knocker. The sound of a dog barking and scrabbling at the door was followed by footsteps.

A tall, thickset man opened up. He was in his late 60s, red faced and with wind-blown, thinning, wild white and ginger hair.

'Hi, is it Brian?' asked Julie.

'Yes yes...you must be Julie and Nick...come in, come in...don't stand on ceremony...I apologise in advance for the dog, she's been out in the fields and I've not had chance to wipe off her paws so I hope you've not got your best clothes on.'

A Dalmatian ran around them giving little yelps of excitement and pawing at their legs. Nick ruffled its ears while Julie stroked it across the back.

'This is a fantastic house, Mr Salmon, and such a nice setting as well. You'd never know you were on the edge of Teesside.'

'Not until you see the chemical works in the distance, anyway,' he laughed loudly. 'Are you both local?'

'I was brought up in Fairfield,' Nick said.

'And I was born in Hardwick and live in Norton; you can almost see my house from here, actually.'

'Ah, Norton. I love the old part, not so keen on some of the new developments, but we need new houses, don't we? I wrestle with it all the time. Should I sell more land for development? Everyone without a house wants new houses but everyone who's got one doesn't want new houses built next to them. It's a catch 22. Come through to my study.'

He led them into a capacious room lined with books. At one end was a large, red leather-topped desk.

'I took the trouble of getting some of these things out from storage,' he said, picking up a box and carrying it to his desk.

'How long have you been farming here?' asked Julie.

'We've had the land since the late 19th century. I took over from dad in 1965. I always had a passing interest in archaeology so every time anything interesting was ploughed up, I'd put it to one side. They may be something or nothing.'

He took off the lid and inside, wrapped in tissue paper, were small fragments of pottery, metal and tiles.

Julie unwrapped a few but they all looked rather anonymous to the untrained eye. They looked like rubble to Nick. While there were hundreds of pieces, there was nothing as obviously interesting as the brooch Susan had found. It was entirely possible that these finds spanned 1,500 years of history. A piece of medieval pottery looks like a piece of Roman pottery to someone whose main job is writing about football.

'Have you ever found anything whole like this?' asked Julie, taking out the picture of Jeff holding the brooch. He peered at it.

'Not really. It tends to be fragments,' said Brian.

'We think the brooch being held by this large hairy man was actually dug up on your land, just east of the golf club, in that copse of yews down there. An academic called Susan Rutherford found it and gave it to him,' said Nick, handing him the photo. 'That's Susan's nephew, Jeff. He found it in his potatoes.'

'Where?'

'In his potatoes.'

'In his potatoes?'

'Yeah, in his potatoes.'

'Good grief.'

He smiled and then stopped and squinted at the picture again, more closely this time.

'It's something to do with Boudica,' added Julie. 'There are theories that she was from around here and not from Norfolk as everybody has always assumed.'

The older man tapped his finger on the photo. 'This does look familiar...very much so. Hmmm,' he scratched his head, 'Susan...who, did you say?'

'Susan Rutherford,' said Julie.

'Ah, ha...yes...yes,' he muttered and began looking along a shelf.

'Have you dug up anything like that before?' said Nick, looking at what appeared to be an old belt buckle.

'Yes I have, many years ago now. Not dug up, but found. I'm just looking for my old photo albums, they're here somewhere. Hold on...ah, here they are.'

He pulled out two leather-bound albums and flicked through them. They were full of old black and white photographs covered in a sheet of tissue paper. The date written on the cover page in pencil was "Jan-Jul 1959".

'When I was a teenager I was sweet - as we rather modestly used to call it back then - on a girl called Susan Hall. She was two or three years younger than me and we used to go walking here on the Blakeston estate because she was from not far away in Roseworth. One day we were walking across a field and...ah yes, here it is.'

He turned the album towards them, tapping a finger at one photo in particular.

It was a picture of a dark-haired man in a tweed jacket and girl in sturdy-looking trousers, her hair in a headscarf.

'Oh, fizzin' hell,' said Julie suddenly, her hand across her mouth.

'What?' said Nick, looking closer at the image.

'That's Susan, isn't it?' said Julie.

Nick went cold. How could she tell? It looked like any old 1950s photo.

'It's me and who I knew as Susan Hall and in her hand, if you look closely, is that brooch your friend is holding in your picture. Or it is one very like it. Let me get a magnifying glass.'

He pulled open a drawer and produced a circular glass magnifier. The girl was clearly holding the same brooch. Nick could even make out the intricate pattern that made up the letter B.

'Wow. That's amazing, Brian. So Susan Hall became Susan Rutherford.'

'It would seem so. '

'You can tell it's her. She has the same small nose and lips,' said Julie, taking the album from Nick.

'It's a long time ago now, obviously, but I think we found that lying in a ploughed field not far from here. She was a lovely girl. Very intelligent. I was very sweet on her but then one day I was told she had moved away all of a sudden. I was heartbroken,' he laughed and shook his head. 'Well, well, well...what a ghost from the past she is. It's been such a long time since I even thought of Susan.'

'I'm afraid she actually died in October,' said Nick.

'Oh. Oh, how sad.'

'She err...well she took her own life.'

'Oh, that's awful. Poor old girl,' said Brian with genuine sympathy.

'Actually Brian, we think she may have returned to do a test pit here at some point in 1996. Do you remember that?'

He frowned and shook his head. 'No, there's never been a dig on our land as far as I know.'

'We have her notes from the dig - it was in that copse of yew trees - could she have somehow done it in secret?'

'I'm sure she didn't come to see me about it. For obvious reasons, I'd have remembered. When did you say she did it?'

'July 1996,' said Nick.

Brian Salmon brought his hands together and clapped once.

'I was living in Canada that year...we have land out there, too - or rather, we did back then - and I was acting as estate manager for a while. I came back home a couple of times but I left the place in the hands of my manager, Frank Yeaman. He could have given permission for a dig of some sort, especially if it wasn't a big affair. He had that sort of authority. Anything major would have gone through me.'

'Could he confirm that for us?' asked Julie.

'Sadly, Frank died three years ago. But I can imagine that's what happened. Oh, dear, dear...it's all such a shame, as I'd like to have seen Susan again. We were only together for a summer but these things tend to stay with you, don't they?'

'Why did she move away?' asked Julie.

He shook his head.

'I never knew. No-one told me and I didn't know her family. Like I said, it was a summer romance. In those days when someone moved away it was very hard to find them again. There really wasn't any easy way to do it so, as one does, I just moved on. Three years later I was married to Grace and the following year we had Stevie.'

They went back into the kitchen and had coffee around the kitchen table.

'Do you live here alone?' asked Julie.

'Yes, I do now. Grace died last year. The kids are all grown up, obviously, so there's just me and my boy here,' he said, stroking the dog. 'It's too big by far but I can't face downsizing. I've lived here my whole life. One can't just uproot oneself like that at my age and I can't see myself living in a care home. For a start, they always have those odd high-backed chairs. Have you noticed? Why do they think us oldies need extra-long backs on their chairs? Very odd.'

They all laughed.

Brian was a good sort. He wasn't as posh as Nick had assumed and was very expressive, with watery blue eyes. Where his son was brash, vulgar and egotistical, his father was softly spoken and polite, and had a fine line in wit and self-deprecation.

'Would it be OK if I take your box of artefacts to Durham University?' asked Julie. 'Just to make sure there's nothing very unusual or interesting in there.'

'Be my guest, Julie.'

'Obviously, I'll let you know if anything is especially interesting or unusual. I think they might be in touch with you soon anyway - they'll want permission to dig the potential Boudica burial site that Susan found.'

'Splendid. I shall welcome them. I shall look forward to the dig with great interest. Land is a mysterious thing. On the one hand it's the soil with which we grow food and such day to day and, on the other, it's a historical document and a connection with all our ancestors. I've always been aware that I am but a custodian of the land. We're all just passing through, aren't we?'

Maybe he'd been a big dope smoker in his youth; he seemed to have the cosmic-tinged outlook on life of an old head.

He waved them goodbye as they turned around on the gravel and took off back down the track.

'What a lovely old chap,' said Nick as they left.

'He's a teddy bear of a man. Almost the exact opposite of Stevie. And he was so good looking when he was younger, too. Very dashing. I could see what Susan saw in him.'

'Yeah, that was a real shocker to see her so young, wasn't it? And how weird for them to know each other. Well, I say weird, but they were local to each other and a similar age, so maybe it wasn't that weird. I wonder why she moved away,' said Nick.

Julie snorted. 'Well, back in 1960 if you moved away suddenly and didn't tell anyone where or why, it was usually only for one reason.'

'What, like?' said Nick.

'Nick! Think about it,' she said, frustrated at his slowness.

He turned onto Junction Road and headed back into Norton. It was noisy after the quiet of the countryside.

'I'm sorry, Jules. It might be obvious to you but it's not to me.'

'Young girls went away to have a baby, didn't they? You couldn't have an abortion. It was a disgrace to have a child out of wedlock, so they packed you off to a distant auntie until you had the child, which was then given up for adoption. Totally disgraceful but it happened all the time.'

'Wow, you think that's what happened to Susan?'

'It wouldn't surprise me. I wonder where she was sent.'

Nick thought for a moment.

'She said to me once at a car boot that her auntie...I think she was called Sylvia...lived near Shandy Hall. That's about 15 miles from Malton. I was talking to her about Laurence Sterne, you know, the bloke that wrote Tristram Shandy, because she had an old copy on her stall. Maybe she ended up living in Malton because she knew it from when she was younger. I mean, it's an odd place to live when most of your academic work is in Durham. It's a 75-mile drive up the A19 - not exactly an easy commute. She must have had a connection to Malton to make her home there.'

'If she was pregnant, who was the father? Has to be Brian,' said Julie.

'He'd have to be the top of the list, but you don't know, do you? Anything could have happened.'

'Oooh, I know what, I'm signed up to one of those ancestry websites,' said Julie. 'We could see if we can find Susan Hall and where she gave birth, presuming she didn't miscarry or anything. We know enough about her to make a start.'

When they got inside her flat in Norton, she turned on her computer and put on the kettle.

'The kids that Susan had later are in their late 30s or early 40s so she must have had them in the 70s. If she did have a kid when she was 17 or 18, she must have had it adopted or Jeff would have known about it.'

She took green tea into the living room.

'Talking of kids, listen, I've been thinking about something for a while now and since you've started talking about moving in together I want to ask you something important,' she said.

'You can choose the curtains and stuff Jules. I'm not bothered about all that.'

'Ha ha. Not interior décor decisions. I'm talking about having kids. Do you want us to have any?'

It was a massive question to just come out with like that. He sat down and she laid her legs across his lap.

'Wow. That's a biggie. Y'know what? I might be ready to think about it for the first time in my life. But I'm scared of it and I'm a bit old, like. I'm not sure an old dad is what a kid needs. How do you feel?'

She winced. 'I just don't feel motherly in any way whatsoever, though I feel a bit guilty about that and it might change as soon as I'm pregnant. I'm scared it won't, though. Part of me feels like I'm being selfish but then you're imposing your life and values on this little thing and maybe that's selfish, too.'

'I know what you mean. I feel like I'm still a kid myself so the idea of having one to look after just scares the shit out of me. I'm not against it at all, but what worries me is if we're both rubbish at it, it really damages the kid, doesn't it? I don't want to impose my shitness on to some innocent new life.'

'Don't be daft. You'd be a really good dad. It's me I'm worried about. I don't think I'd be any good. It's not surprising how we both feel - our parents didn't set good examples.'

'Maybe that's part of it. But we're probably thinking too much about it. Most people just have them and get on with it.'

'Yeah but they're not usually in their 40s. It's a lot less straightforward at my age.'

'And I might not be fertile. I've worn some very tight pants over the years.'

'Gettaway, the amount of the white stuff that comes out of you, some of it must be swimming well enough,' she laughed. 'But I might not have a lot of eggs left for you to fertilise.'

'That makes you sound like a hen. And I'm sure you'd be a great mam, by the way. I'm the loony one. I don't want to pass on that gene. But I think we'd have great kids. Probably really clever, nerdy ones - and good looking, as long as they took after you.'

'You think? It would be amazing to put our DNA together and see what came out. But if we're going to do it, we'll have to do it quite quickly and that means we'd have to settle down somewhere, doesn't it?'

'Yeah, well, I think we might be able sort something out. I can move out at a month's notice and you could put this place on the market or rent it out. But you're forgetting something.'

'What, like?'

'If we're thinking of having kids, we've got to actually have The Proper Sex. According to my O-Level biology class I believe that is essential to the whole process of pregnancy.'

'Well that won't take long, will it? A couple of minutes at best.'

She rubbed his crotch with her foot.

'Y'know...as long as we've got the internet I can work anywhere and OK, you need to be near-ish to Durham for college but that's all sort-out-able. We could even get somewhere on Teesside. We could move within a month or two.'

'You're really serious about doing this now, aren't you? You've really surprised me with all this talk today.' She cocked her head on one side and grinned. 'What's brought all this on?'

'What?'

'This talk about getting a place together so soon. We wanted to make sure we could make it work between us this time. You were, like, massively worried about that and wanted us to go slow. That's what the last six months have been about. Why the change of heart?'

Suddenly, he could see their future. Maybe it was what Marc Lewis had said about changing your life in order to change you as a person. It had happened to both of them or was in the process of happening. Through what had happened to Susan he realised that keeping your illness to yourself was needlessly destructive - you had to deal with it on the days you were well and not just when you were ill. Maybe being sober had helped clear his mind.

'We're both a bit different now, Jules; breaking up changed us for the better, or maybe we're still changing. It's just become really obvious to me. When I'm here like this or earlier when we were on the Blakeston estate, it just feels right being together now, doesn't it? Me and you. It was meant to be. I don't want to go home and be on my own, I want to be with you. It feels like we should share our lives properly, like adults. I'm not sure I really did want that before but now I know I do. And you and Jeff and Marc all reckon the therapy has had a positive effect. I'm older or rather, I feel older, more grown up and a little less fucked up. And I swear I'm more in love with you now than I ever was before, or perhaps I'm just more capable of allowing myself to love you properly. I think that's it, yeah. That's the therapy kicking in. I'm waffling on. Does any of this make any sense?'

It seemed easier to talk about love than at any time in the past.

'Of course it does, you big soppy get, come here.' She held her arms out to him and he fell into them.

'We've probably both grown up and stopped being so selfish and so self-absorbed. When you were depressed it just used to annoy me that you weren't the funny, sexy man I wanted to be with. I felt let down by it, like you were withholding the real Nick from me and that it was my fault somehow.'

'How could either of us have known how to deal with it? I didn't understand it. We both ended up selfishly withdrawing from each other. We won't do that again. Not after what we've been through. Not after all this thing with Susan. It's taught me a lot about being true to yourself.'

'And if you do get depressions again - which seems likely really, doesn't it - I know it'll still be difficult but I think I can cope, and I want to help you cope.'

'You don't mind that?' he said, stroking her hair.

'I'd rather it didn't happen, but it's who you are and I bloody love you, so what am I going to do?'

'I can't promise to be perfect but I will keep working on it all, that much I can promise. I'll keep in therapy. I know I've got to keep open emotionally and not just try and tough it out in my head like I always have.'

She took his hands. 'That's good enough for me.'

They lay in each other's arms stretched out on the sofa. She kissed him and grinned.

'What?' he said, grinning back.

'You.'

'Me? What about me?'

'I can read you like a book.'

'You reckon? And what's written on me, then?'

'That you're very horny and want to have sex, but as usual, you're too shy or polite to ask me. It's allowed y'know. You don't have to look so apologetic.' She let out a gurgling laugh.

He laughed. 'Sorry, well, that doesn't take much sussing out, these jeans are a bit tight.'

She rested her hand on his groin. 'Hmm, they don't leave much to the imagination, do they?'

'Are you sure you don't fancy spending a couple of minutes making a baby?' he said, pulling her close up to him.

She laughed again, 'What are you like? Of course I do. I've been really bloody fancying it for months,' she began to unzip his jeans.

'I'm not sure I can remember what to do, though, Jules,' he said, innocently as she put her hand in his pants.

'There's not much to remember is there? One. Get cock hard. Two. Push in and out of hole until woman makes screaming noise. Three. Add your special gravy. Simple. You've got number one sorted all ready.'

'Add special gravy? Good god. I'll just write that down for future reference. Can you draw me a diagram?'

'We can make an instructional video if you like.'

'Lovely, and you can include some footage of you doing your ping pong ball trick.'

She laughed, put a hand on his chin and guided his face to hers. 'But if you can somehow remember how to do it, you can put on a Durex, loverboy. We need to plan having kids. I've avoided getting up the duff in the heat of the moment since I was 16; I'm not going to start now.'

'Sensible thinking, but I've not got any Durex. I never think ahead, do I?' he laughed and flopped onto his back with a groan. She reached into her back pocket.

'No. But I do, don't I?' She gave silly, toothy grin and took a contraceptive packet from her back pocket.

Half an hour later they sat back down at her computer, both flushed in the cheek after their exertions.

'Well that's a relief.' he said.

'What? Having The Proper Sex? Is it a weight off your bollocks, luv?"

'Yup. I'm about a kilo lighter now, I reckon.'

She giggled a little. 'At least a kilo, aye. I don't know where you get all that stuff from. Now, where were we before we got so randy? We need to think with our brains and not our groins. We know that Susan was 64 when she died so that means she was born in 1942. We should be able to find her birth certificate, which will give us her full name and date of birth. She was born on Teesside, wasn't she?'

'Yeah, somewhere in the Stockton area, Jeff reckoned. And Brian said she was from Roseworth,' said Nick.

She entered the year, Susan's name and Stockton-on Tees in the births register. There was just one.

'Here we are, look, Susan Francis Hall, born April 5 1942 in Billingham. That must be her. To parents Sidney Hall and Margaret Robinson. They were both teachers. Okay, now we've got her full name and date of birth, let's see if there are any records of her giving birth under that name.'

She loaded the relevant page, entered the details and clicked the search button.

This produced one single entry.

Nick leaned forward excitedly. 'Look...look!' He pointed at the screen. 'Susan Francis Hall, a son born on July 25 1961 in Malton Hospital. That must be her! She was pregnant!'

Julie turned to look at him. 'Eeee, fizzin' hell...Susan has a bit of a history, eh? I wonder what happened to the boy?'

'Must have been adopted at birth. Why doesn't it say his name? It usually says the kid's name, doesn't it?'

'Yeah, must be something to do with the adoption. Maybe he hadn't been named before being farmed out or something. See they've put "n/a" in the space for father's name. So she wouldn't say who it was. She was keeping it a secret. Secret secrets, she was all about secrets, wasn't she? Poor Susan. I keep thinking of her being so desperate.'

Nick sat back in his seat and cracked his knuckles. 'You see someone like her and you just don't know the backstory she's carrying around, do you? She had a kid at 18 after a summer romance, she was probably having non-heterosexual feelings at that time too, ended up getting married and having two more kids and all the while must have been at war with her true nature, and that's before we even get to the academic issues.'

Julie sat back and folded her arms across her chest, shaking her head. 'We're often so quick to be judgemental about people when we don't know what they've gone through or where their minds are really at.'

'But it was on those walks with Brian that she got started on her career by finding that brooch. Should we tell Diane, do you think?'

'She might already know a lot of it. Susan probably confided in her at some point,' said Nick.

'Do you reckon?'

'Yeah. I mean, if you'd had a kid, you'd have told me.'

'Maybe she knows who the father was, then.'

He nodded. 'Though I'm not sure it's our place to even ask her, really. It's really none of our business, is it?'

Julie laughed. 'That's a bit too sensitive for you, lad. Considering other people's feelings isn't usually your strong point.'

He ruffled her hair playfully. 'See, I'm changing from a twat into a saint. But you can take her those other finds. I'm sure she'd like to see them. And then she can set about the admin needed to get a dig done on Brian's land.'

'Okay, I'll do that tomorrow. She's usually in her office mid-morning. I'll have more time then and I might take her to lunch, too.'

Jack & Danny's was busy as Nick walked in at just after 8pm. Jeff was in a corner with Luke.

'I see you quickly replaced me as a drinking buddy,' said Nick, sitting down with a glass of fizzy water.

'A man can't ruin his body on his own, it's not healthy,' said Jeff, raising his pint of lager. 'Where've you been?'

'I told you the other day, I went up to Teesside.'

'Oh, the glamour!'

Luke laughed. 'I've never been to Teesside, what's it like?'

'You know California?' said Jeff.

'Yeah?'

'Well, it's nothing like that.'

'Me and Jules met Brian Salmon actually, up at his big farmhouse...nice bloke.'

'A case of like father not like son, then,' said Jeff. 'What were you doing there?'

Nick filled him in about the artefacts found on Brian's estate.

'The thing is, and this will blow your mind, he knew Susan when she was 17 or 18. They had a summer romance. They found your potato brooch - that's what got her interested in archaeology. Then she suddenly moved away from home without telling him or anyone why. Long story short, Susan was up the duff and gave birth to a boy in Malton Hospital. We looked it up on an ancestry website.'

Jeff's eyebrows were raised throughout his tale, his right hand slowly stroking his beard.

'Christ almighty, how many more surprises is she going to spring on us? She didn't move to San Francisco and start singing with Big Brother and the Holding Company as well, did she?'

'If she did turn out to be Janis Joplin I almost think I'd be unsurprised.'

'Aye, well, we did think your dad played bass for Grand Funk Railroad, didn't we?'

'We did.'

'He didn't, did he?' said Luke They both laughed.

'Course not, Lukey. He was on tour with Gentle Giant at the time.'

'So what happened to her kid?' asked Luke, picking at a pluke.

'Adoption, we reckon. Happened all the time back then when kids were born out of wedlock. But there was no information trail that we could find. I'm not even sure it's possible from back then.'

'So you reckon Brian Salmon was the daddy?'

'Can't be certain, but there's a good chance, isn't there?'

Jeff turned to Luke to explain: 'See, this Salmon fella, he's mega-rich and owns loads of land and racing stables. So the kid would have inherited the whole of his estate. I mean, that's worth millions.'

'Only if it were a lad,' said Luke. 'First-born males that inherit innit?'

'He's right. That's how the aristos do it anyway,' said Nick. 'Is Stevie his oldest kid?'

Jeff nodded. 'Aye, jammy fat wanker inherits the lot; he's got a sister who's about five years younger.'

'Julie is going to take Diane Edwards out to lunch tomorrow, tell her about all it and see if she wants to apply to do a dig on Salmon's land at Susan's Boudica burial site.'

Jeff raised a finger. 'Talking of tomorrow, I'm off to Northallerton to look at bikes. There's a garage up there that's got some cheap deals, special offers, like. So I'm going to see if any makes the Evans thighs throb with pleasure. If you want to tag along, Lukey here is minding the fort while I'm out.'

'Aye, alright. I'd fancy riding a bike if it wasn't so bloody cold in this country.'

'Soft shite,' said Jeff.

'And as if to confirm that fact, I'm away home to get some kip and do some work,' said Nick, getting up.

'I'll pick you up at nine,' said Jeff.

Nick put up his thumb and walked home.

He was up early to see the morning light bringing a frosty night to an end with fingers of pink and gold stretching across the North Yorkshire skies. Snow clouds hung like wet duvets over the Pennines. Winter in the north could be magnificent. Cold, hard and cutting, it was capable of being epic, especially if bleak melancholy was your thing. As he'd said to Florence Farrell, he felt there was, at times, an inexplicable mystical feeling to being in the north that he was sure most northerners felt very strongly at some point in their lives. It never left you. It lived inside you like a seed buried deep. It can freeze your bollocks off but stir your soul.

He fried a small fillet of salmon, crumbled it into some scrambled eggs and had only just finished it as Jeff rang his bell.

'I hope this van isn't going to breakdown halfway up the A1,' said Nick as they took off along the A59.

'You're OK, I've serviced it.'

'But you don't know anything about servicing a van.'

'By servicing, I actually mean putting some washer fluid in.'

'Well, thank god for that.'

They went at a steady 40 miles per hour up the A1 on the inside lane.

'Jeff, we're going so slow that old ladies on bikes are overtaking us. This van is emasculating us.'

'You're a fine one to talk. It's you who's given up drinking. Anyway, we're not going slow; it's just that the world has speeded up.'

They took the A684 turning and headed west to the market town of Northallerton, the county town of North Yorkshire.

'Funny area, this,' said Jeff, 'not really Yorkshire, not yet Teesside. All the locals talk in Teesside-type accents but would probably take that as an insult.'

'I've always thought of it as one of Yorkshire's posh market towns. All tweed skirts and men in pink trousers. What is it with the pink trousers and the gold-coloured jumbo corduroys?'

'Yer posh landed types get issued with a list of clothes they're allowed to wear at birth...it's so they can spot one of their own at distance...but they don't want the grubby oiks wearing their uniform so they picked clothes that are so awful that no-one else would wear them. Hence your dudes in the pink pants and all those middle-aged women in head scarves.'

They pulled into a small garage on the outskirts of the town. It had been a petrol station but was now a mixture of motorbike retailer and garage. A man in blue overalls was working underneath a white van.

'Is Mickey around?' shouted Jeff.

He pointed to the showroom.

'How much do you want to spend on this bike?' asked Nick.

'Nothing, but I'll go up to two grand, two and a half, tops.'

It was bright and warm in the showroom.

'Alright, Mickey,' said Jeff, holding out his hand, 'we spoke on the phone. I'm Jeff.'

'Alright, mate. You wanted the Kwaka 2000 didn't you?'

'Aye, I wanted to take a look at it anyway. It was £2,000, wasn't it?'

He led them out onto the forecourt.

'Yeah, I'll not lie to ya, mate, it's been bloody thrashed, hence the low price. I'll throw in an MOT and 6 months tax an' all. If you can tidy it up yourself it's a brilliant bike and a great deal. Still goes like shit off a shovel an' all.'

It was a lovely-looking black and chrome motorbike. The seat was scuffed and torn and there were specks of rust on the chrome. Nick knew nothing about vehicles of any sort, let alone bikes, but this looked good.

'Are the shocks OK? I'm a bear-sized man so I don't want to snap it,' asked Jeff, bluffing that he knew anything about bikes.

'Aye, you'll be alright - and you can get someone on pillion - not as big a lad as you, like, but someone more...less...y'know...'

'Bear-sized,' said Nick, helpfully.

'I like the look of it, Mickey, can we take it for a spin?'

'We?' said Nick.

'Aye, you want a ride on it, don't you?'

'Not especially. I'm assuming you're a lunatic on a bike.'

'See how he treats me, you'd never guess we're married, eh,' said Jeff.

Mickey laughed and went to get two helmets.

Jeff straddled the bike and started the engine, which roared as a cloud of exhaust belched out. He gave Nick a look of delight. 'Sounds magnificent!' he yelled.

Mickey returned with the lids.

'There's half a tank in her so you'll be alright for a few miles,' he said.

Nick straddled the back of the bike. 'Is this just a way to get me to put my arms around you?' he said into Jeff's ear.

'Aye, I've fancied you for years.'

Nick gripped the back of the seat, Jeff opened the clutch and they took off up the Stokesley Road. As they were in open country with little traffic, he took it quickly up to 80. It was exhilarating and terrifying in equal measure. Acres of ploughed field and fencing flew past in a blur of brown, grey and green. It was bloody freezing and he was glad he was wearing a hat and gloves. In the distance the North York Moors stood in the shadow of a rain cloud. Although it was clearly a bit knackered and noisy as hell, the bike could really shift, especially moving from 30 to 70.

Jeff took them east along the A684 to within half a mile of the A19, pulling up in a lay-by.

Nick got off the bike; his legs were buzzing with vibration and his hands and feet were ice cold.

'Bloody hell, that was pretty good, wasn't it?' he said, removing the helmet.

Jeff emerged from inside his own, shaking his long hair and pushing it off his face.

'Fucking magic. It goes like stink.'

'Aye, it's bloody noisy and probably not in a good way - something's going to blow on it sooner than later, but then again, it's cheap, isn't it?'

'Exactly. I'll get greasy Chris Stainton to work on it. He'll do it for beer money.'

'Right, let's get back then and handover the wonga. I'm sodding cold.'

'What are you like? Big Jessie.'

Nick was about to put on his helmet when his phone rang.

He pulled it out of his pocket. It was Julie.

'I'd better just take this,' he said.

'I'm just going behind that bush for a piss, then,' said Jeff.

'Hey, Jules.'

Right away he knew something was wrong. Her voice was breathless and staccato.

'Nick...I've just been to Diane's office, it was open and on her desk was a suicide note - well...it's a letter actually...I can't go into details...there no time.'

His heart leapt. Not another bloody suicide. He could hear other voices near her. Women's voices. She went on: 'Don't say anything, just listen...I'm just about to drive down to the Boudica gravesite on the Blakeston estate. She's going there to kill herself, it says in the letter...I've got to stop her.'

Another voice, more distant shouted at her: 'Quick! Hurry, Julie!'

He recognised the voice. It was Florence Farrell.

'Jules...look, we're only 15 miles from there now...I can't explain...we're on a motorbike...me and Jeff.'

'A motorbike?!'

'Yeah...we should be there in about 20 minutes at most.'

He could hear her getting into the car and starting the engine.

'I'll be there in about the same, maybe a bit more...she's only about five minutes ahead of us, we reckon...' she said. 'I've got Flo and Sophie with me, they were here waiting for her but she's gone. She's had enough. It's finally broken her. We must stop her, Nick... she's going to do the Boudica thing. Die like her. Poison herself.'

'Fucking hell, these bloody drama queens. I'll see you there.'

Jeff emerged from the bushes. 'What's going on?'

'Diane Edwards is heading to the Boudica gravesite in Norton to kill herself.'

He raised his eyebrows. 'Well that'll spoil her day. Why's she doing that?'

'It doesn't matter, does it? Julie found her suicide letter, she's on the way there now to try and stop her but she might not get there in time so we've got to do likewise and at top fucking speed.'

'What? We've got to get the bike back.'

'Fuck the bike, this is life and death. It's only 18 miles or so.'

Nick pulled on the helmet. 'Get a shift on, Barry fucking Sheen!' he yelled, climbing onto the bike.

'Right, you want fast, I'll give you fucking fast,' shouted Jeff.

They flew off and joined the A19, which was choked with heavy traffic.

Jeff dipped into the outside lane to overtake a lorry only to get stuck behind a DHL van. As soon as it pulled in, he opened the clutch, changed up a gear and took off at high speed, hitting 80, 85, 90 and then 95. The bike was shaking and Nick's heart raced with the adrenaline. Would the bike blow up? It damn well felt like it. They went 10 miles in less than six minutes and then hit slowing traffic. The outside lane was closed off for roadworks and was filing into the inside lane. Soon they had ground to a halt. The A19 was choked, gridlocked and at standstill. Nick leaned forward and shouted at Jeff.

'You've gotta weave in and out of this lot to get through it. We'll never make it, otherwise.'

Jeff put the Kawasaki into first gear and slowly began to sneak between cars, vans and lorries. Hopefully no-one would try and block him off.

They got past the closed lane and traffic began to pick up a little as it spread out across the two open lanes. They rolled along at 30 for a mile. Just as there was a sign for Teesport, Thornaby, Wilton, Redcar, it thinned out and Jeff took off again, flying at 90 up a straight stretch of the A19. It felt like a race track. As they sped past the A66 turn off, the industrial magnificence of Teesside began to open up in front of them as they crossed the Tees flyover. In the distance the chemical works belched out white steam and smoke. The river ran underneath, the mighty Tees finding its way to the sea from way up in the northern Pennines.

Traffic jammed up the road again even though it was now three lanes. No matter what time of day or the state of economy, the Tees flyover always seemed to be choked with traffic.

'Do you know where you're going?' shouted Nick as the top of his voice.

Jeff nodded his head. It was an area they both knew like the back of their hands, having grown up in Stockton long before the Tees flyover was finished in 1975.

They passed the A1046 turn off to Portrack Lane. He could hear Jeff singing 'Dickens Home Improvement Hypermarket', a local advertising mantra from the 1970s which always proudly declared its location on Portrack Lane, Stockton. He laughed as they zoomed over the road at speed. Fucking hell, this was brilliant.

Julie had called at 10.29; it was now 10.50 and they had little more than three miles to go. The bike liked being at 50 more than 95 and handled well as he made a sharp turn onto Junction Road, up Station Road and out of Norton into the open countryside. Jeff's sense of direction was perfect.

Now they were in open countryside with tall bare hedges on one side and farmland rising to their right.

'Just take this single-track road until it runs out,' shouted Nick.

Jeff raised a thumb as they passed a farm on their left. As the road twisted in front of them, Nick was sure he caught a sight of a blue car ahead of them. Julie's Peugeot was blue. They rounded a bend - the road was nothing more than a farm track now - and there was her car up ahead. He watched as 300 yards away she screeched to a halt in a cloud of dust.

'That's Jules!' he shouted. Jeff sped them to the end of a track, which petered out into mud. To their right, the land rose on a slope towards a copse of yew trees, the same copse he'd seen from the other side at Brian Salmon's farmhouse.

Jeff applied the brakes heavily as they approached where the Peugeot was parked and the back end of the bike swung out as he did so. In a brilliantly scary manoeuvre they slid sideways to a halt in a cloud of dust and grit, Jeff just keeping control of the machine. Before the bike was even at a stop Nick was leaping off, pulling at his helmet and throwing it aside into the hedgerow.

They had been less than 20 seconds behind Julie. She was already out of the car along with Florence and Sophie.

'Look!' screamed Florence, pointing up the hill towards the copse.

It was Diane.

She was dressed in the long, dark-green velvet coat she had worn at the Boudica Society meeting and was walking in a circle inside the yew copse, weaving in and out of the trees.

She must have taken the top road and parked on the other side of the hill.

Julie vaulted over a wooden fence in one move and began sprinting up the hill. Nick followed behind her. She was five yards in front of him, sprinting at speed.

'Diane! Don't do it!' she shouted as she approached her, but Diane seemed wrapped up in her own thoughts, walking in a circle, talking to herself.

Julie got closer, now only 20 yards away.

'Diane! Diane! I saw your note. It doesn't have to be the end. Come on. We can talk about it. We know you didn't kill Susan! We know what she did,' she shouted in between gasps for air. Diane seemed to come out of her reverie, saw Julie approaching, let out an unholy scream, an invocation to Queen Boudica perhaps, took some capsules from her pocket and raised her hand to her mouth.

Now Julie was just 5 yards from her, Nick less than 10. But it was no use, those last steps seemed infinitely slow in covering the space between them. They were just not close enough to stop her.

Despite the pounding of the blood in his head and the freezing raw air hurting his lungs, he could see her swallow hard just as Julie was upon her.

'No! No you don't! You're not doing this! No! I will not fucking allow it!' screamed Julie and as she reached her, she grabbed her by the face, forced her mouth open with her left hand, and thrust her right hand down into Diane's mouth, two fingers probing down the back of her throat.

'Fucking throw up!' she screamed, shaking her. Diane's face was a mixture of fear and shock at what was happening. She was out to lunch, not really there at all and easily physically overpowered by Julie, who was taller and broader and stronger; she had her in a controlling grip.

The potassium cyanide capsules were already being dissolved by her stomach acid. They'd been inside her for 5 seconds and they would take less than 20 to do their deathly work. Julie held her head back by her hair and thrust her fingers as far down her throat as far as possible. There was no resisting; Diane gagged once, twice and a third time. Julie was in up to her wrist and then out it all came, a flood of beige. She retched the slurry all over Julie's arm, duffel coat and Boro scarf.

'More! C'mon Diane, more! I won't let you die. You've so much to live for...this is not your time,' she screamed in her face and thrust her fingers to the back of her throat again. This time she retched so powerfully that it sent a gloop of semi-dissolved capsules flying out of her mouth onto Julie's shoulder. Diane convulsed forward with the power of the retch, letting out ghostly moans. One capsule was almost whole while the rest came out in a melted lump, their powder not yet released. Julie supported her to stop her slumping to the ground, holding her upright so she could vomit without choking.

Nick stood, his hands on his knees, getting his breath. Behind him came the two girls, both crying now, standing back in fear, scared witless by what was happening, shocked at seeing their lecturer attempting to kill herself out here on a windy slope in rural Teesside. This was a woman they had worshipped, who had been their leader, and here she was choking on Julie's fingers, being forced to empty the contents of her stomach against her will. All the bravado of the Boudica Society, all the dressing up and all the pretend had now dissolved. Reality, as it has a nasty habit of doing, had intruded all too nakedly into their fantasy world. This was life and death and life was only just winning.

Julie was relentless, probing at her throat time and again until Diane's guts were empty and she was retching green stomach bile. Whatever had been in her was now out. But had it been soon enough?

Julie let Diane fall to her knees, the green vomit-splattered coat billowing around her. Julie took a tissue from her pocket and tried wiping her hands and arm.

'You alright, Jules?'

'I think so, and I think she threw them up,' she said, pointing at the melted mulch of capsules now on the ground.

'Well she'd be...' he made a throat-cutting sign, '...by now if it was going to work, wouldn't she?'

Julie nodded and spat out a gob of thick saliva, recovering her breath.

'That was fucking amazing. Look at you. You're all covered in puke - you look like you've had a night out in Middlesbrough.'

She didn't laugh at his joke. Drained of colour and exhausted, she tried to get her breath back.

'I'm so sorry to have troubled you all,' sobbed Diane, adding quietly to herself, 'I wish I was dead.'

She looked up at Nick with the saddest eyes he'd ever seen. She was destroyed. It was sodding heartbreaking to see.

Voices came on the wind from the north. On the brow of the hill two figures approached. It was Stevie Salmon and his father Brian; they must have seen the commotion from the house. It was quite a gathering on his land. He waved at them as they approached. 'Nick...Julie...what...what's going on?' shouted Brian, who arrived ahead of his overweight, wheezing son.

'Bit of a long story. I'll tell you later, Brian - it was a suicide attempt.'

'Bloody hell. What's all this about? This one looks mad and this one's covered in puke!' shouted Stevie Salmon, pointing a finger at Diane and Julie.

Julie turned on him: 'Shut your vile mouth, you pig!'

'Hey, hey, alright sister,' said Stevie Salmon, tugging at his facial hair. Just for a moment it sounded like he was going to deploy his 'talk to the beard' punchline. If he wanted his face to remain unpunched, he should probably resist.

An ambulance roared down the lane with police cars in pursuit, sirens blaring. Jeff came walking up the hill.

'I called 999. Hope that was the right thing to do.'

Nick slapped him on the back. 'Nice work, man, good bit of Berry Sheen-ing there as well - you'd better call the garage or they'll think you've robbed their Kawasaki.'

'Already done that. Some heavy shit has gone down here by the looks of it.'

'You're not kidding, man,' said Nick.

The ambulance and a police car pulled up at the end of the lane.

'Come on lady, let's get you down this hill,' said Julie to Diane, helping her to her feet.

She stood unsteadily, her face drawn and pale except for the red welts on her neck and face left by Julie's hands. She turned to Julie, put her hands on her shoulders and looked in her eyes. A strong cold northeasterly wind blew, streaming out Julie's hair, almost yellow against a grey sky.

'What you just did...Boudica's spirit is in you, my girl...you are a warrior,' she nodded, patting her shoulders. 'Yes...a warrior queen.'

Julie shook her head. 'No, I'm not, Diane, I'm just a Teesside lass...and that's bloody well special enough for me.' She held Diane's arm and began walking her towards the flashing blue lights.

'She's survived, then,' said Jeff, standing alongside Nick as they passed.

'Yeah. Without Julie she'd be a corpse by now. Weird thought, that.'

'She took the rest of the capsules?'

'Yeah, she threw them up just...just there,' he said, pointing at the trail of vomit.

He went over and squinted at them. 'Four, yeah?'

'No, there were six. Susan took six, there were six left.'

'There's only four here...' he said, turning to look at Julie leading Diane by the left arm and, as he did, Diane's hand dipped into her right-hand pocket.

In a split-second the same thought occurred to both Jeff and Nick.

'She's got two in her pocket!' screamed Jeff and took off towards them, covering the 10 yards in huge strides, grabbing Diane around the shoulders, pulling her out of Julie's grip and to the ground like she was a rag doll who weighed nothing. She let out a scream.

Jeff pounced, straddling her and holding her arms in a vice-like grip so she couldn't raise them.

'Get off me, you big brute!' she screamed.

'No chance. Nick, get her hand.'

Nick crouched down and prized open her tight fist. There were two cyanide pills gripped against her skin. He pocketed them.

She screamed again. 'Stop! You have no right! Get off me, you shit! By Christ, it's like mother like bloody son! You fucking people are always holding me back. Let me up!'

'What are you on about?' asked Jeff as two police officers and two paramedics arrived, red faced.

'You! You're just like your mother!'

'You don't know my mother.'

She let out a bitter noise, spit flying in thick foam out of her mouth. 'Gaah! Susan was your mother, you cretin! She gave you to her sister to bring up. Your mother is not your mother and your father is not your father! He is!'

She tried to raise her hand in Brian Salmon's direction and then spat in Jeff's face. A thick, creamy dollop of saliva landed in Jeff's right eye. He wiped it away.

'Eh?! You're insane,' said Jeff, his face knitted into a frown.

'What's going on here?' said the police officer.

Julie began to explain as it all fell into place in Nick's brain. It all made sense now.

'Jeff, remind me when it's your birthday.'

'July 25th, why?'

'In 1961?'

'Aye. Why?'

The policemen were nodding at what Julie was saying. They let the paramedics attend to Diane, who was now weeping tears of hysteria.

Jeff, freed from his role as Diane's shackles, stood up.

'Jeff man, me and Julie found out that Susan's kid was born on July 25th 1961 in Malton Hospital.'

'Coincidence, surely.'

Nick shook his head. He called Brian over. He and Stevie had been standing well back along with the two girls, watching things unfold.

'Brian, this is Jeff... you remember we talked about when Susan Hall went away?'

'Yes...yes...I do,' he said, narrowing his eyes.

'She went away to have a baby, a boy. She was pregnant. Could that have been your child, Brian? I'm sure she wasn't a promiscuous 17 year old in 1960 and she was going out with you before she left.'

He stood with his mouth open, his watery blue eyes now wide.

His son looked at him. 'Dad?! Did you knock someone up?'

'Oh, shut up!' chided his father, red in the face with surprise and embarrassment.

'Hang on, hang on... this is just fucking mental!' exclaimed Jeff. 'If what you're saying is right, my mam is Susan, my dad is Brian and that makes my brother this fucking twat.'

'Thanks very much...the correct term is "this fucking fat twat", actually,' said Stevie Salmon in a way that, right there and then, was somehow exactly like Jeff.

Brian Salmon turned to him. 'It could be true, Jeff. Susan and I did have a...a...physical relationship...I never knew about a child, though. If I had, of course I would have supported her.'

Julie walked up to them. 'I'm going to go to the hospital with Diane and the girls. What's going on?'

'Turns out Jeff is Susan's son and Brian is his dad,' said Nick, nonchalantly.

'Oh yeah, I had that sussed out,' she said, slapping Jeff on the back and winking at Nick. 'I'll call you later.'

She walked off down the hill after the paramedics, who had Diane lashed to a stretcher.

For a few seconds they all stood looking at each other in silence.

Then Jeff held out his hand towards Brian. 'Nice to meet you, dad...nice bit of land this, err...can you lend me a tenner?'

CHAPTER 12

'Here's some good news. I just got all the paperwork about Susan's estate from Annabelle Proctor. Do you want to know the exact amount of money I've inherited?'

'Go on then. Make me jealous.'

Jeff took out a folded sheet of A4 on which various figures were listed.

'Alright, here goes. She left the house to me - that's valued at £395,000. There's a life insurance policy of £98,175, I get that...' he broke off to laugh at the numbers. 'I can't believe this, really...then there are other contents and valuables and money left in deposit and current accounts which is another £19,657, so it all comes to £512,832.'

'Not bad, big man. Not bad at all for doing nothing except be who you are.'

'I know, easiest half a mill I've ever earned. I couldn't believe it when the lawyer rang me up and said "You inherit most of Susan's estate, she's left the lot to you". It's incredible. There's no other word for it. '

'So when will you get your hands on all that?'

'The house will go on the market this week, so who knows how long that'll take to sell? The rest I'll have within a week or two.'

Nick flopped down on Jeff's sofa. A bus rumbled past the window, making the glass shake in the frame.

'So what's on your shopping list?'

'New flat. Got get out of this shithole. We half-millionaires can't live in squalor like the plebs, y'know.'

'Are you gonna buy one?'

Jeff pulled back the ring on a can of lager.

'Nah. I've thought about that. What's the point in sinking all your money into a mortgage at our age? I'll just rent a bigger place like yours. You can only live in one room at a time. As long as I've got a big space to put the records in, that'll do me. I'm not going to turn into lord of the bloody manor at my time in life.'

'Has Brian Salmon been in touch?'

'You mean Daddy?! Still can't believe that. Aye, he's a nice fella. We've had a few chats on the phone, like. He invited me up there but I thought it might look like I was on the sniff for an inheritance, so I've put it off. For now.'

'Big Fish will be bricking it in case Bri decides to make you his heir. First-born male and all that.'

'Ha ha, nothing I'd like better, if only to say to him, when he moans, "Talk to the beard, son...talk to the beard"! He pulled at his own facial growth.

'I should've seen the fucking resemblance between you two, man,' said Nick.

They laughed. Life had made a hard left turn for all of them in the months after Susan's death.

'It's unfortunate that your new brother is a bit of a wanker, mind.'

Jeff shrugged. 'Yeah, he is, but what can you do? You can't choose your relations. At least Brian is a good egg. He's got some interesting 60s stuff in his record collection, y'know.'

'He's got a record collection, has he?'

'Well, I had to ask him, didn't I? Turns out he's got first pressings of the early Dylan albums up to Blonde on Blonde, lots of Beatles, but best of all, a complete set of original Small Faces albums.'

'He's got good taste, then.'

'I know. He went a bit AOR in the 70s though. Eagles, Linda Ronstadt, that sort of thing.'

'I love the Ronstadt.'

'Aye, well, we all love her...it's the music I'm not keen on.'

'How's your mam been dealing with it all? I mean, she kept the fact that she wasn't your real mam from you for her whole life. I can't imagine what it's like holding a big secret for that long and then having it revealed.'

'Aye, it is weird. Turns out she didn't even tell the second husband when she remarried. Once Jimmy - who I thought was my real dad - once he died, she thought, right, I'm locking this in the vault and I'm not letting it come out. To all intents and purposes, only she and Susan and Diane were left alive who knew about it, but she knew it would all come out when the will was read because Susan had always intended to leave most of her money and stuff to me, her loveliest and hairiest son after the other kids had basically rejected her for being gay, which is pretty fucking cruel in my book. I mean, why get so upset about who someone wants to have sex with? I just don't see what difference it makes.'

'People are fucked up about sex, though, aren't they? Some people are, anyway.'

'Yeah, but even if you don't want to get all PC about it, it's just not worth worrying about. So your mam or dad or whoever likes having it off with women or blokes or whatever, so what? There's a lot of shit to worry about in the world and you're worrying about that? It's a loser's mentality.'

'When I met your mam outside the doctors' that day, she did look very worried.'

'I think she thought I might kick off about it all but I just said, "Look mam, I'm an old git, I can deal with this". Y'know...it's not even that uncommon a story. Happens all the time. Had a bit of a heart-to-heart with her about it. I think she's feeling quite liberated now. It's a weird feeling, but not a bad one. In fact, I quite dig it. And let's be honest, half a million pounds makes anything feel good. But obviously, I can see now why Susan always had an eye out for me when I was a kid.'

'Oh, did you hear that Diane's coming out of hospital this week?'

'Out of the loony bin, you mean.'

'The funny thing is that she was in the same place as my mam.'

'Ha. She'll have had enough of being told that the omelettes are being poisoned, then.'

'Well, exactly. That is mother's greatest paranoid hit. Julie reckons that the Boudica Society has fallen apart and disbanded. Without Diane's involvement they had no leader and I think that everyone got a lot of bad vibes from all this business, understandably enough.'

'Well they got what they wanted anyway - digging the site for Boudica's remains,' said Jeff.

'Jules was talking to Diane the other week and found out she never knew what Florence was up to, y'know.'

'What? She didn't know about the bullying and that?'

'Nope. Says she'd never have condoned that.'

Jeff shook his head. 'Really? I was sure they'd all conspired together.'

'Diane didn't even know about the existence of the brooch. Florence had showed her the sketch she'd made from Susan's sketch when she was younger. But no-one had ever actually seen that thing until we found it.'

'That Florence Farrell, she's a law to herself, isn't she? She didn't look so big and grown up at that copse, mind. She was crying, as I recall.'

'Yeah I think the whole thing has shocked a bit of sense into her.'

'What I still don't really understand is why Susan held out for so long on the Boudica brooch,' said Jeff, draining the last dregs out of his can.

'Julie reckons that's because to talk about where the brooch came from meant opening up the whole Pandora's box about her past, about Brian, about having you and giving you up to her sister. She just couldn't face that. It's a kind of psychological thing - you establish an alternative reality for yourself where the bad stuff hasn't happened and just get locked into it. I'm not even sure she was ever at ease with her sexuality. So it wasn't just denying Diane her glory, though it was that as well, it was revealing everything else tied up with the brooch.'

Jeff opened another can of Stella. 'Hang on, though, I thought Diane must have known about that all along, since the 70s like.' Nick shook his head. 'Nope. She'd only just pieced it all together.'

'How do you know that?'

'Jules has visited her in hospital a few times, hasn't she? They're quite friendly now.'

'That girl is a bloody angel. I hope you're not soiling her with your filthy ways.'

'I'm doing my best, believe me. I can't keep my hands and other bits of me off her.'

'I take it the wang, the dang and the doodle is now in full effect then?'

'Ted Nugent would be proud of us. Though that might not be something to be proud of given the fact that Ted is a nutter.'

Jeff laughed and put his thumbs up, frowned and then continued, 'I don't know about you, though, but I keep thinking of Susan. Y'know, just when I'm going about daily business. I still miss her and feel like I should've been able to help her. The fact we never spotted what was going on in her head just...I dunno...I can't get my mind around it. I feel like if someone is going to top themselves it should be more obvious. Were we just too insensitive? It bothers me, that, like.'

'Maybe, but she hid it all very well and she'd been hiding one thing or another her whole life. That's what I get sad about, really. I still miss her, too.'

Jeff nodded. 'It must be very weird for Diane, though; she owes her life to someone's fingers tickling her tonsils. So how did she find out about me and Susan?'

'Like Jules did...on the internet. That's why she was looking at you all funny when we first met. She was making the connection between what she'd discovered and your big hairy self sitting there.'

'But I could have been anyone.'

'She told Julie that she found the date of birth of Susan's kid and that it was a boy, suspected that a member of the family might have been given the child, because it was a common story in those days, eventually got to Jean, your mam, looked her up and found out that there was no record of her having a kid and yet she knew you existed, so where did you come from? It was just a hunch but if you remember, we were talking about you going to Donington in 1980, a month after your birthday, so she finally worked it all out from that.'

'Clever...you don't realise how much information you're giving away about yourself, do you? I still don't see how she knew Brian was my dad, though.'

'Yeah, I wondered that as well but apparently Susan had talked about the fling with Brian without mentioning the pregnancy when she first met Diane. They went over all their past relationships, you know, the way new couples do.'

'I've never really been a new couple so I'll have to take your word for it.'

'So she'd mentioned him in the past, and once Diane found out about the kid and when it was born, she could be pretty sure it was from her summer lovin' with Brian.'

'One thing I don't get. You know we found out that Diane had signed that PO box form for Susan?'

'Aye.'

'Was Susan trying to make it look like Diane was guilty of setting it all up? Trying to frame her, like? I mean, that was the obvious conclusion that I jumped to.'

'I wondered that at first, but I don't think she was. I was talking to Jules about this. Diane remembered Susan giving her the form in her office one week when they were talking to each other. She was in a big hurry, had some other papers to sign and gave her the PO box form and said "Can you just put my name on that?" Diane didn't even really clock what it was. She never gave it a second thought. She thought she was just helping her get some paperwork done. That's why it was Susan's writing on the form but Diane's signature. Julie thinks it was another little act of revenge by Susan on Diane to implicate her in the acquisition of the poison that killed her. Not so that she'd get nicked for her murder but so that she knew, in a way, that she'd helped kill her.'

'Bloody hell. That is properly messed up.'

'Yeah, in hindsight it's easy to see why Diane was on the verge of a breakdown. Jules reckons that last 90 minutes she had with Susan before she killed herself was one long argument and row with lots of tears and recriminations. Diane had brought over that signed copy of The Queen of the Tees for her. Susan had pulled out all those papers and thrown them at her.'

'Ah, so that's why her office was all so untidy. I see now. Another green tea?' said Jeff, pointing to his empty mug

'Aye, go on, then.' Jeff got up to boil the kettle. 'Talking of which - that tea bag - how did that get in the back garden?' he shouted from the kitchen.

'When they legged it out the back door. Diane picked up her empty mug. Put it on the drainer, took out the tea bag and ran, dumping it in the garden and then dumping the empty cyanide packet out in the field. She was in a panic and I reckon she just wanted it to seem like no-one had been there.'

'And that worked. That's exactly what the cops thought.'

'Yeah. The cops were really sloppy, though. It was like you said - they found a narrative and stuck with it. They got the right result though, I suppose that's what they'd say. But if we could work this out, they should have,' said Nick.

Jeff returned with his tea.

'One hippy tea for Mr Healthy. Dunno how you've stuck to being sober for over three months. Don't you bloody crave one?'

He didn't, and had got out of the habit. Now it even seemed a bit of a strange idea to get pissed every night and he'd realised that it was rituals and habits that he needed to make his life work and if replaced the drink ritual and habit with another, he could still keep life together. Then again, his resolve to be sober hadn't been tested by a deep, black mood yet. As such it was best to just think that you'd not drink today and let the future take care of itself.

'But has it made you healthier in the head, do you reckon?' asked Jeff. 'Are you still Mr Loony Tunes?'

'I've not had a really bad depressive thing since I stopped, but it's not been perfect either, like. I still get down and turned in on myself. I still keep doing this sometimes.'

He held up his right hand where his nails had marked the skin.

'But not as often or as bad as I used to, so that's some progress. Julie's helped me out...or at least, she knows how to deal with my moods better, though there's not much she can do to stop them coming on...but still, it's not anywhere near as bad as it used to be and I feel better in myself, like. So maybe being sober is helping. I feel brighter and stronger without it and it doesn't seem to have adversely affected my work. Ironically, the only thing I really miss is actually craving a drink. You know that feeling when you really get the itch to sink something cold and boozy? I miss that sort of excitement. But I don't miss the hangovers or even feeling drunk, weirdly enough, given I've been drunk my whole life.'

'I don't get hangovers.'

'I know you don't, but only because you never sober up.'

Jeff laughed. 'You've discovered my secret! Don't go telling anyone else.'

'I've still got the regular therapy sessions, though. Talking about the shit in your head is quite a good thing for me and it helped give me an insight into how I ended up like this. It seems to have allowed me to get a perspective. We're uptight Northerners by birth, but that's not always a healthy thing. Still want to be a better bloke than I am but that's a work in progress.'

'You do look disgustingly healthy now, like.'

'Mind, I've felt like twatting Marc the therapist on more than one occasion. '

'You should've done exactly that and claimed it was all part of your therapy. I reckon for £85 an hour I'd want to punch him in the balls then flip him over and have sex as well. Get me money's worth, like.'

Nick laughed and shook his head. 'I never got that bloody mental.'

Another bus rumbled past and shook the windows. 'You'll be glad to get out of here though, eh?' said Nick.

'Oh, I dunno. It's been a good few years in here. Okay, it's little more than a squalid cave but it's been home. I was thinking, if you move in with Julie, I could take on your place.'

'Really? That'd be weird.'

'Aye, maybe it would. It's a bloody good flat though and with great views. Plenty of room for records.'

'True, but there's no shortage of places to live in Harrogate. I don't want to have to visit you in my old flat, that'd just freak me out, man.'

'Alright...maybe it would be a bit odd. I might look at places on the other side of The Stray. So any news on the housing front for you?'

'Not really. We've looked at a few places out in the country around Durham but not found anything we like yet. We're checking out an old farmhouse a mile or two south of Yarm next week. Jules will probably have to sell her flat, but she's a bit reluctant to do that.'

'Maybe she wants a bolt hole.'

'Aye, well, after last time who could blame her? She's only had it two years and did it up really nice. I've been staying up there quite a bit. I mean, I can work online anywhere so it's made sense and it's been nice to be together. That's why you've not seen much of me. She might even make a bit of money on the flat when she sells it given the stupid state of the housing market.'

'That's all gonna go boom sometime though, isn't it? Everyone always thinks it won't but then it always does. The good times never last forever. So you're definitely going to do it, though?'

'Move in together again? Yeah, deffo. I really want to, now. No getting married though, sorry to disappoint you on that. We just couldn't think of a reason to do it. We were thinking of having some old pagan, common-law ceremony, jumping over the brush or whatever, but...fuck it, we'll just have a party instead. It's just something the church made up, marriage, isn't it?

'Yeah of course it is...all total shazbat, as our friend Mork from Ork might have said.'

'And you never know, we might even have kids sometime soon, we've talked about it.'

'You're joking me. Is that even legal?'

'Aye, I've got an official licence to reproduce and everything!'

'Bloody hell, they give them out to anyone these days. Well fucking good luck to you, you twisted old pervert, just don't tell the authorities about your self-pleasuring gymnastic abilities.'

'Oh I had a go at that again the other night. Jules showed me her party trick - which I'm not even allowed to tell you about - and then she wanted to see if I could do mine.'

'And could you?'

'Nah. I was an inch short.'

'Aren't we all?'

Nick's phone rang. It was Julie.

'Hey, Jules. I'm at Jeff's, so don't go talking dirty to me.'

'Aw, and I was just going to tell you what I was wearing.'

'What are you wearing, like?'

Jeff sat up and began panting like a dog, his tongue hanging out. Nick laughed.

'I've got big black rubber boots...'

'Oh baby.'

'...and a woolly hat and a sexy red cagoule.'

'You and your bedroom talk.'

'Listen, I was just calling to see if you're doing anything this afternoon?'

288

'Nope. I've all day free and only a good time to have.'

'Well there's a press conference at the Boudica site in Norton. They're going to announce what they've found. Thought we might go over there?'

'Yeah, I'll drive up. Have you heard anything?'

'The whole place is buzzing with rumours about it. They've definitely found other grave goods but they've kept quiet on what it all might mean.'

'Wow. Other grave goods. Boudica stuff?'

'That's the rumours, yeah.'

'Yeah OK, shall I bring the fur ball here with me?'

'Well it is on his land. Yeah, of course. It's scheduled for 3.30.' She rang off.

'We're going to stand in a muddy field in Teesside, Jeff.'

'Why would we be going to do that? Are Ozric Tentacles playing?'

'Press conference about the Boudica dig.'

'Will the musky Flo be there?'

'I should think so.'

'In my mind, I'm already gone.'

Tents had been erected around the yew copse on Brian Salmon's land to keep the archaeologists dry whilst working on the dig. The blue plastic tarpaulins stood out against the brown ploughed field as Nick drove up the track to the Blakeston estate house, where the press conference was to take place.

The gravel track that snaked around the house was littered with press cars. In front of the big house and towards the stables, outside broadcast trucks and satellite dishes had been set up. Others were parked in a nearby field. From the various logos on display, it was clear there were media crews from all over the world. Cables ran all across the yard like thick strands of black spaghetti and little groups of people, some holding cameras, microphones and grey, furry booms, milled around.

'Bloody hell, it's the United Nations of Teesside here,' said Jeff as they parked up on the edge of an adjacent field. 'Look who's over there.'

He pointed to Florence Farrell. She'd dyed her hair a dark brown and was wearing a duffel coat and stood in a group with some other students.

'Shame she's lost the red hair,' said Nick.

'Symbolic that, isn't it?' said Jeff. Brian emerged from the back of the house carrying a large tray packed tightly with mugs of coffee for the assembled media.

'Hey Brian,' shouted Nick.

'Ah, hello, Nick...and Jeff, too. Now then, boys. Come for the big showdown, have you?'

'Have you had a sneak preview of the results of the dig?'

'Not as such. We know they've found more grave goods, though. All very exciting. Would you like a coffee?'

'Not for me, thanks,' said Nick.

'No, you're alright,' said Jeff.

'I think I saw Julie earlier just down by those tables,' he said, gesturing towards some long tables that had been set up at the top of the field on a strip of gravel. TV cameras faced the tables and the site behind.

Just as he spoke, Julie emerged from the crowd in her black duffel coat and black cargo pants and waved at them.

'Hey, you. Isn't this exciting?' she said, giving him a kiss on the cheek. 'Hiya, Jeff.'

'Now then, Jules. Aye, it's an impressive turn out, and all because of my fucking potatoes,' said Jeff. 'All that seems ages ago now, doesn't it?'

'There's supposed to be a big announcement but no-one seems to have been briefed about it. It's not leaked out of the department at all. After Christmas they said they'd found more grave goods that were "of interest" but that's about as far as it went.'

'Who's running the show, then?'

'A bloke called Mike Ezrin is heading it up. He's from Newcastle Uni. I hope Diane's watching on TV.'

'How's she doing?' asked Jeff.

'She's better than she was. Still some healing to do and they've got to stabilise her meds yet, but she'll get there. She's glad she didn't die, so that's a step forward. Come on, let's go down the front. Kick-off should be in a few minutes.'

She took Nick's hand and led him toward the big wooden table, at the front of which was a huge knot of microphones, all adorned with TV station logos. Nick looked around - it was an almost surreal scene, the 21st century media in its full digital regalia set into a rural landscape on Teesside, a small, out-of-the-way place and a small, out-of-the-way unfashionable place at that. A place which had grown out of the industrial revolution but which was more famous for its pollution than its history. And now here they all were, all because of a woman who lived 2,000 years ago.

A tall, bearded man dressed in a blue fleece jacket sat down at the table and was joined on either side by two other colleagues, a man and a woman.

'Okay, shall we get started?' he asked. A buzz of noise dropped away as cameras and microphones began recording.

'As you know, this dig was, in essence, to find Boudica's grave. We focused on the site behind us because of a couple of a notable find and because of the work of my colleague Diane Edwards, described in her book The Queen of the Tees. Basically, we wanted to find out what was under there. I shall give a more detailed archaeological briefing to those who are interested, later. I'll also take questions, of course. After nearly two month's work on the site, some things have come to light, some very interesting things. We have found many first-century artefacts on this site and from field-walking across this and the adjoining land, probably as a result of the plough churning them to the surface.'

He took off the lid of a low, flat plastic box. Inside were pieces of gold jewellery and some coins. He held up some pieces as cameras clicked a strobe of pictures. A couple of items featured the Boudica insignia in part or whole.

'We took all of this out of the site and some of it is very high status. We found this...' He opened another box and, to a stunned low hum of astonishment, produced the hilt of a sword with part of the sword still attached. It was incredibly well-preserved, made from twists of gold and inset with red jewels. It had the Boudica insignia on it.

He held it up. 'Impressive, isn't it? Almost certainly first century and almost certainly a ceremonial sword. This would only be buried with someone of the highest status, someone such as Boudica or one of her generals. But, and this is a big but, we dug this out of a context which wasn't first century. It had been put in the ground probably in the 1920s or early 1930s. In fact, it was sitting on top of an old 1920s beer bottle. The same thing goes for all of these pieces.' He gave detailed explanations of how and where they'd found four of the best pieces of jewellery.

'This could not happen by accident. This isn't just material which has been brought to the surface by the plough like the finds we recovered while field-walking. These have been, at some point in history, buried here. By which I mean they were placed here deliberately.'

'Do you mean they're forgeries?' said an American reporter who was dressed in a suit and tie and sported an odd, plastic-moulded haircut. He looked so out of place in the Teesside landscape.

'No, they're not forgeries or fakes. They're real enough and my guess would be that they were not originally found here but someone in the past, about 80 years ago, decided to bury them on this site. Whether they intended to try and fool future archaeologists or if they were simply hiding them, we can't know. So from that we have to conclude that this place is not the burial site of Boudica, or indeed of anyone else. What we can say is that what we have found is exactly the sort of grave goods we would have expected to find in a highly born tribal leader's grave and, as some of what has been found carries this unique Boudica inscription, an inscription we have never unearthed before but have read reports of in ancient texts, it's not too fanciful to suggest they once belonged to her or her entourage. However, I must stress again that while the artefacts are fascinating and really important in themselves, they have either been placed here to deliberately hoax future archaeologists or perhaps to hide them.'

'So is Boudica a Teessider?' said a local news reporter, insistent on seeking a simple, black-and-white statement, fearing a more nuanced local news report would please no-one.

'I just can't say that. Where did these artefacts come from? Were they excavated locally or somewhere else entirely? We don't know. We only know they are out of context here, where we have found them. I'm sorry. I wish I could be more categorical for you but until we uncover proper stratified evidence, we simply can't be. This is not Boudica's burial place, I can be pretty certain in telling you that.'

Other questions demanding an unequivocal answer were fired in his direction and the other two academics alongside him did their best to reply with shades of grey.

All those years of speculation, research, faith and belief by both Susan and Diane stretching back to the early 60s when she had found that first brooch. All the emotion, intellect and myth, all the grief and heartache, love, lies, denial, destruction and death. This was what it was all for - a big 'don't know', an almighty 'err...not sure'. It gave a little to each side, and it took a little. These were the Boudica artefacts Diane wanted to find but in a false position, a position which meant Susan's old ideas about Boudica could not yet be challenged.

And isn't that just the way with life? The things we build up to be so important, the fictions we're sure are true, all turn out to be mountains of sand in the myth of our own lives.

As the sharp northeasterly wind blew sheet-metal grey clouds across the sky, bringing the latest squall of rain from the North Sea, exactly as it had done for millennia upon millennia, in that moment it was all clear. We are all just another speck of dust in the cosmic eye, you and me and everyone, from the highest-born queen to the grubbiest peasant. And whoever our parents are, whatever we've said and done, we're all unified by the one single truth of the relentless march from birth to death. All of our maps head to the same destination via different highways. And when we get there, all the interests, pretensions and diversions of existence melt away. We have to give them up in the end, no matter how seriously we have taken them in our lives, no matter how much pain or joy they've given, no matter if they were truths or lies. Keeping some love in your life is surely much more important than any of our other affectations and perhaps the only thing to really live on after our death.

A line by the great American comedian George Carlin came to Nick's mind: 'Don't sweat the petty things and don't pet the sweaty things'.

THE END

About John Nicholson

John is a well-known football writer whose work is read by tens of thousands of people every week. He's a columnist for Football365.com and has worked for the Daily Record, The Mirror, Sky and many other publications over the last 14 years.

Other John Nicholson Books
published by Biteback Publishing

We Ate All The Pies -
How Football Swallowed Britain Whole (2010)

The Meat Fix -
How 26 Years Of Healthy Eating Nearly Killed Me (2012)

Books in the Nick Guymer Series
Published by HEAD PUBLISHING

1. Teesside Steal (2013)
2. Queen Of The Tees (2013)
3. Teesside Missed (2013)
4. DJ Tees (2014)
5. Teesside Blues (2014)
6. Tyne Tees (2014)

Kindle/Paperback

http://www.johnnicholsonwriter.com

HEAD
PUBLISHING